"Walk with me, Miss Stone!" he asked abruptly.

"Come, bear me company for a small part of this lonely evening."

"Walk with you?" Her voice quivered as she tried to hide her astonishment. "Why, wherever would we go?"

Even in the flickering light of the wall sconce, Evangeline could see a mischievous smile tug at the corner of Elliot's full, sinfully handsome mouth. "In the gardens," he whispered, leaning into her. "Beneath the light of the moon. Where is your sense of romantic adventure, Miss Stone?"

"I do not think that we should—"

"Ah, Miss Stone! Do something wildly irresponsible for once." Without taking his eyes from hers, Elliot placed his hand on the doorknob of her bedchamber and flashed her a wicked grin. Slowly, he pushed the door open on silent hinges, his big hand splayed against the wood. A wave of desire and uncertainty shook her.

"Your cloak," he answered, in response to her disquiet. Elliot gently tipped her chin up on his finger and looked down into her eyes. It should have been a sweet gesture, but in the darkened corridor, it felt like something quite different. "You are safe with me, Miss Stone," he whispered. "The pleasure of your company is all I seek tonight. But do go in and fetch a cloak, for you shall find the night less benign than I."

Also by Liz Carlyle from Pocket Books

One Little Sin

The Devil to Pay

A Deal With the Devil

The Devil You Know

No True Gentleman

Tea for Two

A Woman of Virtue

Beauty Like the Night

A Woman Scorned

My False Heart

My False Heart

Liz Carlyle

POCKET BOOKS
New York   London   Toronto   Sydney

This book is a work of fiction. Names, characters, places and incidents are products of the author's imagination or are used fictitiously. Any resemblance to actual events or locales or persons, living or dead, is entirely coincidental.

An *Original* Publication of POCKET BOOKS

POCKET BOOKS, a division of Simon & Schuster, Inc.
1230 Avenue of the Americas, New York, NY 10020

ISBN: 0-671-04054-5

First Sonnet Books printing November 1999

10 9 8 7 6 5 4

POCKET and colophon are registered trademarks of
Simon & Schuster, Inc.

For information regarding special discounts for bulk purchases,
please contact Simon & Schuster Special Sales at 1-800-456-6798 or
business@simonandschuster.com

Front cover illustration by Franco Accornero

Printed in the U.S.A.

To my muse and mentor,
my husband

To those red-penned she-devils,
Debbie, Sally, Sandy, and Teresa

And to the eternal optimist,
Lauren McKenna, editor extraordinaire

Team players,
one and all

O, what excuse can my invention make,
When thou shalt charge me with so black a deed?
Will not my tongue be mute, my frail joints shake,
Mine eyes forgo their light, my false heart bleed?
The guilt being great, the fear doth still exceed.

—*William Shakespeare*

My False Heart

❧ Prologue ❧

*Innocence for innocence; we knew not
the Doctrine of Ill-doing.*
—WILLIAM SHAKESPEARE

With an athletic grace, Lord Elliot Armstrong literally leapt from his glossy black traveling coach, just as it rolled to a stop before his future uncle-in-law's town house in Maverton Square. As Elliot's coachman reined in the four fresh grays, a powdered servant jumped down to slam shut the carriage door, left swinging on its hinges in the young nobleman's wake. Vaulting eagerly up the stairs, however, Elliot thought of nothing but his exquisite bride-to-be. He had to see her. Just for a moment. Indeed, he had been formally betrothed to Lord Howell's niece for three whole days now. Surely he had every right to call upon his beloved Cicely, even at such an unfashionably early hour?

After his admittance by Howell's obsequious footman, Elliot strode into the now-familiar morning parlor, where he had paid desperate, passionate court to his green-eyed beauty for all of a sennight. "I must see Miss Forsythe at once, Cobb, if you please," demanded Elliot, tossing his hat and gloves to the servant.

"Miss Forsythe is, er—in the garden with a—a caller, my lord," replied the footman uneasily, motioning Elliot toward a worn settee. "If you would care to relax for a moment?" Elliot did not care to relax for a moment, because an unexpected and arduous journey lay ahead of him. He chose instead to pace the frayed carpet before the French windows, which led onto the flagstone terrace. His reluctance to travel north could be assuaged by nothing less than one last glimpse of Cicely. Immediately, a flash of pink silk caught his eye, and impatiently Elliot lifted his gaze to peer through the glass and into the thick foliage beyond. The sight he beheld sent blood pounding into his temples. *Godfrey Moore!* What was that bastard about? Had he no shame? Had he not heard? Cicely had made her choice, damn him! But Moore appeared disinclined to accept defeat with gentlemanly grace, and Elliot watched in horror as the man touched Cicely, letting his fingertips slide almost seductively across her flushing cheek.

"Howell!" roared Elliot over his shoulder, not breaking his gaze from the fervent scene on the garden bench. *Bloody hell!* Moore had a desperate grip on her wrists now. The hot pounding in Elliot's head grew louder, more insistent, blocking out all logical thought. Instinctively, his hand went for the small dagger which he kept tucked discreetly in his sock, but he found himself clawing impotently at nothing more than the leather of his fine English topboots. *Damnable London manners.* He hissed, wrenching on the door handle. In his Highland home, even in this enlightened year of 1809, a usurper like Moore could well expect to suffer a knife in his ribs for such egregious conduct, and Elliot fully intended to oblige him. Only the sound of heavy footsteps treading into the parlor restrained him from shattering the glass with his bare hands.

"Ah, good morning, my lord!" The baron's voice boomed forth with ingratiating cheer. "Come to call upon my lovely niece, have you?"

Still clenching the brass handle in a white-knuckled grip, Elliot jerked his head toward the baron's terrace. "God damn it, Howell! My future wife is being assaulted under your own roof, and you have the gall to give me *good morning?*" Suddenly slack-jawed, Howell took one look through his French windows and, with a practiced skill, simultaneously kicked and yanked the resistant door, which came free with a wrenching scrape. Muttering a vile curse, the burly baron leapt forward to jerk his niece's red-faced, stammering suitor off the bench. He then propelled Moore smoothly through the room and into the entrance hall.

But Elliot paid neither of them any further heed, for Cicely was now floating in from the terrace, one soft hand outstretched in greeting. Anxiously, he went to her and took Cicely's dainty fingers in his. "Oh, my love!" she breathed, a strained but gracious smile fixed upon her pale face. "What a surprise! Uncle and I did not expect to see you until this afternoon—"

Behind them, the baron interrupted by clearing his throat, his beefy face still florid with obviously suppressed aggravation. Alone, he strode back through the parlor, his whip and hat in hand. "Cicely, Elliot." He nodded at them in turn, as if nothing untoward had occurred. "Just on my way out, I'm afraid. Lady Howell has gone to her papa's and shan't return until tomorrow, but I cannot think why the two of you—er, engaged and all that—cannot spend an hour or two alone."

"Oh, thank you, Uncle dear!" answered Cicely in a honeyed voice as Howell turned to quit the room.

As Cicely pulled him down onto a nearby settee, Elliot forgot his black mood entirely. He forgot, furthermore, to ask Cicely precisely how she had come to be alone on the terrace with Godfrey Moore. And he forgot that he was not supposed to sit quite so close to his fiancée. All these rational thoughts floated up and away as Cicely eased across the settee toward him.

"Oh, Elliot," she whispered softly, lowering her long black lashes. "I have been counting the minutes until I could see you again. To be separated from you, for even a day, is sheer torture. I—forgive me, but it is simply beyond bearing!"

Elliot watched as a little tear formed in a corner of one of her vivid green eyes. "Oh, Cicely, do not cry. It is the same for me, but we must—"

"No, Elliot!" One tiny hand fluttered at her throat. "Do not say 'But we must'! I cannot bear it. But we must wait! But we must use discretion! But we must think of what others shall say! Oh, my love, I am sick to death of *must* and *should!* When can we be married? Do say it shall be soon. I beg of you!"

Cicely clutched passionately at his huge, big-boned hand, and Elliot felt as awkward and as clumsy as a gorilla playing with a china doll. He drew a deep breath. "Cicely—how I dread what I must tell you. Mother has sent for me. I am bound for Scotland at once. My father has taken ill again, and the physicians hold out little hope this time."

Elliot waited for Cicely's quiet words of sympathy, yet he scarcely noticed when they did not come. "At once?" she echoed hollowly, all color draining from her face. "But—but what of me? How soon will you return? I—I must know, Elliot! Why . . . why, you cannot leave me like this—" Her voice choked with obvious alarm.

"Oh, my dearest! I shall never leave you. I'll be gone but a few months, three at most. I promise you, Cicely—"

"Three months?" Her voice was uncharacteristically sharp, and she licked her pouting pink lips uncertainly. "But that is much too long—I mean, it is so very long. I shall surely die—of loneliness, of course."

Elliot suppressed a flash of irritation, reminding himself that Cicely would not carry on so were her love for him less ardent. Indeed, had she not singled him out for her attentions almost immediately upon his arrival in town last month? This despite the fact that he was shy and unsophisticated, while a throng of polished flirts flocked to her side at every *ton* function.

"Darling," he said gently, tipping her sharp little chin up with one finger, "what would you have me do? My father is dying this time, and 'tis only proper I attend his deathbed. Moreover, I shall be required to take charge of the Rannoch estates."

Cicely licked her lips again, her face drawn into the stubborn, taut lines Elliot had quickly learned to recognize. "Very well, then, Elliot," she replied with sudden coolness, staring blindly into the distance. "Let us be wed immediately. You must use your family's influence to obtain a special license this afternoon."

Elliot froze. "This afternoon? Cicely, are you mad? Your uncle would never agree!"

Cicely shook her head and gave a twisted little smile. "Oh, Elliot! You know nothing of what Uncle wants! Howell would have me wed as soon as possible, and I have made it plain that I shall have only you. Indeed, I am sure he will wish us happy."

"I cannot think, my love, that you are correct. Nonetheless, my mother would have an apoplexy! Only think of what people might say about you—"

Cicely sniffed disdainfully. "They would say that we are hopelessly in love, that's what they would say."

"No, darling," he answered with uncharacteristic firmness. "I'll not risk sullying your name. As soon as my mourning is ended, we shall have a grand wedding—the finest St. George's has ever seen! The world must see that you are to be treated with every respect." *Respect,* he had learned early on, was a word that carried great weight with Cicely, and Elliot had vaguely noticed that in some circles his beloved was received with a coolness he did not fully understand.

Elliot's young heart was warmed by the recollection of

how sweetly Cicely had smiled, how eagerly she had grasped his hand, when he had told her that, as the future marchioness of Rannoch, she would be able to look down her nose at those crones at Almack's who had refused to extend her a voucher. Indeed, she would be able to give the cut direct to much of London should she so desire. Elliot almost hoped that she would so desire, for he had had a gut full of the high-handed pomp and English arrogance he had endured during his few short weeks in town.

Cicely smiled weakly and drew his hand to her full, slightly parted lips. "Yes, of course, you are right, my love," she responded in a husky voice. She kissed his hand fervently, then shocked him by sucking one fingertip into the warmth of her mouth, seductively lowering her lashes. Then, slowly, oh so slowly, she withdrew his finger and pressed his palm to her breast. With her other hand, Cicely tugged inexorably downward on the plunging bodice of her gown, dragging the pink silk erotically over her firm, rosy nipples until the lovely white mounds spilled forth. One luscious breast now rested just beneath his eager fingers.

Elliot sucked in his breath and closed his eyes tightly. Never in his life had he seen a lady do such a thing. Whores, yes, but there'd been precious few of them in Elliot's young life. Ayr was a damnably dull town. Furthermore, Elliot's cold, staunchly religious father frowned on such debauchery.

"Oh, touch me, Elliot," whispered Cicely thickly, pulling his fingertips back and forth across the hardening bud of her breast. "I am so very ashamed, but I simply cannot wait—"

Slowly, Elliot opened his eyes, and almost involuntarily he began to caress Cicely's breast. It was as if his hand belonged to someone else altogether, to a disgusting libertine, in fact. His groin tightened, his breathing quickened, and he felt dreadfully uncertain of himself. He was, therefore, greatly reassured when Cicely's head tipped back and her mouth parted slightly in obvious pleasure. Her eyes were dark, glittering slits. A cat being stroked.

Ah, yes! She did love him. And she desired him. She would be the perfect wife.

"Oh, yes, Elliot—please, *please* do not stop." Cicely urged her full breasts forward into his hands. "Touch me. Ah, yes, there. And there—"

Elliot did not stop, though he knew that as a gentleman he should. He touched her there. And there. Just as she asked. After all, they were engaged. In a matter of months, Cicely would be his wife. He had every right to touch her thus, did he not? She wanted him. She loved him so passionately. That much was pleasingly obvious to Elliot.

Slowly, Cicely's head came up, and her green eyes narrowed further still. "*Ahh*, Elliot, please! My aunt and uncle are out. Come upstairs with me. No one will know. I—" Her lashes fluttered demurely. "I simply must have you now. I cannot wait." When Elliot found himself stunned into utter silence, Cicely slipped one delicate hand down his waistcoat, then lower still, until Elliot gasped.

As she caressed her own breasts with one hand, Cicely began to massage his swollen member with the other until Elliot was sure he was going to disgrace himself right there on the baron's brocade settee. Then, somewhere deep inside the house, a servant's voice echoed, dragging Elliot back to the grim edge of reality. Frantically, his Presbyterian upbringing fought his libidinous urge to the ground and wrestled it into a chokehold. He pulled away from Cicely and gently tugged upward on her bodice.

"Cicely, my darling," he whispered hoarsely, "I could

never take you outside the bounds of matrimony. You are too special. Too worthy."

Sitting stiffly back against the settee, Cicely crossed her arms, tossed her raven curls, and fixed her lips into a lovely pout. As always, Elliot was utterly charmed. With gentle deliberation, he leaned forward to kiss her dainty nose. "Soon, sweetest, soon," he promised, with all the reassurance he could muster. But Elliot was stunned to see that Cicely's green eyes had pooled with tears and she was now crying in earnest.

Eighteen-year-old Evangeline Stone leaned wearily across the boat railing, sighing in abject frustration as their westbound Ostend schooner sailed into the ancient Cinque Port of Dover at precisely the same moment as the afternoon packet came in. As ill luck would have it, the crowded ship, despite running late as usual, came in on the tide and managed to beat their chartered boat by a breath. On the distant quay, stevedores began to swarm like industrious ants, stirring in anticipation of the incoming vessels. In the background, carriages ranging from the finest barouche to the simplest farmer's gig lined the lower road which curved up and into the town proper. Despite the fact that war raged on the Continent, business struggled on.

Standing on the deck beside her, little Nicolette began to whine, shifting anxiously from one foot to the other. Their exodus from occupied Flanders had been both expensive and harrowing, and the children were now weary to the point of agitation. Urgently, Nicolette tugged at her elder sister's hand, a now cold and seemingly bloodless extremity which the child had clutched tightly in her own sticky little paw for the last two hours or more.

"Evie," wailed the round-faced toddler plaintively, "I *have* to go!"

Slumped against the rail beside Evangeline, her grief-stricken father said not a word. His thick hair, always too long, was now tossing aimlessly in the channel breeze. The rich brown locks had turned to a dull gray, seemingly overnight. Only the briefest movement of his flat blue eyes, flicking up to the soaring heights of Dover Castle and back down into the churning surf, gave any indication that Maxwell Stone was even vaguely aware of his surroundings.

Evangeline inhaled deeply, threw back her narrow shoulders, and sent up a silent prayer for strength, but little Michael chose this ill-timed moment to begin screaming his displeasure at the delay, and, no doubt, at the brisk channel breeze.

"*De pis en pis,*" muttered his French nurse darkly, shifting the plump infant to her other hip. Weakly, she mopped her clammy brow with the back of one pale hand.

"*Ça va sans dire,* Marcelle. From bad to worse, indeed," answered Evangeline with as much gentle equanimity as she could dredge up. "This entire journey has been a dreadful nightmare, yet we can do nothing but march onward as best we may." Sympathetically, she turned toward the seasick nurse and reached out her hands for the screaming infant. "Go back down below, Marcelle. You are not well. Take Nicolette with you. Regrettably, it will now be quite some time before we can disembark."

At this remark, Nicolette began to snuffle moistly. "No, Evie! I don't want to dis-dis-disinhark! I want to go back home! I want Mama! And I want Mellie and Harry back, too!" The little girl's pleas rose to a keening cry of urgency as she tried to hurl herself into her inattentive father's arms. "Please, Papa, please—let's go back to Flanders! I hate it here. I hate it already."

Maxwell Stone merely looked at her, unblinking.

"Tut, tut, *ma petite*," murmured the nurse softly as she knelt down to smooth Nicolette's pale hair back from her forehead. Gently, she took the little girl's hand and turned to lead her down below. "You shall like England very much. We are simply—*dépaysé. Oui,* merely homesick. Winnie and the cousins shall soon come to visit, and you shall see that Essex is a fine place."

"How do you know?" grumbled Nicolette, eyeing her nurse suspiciously. "You're not English, either! And it's far away, so you've never been there!"

Evangeline turned to watch the sullen child depart. It was, she inwardly acknowledged, a very good point. How did they know? They were not English. Not in any way that mattered. *Was* England a fine place?

She bounced the fussing infant, whom she now held nestled in the crook of her arm. Dear Lord, these three people, whom she loved with all her heart, were her responsibility now. At her mother's deathbed, Evangeline had given her promise to care for them. Nicolette, Papa, and Michael. Drowning in grief, Papa seemed almost beyond help, but Michael needed her desperately. Yes, he would need her most of all, she realized, as she chucked him gently beneath his plump little chin. Her baby brother responded with his irresistible toothless grin and gradually began to quiet.

With a sigh born of fatigue and sadness, Evangeline turned to face the Kentish coastline once more. Her hand trembled slightly as she smoothed back the tendrils of hair which now blew wildly in the breeze.

Had she made the right choice for her family? *Had she?*

❧1❧

Give due light to the misled and lonely traveler . . .
—JOHN MILTON

London, May 1819

The splatter of ice-cold champagne hit the marquis of Rannoch full in the face like a blast of well-chilled reality. From his lap, a buxom brunette leapt to her feet with an annoying scream, brushing ineffectually at the rivulets of wine that now marred her pink silk evening dress.

In a dimly lit back room of the Theatre Royal, Antoinette Fontaine stood before the fashionable après-theatre crowd, weaving unsteadily as she raised her empty glass in mock salute to the dark, surly man sprawled with casual arrogance before her. Already, the actress's flaming red hair was tumbling from its elaborate coiffure, while kohl-tinged tears trailed hopelessly down her face.

"Reas—reason and love keep lit—little comp'ny together now'days," she quoted, hopelessly slurring the words as she staggered toward him. In the background, several people tittered discreetly. Heads craned, and quizzing glasses came up to survey the commotion.

"You spiteful bitch!" wailed the brunette, still dabbing at her ruined dress. "Look what you've done to my best gown!"

"Shut up, Lily," growled Rannoch, unfolding his huge body from the chair and rising smoothly to his feet. "I can easily buy you a dozen." He crooked his finger at the weaving woman who now stood, her lips a sulky pout, in the center of the room. "To your dressing room, An-toinette. Go! Now."

"Better, my lord, that I sh-should burn in hell," spat the drunken woman through her choking sobs. "I'm done wi'ch you, Elliot, you m-mean-spirited bash—bashtard." As if to make a point, she hurled the wine glass at his skull. Clearly, the alcohol had not greatly impaired the actress's aim. A spray of crystal bounced off the wall just above Rannoch's head.

The ruined dress now quickly forgotten, the brunette screamed again, bolting for cover in a streak of pink silk. Rannoch paid the fleeing woman no heed at all. Easy come, easy go; that was his motto. Another whore—or another mistress, for that matter—was a simple enough thing to find. Elliot Robert Armstrong, fifth marquis of Rannoch, seemed literally to trip over them everywhere he went. Sometimes it was almost tiresome.

With an indifferent shrug at the fleeing Lily, he re-turned his attentions to his current mistress. "You, An-toinette," he warned silkily, "are not finished with me until I am finished with you."

"Oh, bend over an' bugger yourself, you heartless pig," Antoinette snapped, her eyes narrowed into glittering slits. As if to yank it from her neck in disgust, she twisted one hand into the heavy, ornate necklace that trailed a dozen blood-red rubies around her stark white throat.

"Oh, I strongly recommend you keep that little trinket, my dear," whispered Rannoch. "You may soon have dire need of it."

Releasing the necklace, Antoinette raised a well-manicured finger and struggled mightily to point it in the marquis's direction. "Hah! I can do well enough w'out you, Elliot," she taunted, spitting out the words in a surly tone of drunken bravado tinged with pain. "Plenty of other men w'glad—gladly keep me. An' do a better job, too, if you take my meaning." She gave another little lurch and hitched up the bodice of her disheveled gown.

Rannoch heard soft laughter ripple through the crowd again and felt himself go wild with anger. Forcing his voice to be calm, he wrapped his massive hand hard around her wrist and jerked her roughly toward him. "Then, by all means, Antoinette, have them," he whispered in a menacing tone, "and all at once, if you wish. I hardly think I give a damn."

Suddenly, a muscular, well-dressed gentleman stepped from the shadows. Wondering who had the audacity to trespass in the middle of such personal indignation, Rannoch lifted his eyes to threaten the man back into the crowd.

Major Matthew Winthrop. There was no mistaking his dark hair and military bearing. Rannoch felt himself relax fractionally.

"Rannoch," said Winthrop in a soothing tone, "it would appear that Miss Fontaine is rather overset tonight. Will you give me leave to escort her home? I daresay it would be for the best."

Elliot nodded stiffly and stepped back from Antoinette. "You are very obliging, Winthrop. I should be most grateful. And as to you, Antoinette"—he lowered his voice—"I shall wait upon you tomorrow at five, and we shall resolve this unpleasantness once and for all. Make certain that you are in. Do I make myself plain, woman?"

Antoinette merely shot him a sidelong glower of drunken rage as Winthrop wheeled her about and urged her gently toward the door. With a bitter, gnawing sadness, which Elliot would rather die than confess, he coldly watched them go, listening as the titters and whispers slowly subsided. It was time, he realized as he picked up his glass of whisky from the side table. Time to make a drastic change in his life. A new mistress, certainly, for Antoinette had just become far more trouble than she was worth. Unfortunately, the thought of another Antoinette did little to lift his black mood.

Four days later, the mid-morning sky was already gray and bleak when the marquis set out from London. A wiser man might have heeded the dark, scuttling clouds that were fast sailing in on the heels of a two-day rain. Indeed, Elliot did see them, but in his black, boiling anger he did not care. His disrespectful, ill-tempered, ungovernable mistress had deliberately ignored his orders, and he was nearly blind with unspent rage. Elliot flicked his whip hard against his topboot. A twenty-mile ride in pouring rain might, he wryly considered, cool his still-burning urge to choke every last gasp of breath out of Miss Antoinette Fontaine, who was, he had not been surprised to discover, nothing more than a jumped-up country girl. Annie Tanner, daughter of an innkeeper from Wrotham Ford, Essex.

In any event, the chestnut was a worthy mount, not the most spirited of horses but good and solid, perfect for a long, damp journey. Elliot had every confidence of making excellent time and being back in town before dusk. Shoving his hand deep into the pocket of his greatcoat, he assured himself that the ruby bracelet was still secure. But touching the velvet case reminded him of Antoinette's skin. *That bitch!* He ought not trouble himself to give her a damn thing after the way she had behaved. How dare the woman challenge him in such a public way! And now to refuse his letters! Indeed, to refuse to so much as open the door to admit his messengers! Why, technically speaking, it was his damn door. Rannoch money had paid for it, and very nearly everything inside as well. Elliot decided that he ought to have the bloody thing knocked in with a sledgehammer.

But Antoinette was not inside. He knew that now. She had not been seen in town for three days and had missed her last two rehearsals at the Theatre Royal. No doubt about it, the woman had turned tail and run home to wait out Elliot's temper. Well, this time the mercurial actress had pushed him too far. This time it was over, and he would find her and tell her so.

A proverbial ill wind was whipping up from the east by the time Elliot managed to locate the crossroads that led to Wrotham Ford. Unfortunately, the adjacent road marker had been the recent victim of what looked to be a nasty encounter with a hay-laden tumbril and now lay almost flat on the ground, protruding crookedly from the mound of loosened earth at its base. Scattered about in the muddy roadway lay the damning evidence. Tufts of hay had blown hither and yon, some to be ensnared in the adjacent hedgerow but most to be ground beneath hooves and wheels into the two days' accumulation of mud that seemed to constitute the only road to Wrotham Ford.

With a hiss of aggravation, Elliot dismounted from the chestnut. As he swung his right leg down, however, the old wound in his hip cramped violently, aggravated by the pervasive damp. Rubbing his buttock, Elliot hobbled to the signpost, which lay on the far side of a long, nasty puddle. Stepping impatiently across it, Elliot watched in increasing frustration as both his glossy topboots became splattered with mud and worse. Damn, Kemble would go off on a pout over this. But there was no help for it. In disgust, Elliot pinched one wing of the signpost between the thumb and forefinger of his snug calfskin glove and lifted it carefully from the mire.

London. No. He twisted the post. *Wanstead.* No. *Tottenham.* Hardly. With another hiss, Elliot scraped a dollop of mud from the wing that pointed in the direction opposite London. *Wrotham something.* Yes, that would be it. Due north of London. Good Lord, but his arse hurt, an eternal reminder of Jeanette, whose husband had had such poor aim. Oh, yes! There was yet another selfish bitch who had brought him more pain than pleasure. Elliot hurled the signpost back to the ground with such a force that the barely buried end popped up out of its loosened base, flicking him head to toe with chunks of moist, soft dirt. Elliot hissed for the third time in as many minutes, limped back to his mount, and threw himself wearily into the saddle.

And then the deluge of rain began.

Two hours later, the marquis of Rannoch was well and truly lost in the countryside of rural England, or someplace that certainly seemed to him like the wilds of a distant, godforsaken land. Elliot, who hated to venture beyond London, rarely even bothered to visit his Scottish earldom. He certainly had no further interest in plodding through the remaining hills and vales of lower Essex. Yet here he was, plodding indeed, for since leaving Wrotham crossroads, he'd had the misfortune of seeing only one wide spot in the road, and the crumbling church, narrow pub, and half-dozen ancient houses could hardly have been termed a village. Even that meager spot was now long gone in his wake. Certainly, it had contained nothing that might have been mistaken for the inn owned by Antoinette's family, where he strongly suspected she would be found.

Elliot was cold, wet, hungry, and splattered with mud. It was time, he realized with a resigned sigh, to ask for directions. But where? Should he turn back two miles to the tiny pub? Suddenly, as if conjured up by fate, a well-lit house appeared around the next bend, some fifty yards from the main road.

Elliot stared through the mist at the tempting sight. A

neatly kept drive swept up through informal gardens
filled with spring flowers, then made an elegant circle in
front of the wide, welcoming entrance. The house was far
larger than almost any he'd seen since leaving London.
But it was not grand. No, not grand. Pretty. Peaceful.
Even elegant, perhaps, despite its hodgepodge exterior of
sandstone and brick. The oddly pitched roof lines lay at a
variety of angles, as if the original manor house had been
frequently expanded down through the ages. The obviously ancient north end, primarily stone, was little more
than a squat, four-story tower snaked with ivy. The main
house consisted of three stories with a sweep of windows, at least six on each level. Toward the rear, Elliot
could barely see a row of half-timbered cottages and a
moderate carriage house. Beyond that, he saw nothing,
though his sense of direction told him that he must be
near the River Lea.

The rain still drizzled, bringing with it the warning of
a premature dusk. In the house before him, Elliot could
see that a soft, welcoming light already shone in almost
every downstairs window. The warmth tugged at him,
drew him nearer, and Elliot impulsively wanted to wade
through the swirling mist, peer through the windows,
and see what the people inside were doing. No, no. He
wanted to hurry back to Richmond, light all his windows, and rush outside to see if the effort had any warming effect on his home.

But it would not. Elliot knew that much for certain.
With a soft flick of his whip, Elliot urged the chestnut up
the drive, dismounted, and bounded up the two steps to
the threshold of the charming house. His fatigue lifting,
Elliot no longer noticed that his boots made a moist,
squishing sound when he walked, or that his coat was
filthy, his gloves muddied.

Following his brisk knock, the door swung wide open

into a warm, lavishly carpeted hallway filled with good smells and cheerful sounds. No less than three arrangements of fresh flowers sat stationed about the hall. Laughter and music rang through the corridors. A house party, perhaps? Elliot turned his attention to the plump, pleasant-looking woman whose black bombazine and starched linen made plain her status as housekeeper. A shiny ring of keys hung from her waist, jingling delightfully as she stood smiling on the threshold, anxiously beckoning him inside.

"Oh, bless me, sir! Here ye be at last, and what with Bolton already givin' up on your ever coming!" Elliot merely stared at the cheerful woman, who immediately seized his hat and whip. "Now, give me your gloves, sir. Ah, bad luck in the mud, I see." She dangled the thumb of his glove between two pudgy fingers. "Indeed, what a foul, foul day! I do declare, you've had a nasty trip up from London, have ye not? Let's fetch you a nice dish o' tea. Miss will insist upon it, to be sure."

From the far reaches of the hall, the smell of cooked apples and warm cinnamon wafted out. In the back of the house, a maid scurried across the corridor with a well-laden tray, two fat tabbies trotting expectantly behind. This house, tucked into the middle of nowhere, looked, felt, and even smelled like a home should. Someone else's home, of course, since Elliot had never known such a place in his life. But this house was nonetheless tempting, for it seemed at once vaguely familiar and oddly foreign.

"Coat!" demanded the plump woman with brisk cheer, and Elliot snapped to attention, looking at the housekeeper in mute amazement as he obediently handed her his greatcoat. Surely he was not invited to stay? Reluctant to say anything that might break the strange spell, Elliot looked anxiously about the inviting home, feeling as if he'd somehow been transported into a cozy fantasyland of warmth and laughter. From deep inside the house, a pianoforte tinkled, then burst into a strange, rousing tune which Elliot couldn't have named if someone had held a gun to his head. A fit of feminine giggles burst forth.

"A waltz! I want a waltz!" insisted a youthful male voice, and the laughter burst forth again. "Who shall be my partner?" The females merely tittered.

"Fritz!" cried a laughing girl. "What's become of Fritz? Surely he will give you a dance!"

At last, Elliot managed to stammer, "My good woman, who—whose house is this?"

The plump housekeeper paused, his sundry items of dripping apparel in hand, and blinked at him oddly for a long moment. "Hmm . . . why, it queers me to guess, sir!"

"You—you do not know, either?" Elliot was feeling seriously confused. But in an exceedingly warm and pleasant way.

The housekeeper pursed her lips as if in deep thought. "Well, I should venture to say that, technically speaking, 'tis prob'ly Mr. Michael's house."

"Mr. Michaels?"

The housekeeper shot him a sideways glance laced with amiable warning. "Aye, but it's Miss Stone who be in charge here, and no mistake! Now, let's get you out o' those wet boots and into the studio before she has a fit. You know what artists are like! Though, in truth, Miss Stone's really as much an angel as her name implies."

"Stone?" asked Elliot, a quizzical smile beginning to tug at his lips. The name certainly did not sound celestial.

The housekeeper's brow furrowed. "Oh, no! No, indeed! Evangeline! But, no . . . you probably came looking for someone else entirely, did ye not?" Her eyes narrowed shrewdly even as she beamed at him.

Elliot nodded, trying to hide his disappointment at being found out. "Yes, I did. I was wondering when you might realize it."

The housekeeper nodded sagely. "Aye, happens here often enough. Like as not, you expected to find some stuffy gentleman named Edmund or Edgar van Artevalde, did ye not? Well, you're in for a pleasant surprise, indeed."

Elliot was on the verge of admitting that he'd had nothing but a series of pleasant surprises these last two minutes and that he hadn't a clue as to who Mr. van Artevalde might be, but the housekeeper was motioning impatiently for his boots again. "Er—no, ma'am," Elliot averred. "I daresay I ought to keep my boots—"

"Well, suit yourself, I always say!" interposed the woman with a shrug. "But you'll catch your death, mark my word. And we stand on no ceremony here at Chatham Lodge, so you may as well have 'em off."

Chatham Lodge. How pretty it sounded, though it meant nothing at all to him. Elliot was struck with the fleeting impression that if he should turn and walk back out the front door into the mist, he might return here tomorrow to find that Chatham Lodge had never existed. It seemed that fanciful to him.

Almost immediately, a wide door in the rear of the hall burst open, and another housemaid darted out. A small black dog shot from between her legs, pink tongue dangling, and headed undoubtedly toward the lively crowd. "Mrs. Penworthy!" called the maid, clearly oblivious to the skittering animal, "Miss Stone says to fetch the London gent straightaways to the studio. She says as how the good light is fair to disappearin' on account of the rain, and she's ter'ble anxious to see him."

Elliot decided that he was as terrible anxious to see the mysterious Miss Stone as she was to see him.

"Oh, oh—yes, indeed," murmured Mrs. Penworthy, and, with one last resigned glance at Elliot's boots, she darted down the hall with impressive haste, motioning for Elliot to follow.

Well, *what the hell!* As the Iron Duke always said, "In for a penny, in for a pound." Elliot caught up with the bobbing, jingling housekeeper halfway down the hall, passing, as he joined her, a drawing room filled to overflowing with young people. In the center of the laughing crowd, a handsome youth with a fichu tied dramatically about his head seemed to be dancing a boulanger. Aloft, he held his partner—the small black dog. Apparently, the errant Fritz had returned, and with an empty slot on his dance card.

Elliot suppressed a snort of laughter, but just then the housekeeper turned abruptly down a short corridor that shot off to the right and threw open the double doors that lay at the end.

Elliot was escorted into a cavernous, whitewashed chamber with a bank of high, vaulted windows that ran along the south end of the room. Above, a narrow gallery ran along the southerly and westerly sides, and below, a huge blank canvas stood propped against the wall, as did several easels and a half dozen partially completed paintings. The ancient stone floor was bare, save for a matching set of opulent Turkish carpets. One was spread beneath the desk, which sat, along with two side chairs, in the northeast corner. Opposite the desk, a long, rough-hewn worktable held pots and jars of assorted shapes. On the farthest wall, a long, well-worn leather sofa and a pair of carved armchairs were grouped into a sitting area upon another carpet. Paintings, both watercolor and oil, in varying sizes and styles, covered almost every expanse of wall. In the few blank spaces that remained, pencil sketches had been neatly tacked into place. The thick, sharp tang of solvent and oil hung heavily in the air.

Near the center of the room stood an easel, and rising from the chair beside it was quite possibly the most beautiful woman Elliot had ever had the pleasure to encounter in all of his thirty-four nefarious years. The mysterious Miss Stone, he presumed. She was a dainty, fine-boned woman in her late twenties, with a sensually full mouth and strong, high cheekbones. Her eyes were china blue and wide-set, her nose a serious straight angle, and her neatly braided hair, the color of rich buttermilk, was twisted into a plain yet elegant arrangement. Attired in a simple dark blue dress, Miss Stone also wore a coarse smock liberally blotted with stains in a rainbow of hues.

She came quickly toward him with a strong, purposeful step that seemed out of character with her size and appearance. "Thank you, Mrs. Penworthy," she said in a low, rich voice which held a distinctly Continental accent that Elliot could not identify. "You may leave us now."

Miss Stone closed the short distance between them, her face bright and smiling and one hand extended just a bit too high for a handshake. Suddenly, she was near enough to touch him, and, surprisingly, she did so, reaching higher still to grasp his chin in her hand. Elliot suppressed a sharp gasp as her warm fingers touched his jawbone. Slowly, methodically, she twisted his face this way and that. Her grip was sure, her fingers surprisingly strong.

"Excellent bones," she murmured, staring up into his face with open admiration. "You are most striking, Mr.— Mr.—" Appearing suddenly embarrassed, she turned to scrabble about in the papers on her desk. "So sorry—I'm sure I must have Peter Weyden's letter right here. You wanted . . . let me see, you wanted . . ."

Miss Stone continued her frantic search, then finally turned to him in surrender. "I must beg your sincere forgiveness, sir, for I do seem to have misplaced the note. Perhaps you would be so kind as to tell me your name, and explain to me exactly what you had in mind?"

"My name?"

Miss Stone's face seemed fixed in anticipation, and Elliot suddenly realized that she really had been expecting someone else altogether. Someone from London. Someone who had not come. There was no magic spell. He did not belong here. And if he told this warm, beautiful woman his name, she might very well recognize it and pitch him right back into the cold, dreary day from which he'd just come. But he had no choice. A black-hearted devil he might be, but Elliot prided himself on being an honest one. With a resigned bow, he reluctantly answered, "I am Elliot Robert—"

Suddenly, a crash of glass echoed down the hall, and the tinkle of the pianoforte came to an abrupt halt. A long, dead silence fell across the gaiety that had previously drifted from the drawing room. "Good Lord," muttered Miss Stone, one hand fluttering to her temple. "Please excuse me, Mr. Roberts! I collect we've just lost another vase. Or a mirror perhaps. I do ask that the boys not cavort or play catch in the long hall, but, well—such temptation! And on such a dreadful rainy day . . ." Miss Stone let her explanation trail away behind her as she headed for the door.

Mr. Roberts? Mr. Roberts. How simple. A nice enough name, really. And certainly he had not *said* that he was Mr. Roberts. Indeed, that misconception was one that Miss Stone had drawn entirely of her own accord. And he really did want to stay, if only for a few moments. Just a little bit ashamed of what he was considering, Elliot stared down at the toes of his ruined boots. It was then that he realized that his huge foot had come to rest on a folded scrap of paper. Slowly, Elliot bent down to pick it up. It was a tiny note addressed in a stiff, old-fashioned copperplate to *Miss E. Stone.* Obviously, the missive had been hand-delivered, since the note gave no direction.

With another wave of shame, only the second Elliot had felt in about a decade, he flipped open the note to stare at the scrawled signature. The body of the note was written in neither English nor French, the only two languages Elliot had ever troubled himself to learn. Nonetheless, at a quick glance, he made out the signature. *Peter Weyden.* This was Mr. Weyden's letter. Miss Stone's footfalls sounded back down the hall, and Elliot spun toward the door, clutching the note behind his back.

Miss Stone, looking slightly vexed, appeared on the threshold. "Vase? Or mirror?" he asked, trying to be charming and cordial. It was a bit of a stretch for Elliot, who, generally speaking, bothered to be neither.

"Worse," muttered Miss Stone, apparently unimpressed with either his charm or his cordiality. "A window."

Elliot's discerning eye swept Evangeline Stone's lithe figure, noting the elegant sway of her hips as she stalked back into the room. "How unpleasant," he murmured, ruthlessly shoving the note deep into his coat pocket.

Miss Stone merely shrugged and shot him a resigned look. "I shall summon the glazier tomorrow. In the meantime, I have tasked Michael and Theo with sweeping up the glass, since they are the guilty parties."

"Michael and Theo?"

Miss Stone smiled somewhat wearily. "Yes, my impish younger brother and my—my cousin. Theodore Weyden."

"Weyden?" Elliot parroted stupidly.

Miss Stone withdrew to take the seat to the right of her easel and motioned him toward a chair opposite. "Yes. But of course! I forget that you are acquainted with Peter Weyden. Theo, you see, is his nephew."

"And your cousin as well?"

"In a manner of speaking." Miss Stone's cool blue eyes flicked up at him as she turned the page in a sketchbook and then replaced it against the easel. "Now, tell me, Mr. Roberts, what do you have in mind?"

Elliot swallowed hard. "I daresay that just . . . just the usual should suffice, I think."

A faint smile played at Miss Stone's lips as she fixed her gaze on him. They were very close, not more than six feet apart, and Elliot could see her eyes narrow perceptively. "Just the usual? Nothing exotic? Symbolic? Abstract?"

She was toying with him, and Elliot felt exceedingly stupid. Big and stupid, like the raw-boned Scottish boy he'd been ten years ago. Stiffly, he inclined his head. "I beg your pardon, ma'am. I fear I have no notion—"

Miss Stone did laugh then, a rich, musical laugh that made Elliot think, oddly enough, of clean, cool water flowing through green lowland braes. "Very well, Mr. Roberts. I shan't torture you. After all, your heart is apparently in the right place, since this is to be a gift for your fiancée—?"

"My . . . fiancée?"

Miss Stone frowned. "Indeed, I have that much aright, do I not? I recollect that is what Mr. Weyden said in his letter, that this portrait is a betrothal gift."

Elliot hedged, artfully avoiding her question. "I would like for you to paint my portrait, Miss Stone, in keeping with your tastes. Certainly, I have no preconceived notion as to how such a thing ought to be done."

"And as to your fiancée's preference?"

"I rather doubt, Miss Stone, that any woman's judgment in such things"—Elliot let his gaze drift over the beautiful works that hung from the walls—"could equal yours."

His hostess nodded curtly. "Very well," she murmured. "And Mr. Weyden has informed you of the price of this commission?" Miss Stone, her head tilted to one side, had begun to make light pencil marks upon the sketchpad.

"I—whatever your charge, I am willing to pay it."

Miss Stone's brows arched elegantly at that. "Indeed? But you should understand that there are a dozen competent portrait artists conveniently located within two miles of the City of London who will do this work for half of what I shall ask."

"That doesn't signify," Elliot interrupted. "I want you to do it, and besides, I rather enjoyed my ride in the country."

"How unusual to enjoy riding in a drenching rain," murmured Evangeline Stone. "I fear you shall be inconvenienced by several such rides before this portrait is completed."

Elliot paused. He had not considered such a thing. In fact, he hadn't considered anything at all. And regrettably, he was not the least put off by the thought of spending a great deal of time sequestered with Evangeline Stone in her studio.

Good Lord—what was he doing here? In the middle of nowhere, pretending to be someone he was not, and watching this breathtaking woman sketch his likeness? It was insane. But Elliot could bring himself neither to explain, to apologize, to leave, nor to do any of the things he ought to have done long since. He felt transfixed by— no, drawn to this place. And to this woman. Abjectly, he raised his eyes to meet her pointed gaze. "I just want you to paint my portrait," he answered honestly, his voice soft.

Miss Stone made no answer, but she began to sketch in earnest, her hand sliding back and forth across the paper in bold, sweeping motions. As she worked, her eyes flicked back and forth from the paper to his face, over and over again. Twice, Miss Stone stopped suddenly to focus on his eyes, holding his gaze in long, timeless moments, her hand frozen elegantly in mid-stroke.

Elliot sat stoically, watching her work. It was fascinating. No, mesmerizing. He wondered what she saw when she stared into his eyes so boldly. What was she sketching? What did she see when she looked at him?

"I am merely studying your face at present," she commented, as if in answer to his unspoken queries. "I prefer to begin with a few sketches to familiarize myself with your bones, the way the planes and angles catch the light. Turn your head, please, Mr. Roberts. Just slightly to the left—yes, that's it. Thank you." She resumed her work and continued thus for another quarter hour or longer.

Elliot, still transfixed, eventually lost track of time. He was, therefore, surprised to hear himself blurt out a question into the protracted silence of the studio. "How long have you been a portrait painter, Miss Stone?" The soft whisking of her pencil stopped abruptly. "I'm sorry," he belatedly added. "I should have said an *artist*. How long have you been an artist?"

"Portrait painter will suffice, Mr. Roberts. You need not fear insulting me. I am well aware that most portraits, unlike landscapes, for example, do not carry great artistic weight at present. Nonetheless, I take great pride in all my work."

"And you do other types of work, do you not?" His gaze floated over the room's north wall, the upper half of which was covered in landscapes.

"Not all of those are mine, Mr. Roberts. But yes, I do the occasional landscape. However, society's obsession with immortality ensures that the business of portrait work is both consistent and lucrative."

"You make no apologies. I rather like that."

"I cannot afford to," she replied briskly, ripping away one sheet of paper and laying it carefully to one side. Elliot was disappointed to see that she placed it face-down. "And to answer your question, I have been painting all my life, but only in the last seven years have I built my—my reputation. Such as it may be," she added.

"Forgive me, Miss Stone, but you have a lovely accent—almost French. Did you study abroad?"

"Yes," she said simply, but Elliot saw that her expression had begun to soften.

"What a wonderful opportunity for—for . . ."

"For a female?" Her gaze caught his again, and Elliot could see a flash of blue fire. "I am Flemish, Mr. Roberts. My father was an English artist who met my mother in the studios of Brugge. Since neither his work nor his bride was acceptable to his family, my parents found life abroad much more to their liking."

"Ah, I see. And how long have you been in England?"

"Since my mother's death, almost ten years now."

"And your father?"

"My father passed away five years ago."

"I am sorry, Miss Stone. Have you no husband, no family, save your brother?"

Evangeline Stone's cool gaze came to rest squarely on his face, and Elliot realized that he had overstepped himself. Badly. What had possessed him to ask such impertinent questions? Belatedly, he tried to apologize, but Miss Stone cut him off with a toss of her hand.

"Pray do not regard it, Mr. Roberts. I can hear the

kindness in your voice. I have also a younger sister, Nicolette, and a cousin, Frederica. Michael is eleven."

"Surely you cannot be responsible for them?" he asked incredulously.

"Most assuredly, sir, I am. Fortunately, I have assistance. Peter Weyden was my father's business partner for many years, and he now serves us in many ways, as a sort of uncle, a trustee, and a guardian. He helps oversee our investments, he supervises our estate manager, and he screens my commissions; all other matters he leaves to me." Her face was fixed in a tight smile. "We are in good hands, Mr. Roberts. And far from destitute, I can assure you."

"I'm sorry, Miss Stone. I certainly never meant to imply—"

"I'm quite sure, sir, that you did not. Pray lift your chin just slightly, please. Yes, that is—*ah,* perfect." She made three or four quick marks, then set down her pencil. "Mr. Roberts, the day grows quite late, and the light is fading. We can do no more today, I am afraid."

Elliot suppressed a wave of disappointment. "I see."

"When might it be convenient for you to return?"

Elliot opened his mouth to answer, but his reply was forestalled by yet another commotion in the hall. Suddenly, the door burst inward, and a pretty, round-figured woman attired in a gown of brilliant purple sailed through the door. A boy and a girl, whom Elliot had spied earlier among the crowd in the drawing room, followed hard on her heels.

"Evie, my darling! You shall never guess who—" She stopped short as she spied Elliot from across the room. "Oh, my dear! Pray forgive me, for I did not know that Mr. Hart had finally come!"

Elliot froze. *Mr. Hart.* Not Mr. Roberts. How humiliating to have his silly ruse found out. With a sigh of regret,

Elliot forced himself to rise and make a weak bow to the lady. Miss Stone was by now on her feet.

"Aunt Winnie! See! See! We tried to tell you," insisted the eldest child, a flaxen-haired boy. He was undoubtedly Michael Stone, for he was the very image of his elder sister. "Evie has a guest, just as we said."

"Well, so she does, my dears!" The woman in purple was blushing now. She was remarkably attractive, in a bold, voluptuous sort of way, and appeared to be in her middle to late thirties.

"Not at all, Winnie," interjected Miss Stone, "for we were just finishing. Do come meet Mr. Elliot Roberts. Mr. Roberts, this is my companion, Winnie Weyden, who is Peter Weyden's sister-in-law. And this is my young brother, Michael Stone. And my cousin, Frederica d'Avillez."

The two children, who looked to be perhaps ten and eight, greeted Elliot amiably. Then, almost immediately, the girl, a slight child with black hair and olive skin, seemed to slip shyly behind Evangeline Stone's skirts, very nearly disappearing.

"Mrs. Weyden," murmured Elliot politely, nodding to them in turn. "Michael. Miss d'Avillez. It is a pleasure, to be sure."

"Oh!" chirped Winnie Weyden, still blushing. "Hart? Roberts? They sound not at all alike, do they? Pray forgive me," she said, her rich golden ringlets dancing nervously about her round, pleasant face. "I vow, I cannot remember the names of my own children, let alone anyone else!"

Elliot breathed a sigh of relief. "Pray think no more of it, Mrs. Weyden. As it happens, I am just taking my leave."

"I shall see you out," murmured Evangeline Stone, making her way around the chairs and past the newcomers. *Evie.* He rather liked that name.

"Yes, to be sure," agreed Mrs. Weyden. "But do have a care, Mr. Roberts. The rain has worsened considerably, and this road is now barely passable. I have just come from the vicarage and very nearly did not make my way back—"

The group rambled down the hall with Miss Stone in the lead. The boy and girl, laughing and chattering, followed Elliot like good-natured puppies as Winnie Weyden continued her rambling exhortations. "—and our coachman said in all his seven and fifty years he's never seen the like. Mud nigh up to our hubs! I do hope, Mr. Roberts, that you've come to us on horseback? For I cannot think that a coach could safely make its way back to the London road this evening."

The elderly housekeeper, Mrs. Penworthy, met them in the hall, Elliot's hat in hand. Just then, the door flew open to admit a burst of whipping rain, followed by a stooped, elderly man in a long black coat. "Bolton!" cried the housekeeper, setting aside the hat to pull off the man's drenched coat. "Pray, how did you find your daughter? And whatever took ye so long?"

The elderly man, whom Elliot now saw was dressed in formal butler's garb, seemed unfazed by the half dozen people crowding his hall and was obviously returning to his post from an unpleasant excursion in the rain.

"My good woman," the butler answered Mrs. Penworthy as he handed her his sodden hat, "I was quite unable to see my daughter. However, Squire Ellows, whom I met at the bridge to Wrotham Ford, tells me that she and the new babe go on very well."

"Haven't seen her?" echoed the cheerful housekeeper. "Gone all that way in this torrent and haven't seen her?"

"No, indeed, madam. The bridge washed out, and none can pass through. I was obliged to shout at Squire Ellows across the water and could do little more. I've spent these last two hours pushing carriages out of mud, and I am none the better for it, I can tell you!"

"Pushing carriages! At your age?" The housekeeper tugged on the bell. "Are ye daft? Best send for more tea, or we'll likely have both you and Mr. Roberts here dying of lung fever or such like, what with the both of you nigh drowned a-traipsing about in it."

At this, the elderly butler looked at Elliot with what appeared to be perfectly amiable disinterest. "Indeed, sir. Indeed. And I shouldn't go back out, if I were you." As if to give credence to the old man's warning, the skies opened wider still, and the rain began to hammer unmercifully at the front door. From the narrow window, Elliot could scarcely make out the front walkway, let alone the gardens beyond.

"Hullo, Mama!" chimed a pleasant voice, and Elliot turned to see a young man striding down the hall from the drawing room. It was the same fellow he'd observed earlier dancing madly about with the fichu tied around his head. He smiled warmly at Elliot. "And Evie, who's this? Have we a guest?"

Evangeline interrupted. "Mr. Roberts, this is Augustus Weyden, Mrs. Weyden's eldest. Gus, this is Elliot Roberts."

"Indeed, Gussie," added Mrs. Weyden as Gus pumped Elliot's hand up and down with the youthful enthusiasm of one who hopes he has met a kindred spirit. "Mr. Roberts has come to have his portrait done. He was just on his way back to town."

"Shouldn't recommend it, sir," insisted Gus Weyden, shaking his head. Elliot gazed at the young man appraisingly. He was young—twenty, perhaps—tall and lanky, with his mother's gold-brown hair. A handsome fellow, Augustus Weyden was dressed for the country in a simple, well-cut blue coat and fawn trousers. Nonetheless, a hint of the youthful dandy lingered, evidenced by a fine cravat *en cascade.* "Best rack up here for the nonce," finished Gus with an amiable shrug. "Lots of room, and Cook turns out an excellent joint." Just then, a second young man, obviously another Weyden, stepped out of the drawing room and nodded politely in Elliot's direction. Undoubtedly this was Theo, the rambunctious window breaker.

Winnie Weyden smiled at her younger son, then turned to Miss Stone. "Indeed, Evie, dear. I daresay it would be best if Mr. Roberts stayed. I shall have Tess lay another place for dinner," she added, as if the matter were settled.

"Thank you, Mrs. Weyden," interjected Elliot. "You are exceedingly kind, but I do not go back to town tonight. In fact, I have business . . . nearby."

"Bridge is out," mumbled the butler in a tone that implied he found Elliot's intelligence wanting.

"Yes, but I haven't got a carriage. Surely a horse—" But Elliot's protestation was cut off by a warm hand encircling his arm. He looked down into the bottomless blue eyes of Evangeline Stone, and an enigmatic, nameless longing seized him, stealing his breath and taking him quite by surprise. The sweet emotion twisted roughly inside his stomach, fast bringing him to the edge of pain.

"Please stay, Mr. Roberts," she softly insisted, so near that he could smell her warm fragrance. For the briefest moment, Elliot ceased to think. "It is perfectly proper, I can assure you," continued Miss Stone, apparently oblivious to the effect she was having on his senses. "We entertain frequently here, and I would be exceedingly glad for your company tonight."

"I should not like to impose."

"Not at all." She shook her head. "As you can see, we always have a jolly house full, and one more can be no inconvenience. Indeed, if you are an early riser, then you'll find that the morning light here is of an excellent quality. Spare me two hours tomorrow, and I shall begin your portrait, yes? Then the water will no doubt have receded, and you may ford the stream."

Miss Stone's warm hand slipped slowly away from Elliot's arm, and with it went his resolve. Staying the night made some sense, he reassured himself. And although Elliot generally gave no consideration whatsoever to the propriety of his actions, he now paused to give a passing thought to the matter. However, his hostess was a grown woman, chaperoned by a mature companion and a gaggle of cheerful young people, so surely his remaining—or at least the honorable Elliot Roberts's remaining—would not be improper.

And indeed, if he managed to reach Wrotham Ford this late in the day, he would simply find himself obliged to put up for the night at Mr. Tanner's inn. Not a very pleasant prospect, that. *Far better,* whispered the devil perched upon his shoulder, *to go tomorrow when the weather has cleared.*

"Ah, come on, Roberts," cajoled Gus Weyden, apparently in cahoots with Elliot's personal demons. "Stokely, Theo, and I need a competent fourth for cards tonight. Evie don't like 'em, and Mama's dreadful!"

"Augustus!" scolded his mother, rapping him soundly on the hand. "You should be grateful that I—"

"Quiet, please!" called Miss Stone sharply over the din. "We are inundating our guest with people whose names he cannot possibly remember. Let us not add confusion and quarreling to the mayhem just yet!"

"Indeed," murmured Winnie Weyden in agreement. "There are far too many of us!"

"Mrs. Penworthy," directed Evangeline, "please show Mr. Roberts to the Tower Room. Frederica," she said, looking at her little cousin, "go tell Cook there shall be nine to dinner. Michael, find Polly and tell her to prepare hot water for Mr. Roberts's bath, for he's been soaked to the skin."

As Miss Stone's young brother trotted off to do her bidding, Elliot opened his mouth to protest, but his hostess was still issuing orders while the people who filled the hallway stood at attention. For a moment, the directives seemed out of place coming from such a pretty, delicate thing, and it struck him that Evangeline Stone was a woman of great contrasts. Looks could, indeed, be deceiving, for there was apparently nothing delicate about her.

"And Bolton shall see to the brushing of your jacket and trousers, Mr. Roberts. Now, Gussie," Evangeline continued, turning her gaze firmly upon the elder Weyden son, "go to the stables and tell Hurst he's to stable Mr. Roberts's horse for the night."

"Oh, Evie! It's pouring!" whined the young man pitifully.

"Then shut your mouth, Gus, and you shan't drown," replied Miss Stone firmly. "Now, Theo," she said, turning her attentions to the younger Weyden boy, "finish cleaning the broken glass in the drawing room. And where is Nicolette? What has become of my sister?"

"Here," said a soft voice from the drawing-room door. A beautiful young woman who looked very like Miss Stone darted into the crowded hall.

"Nicolette, I'm finished painting for the day. Will you clean brushes for me?" asked Miss Stone, and the girl nodded. "Later, we shall begin work on pigments for tomorrow, since Mr. Roberts has agreed to stay the night."

Elliot was just about to point out that he'd agreed to no such thing when he was struck by two dissimilar thoughts. The first was that one did not easily disagree with Evangeline Stone's instructions, and the second, even more surprising thought was that he really had no wish to disagree with her. Indeed, it was pleasant to have someone see so efficiently to his comforts—a bath, clean clothes, a warm meal, and good company. Someone who was not even being paid to do so.

After all was carefully considered, Elliot could think of nothing he'd rather do than spend the evening enjoying the odd companionship of this very large, very strange family.

Just for tonight, whispered the devil. What could be the harm?

&2&

True it is, she had one failing; had ae woman ever less?
—ROBERT BURNS

*D*espite her outward calm, Evangeline watched with unsettled emotions as, one by one, the crowd trundled down the thickly carpeted hall to do her bidding. The housekeeper, still rattling on about the dreadful health hazards of damp weather, was slowly leading a rather dazed Mr. Roberts up the front staircase, and Bolton, the butler, had made an expedient escape to the warmth of the kitchen.

Beside her, Winnie Weyden gave a deep sigh of feminine satisfaction. "Oh, Lud!" she whispered. "What a charming, handsome man!" By far the shorter of the two, Winnie tugged on Evangeline's sleeve. "Do you not find him handsome, Evie? I vow, he puts me so very much in mind of my dear Hans."

"Winnie, every stunning looker over six feet puts you

in mind of Hans," interposed Evangeline with feigned disinterest, remembering all too well what she had felt upon seeing—truly seeing—Elliot Roberts for the first time. Holding his chin in her hand and letting her normally impartial artist's eye roam across his hard, strong-boned face, Evangeline had felt a sudden knifing heat and a disturbing, inexplicable sense of intimacy. And he *was* handsome, Evangeline had to admit. Not classically beautiful but darkly seductive, in a fascinating, rugged way. Even now, watching his long, booted legs as he strode effortlessly around the final turn of the staircase, Evangeline could still feel the sensation of vibrant energy beneath her fingers as she had laced them tightly about his arm.

Good Lord, whatever had possessed her to clutch at him so? And why had he, a virtual stranger, looked back at her with such sudden and unsettling intensity? Evangeline had spent just over an hour alone with him, studying and sketching and . . . yes, enjoying the enthralling shadows and angles of his extraordinary face, and every moment had been an unexpected test of her artistic detachment. Not to mention her composure.

He had undoubtedly thought her serene, perhaps even distant, for such had been her intention. And yet, when she had laid her hand upon his arm, he had responded to her with a look so intimate and so unexpectedly penetrating that Evangeline had been almost frightened to return his gaze. But return it she had, and in it she had seen shock and warmth and something more. *Need?* Yes, for the briefest of moments, she had looked up into those stunningly clear gray eyes and had glimpsed a need that had very nearly mirrored her own.

But no, that simply could not be. She was perilously close to making an utter cake of herself, while Mr. Roberts was simply a client, a pleasant, handsome London gentleman who intended to gift the woman he hoped to wed with a betrothal portrait. Heat? Need? Intensity? What fanciful ideas she was beginning to have! And at a time when she could least afford them, too.

Winnie Weyden made a vague pout and, taking her friend by the arm, pulled her gently into the library. "Oh, Evie! Must you spoil a poor widow's fantasies with your cool realism?"

Evangeline suppressed a sharp, bitter laugh at her companion's misjudgment. Determined to maintain at least the semblance of composure, Evangeline collapsed into a chair by the hearth and watched as her best friend and former governess withdrew to a nearby table and poured two glasses of wine.

Deliberately, Evangeline shot her friend a teasing smile. "May I remind you, dear Winnie, that Mr. Roberts is not yet wed? Why do you not wear your red dress to dinner? The one with the bodice cut down to here"— Evangeline skimmed her index finger low across the swell of her bosom—"and he shall quickly be convinced of your many fine qualities. Particularly so, should one of them tumble out onto the tablecloth!"

Winnie returned to thrust a glass into Evangeline's hand. "Madeira, darling," she announced. "Perhaps it will restore a touch of color to your cheeks. Your pallor suggests that I am not the only one felled by the charms of our houseguest."

Gratefully, Evangeline sipped at the wine. It was pathetically true, but even with Winnie, Evangeline was afraid to give voice to such a new and frightening emotion. Yes, despite Winnie's good-natured teasing, any woman with an ounce of blood in her veins could see that Elliot Roberts was an artist's dream come to life. His was a face that she knew as if it were her own, for indeed she had studied it well.

Many years ago, Evangeline's mother, in the interest of expanding her sixteen-year-old daughter's artistic horizons beyond those of France and Flanders, had taken her abroad to study the Italian masters. There, in the grand palazzo of a Florentine nobleman, had stood the bronze statue that was almost the very likeness of Elliot Roberts. Although painting had been Evangeline's only passion for as long as she could remember, that godlike Etruscan sculpture had drawn first her eyes, then her hands, and ultimately her pencil, as if she were bewitched by it. Much to her mother's consternation, Evangeline had insisted on spending hour after hour sketching the bronze from every angle while Marie van Artevalde had been left to stroll the piazzas of Florence with their remarkably hospitable host. Her daughter's "obsession," Marie had called it. And obsession was surely what Evangeline felt when she looked at Elliot Roberts.

She had felt the lure of his attraction, even before she had laid her hand upon his arm. No, he was not an Etruscan hero, made of once-molten metal which had long since cooled. He was hot blood and hard bone, lavish shades of light and dark, pulsing with life, breathing and wanting. And making her want. She had sketched him today like a madwoman, afraid that he might leave, for in him she had also sensed an uncertainty and an apprehension which she did not fully comprehend.

Peter Weyden referred Evangeline few portraits these days, for her other work had become far more profitable. Yet, after one glance at Elliot Roberts, it was obvious why Peter had recommended this commission. The man possessed the sort of rare, unrefined beauty almost never seen among the English. A hard, huge man with long legs and arms, Roberts had a hard, chiseled face to match. Black hair, heavy, straight, and far too long, emphasized Roberts's strong jaw and square, stubborn chin. Cool eyes the color of smoke gave way to a nose that was too prominent, too arrogant, and slightly crooked, while his forehead was high and aristocratic. The man was too much of everything. The combined effect was over-whelming.

From across the expanse of her studio, Roberts had immediately commanded her attention, and she had been unable to restrain her hand, which had been drawn, inexplicably, to touch his face. There had been something in the sharp, assessing light of his eyes that had made her instantly aware that she was not only an artist but a woman as well. And that he was, in every sense of the word, a man. In that one unexpected moment, Evange-line had felt the sharp, sudden pain of emptiness, of yearning for what she had never known and could not afford.

Despite his overwhelming height, the man was lean, narrow-hipped, and broad-shouldered, and for the first time in her life, Evangeline Stone found herself wishing that she were a sculptor instead of a painter. Two dimen-sions could not possibly do justice to Elliot Roberts. He was an artist's gift, this man, so starkly beautiful that she'd finally yielded to her foolish inclination to wrap her hand around his arm and beg him to stay. What would it be like, she wondered, to run one's fingers over the lean, hard muscles of Elliot Roberts's back? To shape and mold his—

"Evangeline! *Evangeline!* Do attend us, please!"

Wine glass still clutched in her hand, Evangeline looked up to see both Winnie and the cook, Mrs. Crane, standing very near, peering owlishly at her. "Oh . . . very sorry," she answered, straightening herself in the chair. "You—you were saying?"

Winnie's lips turned up into a sly smile. "Cook is ask-ing about the pippin tarts."

Mrs. Crane, wiping her hands on her apron, nodded energetically. "Aye, miss. We've enough left over, for them as may want 'em. And the rice—to be stewed with the beef as usual?"

Between dragging out the extra blankets and supervising the pouring of Elliot's bath, Mrs. Penworthy had made it plain to him that Chatham Lodge kept country hours and that the household would sup promptly at half past six. From her warm but precautionary tone about the early dinner hour, Elliot could easily surmise that he was not the first London visitor to occupy the Tower Room, and he found himself wondering what sort of guests the Stones were in the habit of entertaining.

"There, sir," said Mrs. Penworthy, rising with a little grunt from her stooped position over the tub. " 'Tis hot enough, I vow. And if there be aught else you're wishful of, you're to pull the bell straightaway. Miss Stone does like her guests proper treated, I do assure you!"

"Thank you," murmured Elliot, "but I shall try not to inconvenience anyone. Do I take it that Miss Stone entertains with some frequency?"

Mrs. Penworthy nodded and beamed at him. "Oh, indeed! I don't scruple to say this house loves a guest here better than any I ever saw. Expect 'tis because they don't go about much." The housekeeper threw open an ancient, heavily carved armoire, tugged out a stack of thick towels, and dropped them onto a stool by the tub. "But I do say that Quality will tell, and a proper English gentleman—for I can plainly see, sir, that's what you are—is a fine treat for house and staff alike."

Elliot rose from his seat by the deep, mullioned window and strolled slowly toward the tub, lifting his gaze to watch the housekeeper carefully. "Does Miss Stone not normally entertain Quality?"

Mrs. Penworthy's eyes widened in obvious consternation. "Oh, no, sir! I mean, indeed, sir, she does—nothing but the finest ladies and gentlemen, to be sure! But foreigners, mostly. Sometimes a London customer, but usually Frenchies and Italians and, oh, I don't know what all! All friendly enough, too, I suppose—could you but understand a word what gets said. 'Twas a regular Tower of Babel here when that nasty little Corsican got loose, and no mistake! Mrs. Weyden and the young miss had foreigners tucked into every cupboard and cranny."

"Ah, yes. I see." Elliot nodded, choosing his next words carefully. He had to evaluate his risk of exposure. "And, of course, I expect Peter Weyden is here regularly?"

The housekeeper was smiling broadly again as she picked up the top towel, threw it open with an efficient snap, then spread it carefully alongside the tub. "Oh, yes, sir. Regular's what he is," she answered cheerfully, but Elliot's momentary alarm was quickly allayed. "Reliable as the calendar, that one! Comes two hours afore Christmas Eve dinner and then leaves a' Plough Monday at first light. 'Tis his curious way of things, you know. A right partic'lar fellow he is!"

Elliot felt himself relax and bent to dip a finger in the deep tub. It was, indeed, pleasantly hot. "And Miss Stone's family—I expect they are regular visitors as well?"

At this, Mrs. Penworthy's sharp eyes narrowed, but her smile did not waver in the slightest. "No family but what's under this roof, sir. Leastways, none as I've ever heard tell of, and I've done for the Stones since the young miss took me on in 1810." And with that, the housekeeper bade him enjoy his bath and trundled out the door, pulling it shut with a hearty thump.

Though Elliot had certainly never considered provincial family life interesting—indeed, he found little that interested him these days—such an odd mix of people living in apparent harmony under the same roof nonetheless intrigued him. Mrs. Weyden, Evangeline had said, was her companion. She was also Peter Weyden's sister-in-law. Yet Mrs. Weyden had two sons: the handsome, irrepressible Augustus and the accident-prone Theodore, both of whom appeared to reside in the house.

In addition to her brother, Michael, and her sister, Nicolette, Evangeline Stone had an unusual cousin, the exceedingly pretty and obviously foreign Frederica d'Avillez. An interesting child, that one. And given her olive skin and black hair, there was an interesting story to go with her, Elliot had no doubt. And who the hell was Stokely? Another cousin? Another uncle? Elliot, who had very little family at all—and certainly one couldn't count his bloodless mother—was already struggling to keep up with the identities of the pleasantly rambunctious crowd occupying Chatham Lodge.

Slipping deeper still into his steaming bath, Elliot asked himself why he cared. It was the painful contrast, he supposed. Though he'd never considered his home precisely cold, he had certainly felt it to be so this afternoon when he had stood outside looking into this lovely oasis. But Elliot's home was lovely, too, and far more grand. Nonetheless, his stately residence, soaring four stories above the south bank of the Thames, seemed always empty, despite the fact that his infamous uncle, Sir Hugh, maintained extensive second-floor apartments within. But Sir Hugh, when his gout permitted, preferred to warm the beds of London's middle-aged widows and neglected wives, who were always, he argued, generous with their brandy, obliging in the boudoir, and willing to listen to his war stories. Oh, he and Hugh were exceedingly fond of each other, albeit in that "hail fellow" way that was so common among men. But Sir Hugh was a busy fellow, more apt to be seen across the river in Chelsea than in Richmond where Elliot's vast house was located.

And then, of course, there was Zoë. Elliot felt a rare and unexpected wave of guilt for having left his eight-year-old daughter behind, but surely by now she was used to it. Zoë had never known her mother, who had been but another of Elliot's many affairs gone awry. Maria had been a capricious Italian dancer who had cheerfully deposited her babe on Elliot's doorstep en route to a carefree life on the Continent. Now, Elliot himself was often absent for days at a time, and Zoë had learned never to question his absences. With her innate sensitivity, she seemed to know what was expected. And what not to expect. It was his own doing, too, for in his inexplicable, withdrawn way, Elliot knew that he had deliberately isolated himself from her, for he did not know what else to do.

But he loved her. God, yes, he loved Zoë. He loved his child with all his heart, black though it most certainly was. He had not, however, loved Maria. Indeed, Elliot had allowed himself to need no woman since Cicely, yet the abiding love he felt for his daughter was like a sure and frustrating ache in his belly. Elliot had no notion what one did with such an overwhelming emotion. He wanted to tell her, to show her, to hold her. And yet he rarely touched her and almost never conversed with her. Not in any meaningful way. Why? Elliot was not certain, but in the dark of night, when he was sober enough to think clearly, Elliot sometimes began to fear that perhaps he was far more like his father than he wanted to be. Was Zoë paying the price for that shortcoming, too?

It was a horrifying notion, and Elliot did not realize that he held a death grip on the soap until it spurted from his hands and skittered aimlessly across the floor. He looked about himself, taking in the antiquated but comfortable bedchamber Miss Stone had provided him. The room was small, warm, and richly furnished. Outside, the chilling rain continued to hammer at Chatham's ancient, mullioned windows, cutting him off—no, sheltering him—from the vast emptiness of the world beyond this place. His bath now tepid, Elliot looked down to see that his toes, and a few other things, had begun to shrivel. With an inward sigh, he shoved away his fanciful thoughts, then heaved himself from the tub in a cascade of soapy water.

The dining parlor at Chatham Lodge was large, well proportioned, and elegantly fitted with all the appointments necessary to a genteel country house. Nonetheless, as with every nook in the Stone-Weyden household, it was warm and comforting. The tableware was sturdy Chinese export, while the delicately carved table itself was long and narrow and laid with good linen. Across the corridor, Elliot noticed what must once have been a breakfast parlor, which, being far too small to accommodate a family of this size, had been converted into a schoolroom. In the rear was a door that undoubtedly connected to Evangeline's studio.

Elliot was greeted at dinner with all the bonhomie and felicity due an old friend, an honor that served to warm his heart while heightening his guilt. It soon became obvious that the entire family dined together, an unfashionable practice but one that Elliot found oddly charming. At the table, Evangeline and Mrs. Weyden were seated at the head and foot, and as a practical matter, the smallest children, Frederica and Michael, sat to their left sides. Much to Elliot's satisfaction, he was placed at Evangeline's right and somehow managed to fold his awkward length into the delicate chair without accident. As they were seated, the remaining family fell automatically into their places, filling every chair.

Elliot, piously dropping his chin as Mrs. Weyden said grace, sent up his own fleeting prayer that a thunderbolt would not descend from the heavens to send his aberrant Presbyterian soul straight to the perdition it undoubtedly deserved. But Elliot evaded the well-deserved lightning strike yet again and, following the soft chorus of *amen*, relaxed in his chair and began to survey his lively companions, mentally summarizing what he had learned. Augustus, Mrs. Weyden's elder son, sat across from Elliot. The young man, who looked about nineteen, was possessed of all the good looks, dapper elegance, and youthful charm of a Bond Street beau in the making. On the verge of adulthood, his brother Theo was about three years younger. Nicolette, Evangeline's sister, looked about Theo's age and seemed serene and rather sweet. The youngest Stone, Michael, was the typical, effervescent English schoolboy, with his blond hair, blue eyes, and easy laugh.

On Mrs. Weyden's right sat Harlan Stokely. Introduced to Elliot as the children's tutor, Stokely was a thin, shortsighted fellow with narrow shoulders and soulful eyes that seemed permanently fixed upon Evangeline. Scanning the crowd, Elliot was left to wonder who normally took the chair at Evangeline's right. The fact that he did not know was strangely disconcerting. From across the table, the youngest child, Frederica d'Avillez, looked up at him expectantly. "This is Wednesday," she announced in a shy voice.

"Indeed it is," agreed Elliot, secretly pleased that the child seemed drawn to him but quite uncertain as to the significance of her statement. His confusion must have shown.

"On Wednesday, we speak only German at dinner," explained the little girl with a rueful sigh, "but my German is very poor. Thursday is Italian, and I am quite good at that." Her gaze dropped back down to study her plate.

Evangeline paused, a basket of bread in one hand. "Not tonight, Frederica," she corrected the child gently. "Since we have a guest, tonight we shall speak only in English, please. Mr. Roberts would not wish to suffer through our rather rudimentary vocabulary."

Elliot glanced at her but saw only kindness in her blue eyes. She knew, he suspected, that he spoke not a word of either German or Italian and was giving him a gracious way out. "Thank you, Miss Stone," he replied solemnly. "As it happens, I cannot speak it at all and must prevail upon Miss d'Avillez for future lessons." His efforts were rewarded by a beaming smile from Frederica.

To an outsider, the interaction of the dinner party was a fascinating exercise in group dynamics. Other than Gus, each child deferred readily and equally to both Evangeline and Mrs. Weyden in matters of discipline and direction. Together, Gus and Evangeline interacted much like grown siblings, while the two ladies obviously held each other in great esteem and genuine fondness. This circumstance appeared to Elliot an aberration of nature, for in his vast experience with the opposite sex, females were invariably treacherous and territorial.

As the younger children struggled with the soup course, Evangeline initiated what Elliot learned was a routine of discussing current events over dinner. Each person in turn was asked to raise a topic of interest to the group, and then a few moments of lively discussion— and occasionally a fierce argument—ensued. The subjects ranged from Mrs. Weyden's interest in the regent's latest bilious attack to Nicolette's mention of the newest member of the royal family. Although undoubtedly too ill to comprehend the significance, George III had been blessed with a healthy granddaughter. A legitimate one, for a change.

On the matter of the babe's future, the table was loudly divided. The females agreed that the profligate royal dukes ought now to do England the favor of dying off without further issue and allow a woman to ascend to the throne. However, the men argued that the obnoxious duchess of Kent should be sent packing to her German relatives and the newest heir sent with her.

"My dear friend Lady Bland has written me from town," interrupted Mrs. Weyden in a gossipy tone. "Rumor has it that the regent has refused his brother's request to name the baby Georgiana, in his honor. Instead, she is to take a Saxe-Coburg name, Alexandrina Victoria!" Upon this cruel bit of news, the entire table promptly agreed to throw their collective support squarely behind the new Lady Alexandrina Victoria and urge her forward to the throne.

Given the lively enthusiasm and pithy commentary that followed, Elliot experienced a moment of concern on behalf of the royal dukes, worthless laggards though they were. But his worry was quickly forgotten when Theo seized his turn and commenced a dark and detailed narrative about the infamous exploits of a local highwayman who had been hanged just the preceding week. When, however, Theo began to expound upon the vivid specifics of the actual rope, platform, and gallows, as described to him in lurid detail by Crane the footman, his mother set down her wine glass with a sharp chink. "Oh, Theo! I vow, that is quite enough, if you please! Nicolette"—she gestured encouragingly down the table—"I collect 'tis your turn. Pray speak of something pleasant."

Nicolette cut a sly glance down the table toward her

sister, then returned her gaze to Mrs. Weyden. "I call for a debate!" she announced regally.

"A debate!" agreed Gus cheerfully.

"Yes, let's do," chimed Theo. "Choose sides and throw us a topic, Nick!"

Nicolette's full mouth curled up into a mischievous smile. "I propose we debate upon the subject of who has been the handsomest guest to grace our table of late—is it Mr. Roberts or Squire Ellows?" Beside him, Elliot heard Evangeline gasp as if horror-stricken.

"Oh, that's gammon, Nick!" groused Theo. " 'Tis of no consequence to us fellows!"

"I vote for Mr. Roberts," piped Frederica.

"Oh, indeed!" chimed Michael. "I agree with Frederica. Squire is losing his hair on top."

"Children, children!" Mrs. Weyden's voice was shrill now as she flapped her napkin admonishingly. "Such a want of comportment! I vow, this can hardly be described as proper entertainment for—"

"Oh, on the contrary, ma'am," interrupted Elliot dryly, pausing with his wine glass aloft, "I find it to be highly entertaining."

Mrs. Weyden stilled her napkin and turned to coo at him soothingly. "Poor Mr. Roberts! First we ignore you whilst we quibble amongst ourselves like barbarians. Then we scrutinize you, as if you were naught but some odd Elgin marble!"

"Thank you, ma'am!" Elliot replied cheerfully. "Though I have hardly felt ignored, and surely every man must desire comparison to—to marble, was it?"

Farther down the room, Gus and Theo snickered, having obviously chosen to misinterpret Elliot's repartee. Across the table, Elliot spied Frederica giggling softly behind her hand. "Psst—Miss d'Avillez!" he hissed. "Whatever *is* an Elgin marble?"

Her brown-black eyes danced mirthfully. "Grecian sculptures," she whispered back. "From the Parthenon."

Winnie Weyden glared at them, then deftly changed the subject. "Do tell us something of yourself, Mr. Roberts, since you seem to be a subject of much interest. Have you, for example, a profession?"

"No, ma'am. None to speak of," replied Elliot, acutely aware that he was now the center of attention. He hoped desperately that the thorough brushing of his expensive but previously filthy clothing did not completely give him away. Apparently, it did not.

"Down on your luck, eh?" chortled Gus. "Well, you've come to the right place, then. Evie's a good 'un. She'll take you in—even a profligate wastrel like me, rusticated from Cambridge 'n' all that." Gus hung his head in mild embarrassment. Elliot suppressed a laugh.

"Pray do not be foolish, Gussie!" snapped his mother. "And I beg you will not mention your ill-timed exploits at school. I think it obvious that Mr. Roberts is a gentleman born, and he has simply come to have his portrait painted for his fiancée—"

"Oh, indeed, I think that's romantic!" breathed Nicolette, a fork full of parsnips suspended in midair. "Do you not think it romantic, Mr. Stokely?"

"Indeed, I do, Miss Nicolette," agreed Mr. Stokely, still staring at Evangeline. "But what does your sister think?"

"Oh, I find it infinitely romantic," murmured Evangeline, looking somewhat impishly up at Elliot from beneath a sweep of thick lashes. "All the more so since it takes money from Mr. Roberts's pocket and puts it into mine."

"Miss Stone!" Elliot said in feigned mortification. "Your callousness alarms me. I was given to understand that all great artists were possessed of a fiery, romantic nature."

"Hah!" snorted Gus. "You thought wrong, indeed. Evie ain't got a romantic bone in her body. Unless, of course, she's working on—"

"Augustus!" Evangeline's voice held a distinct warning.

"—those great battle scenes and allegoricals."

Elliot looked at his hostess in some surprise. "Indeed, Miss Stone? I assumed your work was limited to portraits and landscapes."

"That's 'cause Uncle Peter carts the good stuff off so fast we never have any of it hanging around here," muttered Gus as he chewed around a mouthful of beef.

Elliot watched as Evangeline began to twist uncomfortably in her chair. "Does he indeed?" he asked softly.

Gus continued. "Aye—she's getting prodigious famous, too. But Evie don't use her full name—just her first initial and her middle name." He put down his fork with a clatter. "Do you know art, Mr. Roberts?"

Elliot paused. "Well, I know what I like, but isn't that what everyone says?" He turned his gaze upon the woman to his left. "Pray what is your professional name, Miss Stone?"

His hostess looked thoroughly vexed now.

"Van Artevalde," supplied Gus obligingly. "E. van Artevalde."

As was customary after dinner, the family retired to the drawing room for music, reading, and cards. Evangeline could not help but notice that Elliot Roberts hesitated, lingering by his chair until the dining parlor was all but empty. With a discreet sideways glance, Evangeline let her artist's eye take in his tall, rangy length as he stood, arms braced casually against his chair, watching the stragglers file out of the room. Long, elegant fingers fanned across the chair's front, almost touching in the center. But despite his easy manner, Evangeline could sense the restlessness and doubt that radiated from him. What was it that so troubled this man? Something most assuredly did . . . but perhaps it was nothing more than boredom. And why not?

Though Evangeline made no excuses for the tranquil, secluded lifestyle her family chose to lead, she inwardly acknowledged that theirs was by no means a sophisticated company. And from the look of weary boredom that seemed eternally etched on his harsh, handsome face, Elliot Roberts had experienced a lifetime of worldly sophistication. Indeed, she wryly considered, if more of the same was what he sought, Mr. Roberts had most assuredly come to the wrong place. And yet she wanted him to stay at Chatham Lodge with a desperation that bordered on the irrational. It was the desire to paint him, she reassured herself again, her irrepressible artist's urge to commit physical beauty to virgin canvas. Her other foolish emotions would soon abate, but her hunger to paint him would endure.

As Evie finally remembered to summon Tess and Polly to clear the last course, she saw Mr. Roberts nod and exchange a few low words with Gus. Though her guest had been relatively quiet at dinner, it had become readily apparent that Mr. Roberts was not a shy man. His clothing, still slightly rumpled from exposure to the elements, nonetheless identified him to be, as Gus would say "tol'rably well blunted." Moreover, despite his subdued demeanor, Mr. Roberts's manner, motions, and voice bespoke a man obviously accustomed to issuing commands. For a moment, Evangeline experienced a wave of discomfort, realizing how dully provincial they must seem to a man of such sophistication. As Gus turned to quit the dining parlor, Elliot finally strolled from behind the table and walked toward her.

"Mr. Roberts, we normally have no need to serve port after dinner here, but if you and Gus should like to partake—"

Her guest interrupted with a shake of his head, then offered Evangeline his elbow. "Thank you, Miss Stone, but no. May I see you to the drawing room?"

Evangeline managed a warm smile, but she did not take his proffered arm. "Mr. Roberts, I sense that you are not . . . perfectly at ease. And, of course, I realize this cannot compare to town. Believe me when I say that you need not join in our after-dinner gaieties, since I daresay they are not at all to your taste."

Mr. Roberts seemed greatly taken aback, and Evangeline had the fleeting impression that perhaps she'd insulted him. "I—of course," he stammered. "I would not wish to intrude."

She *had* insulted him. "You misunderstand me, sir," she responded smoothly, curling her hand around his arm as they made their way out. She tried to ignore the familiar feel of his taut, powerful muscles beneath the fabric of his coat. "I simply have no wish to compel you to entertain my charges with a game of backgammon or cards, for following that you shall no doubt be called upon for a song, if not a hornpipe jig. And that, I can assure you, shall only lead to Blind Man's Bluff or worse."

"Worse?" he cried in feigned shock, pressing his fingertips into his chest. "Pray whatever could be worse?"

"There's always Hunt the Slipper, Mr. Roberts," Evangeline answered, deliberately forcing a light, dry tone. "Have you never played it?"

"No, indeed," he said gravely. "I have not."

"Avoid it at all costs, sir," she warned. "It is a bruising sport."

"I see," he answered solemnly. By now, they were alone in the darkened hall. Unexpectedly, Mr. Roberts pulled her to a stop and spun on one booted heel to face her. His narrowed gray eyes seemed to glitter, sending a wave of unexpected heat coursing through her. He stood close, too close. And when he spoke, his voice was a low, soft whisper, a subtle, almost irresistible invitation to draw nearer. "Pray tell me, Miss Stone, what other perils do I risk by remaining overlong in this enchanting place? And in this bewitching company?"

Evangeline felt her breath catch, and she fought the urge to lean into him. Elliot Roberts was standing so near that she could feel the warmth radiate from his body. His hand had slipped up to catch her gently by the elbow with a grip that seemed suddenly unrelenting. His fingers warmed her skin through the silk of her gown, and she could smell the soft scent of expensive tobacco. Even in the dimly lit corridor, she could see the shadowy outline of his heavy beard and the burning emotion in his smoky eyes.

"I—I, ah, well, there is the gooseberry wine," she managed to stammer, struggling valiantly to sound light. Good Lord, but he was a dangerously handsome man. Someone else's handsome man, she reminded herself, to little avail.

"Ah, yes. The gooseberry wine," he repeated in a quiet, silky voice. "Might it dull my senses, Miss Stone? For I should fear that above all else."

"If you dare to drink it, naught shall be dulled but your taste buds," she managed to answer, daring to look up at him. "Winnie makes it herself and takes a sadly misplaced pride in that fact."

Mr. Roberts seemed briefly to ponder this dire consequence. "Hmm—well, then, I shall avoid it altogether, for I value my sense of taste very highly," he responded, still holding Evangeline's gaze.

"Do you indeed?" In unwitting invitation, Evangeline licked her lips nervously, suddenly very much aware of Mr. Roberts's towering height and physical intensity. It felt as if they drew incrementally closer, and Evangeline was not sure if she had willingly stepped toward him or if he had subtly drawn her nearer. Uncertainly, she placed the flat of her hand against his chest, wanting to push him away yet yearning to dig her fingertips into the fabric of his shirt. She felt his heart beating, hard and steady, and once again the heat and vitality of him flooded her senses, washing her in desire.

"Oh, absolutely," he replied, leaning closer still, his lips very nearly brushing the curve of her ear, "and some of my other sensory skills are equally well developed."

In sudden panic, Evangeline jerked away and tried to step backward. "I—please excuse me, Mr. Roberts," she responded breathlessly, feeling her face flame as she pulled from his powerful grasp and began to back down the hall toward the drawing room. "I—I should go. I must turn pages for Frederica. At the—the pianoforte. I always do so after dinner."

Suddenly overwhelmed by uncertainty and guilt, Evangeline whirled about and strode rapidly toward the drawing room, finding it already filled with children. Blindly moving through the crowd and toward the pianoforte, she unexpectedly sensed the hot press of tears behind her eyes. What was wrong with her? What was she about? She had no business allowing—yes, *allowing*—a client, a betrothed gentleman, to begin a silly flirtation with her, merely because she enjoyed his attentions. Such playful banter undoubtedly meant little to Mr. Roberts, but the words left her feeling raw and inexplicably vulnerable.

Oh, Evangeline understood that in polite society, flirting meant next to nothing. Indeed, it was deemed as necessary a social skill as dancing or gaming. Nonetheless, she was not versed in the shallow ways of English society, as Elliot Roberts almost certainly was. She was an outsider. For Evangeline, words were still serious things, and passion was something she could afford to express with oil and canvas only. In this handsome gentleman, Mr. Roberts, she had found herself unexpectedly out of her depth and a little ashamed of her response toward him.

Deliberately, Evangeline stared across the length of the drawing room, watching as her brother Michael cheerfully pulled a chair toward the mahogany card table. The child was so innocent, so carefree. Pray God he could remain so. At that very moment, Michael tilted back his head and laughed gaily at some jest of Theo's. Strangely enough, the vision of her brother's happiness soothed Evangeline, suffusing her with an almost calming sense of duty. Her composure slowly returning, Evangeline picked up Frederica's music and spread it open, just as Elliot strode into the room.

Only moments later, Elliot found himself making up a fourth for cards with Gus, Theo, and Michael, Mr. Stokely having taken up a book of poetry instead. Much to Winnie Weyden's consternation, the boys had persuaded Elliot into a rowdy game of loo played for ha'pennies. Despite such impecunious stakes and Elliot's notorious cunning at the gaming tables, he soon found himself well on his way to being fleeced as a result of his impaired concentration.

True to her mumbled explanation, Evangeline now sat stiffly upon the pianoforte bench beside Frederica at the opposite end of the vast drawing room. Carefully positioning himself at the card table in such a way that he might observe the pair, Elliot watched as Frederica performed with admirable skill for one so young. He could not help but notice, however, that the child stumbled frequently, and the cause was almost always Evangeline's failure to turn the page in a timely fashion.

She had been discomfited by his flirtation, that much was obvious. Why, Elliot asked himself, had he done such a heartless thing? Despite her age and demeanor, Evangeline was plainly unaccustomed to the attentions of an accomplished flirt, having instantly stammered and blushed at his intimations. What had he hoped to gain by such coarse behavior? Had he sunk so deep into dissolution that he took some pathetic pleasure in the discomfort of a gently bred woman? Such a thought disgusted him, and yet he knew that he had deliberately stood too close and implied too much, all the while reveling in his ability to disconcert her.

It had been a test, he realized with a shock. Yes, a test of sorts. He'd wanted to see for himself what her response would be. All of the women Elliot knew, even those few who made a passing bid at respectability, were more than capable of rising to the challenge of an arrant scapegrace like himself. But Evangeline Stone, clearly, was not. Not yet.

At last, the closing chords of Frederica's sonata sounded amid her cousins' gracious cries of "bravo" and "well done." Evangeline quietly withdrew to a sofa by the window as Nicolette Stone laid quick claim to the pianoforte. Curled on a rug with the cats, Fritz the dog lay by the hearth where coals hissed warmly in defense against the insidious damp. Evangeline flipped open a book, and Mrs. Weyden sat, as she had done since dinner, sewing in an oversized armchair. Beside the fire, Mr. Stokely appeared to be very nearly asleep. Shyly approaching the card table, Frederica curled around Michael's chair to peer at his hand. It was a scene of utter domestic harmony, an oasis of peace. And it brought with it a sense of comfort that even Elliot could not miss.

As the cards continued to fall, Elliot began to relax; though he continued to observe Evangeline out of the corner of one eye. "I say, Roberts!" gloated Gus as Elliot's next card fell. "Expected better from a real town gamester." Energetically, the young man leaned forward to sweep the loo into his corner.

"Oh, aye, that's a whole quid you've taken 'im for, Gus," added Theo, his mouth curling sarcastically as he dealt another hand. "No doubt we'll be rich as nabobs any day now."

"I do not suppose, Mr. Weyden," said Elliot dryly as the play resumed, "that this inadvertent hiatus in your Cambridge career had anything to do with your card skills, hmm?"

Theo, a handsome lad who looked to be about sixteen, snorted disdainfully as he made his play. "He wishes!"

Gus colored slightly. "Er—not exactly," he replied, tugging at his cravat.

Theo winked at Elliot conspiratorially. "Nothing so sophisticated as all that, sir! Gus 'n' a vicar's son got a touch bosky. Shinnied up an oak tree and flashed their bums at the vice chancellor's old auntie!" At this remark, Elliot was simply beyond restraint. He burst into a sputter, which advanced rapidly into an undignified guffaw, immediately sending Michael and Theo into peels of hilarity. Across the room, Evangeline and Mr. Stokely turned to regard the four card players with mild interest.

"Theodore!" Mrs. Weyden's tone rang out sharply. "Hush this instant, or your bum will be exposed to my riding crop! And do not you, Mr. Roberts, be so wicked as to encourage them!"

"Yes, ma'am," agreed Elliot soberly, wiping a tear from

his eye. He looked down to see that Gus was again sweeping up the pot. "Mr. Stokely!" Elliot called out to the instructor in the most companionable voice he could muster, "come save me from this lubricious gang of Captain Sharps, for I'm down to my last shilling."

"Oh, you're a clever fellow, Roberts," jeered Gus good-naturedly. "Best admit it when you've been done in by professionals!"

"Aye, come on, Stokely!" added Theo. "Roberts is pressed to quit, else he'll not be able to afford Evie's commission, and she'll toss him out on his ear."

Shoving his spectacles up his nose and laying aside his verses, Stokely stirred himself and obligingly took Elliot's seat.

Elliot, ever the opportunist, slipped across the room to stand alongside Evie's sofa. "May I join you?" he asked as humbly as he knew how.

Evie looked up from her book and blinked twice. "By all means, Mr. Roberts," she replied, with stiff civility.

Settling himself onto the empty half of the sofa, Elliot peered at her book. "Fielding?" he asked, keeping his voice deliberately low.

"Yes." Her throaty voice was cool but cordial.

"Ah! Which one?"

"*Amelia*," she replied succinctly.

"Oh, too serious, Miss Stone!" Elliot shook his head. "I much prefer *Tom Jones*."

Over her small, elegant nose, Evangeline fixed him in a pointed stare. "Indeed? The adventures of a charming libertine. I might have guessed."

Elliot choked. Evangeline Stone might not be worldly, but she was a quick wit. His gaze swept the room. Over the chords of the pianoforte and the din at the card table, no one in the room paid them any heed. He drew a deep breath and subtly leaned in toward her. "Ah, you need say no more, madam! I perceive that I have distressed you. Let me try again—"

"Try what again?" she interrupted sharply.

Elliot dropped his gaze and tried to look repentant. "Miss Stone, I owe you my deepest apology for giving even a moment of discomfort earlier this evening. I have not the slightest notion of propriety, I fear, since I was most shamelessly attempting to flirt with you."

She flicked him an icy look. "Flirting?"

"Yes, and I am sorry for it. As you so carefully pointed out, this is not town. Moreover, I am a grateful guest in your home, and I have partaken of your generous hospitality. It was wrong of me to put you so out of countenance."

"Out of countenance?" A touch of humor brightened the perfect oval of her face.

Elliot tried to smile innocently and lightly touched her hand where it lay upon the sofa. "Miss Stone, you are doing naught but echoing my words. You must smack me! Scold me! Tell me that I am not fit to kiss the hem of your skirt. For I am not, you know," he added in a low voice.

Evangeline watched her handsome guest's gray eyes soften, and suddenly she found herself laughing, quite against her will. Elliot Roberts was trouble indeed, she realized yet again, for she could no more resist his charming entreaties than his subtle overtures. "Good Lord, Mr. Roberts! That's quite enough! All is forgiven."

"Thank God!" he whispered melodramatically, falling back against the sofa. "I thought to be forever in your bad graces."

Deliberately, Evangeline broke away from his hypnotic gaze and forced herself to stare into the depths of her book. "With such skillful groveling as all that, Mr. Roberts, I shouldn't expect that you remain in the bad graces of any woman for very long."

"Miss Stone!" he whispered softly. "I must warn you that you are now perilously close to flirting with *me!* It's not at all the thing, either, since I'm a client."

Evangeline squared her shoulders and tried to look stern. "Mr. Roberts, I have taken you in, had you brushed, bathed, and fed—"

"—like a stray dog, I know," interrupted Elliot, hanging his head mournfully.

"And you've paid me not a penny so far, so I fail to see—"

"Come, Miss Stone." Elliot sighed and extended his hand. "You are right on every villainous count. Ere someone suggests I sleep with Fritz, please take me off to your Tower. It is where I belong, no doubt."

"No doubt," she muttered, laying aside her book. Then, resolutely, she lifted her gaze to catch his once more. "Though I almost fear being alone with you, Mr. Roberts. You have altogether too much charm," she added grimly.

Her guest seemed taken aback by her forthright confession, his teasing expression immediately gentling to one of grave concern. "I am exceedingly sorry, Miss Stone. I give you my word as a gentleman that in the future you shall have no cause to feel even a moment's discomfort in my company." So saying, he rose smoothly to his feet and offered her his arm.

With a sigh of resignation and an irrational sense of disappointment, Evangeline rose, then politely escorted her guest back up the main staircase, down the second floor, and around the twisting tower stairs to his third-floor bedchamber. Elliot promptly made a very proper thank you, then bid her a pleasant good night.

It was precisely half past midnight when the ancient butler, MacLeod, swung open the heavy door at Strath

House, the century-old Richmond residence of the marquises of Rannoch. The knocking had been loud, intense, and unremitting. Fully expecting, therefore, to see his exhausted master standing on the threshold, MacLeod was taken aback to find instead Major Matthew Winthrop and his cohort, Aidan Grant, Viscount Linden, weaving unsteadily and begging admittance.

"Evening, MacLeod," called Linden jovially, holding his gold-knobbed walking stick aloft in his fist. "We come bearing news of a most ursh—urk—no, *urgent* nashure. For his lordship!"

"Gossip!" echoed Winthrop with another drunken wobble. "For Rannoch!"

MacLeod peered through his silver spectacles and down his hooked nose at the two strikingly dressed and cheerfully drunken gentlemen who stood staggering upon the broad marble steps of Strath House.

"Verra sorry, my lord and Major Winthrop," replied MacLeod civilly. "Lord Rannoch is oot and hasna returned." The butler watched as the two men glanced at each other with what was obviously crushing disappointment.

Other than the aura of privilege and the odor of alcohol, both of which copiously emanated from them, the two men were a contrast in every possible way. Winthrop was raven-haired, broad-shouldered, and attired in a dark, conservative coat of a military cut, while Linden, tall, blond, and angelically handsome, was every inch the immoderate town dandy. How the irrepressible pair had come to be the partners in debauchery of Elliot Armstrong was no secret to the elderly butler.

It was astonishing when one now considered it, but in his youth Lord Rannoch had been worse than unsophisticated. He had been recklessly naïve. By the close of his first year in town, Rannoch's reputation lay in ruins. The young lord then set about worsening matters by steeping himself in that most volatile of concoctions: alcohol, mixed with heated despair, topped by a froth of high-stakes gaming.

Late one night, following a remarkably profitable run at hazard, the inebriated marquis had found himself on the wrong end of a disgruntled competitor's sword. Unarmed and friendless outside a London stew, Rannoch had been fortunate indeed when both Linden and Winthrop, only marginally more sober, had leapt to his defense. Rannoch's wounds had healed quickly, his vengeance had been swift, and ever after the effervescent viscount and the dour army officer had been the marquis's best—indeed, his only—companions.

MacLeod knew that the gentlemen were to be afforded every courtesy. Eyeing them up and down, the butler cleared his throat ceremoniously. "Weel, gentlemen . . . might I suggest that these verra important tidings be best carried tae Sir Hugh? He is in, being laid up with the gout, but no yet abed."

"Capital idea, MacLeod!" boomed Major Winthrop.

"Indeed!" concurred Linden cheerfully. "To Sir Hugh!" Eagerly, both men charged toward the door at precisely the same moment, resulting in a most maladroit tangle of elbows, legs, and walking sticks. Once MacLeod had restored Winthrop to his feet and disentangled Linden's cravat from his cane, he bade them both be seated while he informed Sir Hugh of their presence.

"If you want brandy, fetch it yourselves," grumbled Sir Hugh Benham from his favorite wing chair. The elderly gentleman's bare, swollen foot was extended before him, propped high upon a stack of feather pillows perched atop a footstool.

"I say, Sir Hugh," exclaimed Lord Linden, weaving unsteadily as he peered down at the foot. "Nasty mess, that." Still carrying his elegant walking stick, from which he had illogically refused to be parted, the dandified viscount made as if to poke at the inflamed joint of Sir Hugh's great toe.

"Touch it and die, you son of a bitch," growled Sir Hugh irritably.

"I say, Hugh! What's got your wind up?" asked Winthrop, carrying a fresh drink over to join the pair. Even half sprung, the man still looked every inch a soldier.

"Needs a woman, belike," explained Linden cheerfully, completely unoffended. He plopped down alongside Winthrop on a leather sofa. "Curse of the Benhams, ain't it, old boy?" He turned his bleary gaze upon Sir Hugh for confirmation.

"Been trapped up here for three damn days," grumbled Sir Hugh, twisting irritably in his chair. "Feels more like three bloody months. And Olivia Johnson's husband just left for Rome, damn it all."

"Curse of the Benhams," repeated Lord Linden in his languid drawl. "Oversexed. Rannoch's got it, too, don't he, Hugh?"

"Quite right," interjected his dark-haired companion unexpectedly. "Why we're here an' all that." Major Winthrop struggled to focus his normally piercing gaze upon Sir Hugh.

Lord Linden turned to his friend in bewilderment. "On account of the Benham curse?"

"No, no," replied Major Winthrop.

"Livie sent you?" asked Hugh suspiciously.

"No, no!" The major shook his head, sloshing brandy across his thigh. "Here about Rannoch! All the old talk. You know—" Winthrop looked at his dandified cohort for assistance, but Sir Hugh interrupted.

"You mean about that shot in his arse?" Sir Hugh's voice was gruffly impatient. "That trifling spat with Jeanette's husband?"

Major Winthrop shook his head again. "No, no, not that! The other. Cranham."

Lord Linden resolutely thumped his stick upon the floor. "Righty-ho," he agreed, and turned to Sir Hugh. "Cranham. Thought Elliot ought to be prepared. He's back."

"What, from the dead?" Sir Hugh stared at Linden incredulously. "Boys, put away your cups! That old goat died eight months past."

Major Winthrop shook his head. "The *new* Baron Cranham. Walked right into Brooks's tonight. Back from Baipur a month or more. Bit of a nabob now."

"All the talk, don'tcha know," chimed Linden, jerking backward with a little *hic!* One thick lock of his perfectly groomed blond hair tumbled forward to bounce, apparently unnoticed, before his left eye. "Found his mother's marriage lines—"

"—stuck in her father's family bible!" chimed Major Winthrop.

"Looks like they're valid." Lord Linden nodded.

"Not the bastard we thought he was," snickered the major. "In one way, at least."

"Elliot ought to kill him this time," added the dapper viscount with a cheerful certainty.

Sir Hugh looked at the men in mute amazement, his eyes traveling back and forth between them. Then, abruptly, Sir Hugh snatched a small brass bell from his side table, and a footman immediately oozed from the shadows. "Fetch me a damn drink!" the elderly baronet barked.

❧ 3 ❧

Doubtful thoughts, and rash-embrac'd despair.
—WILLIAM SHAKESPEARE

Good night had suddenly become little more than a trite expression to Evangeline, as she tossed miserably in her second-floor bedchamber. She thumped her pillow unmercifully, until finally, with a sharp exhalation, she felt compelled to pitch it onto the floor. Surely it must be nearly four o'clock by now, since eons had passed since the hall clock had struck three. It was him, drat it all. The sculpture. The man. Elliot Roberts. What unholy urge had possessed Peter to send such a man to torment her nights?

But indeed, despite the man's stunning appearance, Peter had probably never given Elliot Roberts a thought. Because Peter, along with everyone else who knew her, thought Evangeline wholly impervious to male charm. And regrettably, she was . . . or had been. Precisely why this was so, she could not say, but despite the aching emptiness that had begun to gnaw at her these last few years, Evangeline had never met one man who could turn her head with anything other than mild artistic interest.

Perhaps that was why her portraits brought her so little satisfaction and she felt compelled to turn to epic—and often imaginary—heroes to bring her canvas fully to life. But despite his elegant manners and physical beauty, she must remember that Elliot Roberts was just a man, not a hero. There was nothing obvious in his demeanor that should have given Peter a moment's concern. And Peter, with his odd, meticulous ways, would never have referred a client who was disreputable in any way, for despite his constant travels, Peter was an attentive trustee and a devoted friend. Nonetheless, there was something not quite right about this man he had sent to see her; an enigma, an ephemeral feeling ... but she would come to understand it eventually. Perhaps tomorrow, when the painting began, matters would come clear. Perhaps in the light of day, she would get a grip on those turbulent sensations his presence aroused and his touch inflamed. Perhaps, she wryly considered, she should avoid touching him altogether.

But she was obsessed by far more than good looks and a gentle touch. In every respect, she was altogether too charmed by Elliot Roberts, who, with his low, silky voice, had a way of saying "May I pass the parsnips?" and making it sound like a far more intriguing offer. Admittedly, he had disconcerted her with his rather blatant flirtation, yet now that the curling, insidious warmth had left her stomach and the jelly in her knees had solidified, Evangeline had to ask herself what harm there was in flirting. It was hardly the first time a man had flirted with her, though few had done so with such practiced skill, and none to such a disquieting effect.

Indeed, had she not known perfectly well what he was about last night in the hall? Yet she had remained, to stare into his hypnotic gray eyes and to allow herself to be pulled far closer than was wise. To his credit, Mr. Roberts had not pressed his attentions upon her. Rather, he had ultimately apologized. And very prettily, too. It had been rather a disappointment, that apology. Despite her initial panic and subsequent urge to cry, Evangeline had still harbored a foolish, secret hope that Mr. Roberts might shoot her that fast, wicked smile, then resume his flirtation in the corridor outside his bedchamber.

Angrily, Evangeline let her head drop back with a harsh thump against the headboard. The timing of such discomfiting emotions could not possibly have been worse, and her shame could not have been greater. Lord, how she wanted him. An Englishman! And another woman's fiancé, no less. Why could not things have worked out differently? Had she not been courted by a half dozen perfectly agreeable suitors while Papa was still alive? Among them had been a Bavarian nobleman, a Russian painter, and even one young Italian banker. Friends of Papa's, associates of Uncle Peter, none of them English. And all of them, if words could be believed, utterly devoted to her. More importantly, while Papa lived, Michael had been safe. But now, well . . .

Bloody hell! Such thoughts were madness. Evangeline gave the coverlet a sharp yank. She needed to keep at an emotional distance from Elliot Roberts. Whether or not she wanted, for once in her life, to exchange flirtatious comments was beside the point. He was betrothed. And she was busy. Exceedingly busy. Her life was filled with duty and responsibility. Indeed, she had no business flirting with anyone when eleven-year-old Michael had a veritable ax hanging over his head. Exasperated, Evangeline tossed off the bedcovers, bathed her face in cold water, then dressed quickly. Yes, she could work by lamplight until the sun was up. After all, she had yet to prepare the freshly stretched canvas for her morning's work. That would take some time.

Just as his lovely hostess had predicted, Elliot had arisen to find that the torrents of spring rain had finally given way to a brilliant May morning. Muted sunshine now flowed through the high south windows of

Chatham's studio, warming the flagstone floor and heightening the colors of Evie's masterpieces.

And they really were masterpieces, Elliot realized as he strolled through the room, the heels of his heavy boots echoing forlornly through the empty chamber. He wished that Evangeline would come and fervently hoped she had forgiven his shocking lapse of propriety, for he was resolved that it would not happen again. Much to his disappointment, his hostess had not appeared at breakfast, though he saw evidence that she had already been at work in the studio.

At the north side, he paused. A collection of landscapes was suspended from the wall at its highest level. Beneath them hung a row of portraits, and below that more sat propped against the wall, almost all completed. In comparison, however, even Elliot could see that the artistic style between the portraits and the landscapes differed greatly. Over and over, the landscapes pulled his gaze aloft, as he moved from right to left. Each was unique and exquisite—rolling scenes of pastoral beauty, rushing streams in hues of frothy green, windmills whirling against scuttling clouds, threshers toiling in golden fields, the next more beautiful than its neighbor.

As Elliot reached the northwest corner, however, his eye was distracted by a vast canvas propped upon a sturdy easel and turned back against the wall. Carefully sliding himself into the corner between the wall and the canvas, Elliot stared at the massive oil painting and involuntarily sucked in his breath.

Although Elliot was ready to confess near ignorance on the subject of art, the piece his eyes took in was dramatic beyond anything he'd ever witnessed. Before him, a medieval battle scene unfolded in the background. Crested helmets rose to meet a cloudless sapphire sky as multihued banners snapped in the wind. From the left, mounted knights charged, advancing into the fray through the swirling dust of a plateau battlefield. Hacking forward from the right came obviously enraged hordes of thickset foot soldiers, swinging long, wicked halberds as they marched. Men of arms bearing deadly spears stabbed randomly into the melee.

Elliot could smell the sweat of the charging warhorses as their eyes flashed white with fear, and he could hear the crash of arms and armor as man after man fell to be trampled beneath pounding hooves. It was a scene charged with raw power; a majestic fusion of motion and emotion. Yet even as the background seemed literally to move before the viewer's eyes, the foreground stood still, frozen in time. A hero in golden armor lay dead, cleft through the heart by a bloody halberd. The knight's towering crest of peacock feathers was splayed in a contrasting swath of color against his fallen banner. His right arm lay outstretched, a glinting sword still clutched in his hand.

The piece was at once horrific, epic, and frighteningly beautiful.

The rasp of door hinges pulled Elliot from the spell of the painting, and he stuck out his head to see Evangeline entering through the schoolroom door. The stout black dog trotted dutifully behind, his tiny claws clicking rhythmically upon the flagstone.

"Good morning," called Elliot, stepping carefully from behind the canvas.

Her veiled gaze shifted toward him. Evangeline wore another dark blue dress over a muslin chemisette this morning, and in her hand she clutched a sheaf of papers. "Good morning," she replied as she strode purposefully through the studio toward her desk.

Elliot felt compelled to explain himself. "Good morning, Miss Stone. I hope you do not object? I saw this, and I wanted to examine it."

Evangeline put a few loose papers down on the desk-top, then turned back to face him. "No, Mr. Roberts," she answered, looking almost resigned. "I have no objection."

"Miss Stone, I must confess, I have never seen any-thing to rival this. It—it is your work, is it not? I mean, I can tell that it is . . . somehow."

"Yes. It is mine," she answered, strolling slowly across the room to where he stood. "I do try to keep my com-mercial portraits separate from my other work, but as you can see, I do both."

"And under different names?"

"Yes."

"Because you are a female?" he guessed.

She threw him a quizzical smile. "I think it makes for better business," she admitted.

"What do you call this piece, Miss Stone?" he asked softly, gesturing toward the huge canvas behind him.

"*The Fall of Leopold at Sempach*."

"A truly remarkable painting," he murmured.

"It is almost finished," she answered noncommittally. "Soon it will be taken down to London, and Uncle Peter will put it on the market."

"Must you sell it?"

"Yes, we need the income," she admitted crisply. Then, apparently noting the surprised expression on his face, she added, "I prefer to keep our capital in the funds, and the estate income is needed to maintain our tenant farms."

Elliot nodded, sensing that she did not wish to belabor the subject. "It would appear that you have a remarkable range of style and technique," he commented, returning his gaze to the landscapes mounted high on the north wall.

"Those are my father's," she replied quietly. "They are not for sale."

Elliot looked at her uncertainly, then nodded. "Somehow, I did not think they had the look of your work, though they are very fine. Your father was exceedingly gifted, was he not?"

"Oh, yes," she answered, but the blue sheen in her eyes had suddenly dulled. "Very gifted."

"I can see that. His work is exquisite. But this! This is—not exquisite." Elliot reached out to touch the battle scene lightly. "Indeed, Miss Stone, this work defies my descriptive powers."

"Thank you—I think," she responded politely.

In his absorption, Elliot missed the note of uncertainty in her tone. "What is this, exactly? I mean, what is it about?" he asked, his tone reverent. "I feel as if I am there."

"I visited that battlefield, or what remains, many years ago," said Evangeline with a shrug. "The painting is a scene from Leopold's march through Switzerland. It has been depicted on canvas often enough, and I expect this one shan't be the last."

"What sort of march?"

"To suppress the forest cantons' rebellion against growing Habsburg rule. You see here the banner of Lucerne, yes?" Elliot nodded. "And to the far right lies the body of de Winkelried, a knight of the Unterwalden. Do you see here?" She pointed at a tortured figure. "Legend says that he impaled himself onto the Habsburg pikes to open a gap in the enemy wall."

"Good Lord!" replied Elliot with a shudder. "Who are these mounted knights?"

"Those are the mercenaries of Hawkscastle, the dynasty we now call the Habsburgs. On this battlefield, in the late fourteenth century, the Austrians met the rebel *Schwitz*—the Highlanders, if you will."

"I'm shamefully ignorant of history, Miss Stone. Was this battle significant?"

"It certainly was to the Austrians." She chuckled, seeming to warm to the topic, the blue spark returning to her eyes. "It was quite an unexpected defeat for the Habsburgs. The Swiss foresters, though disorganized and foolhardy, were savage and fearless."

"This golden knight, then, is Leopold?"

"Yes, but again, the gold armor is no more than a legend." She turned to him, her face fixed in a calm smile. "I think that is enough medieval history for one morning, Mr. Roberts. Shall we turn our attentions to you?" Lightly, she touched him on the elbow and guided him toward the easel and chairs which were positioned in the center of her studio.

For more than an hour, Elliot silently endured the ceaseless scrutiny of Evangeline Stone's cool blue gaze. Elliot could see that she'd earlier prepared a large canvas and mounted it on the easel. In her left hand she held a palette, and in the long, slender fingers of her right, the brush. From time to time, Elliot could hear her mutter a low, unladylike oath, and then he would see a flash of her palette knife. It was frustrating. He could not observe her—at least, not to his satisfaction. Nor could he see what she was painting. All he could see was Evangeline's penetrating eyes. Sharply focused. Brilliant. What would it take, Elliot mused, to make those deep blue eyes glaze over? What would a man have to do to make Evangeline's lips part invitingly and her heart race? For the right man, very little, he guessed. The thought made his loins tighten, and he suppressed a groan.

Focusing on the long, graceful turn of Evangeline's neck, Elliot wanted, inexplicably, to press his lips to the warmth of her throat, to touch her ivory skin lightly—yes, just there—with his tongue and feel her pulse throb beneath it. Yes, he wanted to feel the warmth and life that surged within her, for, most assuredly, Evangeline Stone

was alive. Despite her outward calm and deliberate reserve, Elliot was convinced the woman sheltered a passionate soul. Moreover, one could not lend life and
passion to canvas as powerfully as this woman did without possessing a heart filled near to bursting with it.

Good Lord. *Soul? Heart?* From what foolish recesses of
his mind had such drivel been dredged? He simply wanted to seduce Evangeline Stone. Putting pretty names to
his baser instincts made them no better than what they
were. Damn right, he wanted her. Moreover, while wanting a woman was as common as an itch for Elliot, and
about as easy to remedy, wanting a particular woman was
a luxury he no longer allowed himself. In any event, the
temptation was not Evangeline. It was this place. No, perhaps it was nothing more than the contrast with the cold
despair that had been left to bear him company in the
wake of another affair gone sour. It had to be caused by
something; this sort of obsessive desire was appalling.
But admittedly, Elliot had become painfully aware of his
need last night in Evangeline's dimly lit hallway, when
she did not pull away from his grasp.

Yes, that, too, was interesting. Until the very last moment, when she'd run for cover, Evangeline had held his
gaze steadily as Elliot commenced his age-old routine of
seduction. Within Elliot's usual social circle, a little seduction along with a trinket or two could persuade almost any woman to overlook his hulking size, nasty
disposition, and scandalous reputation. Indeed, within
the demimonde, it was a routine that never failed to meet
with success, and he had begun to suspect it might work
on Evangeline.

Elliot had watched intently as her breath quickened at
his touch last night. It was an almost unmistakable sign,
that. A bad one, too, perhaps. His folly in lingering in this
house no longer had anything to do with his being tired,

wet, and frustratingly lost in the rain-swept English countryside. It had everything to do with this hauntingly beautiful and damnably innocent woman.

"Mr. Roberts?" Evangeline's rich contralto voice brought him back to reality. "Would you kindly turn to the right just a trifle? Yes. Thank you." She flashed Elliot just a hint of a smile and returned her eyes to the canvas.

"Miss Stone?" He watched as Evangeline's head jerked up, her brush poised halfway to her palette. Desire and uncertainty washed over him. "Yesterday afternoon, you said that you found me . . . striking. What, precisely, did you mean? Striking?"

"Mr. Roberts, I am not at all sure I understand your—"

"What I mean to ask is," he interrupted bluntly, "was your remark intended as one of those backhanded compliments? Such as when one tells an exceedingly ugly woman that her face has great character?"

A playful smile began to tug at Evangeline's full mouth. "Indeed, your face does have great character, Mr. Roberts, and that is, after all, the most important thing. When I paint a really good portrait—one that comes from my heart—the subject's character *is* what I paint."

At this explanation, Elliot inwardly shuddered. Certainly, he had no wish to view an artistic rendition of his character and couldn't imagine Evangeline taking any pleasure in it, either. What would such a piece look like? A vast, gaping black hole? Or worse?

As if she could read his thoughts, Evangeline's gaze flicked up at him again. "Have a care, Mr. Roberts. I can tell a great deal about a man by simply studying his face, so I give you fair warning."

Elliot drew a deep breath and tried to keep his mouth shut, but his cold Scottish reserve seemed to melt in the presence of this woman. "Very well, Miss Stone, what do you see in my face?"

Evangeline put down her brush and stared at him for a long moment as if she did not wish to answer. When at last she spoke, her words were soft yet precise. "Intelligence, certainly. The potential for goodness. Despair. Dissimulation. And . . . great anger, I think."

"I see," he softly replied, suddenly no more eager than she to expound upon the subject. He felt a sudden urge to flee. Her perception was too disconcerting. But he could not tear himself away. "You did not answer my original question," he said, trying to maintain a teasing voice.

Eyes now focused on the canvas before her, Evangeline flushed slightly and refused to meet his gaze. "Mr. Roberts, I am quite certain that you are well aware of how unusually handsome you are, since innumerable women have no doubt told you so."

"Handsome? Perhaps a few women of my acquaintance have used that term," he admitted grudgingly, "but gratuitous fawning can be motivated by some ugly and unpleasant things, can it not?"

Evangeline's eyes flicked up at him again as she dropped her brush neatly into a jar of solvent. Her rich voice was cool and steady. "Contrary, perhaps, to some of your past experiences, Mr. Roberts, my remarks are artistically, rather than economically or carnally, motivated."

"*Touché*," he murmured softly, amazed at her audacity.

"Your face is uncommon yet beautiful in a strong, stark way," she continued dispassionately. "And it is far more pleasant for the artist when one's subject is inherently beautiful, as you are. Then one feels no need to pretend."

"Pretend?"

"Yes. That is to say, I need not paint superficially. I can be honest with my canvas without fear of the customer's disappointment."

"Ah, I see."

"Do you? I wonder. Tell me, Mr. Roberts, is this portrait really intended for your fiancée? I must admit, you seem more than a little indurate. Moreover, you have neither the look nor the demeanor of a man in love. And a man who goes to such trouble is, generally speaking, passionately so."

Elliot paused to consider carefully how best to respond to such extraordinary incisiveness. "How perceptive, Miss Stone. You have found me out."

"Indeed, Mr. Roberts, precisely what have I found out? I must say, it is not at all clear to me."

"My betrothal was . . . has been ended," he responded slowly. That much, at least, was true.

"I see. And yet here you are."

Elliot shrugged. "Well, I really did not intend to have my portrait painted. However, when I saw you, er, saw your work—"

Evangeline's brow furrowed. "Do you mean to say that you rode all the way to Wrotham-upon-Lea just to tell me—"

"To—to where?" In his confusion, Elliot forgot his ruse. *Good heavens, was he in the wrong damned village?*

Evangeline froze, her brush hung in mid-stroke. "To Wrotham-upon-Lea," she repeated slowly and distinctly.

"Yes. Yes, to be sure! To Wrotham-upon-Lea." Elliot turned his palm upward in a gesture of apology. "Well, as it happens, I thought that a ride through the countryside might be pleasant—"

"In the mud and the rain? Merely to tell me you didn't want a portrait?"

Caught in his first real lie, Elliot hesitated, beset by sudden guilt. It was a surprising reaction, and he was taken aback by the realization that he did not want to lie to Evangeline Stone. Nor, however, did he wish to tell her the truth. Something in the middle would have to suffice. Blandly, he smiled. Evangeline was still poised with a clean brush aloft. "Well, to be a trifle more honest, Miss Stone, I had other business in the area, and when I saw how beautiful you—your work was, I just couldn't resist."

Evangeline blinked, then lowered her brush. "How odd!" was her only comment, and then she bent to resume her painting. For the better part of an hour, they continued thus, each watching the other, neither speaking a word. When at last Elliot felt his legs begin to grow numb, he rose and slowly began to stroll about the room, staring at but hardly seeing the paintings that hung on the walls.

It was time. Time to go. Elliot could no longer postpone the inevitable, and the reasons he should leave were many, while the reasons he had stayed bordered on the insane. Evangeline Stone saw far too much. And the ugly business with Antoinette remained, hanging over his head like a rusty blade. And as always, pressing business awaited him in town. Zoë awaited him as well, and it was long past time that he saw to her. He missed her, and in some way the children of Chatham Lodge made his loneliness and frustration all the more poignant when he thought of his daughter.

Once he returned to Richmond from this pleasant diversion—and that was all it had been, a spontaneous, selfish, and ill-conceived diversion—he would immediately send a letter to Evangeline by private courier. He would enclose a cash payment for the commission and make some vague excuse for his inability to continue sitting for the portrait. That would be best for all concerned. Certainly, it was best for her. Indeed, a prompt and permanent disappearance was the only logical alternative left to him now that he had initiated this dratted mess.

"Miss Stone," he said quietly, still facing the wall, "I am afraid that I must take my leave. Not only have I imposed upon you far too long, but I have business to which I must attend."

He heard the clack of Evangeline's brush as she put it down and the rustle of her skirts as she rose to pull the bell. Almost immediately, the sullen housemaid called Polly appeared at the door, and Evangeline gave orders to have Elliot's mount brought around from the stables. Then she crossed the width of the room to join him by the broad south windows and tilted her head to look up at him. She seemed so small yet so vibrant, full of life and warmth. "I apologize," she said softly, "for my tasteless remark about your paying me. It was not something a well-bred lady should say. But I was disturbed by your—your unwarranted self-deprecation."

In the brilliant sunlight, her blond hair was shot with glimmers of gold, and the blue of her eyes deepened to a rich shade of azure. A faint smear of white paint marred one otherwise perfect ivory cheekbone. He watched her as, almost uncertainly, Evangeline's mouth curled into a serene yet alluring smile. "It has been a pleasure—no, a great pleasure—to begin painting you, Mr. Roberts," she continued quietly, "and I hope that you really will return."

Elliot could not resist the urge to touch her. Slowly, he raised his hand and brushed his thumb back and forth across the oily smudge. "Paint," he murmured, pulling out his handkerchief to wipe his hand clean. Elliot watched as her color heightened almost imperceptibly, enhancing her beauty. *If I were an artist, Miss Stone, I would paint you,* he wanted to say.

But he did not. Elliot Armstrong was a great many things, none of them good and none of them remotely associated with life's finer arts. His skills, such as they were, lay elsewhere, and they most assuredly should not be practiced on Evangeline Stone.

At some point, Elliot had ceased to be fully aware that he was still staring into Evangeline's eyes. "You will return, will you not?" she asked, her voice laced with doubt.

She saw through him intuitively. She sensed his uncertainty. Elliot knew it, and he forced himself to smile. "Are you sure you want me to, Miss Stone, having now discerned but a few of my dark secrets?"

Evangeline's brows came together in confusion. "More than ever, as it happens," she answered as if it were obvious. Slowly, they made their way through the house toward the door. For once, neither Bolton nor the housekeeper was anywhere to be seen. Indeed, the entire house seemed unusually empty. Evangeline retrieved his hat and gloves, handing them to him with what Elliot hoped was a measure of reluctance.

Suddenly, all of his resolve gave way, collapsing onto the floor in a sinking, sliding heap. "When, Miss Stone?" he asked hollowly. "When shall I return?"

Evangeline spoke without hesitation. "Next week? And plan to stay, if you can? The children greatly enjoyed your visit, and I hope you do not find them tedious. Until then, I must work on *Leopold* for Peter, but thereafter I would very much like to return my attentions to you."

Elliot bit back a rather impassioned response to that statement and merely nodded, curling his fingers hard into the fabric of his hat brim. "I shall return next week," he agreed softly.

Evangeline smiled. "Do you know, I rather like you, Elliot Roberts? Though you are a bit of an enigma—but that, of course, is something no true artist can resist."

She liked him? No, Miss Evangeline Stone surely

would not like him, should she have the great misfortune to know him. Nevertheless, she liked Elliot Roberts well enough, and he was a fortunate man indeed. Again, Elliot found himself wondering what it would be like to be Mr. Roberts. It was odd, really, but Elliot was struck with the fact that the marquis of Rannoch rather wanted to be someone else. At what point had the deliberately mind-numbing whirlwind of debauchery ceased to bring him satisfaction? Or had it ever done? Elliot honestly did not know.

His was an affluent lifestyle, of that there was no doubt. Elliot's ruthless gaming sustained it, and his wealthy estates ensured it. Evangeline Stone was merely comfortable, yet here she stood, the very picture of domestic contentment. Furthermore, her extended family seemed blessed with all that was good and peaceful. The mere thought of leaving brought a jaded weariness pressing down upon him. Elliot stared at the gentle, elegant lines of Evangeline's face and tried very hard to remember the last time he'd felt contentment. And then he tried with equal effort to remember a time when he had not felt angry.

It was no use. The memories, if there were any, would not come to him. An untoward sound of frustration must have escaped his lips, for Evangeline took a sharp step backward, and it was then that Elliot realized that she'd been standing very close to him, his long black greatcoat laid in neat folds across her slender arm.

He reached out to take it from her, then slowly lifted his gaze to hers. "Next week, Miss Stone," he repeated softly. "Until then, I shall count the minutes." Impulsively, he grasped her hand and pressed his lips to it, and as Elliot felt the heat of her skin against his mouth, he knew that without a doubt he would come to her again. And again. And again, until he was found out for the scoundrel that he was. Or until he dredged up enough courage or choked on enough guilt to tell her the truth and face the ugly, unbearable consequences. Rocked by this chilling realization, Elliot spun about and walked rapidly down the steps and into the drive.

Evangeline watched him go, her mind caught in a whirling vortex of emotion. She stood in the doorway as Elliot mounted his horse with an easy, languid grace, throwing one long booted leg across the saddle and urging the big horse forward in a smooth, flowing motion. Then, reining the prancing chestnut into a tight circle, Elliot held her eyes briefly, smartly touched his hat, and cantered down the long drive in a spray of gravel. At the end of Chatham's lane, horse and rider turned north toward Wrotham Ford, quickly disappearing from sight. Elliot did not look back again.

Evangeline remained standing in the doorway, unaware that Winnie had slipped into the hall until she felt a warm, familiar arm circle her waist. Winnie sighed and pulled her close. "Oh, Lud, Evie. I saw how he kissed your hand! He's perfect. Perfect for you. What ill luck that such a man should be already betrothed."

Evangeline heaved a sigh, too. "Well, Winnie, there's the rub."

"Oh, my dear!" Winnie clasped her hand to her chest. "You've fallen for him, have you not?"

"He isn't betrothed."

Winnie's hand flew to her mouth, and suddenly Evangeline found herself abruptly shoved into the library, the door thumping shut behind her.

"What do you mean, not betrothed?" Winnie demanded, leaning back against the door. Her hands were splayed stubbornly against it as if she feared Evangeline might attempt to escape her interrogation.

"Mr. Roberts's engagement has been ended, Winnie,"

answered Evangeline softly, dropping down into her usual chair. "That is all I can tell you."

Winnie came slowly away from the door and wrapped her arms uneasily around herself. She walked to the front window to stare pensively across the gardens. "Evie, a broken engagement is all but unheard of. Did his fiancée cry off?"

Evangeline pressed her fingertips hard into her temples in a futile attempt to forestall an approaching headache. Winnie was right. A sickening uncertainty pressed down upon her. "I do not know, Winnie. He simply said it was ended."

Winnie turned from her place by the window and began to flit throughout the library in quick, anxious motions, pausing to straighten books that were not crooked and to rearrange ornaments that were not out of place. As she moved, she spoke softly. "My dear," she began in the low, thoughtful tones she so effectively employed with upset children. It was her governess voice, Evangeline always thought. "Peter does trust me to look after your best interests, though why he thinks I might do so effectively is quite beyond me, for I am the featherhead and you are the sensible one." She paused to fuss with a floral arrangement that was already perfect. "Nonetheless, I find nothing disagreeable in Mr. Roberts's countenance, and I think we must accept what he says at face value."

Suddenly, Winnie ceased her flitting and turned to face Evangeline's chair. "Indeed, Evie, he seemed quite charmed by you. He scarcely took his eyes from you throughout the whole of dinner last night. I vow, he's as besotted as poor Stokely."

Evie dropped her hands into her lap. "Winnie, given my responsibilities here, I hardly think—"

Unexpectedly, Winnie cut her off with a sharp toss of

her tiny hand. "Oh, I know, I used to be your governess, and Peter depends upon me to lend countenance to your present situation, but dash it all, Evie, you aren't getting any younger. Consider your future!"

"That, dear friend, is precisely what I do consider! And Michael's, as well. Oh, Winnie, the child is but eleven! What shall we do if my grandfather dies and they try to take Michael away from me?"

"Bah!" snorted Winnie with another hand toss. "Old Lady Trent has said she'd rather roast on a rusty spit in hell than acknowledge your—"

"She lies!" hissed Evangeline. "Oh, she disowned my father quickly enough when he followed his heart. And she did not hesitate to make certain that my grandfather took no interest in any of his grandchildren. But mark my very words, Winnie, she will take a remarkable interest when Grandpapa is dead. She will rip that child from the heart of this family and thrust him into a nest of vipers if I let her."

Winnie nodded weakly. "Oh, Evie, I fear you may be right."

"Depend upon it," replied Evangeline grimly. "And when she makes the first move, we return to the Continent at once."

Winnie looked vaguely hopeful. "Yes, but a . . . an alliance with a gentleman like Elliot Roberts could go a long way toward frightening off Lady Trent, nefarious old bag of bones that she is. Peter, as Michael's trustee, is naught but half English, and foreign-born at that. However, an English husband would be something altogether—"

Evangeline forestalled Winnie with an upraised hand. "Yes, any honorable man would wish to be helpful under such dire circumstances, but let me remind you of the power and influence wielded by Lady Trent and the

Stone family. Yes, Mr. Roberts looks to be a gentleman and is no doubt reasonably well set up. But she! She is a peer, a staunch Tory. Rich and ruthless beyond measure."

"Well, yes . . . that's all too true, but—"

Evangeline exhaled sharply. "Winnie, a commoner like Mr. Roberts has no more influence than Peter. Moreover, Mr. Roberts would have no notion how to manage such a witch. And from the looks of him," she added dryly, "he isn't much given to martyrdom."

Winnie took her customary seat opposite Evangeline, her brow furrowed in thought. "Yes," she mused, pensively staring at her tiny feet. "And unfortunately, he's Scottish. Did you notice his voice?"

"Scottish?" Evangeline's voice was sharp. To her Flemish ear, all the King's English sounded very much alike.

Winnie nodded slowly and lifted her gaze from the floor. "Yes, I think so. No—I'm sure of it, Evie. A touch of an accent remains . . . 'tis very slight, when he makes a joke or such. I may have spent half my life in Flanders, but I'm an old Newcastle girl, and I know a burr when I hear one."

"Yes, the name probably is Scottish," considered Evangeline, fixing her stare on the cold hearth, "which only reaffirms how very little we know of him, Winnie. And we can ask nothing of Peter until he returns from Italy."

"La, dear, you are too cautious! Must your life be an endless path of seriousness and suspicion?"

"Yes, to be sure," responded Evangeline, returning her gaze to Winnie. "A great many people depend upon me. Seriousness and suspicion have thus far stood me in good stead."

Restlessly, Winnie sprang up from her chair and began to drift through the library once more. "Oh, Evie! I would not encourage you to be imprudent! I simply wish for you what I had with my darling Hans. Indeed, it is my fondest dream! I want you to have the happiness one finds only with one's soul mate, and I cannot help but wonder if Mr. Roberts is not the one for you."

"Why?" asked Evangeline softly, genuinely mystified.

"Why?" Winnie whirled again, now nervously twining a linen handkerchief back and forth through her fingers. "I do not know!" she responded plaintively. "I just see it, that's all. There is something in the way he looks at you, the way he seems to belong here. And the children! They were taken with him at once. Elliot's face has this compelling expression—somewhat baffled and charmed and happy all at once."

"Ah, Elliot is it now?" Evangeline's tone was arch. "Winnie, indeed! You are foolishly romantic. I think Peter looks to me to guard *your* virtue!"

Crossing her arms stubbornly, Winnie turned to gaze out the window once more. "And I agree with Augustus, much as the admission pains me, that you haven't a romantic bone in your body!"

So chastised, Evangeline rose and crossed the room to join her friend before the window. Apologetically, she snaked one arm around her companion's waist. "I daresay, Winnie, that you may be right, and I take no pleasure in it. I shall try very hard to change. But you must admit, there is something mysterious about Mr. Roberts." Slowly, she leaned forward and pulled back the drapery to peer intently into the sunlight, as if the truth might be hidden within Chatham's front gardens. "Something is missing; some bit of information is wanting."

"Oh, bother!" fussed Winnie impatiently. "The only thing that big, strapping man is wanting is a kilt! Just think of what his knees must look like!"

At this, Evangeline threw back her head and laughed. "Ah, Winnie, you are too awful! He shall return in a week's time. You must simply ask to see them."

"Why do not you ask, Evie?" quipped Winnie with asperity. "After all, darling, you're the artist."

It was a tempting thought, that.

The Wrotham Arms was little more than a shabby coaching inn that had undoubtedly seen better days, all of them occurring in the preceding century. Even in his weatherworn clothes, a man of Elliot's intimidating size and imperious demeanor garnered swift attention, yet the increasingly foul mood that had seized him upon leaving Chatham Lodge was barely pacified when a thin, nervous potboy agreed to show him directly to the innkeeper. Following the lad through the squalid taproom as he darted between the rickety tables and worn settles, Elliot made his way to the back of the chamber and down a filthy corridor into a narrow office.

Seated behind a stout worktable piled high with dishes was a corpulent, garishly dressed woman, marginally occupied with wiping out tankards. Her age was uncertain, but her station clearly was not. "I said *innkeeper!*" barked Elliot to the skittish servant, then instantly regretted his words when the potboy jerked backward, flinching. In all likelihood, this wasn't the lad's fault. "I'm wanting the innkeeper, Mr. Tanner," he repeated to him, softening his tone.

"Aye, an' who might you be?" rasped the woman at the table, spitting violently into a tankard then ramming in a rag with one meaty fist. She jerked her head toward the door, and the round-eyed servant immediately skittered back down the hall.

"I'm an acquaintance of Mr. Tanner's daughter," answered Elliot stiffly, turning his full focus on the tawdry woman. Beneath the tumble of wiry red and gray hair that spilled from a yellowed mobcap, her eyes were like bright jet beads set deep into the folds of a florid face. A thick, beefy nose hung between heavy jowls and over thin lips, set in a visage that could never have been pretty.

She grinned sarcastically, showing off a set of nearly complete but blackened, stubby teeth. "Which 'un do ye want? But I needn't ask, do I, sir?" She chuckled to herself. "Not me poor Mary, I'll wager, for she'd have no use for the likes of a fine gent such as yourself."

"Annie Tanner," interjected Elliot irritably. "I am looking for Annie Tanner."

"Aye, above half the gents in Lunnon be acquainted with me Annie," replied the woman, nodding shrewdly. "And them as ain't likely will be." The tankard, now apparently cleaned to her satisfaction, was put down with a hearty thump, and she returned her narrow gaze to Elliot.

Watching the woman clean the dishes, Elliot paused to thank God he'd avoided putting up for the night in this rat hole. No matter how much physical discomfort his unslaked desire for Evangeline had given him, it was better than a bad case of the bloody flux. "I'm the marquis of Rannoch," he said coldly. "And I wish to see Mr. Tanner. Now."

The woman jerked her thumb back over her shoulder and cackled obnoxiously, her bosom and mobcap shaking in unison. "Do ye, indeed? Well, 'ee be right across the lane there, m'lord. Third grave left o' the small oak tree."

"Dead?"

"Aye, gone on to 'is eternal reward these three weeks past," she replied sarcastically.

"And pray who are you, madam, if I may ask?"

"I'm the grievin' widow, thank ye kindly," replied the woman, still grinning. "And I'm just settling up matters here."

Good Lord. *Antoinette's mother.* He might have

guessed. "Then where, madam, might I find your daughter?"

The woman eyed him suspiciously with her sharp black gaze. "Annie? Can't rightly say as I know." She shrugged nonchalantly. "Me Mary housekeeps for a fine family in Mayfair—mayhap she's heard from 'er."

Elliot suppressed a rising tide of aggravation and anxiety. God, but he wanted this over and done with. Antoinette's wardrobe girl had said the actress was returning to Essex. Damn it, she had to be here. Undoubtedly, she was still hiding from him. "Mrs. Tanner, I have business to settle with Annie, and I should like to get on with it."

Mrs. Tanner squinted at Elliot appraisingly, scanning his length with one dark, beady eye. "Aye, a great buck of a man like you, I 'spect you've business aplenty for her!" The woman cackled again, then promptly stopped, narrowing her gaze speculatively. "But I'll be seein' me Annie soon, no doubt. She'll turn up 'ere, or I'll go down to Lunnon once I get this place done for."

Elliot swallowed hard, desperate to shove Antoinette and all that she represented into his past where it belonged. Impulsively, he reached a decision and dug deep into his pocket to pull forth the velvet case. He slapped it onto the desk with a harsh clack. "See that she gets this, Mrs. Tanner. And the note that is enclosed."

A burning light in Mrs. Tanner's eyes flared, then just as quickly died again. She shifted her gaze away to pick absently at the worn fabric of her bodice, then sniffed pitifully. "Aye, that's all very well for me girl, but I'm a poor widow woman. 'Tis a long trip to Lunnon—"

Elliot tossed a handful of coins onto the tabletop, and they clattered against the plates and tankards. "That should make it worth your while," he replied in a soft, cold voice as the woman began to rake the money into her apron. "But make no mistake, Mrs. Tanner. Should I have the regrettable misfortune to discover that Annie did not receive that box or my letter, you'd be well advised to dig another hole under the oak tree." Then Elliot turned hard on his boot heel and strode back down the hall toward the filthy taproom, almost tripping over the nervous potboy who stood hidden deep in the shadows.

Suddenly, the atmosphere inside the repulsive tavern seemed thick, stale, and dirty. Anxiety began to claw at his gut, and Elliot was seized with an almost overwhelming need to draw the sharp, pure air of Essex down into his lungs. He burst forth from the stooped, narrow doorway and into the packed dirt yard, jerking his head toward the stables and muttering a blunt command to the dim-witted ostler who had taken his horse.

As he waited for his mount by the roadway, the feeling of anxiety churned, shifted, and became dread and then something worse: a gnawing sense of loss and fear. Of what? He was impatient to escape this wretched place, yet he had no wish to return to London. Nor, in fact, to his life. He was the all-powerful, much-reviled marquis of Rannoch, and he suddenly found himself liking that fact no better than did anyone else. Nonetheless, that was precisely who he was, and the reality of it would never change. The stench of this wayside clung to him like the knowledge of what he had become: jaded, sated, base, and bored.

❦ 4 ❦

Tell me, Muse, of the man of many tricks.
—HOMER

It was perfectly obvious that the much put-upon MacLeod had been compelled to suppress a gasp of horror when his travel-worn master returned to Strath that evening and announced his shocking intention of taking an early supper in the schoolroom with his daughter. Without comment, however, the butler dutifully conveyed his lord's command belowstairs, thereby pitching Henri and his kitchen staff into a fit of French anarchy. But since Miss Zoë was known to be the particular favorite of the hard-nosed MacLeod, in very short order a trio of footmen arrived at the schoolroom door, bearing great silver trays laden with cold ham and warm beef, along with all the wines, vegetables, and breads that would normally have been laid out in the great dining room. More importantly, they brought along Zoë's favorite, a raspberry tart, to finish.

By the time the schoolroom clock struck eight, however, the covers had long since been removed, and Elliot found himself rather awkwardly wiping a smear of raspberry filling from Zoë's chin. With a sticky napkin still clutched in his hand, Elliot leaned back into his chair, stretched his feet toward the cold hearth, and studied his daughter assiduously. She was a part of him, this lovely little thing. In Zoë, he could see his own mother's dark, curling hair, framing his late father's solemn, steady expression. Her sharp little chin probably came from Aunt

Agnes, but the strong, stubborn jaw . . . well, that was undeniably his very own, and only God could guess at its origin.

Yes, she was indeed his child, and he cherished her, yet she had scarcely uttered above a dozen words during dinner. And was there any wonder? Zoë doubtless thought her papa had gone perfectly mad, for Elliot rarely saw the inside of the schoolroom, usually dined alone, and never, ever wiped his daughter's face. Sitting there amidst the books and globes and tiny chairs, Elliot felt—and probably looked—just about as awkward as a tricked-out cyprian at an Almack's assembly. Perhaps, he wryly considered, he really had gone mad. It was not the first time such a thought had crossed his mind. Resolutely, he shoved it away. He was determined to do a better job of this thing, this parenting, or nurturing, or whatever one called it.

Deliberately, he forced a smile. "Zoë, why do you not fetch that book you like so much? Let's have a look at it together." Zoë gave him a rather blank stare, and in desperation Elliot began to dig around in his memory. "The picture book, sweet? I believe it had to do with, er, animals in the zoo or some such thing?"

Zoë blinked, her brown eyes luminous in the lamplight. "I am too old now, Papa, for picture books."

Good Lord . . . how stupid he was! Of course, a girl who read as well as Zoë would have long ago lost interest in her picture books. Elliot shot her a shamefaced grin and was pleased when she gradually returned it. "Then fetch a book you do like, sweet. And tell your foolish, forgetful papa what it is about."

Dutifully, Zoë slid from her chair and padded across the carpet to rummage through a stack of small, well-worn books. She returned to her father's chair, clutching one in her plump, girlish fingers. "It is about a yellow kitten," she softly explained, extending it toward him. "He has adventures, but some of the words are too hard."

Elliot smiled again, and it felt less forced this time. Perhaps this would indeed become easier with practice. Gently, he reached out to tuck a stray piece of hair ribbon back from Zoë's heart-shaped face, then tweaked Aunt Agnes's chin for good measure. "Then Papa will read it to you, sweetie, and we will work on the hard words together. Would you like that?"

Wordlessly, Zoë nodded, her solemn eyes widening with what looked like anticipation. Gently, Elliot leaned forward and kissed the tip of her nose. Silence hung in the air for a long moment. "Well," said Elliot briskly. "How shall we go about this, Zoë?"

"How shall we go about what, Papa?" she echoed sweetly.

Inwardly, Elliot kicked himself. Had he truly never read a book to his daughter? Damn it all, he knew perfectly well he hadn't. It was not that he had never wished to read to her, yet Elliot could not precisely say why he had not, or explain what it was that held him back from a child he loved so much. His child. She stood before him, so small yet so grave and uncertain. His daughter hardly knew her own father, and it was his fault. He was all that Zoë had left, yet it should have been more than enough.

Indeed, a loving father was far more than many children had, and love her he surely did. None of the boys and girls at Chatham had a father, and yet they flourished, while his daughter floundered. "Come up into my lap, Zoë," Elliot answered with a sudden certainty. "Come up, and I will hold you, and together we shall see what adventures this yellow kitten of yours has got himself into."

At last, Zoë smiled. It was a smile that did not quite

reach her eyes, but as she lifted her arms to touch her father's shoulders, it came close. Very close. *Ah, yes,* he reassured himself. It was a start. But the start of what? Elliot did not know, but he was working on it.

At half past nine, Gerald Wilson paused on the threshold of the marquis of Rannoch's library and asked himself what the hell he was doing there. Oh, he knew very well that the marquis had summoned him. And in his usual high-handed manner: an overwrought footman bearing a scribbled note which read "Library now," with a thick, black *R* boldly slashed across the bottom. It was time, Wilson told himself. Long past time, in fact. He should have begun seeking a new position months ago.

With his impeccable references and experience, Wilson prided himself on being a consummately professional man of affairs. Two years earlier, he had reluctantly accepted employment with Rannoch, for at the time, the exorbitant salary the marquis offered him had made living in hell seem worth the price. Now Wilson harbored grave doubts, and he had learned a hard lesson about why Rannoch paid so well. Worse still, the marquis went through staff like a scythe through wheat, cutting fast and close to the ground. Wilson winced at the analogy. He could almost see the glittering blade slicing toward his kneecaps.

Oh, Lord. That was it, then, wasn't it? He was going to be fired.

Wilson could fathom no other reason why the marquis would have sent for him at such an unusually late hour. And though he had indulged in many a fantasy about marching into the marquis's dark library and cavalierly tossing down his resignation, Wilson had never in his wildest imaginings dreamed that Rannoch might turn *him* off without notice. Why, had he not given exemplary service? Had he not tolerated Rannoch's harsh demands and vile moods with nary a whimper?

Throughout two godforsaken years, he had done the marquis's dirty work. He had trafficked with free traders who would have cheerfully knifed him over a case of brandy, paid off occasional bribes when needed, and bailed the randy old baronet, Sir Hugh, out of various and sundry foul predicaments. He had routinely collected crushing debts of honor from dozens of near-bankrupt gentlemen, two of whom had blown their brains to kingdom come as soon as the door clicked shut behind him.

Yes, Wilson allowed that in the service of the marquis of Rannoch, he had stared over the precipice and into the blackest pit humanity could offer up. To be sacked after all that he had suffered was too much to be borne, but best to have done with it quickly. With a steely determination, Wilson squared his shoulders, rapped upon the thick oak door, then entered the marquis's inner sanctum.

"Ah, Wilson!" exclaimed his employer, putting down an unlit cheroot and rising with uncharacteristic politeness from his sprawled position behind the desk. "Thank you for coming so promptly—and so late in the evening."

Thank you for coming?

The civility of the remark was disconcerting, and Wilson paused uncertainly just inside the cavernous chamber. The marquis was obviously dressed for the privacy of his home, having removed his usual coat and waistcoat. The fine cambric of his shirt looked limp, and Rannoch's sleeves were rolled partway up his forearms, revealing dark hair sprinkled over taut muscle. A day's growth of heavy beard shadowed his harsh face. Wilson swallowed hard, for despite his employer's opulent surroundings, the Scotsman always looked brutal. Absent the civilizing effect of formal clothing, he looked barbaric.

"Well, come in, Wilson! Good God, man, come in and pour yourself a brandy," offered Rannoch convivially, waving toward a set of crystal decanters. "It is, after all, well past your regular working hours," he added, strolling from behind the desk to peer through the heavy damask draperies. "Tell me, Wilson, has the fog worsened outside?"

Good God, Rannoch was discussing the weather. And offering him a drink. His employer's usual conversational vein ran more to an occasional grunt, a half dozen words of command, followed by a curt dismissal. Gratefully, Wilson headed for the brandy, now fully convinced that he was going to need it.

Looking unusually relaxed, the marquis turned from the window and sat back against the corner of his desk, cradling his customary glass of scotch whisky negligently against one big leg. Even perched on the desk, the tall man towered over Wilson. Anxiously, his brain scrabbled for a foothold on the conversation. If Rannoch had intended to dismiss him, he would have had done with it by now. Wilson had witnessed it often enough. Rannoch turned on a man like a cobra struck: fast, blinding, and agonizingly painful.

So the marquis wanted something else—but what? Wilson put down the decanter with a careless chink. This newest task must be something dreadful indeed to warrant such uncharacteristically pleasant behavior from the marquis. Earlier this week, Wilson had been tasked with tracking down, or attempting to track down, Rannoch's errant mistress. What a hopeless job that had been! Then, immediately thereafter, he had been dispatched to the jeweler's to purchase an extravagant ruby bracelet to match the necklace Wilson had chosen as her Christmas gift.

The bracelet had been a bad sign. Wilson knew exactly what it meant. Perhaps, he sarcastically considered, he was now to procure a new mistress. There was nothing unusual in that, for it had been Wilson who had secured Miss Fontaine's services last year. On that memorably unromantic occasion, Rannoch's orders had been coldly succinct. Discover the name of Lord Clivington's mistress, make certain she was reasonably attractive, ascertain his financial arrangements, and offer her twice as much.

It had been widely rumored that Clivington had badly cheated Rannoch at hazard the preceding week, but with tactics that had been quick and clever. No gentleman, not even Rannoch, would be so forward as to make an accusation that could not be proven. Therefore, the treacherous marquis of Rannoch, as he so often did, simply exacted his revenge by other means.

In short order, Clivington had been forced into the laughably awkward position of pretending, with no success whatsoever, that he had lost interest in Miss Fontaine. He did not dare call Rannoch out; few of Rannoch's victims were so foolish. Those who were soon regretted their impetuousness. In fact, given Rannoch's usual methods of retribution, Clivington had escaped relatively unscathed.

Uneasily, Wilson turned from the side table to face his employer. "Indeed, my lord," he replied at last. "It is unseasonably foggy tonight."

Rannoch still looked, relatively speaking, benign. Nevertheless, Wilson feared he was little more than a languid, sated panther that had recently dined on plenty of red meat. "Sit down, Wilson. Sit down," the marquis suggested, motioning affably toward a chair. "I fancy you look rather pale. Perhaps you've been working too hard?" Casually, the marquis retrieved his cigar, lit it from a desk candle, then exhaled a curling cloud of smoke into the dimly lit room.

Wilson sat. "No, my lord. I am quite well, I assure you."

"Good, good," replied Rannoch, absently studying the cheroot in his fingers. He paused for a long moment as if searching for something to say. At last he spoke. "Tell me, Wilson, I never think to ask, how does your family go on? You have an elderly mother, I collect?"

Wilson was stunned to know that the marquis was aware he had any family at all, let alone a mother. "Indeed, Lord Rannoch, my mother and family fare quite well."

"Ah, yes. Good." The marquis picked up his glass and sipped at his vile scotch whisky pensively.

Wilson took a very healthy swallow of his drink, too. "My lord?"

"Yes, Wilson?" The marquis's slashing black brows arched inquisitively.

"Was—was there something you wanted?"

Rannoch regarded him from his perch on the desk corner, looking for all the world like a huge black bird of prey which might at any moment unfurl its broad wingspan to swoop down upon an unsuspecting rodent. "Yes!" replied the marquis, startling Wilson. "Do forgive me. I forget that you must be desirous of returning to hearth and home."

"Yes, well . . ." Wilson let his words trickle weakly away.

"Ah, indeed! Hearth and home," repeated Rannoch almost pensively, "and on such a dreary evening. I must say, Wilson, having now considered my behavior, I regret having been so thoughtless as to drag you from such a pleasant place so late at night."

Wilson, rapidly sipping his employer's very fine

French brandy, was on the verge of explaining that given Rannoch's extraordinarily affable mood, the marquis's dark library was beginning to seem somewhat more agreeable than Mrs. Wilson's chilly hearth, but he withheld his sentiment out of an abundance of reserve. "Do not regard it, my lord," he replied instead.

"You are a good man, Wilson. More than once, I have been glad of my decision to retain your services. I shall come straight to the point." Rannoch passed Wilson a small slip of paper bearing two names.

James Hart. Peter Weyden.

"I do not know these men, my lord," replied Wilson uncertainly.

"Nor, Wilson, do I," agreed the marquis amiably. "But I should very much like to know something of them. Discreetly, of course. Both reside in London, though they probably do not move in the highest circles. The first I collect is betrothed. I should like to know to whom, and the status of the betrothal."

Wilson nodded mutely.

"And the second is a Flemish art expert who imports a great deal of work from the Continent. It would appear that he travels extensively, and I suspect he has connections at the Royal Academy. He also refers commissions to . . . to various artists."

Wilson blinked his eyes slowly. "And what would you have me learn of this man, my lord?"

Rannoch took another languid draw on his cheroot, then slowly exhaled. "I merely wish to reassure myself that he is a man of unimpeachable character, which I daresay he is."

"Ah, I see, my lord. You are in the market, then, for a work of art?"

Rannoch nodded slowly. "Suffice it to say, Wilson, that I am rapidly becoming an admirer."

"Am I to purchase something, my lord?" he asked uncertainly.

Rannoch turned to stare at him for a long moment, his quizzical expression slowly shifting to one of bemused satisfaction. "What a splendid idea, Wilson!"

"Indeed, my lord?" Wilson tried not to look confused.

"Yes!" responded Rannoch, then dropped his voice to an almost conspiratorial tone. "Seek out Mr. Weyden. Tell him that your employer—do not use my name—wishes to buy a van Artevalde."

"A *van Artevalde*, my lord?" Wilson blinked nervously, then swallowed hard. "I must tell you, Lord Rannoch, that they are exceedingly difficult to get hold of. Rare, and rather costly as well."

Wilson waited for the spewing verbal torrent, but none came. Rannoch merely crooked one dark brow. "You are familiar with the work of van Artevalde?" he asked respectfully.

"I—why, yes. I have some limited knowledge," stammered Wilson. "My previous employer, you may recall, was a collector of some serious devotion. Van Artevalde is a young Flemish painter but of no small merit."

"Is that so?" asked Rannoch, looking most intrigued.

"Oh, yes, my lord. His allegoricals are often compared to Rubens's work. His use of color and light is exquisite; very like van Eyck's. Indeed, his works have begun to fetch high prices, particularly abroad."

"Excellent, Wilson," murmured Rannoch. "Your skills never cease to amaze. Tell Weyden, or whoever runs his business, that you want a van Artevalde immediately, something glorious and epic. Soon he shall no doubt show you a piece called *The Fall of Leopold at . . .* someplace."

"That's *Sempach*," corrected Wilson, then winced.

Rannoch merely nodded, rubbing his harshly stubbled

chin. "Aye, that sounds right. Pay him in gold. The price is of no consequence."

"Yes, my lord," replied Wilson dutifully. "Will there be anything further?"

"Yes," said Rannoch slowly, drumming his long fingers on the desktop. "Tell Weyden's people that you want first option on every van Artevalde that happens onto the market, until further notice. Buy . . . buy them all."

"All?" Wilson was stunned.

Rannoch's brow furrowed deeply as he stared into the shadows of the room. "No. Not all," he corrected thoughtfully. "We would not want to restrict Ev—er, van Artevalde's exposure to the marketplace." The marquis's gaze sharpened and returned to Wilson. "Buy about every second painting—you choose which. God knows I have no taste in art."

"But, my lord, that will drive the price up prodigiously!"

Rannoch grinned. His perfect white teeth seemed to gleam ominously in the candlelight. "Will it, indeed? So much the better, then."

Shortly thereafter, Wilson tucked the little slip of paper into his pocket and departed, greatly reassured yet exceedingly confused. With both blood and brain slightly numbed by the brandy, of which he had ultimately imbibed two ample servings, Wilson very nearly tripped over Kemble, the marquis's very proper gentleman's gentleman, as he entered the library.

Exhaling a long column of smoke, Elliot stared up from his chair in veiled amusement at the willowy, middle-aged man who now stood sniffing disdainfully before him. Kemble, who made no secret of his abhorrence of cigar smoke, flailed a cambric handkerchief ineffectually back and forth in a gesture designed solely, as they both knew, to annoy the marquis.

Why, Elliot asked himself for the thousandth time, *do I put up with my valet's snubs, snorts, and pouts?* Because, simply put, the man was an unparalleled genius. Ten years earlier, Kemble had willingly taken Elliot in hand, burned his kilt, and transformed a dour, hulking Scottish lad into a well-groomed, impeccably attired London gentleman. The regrettable fact that, during those first few months, Elliot's level of worldly sophistication had lagged lamentably behind his tailoring was in no way Kemble's fault. Moreover, throughout all the debacles that had followed, Kemble had stuck by Elliot. He could always count on Kemble to dress him to perfection, shave him flawlessly, and recollect which paramour preferred what cologne.

In addition, Kemble also excelled at less traditional tasks such as knowing who among the *haut monde* tended to have undesirable tendencies such as cheating at cards, reneging on vowels, or sleeping with other men's mistresses. Kemble knew the best remedy for a hangover, how to pick locks, and who among the fashionably impure had contracted the French pox. In addition, he possessed an unfailing technique for the reduction of facial swelling in the event of a misjudged punch and was on gossiping terms with every demi-rep, housekeeper, under-butler, scullery maid, pastry chef, and bootblack in London. Furthermore, he knew their secrets as well as their foibles.

It was, therefore, with a resigned sigh that Elliot calmly stubbed out the cheroot and addressed the only servant he did not dare upbraid, humiliate, or threaten. "This is about the topboots, isn't it, Kem?" He eyed the valet narrowly through the dissipating cloud of smoke.

Kemble's tightly pursed lips trembled, and his hands fluttered up and down at his sides in apparent agitation. "My lord! How could you? Their condition is an abomination! They are ruined—ruined, I tell you! Exceedingly, irrevocably, hopelessly—"

"Spare me the theatrics, Kem. Couldn't be helped. I'm sorry."

"Sorry?" The valet rolled his eyes wildly. "I'm very sure that you are! But do tell, my lord, where in heaven's name did the irrepressible urge to roll about in the mud like some swine come upon you?"

"Er—Essex, it was. The urge came upon me in Essex." Elliot forced himself to suppress a bark of laughter, since Kemble's scoldings were very nearly the only thing remotely resembling care or concern in his life. "Perhaps," he added teasingly, "I have merely become the pig I have so often been called."

"Umm," replied Kemble sagaciously, still pursing his lips. The valet crossed his dangling arms over his chest in a familiar posture of recalcitrance. Elliot did not bother to look, but he knew from experience that the valet's toe was busily tapping out an angry tattoo upon the carpet.

"Sorry, Kemble. Truly. Now listen, old fellow. I need some new—no, some *different* clothes."

Kemble's fine, angular brows arched even more dramatically. "I do not doubt it at all, my lord, for if you anticipate that this propensity for traipsing about in the filth of the countryside shall continue—"

"That I do," interrupted Elliot bluntly, his aggravation allowing just a hint of Highland burr to creep into his tone. "And I'll be wanting some things that do not look quite so . . . so expensive."

"Indeed?" sniffed Kemble disdainfully. "Pray be specific. I know very little of *such things*," he added, pronouncing the words as if they were Hindustani for *chamber pot*.

Elliot sighed. "I'll want two pairs of ordinary buckskin breeches, two pairs of plain wool trousers, a half dozen ordinary linen shirts, a frieze coat, a couple of neutral waistcoats, and—oh, the old topboots."

"What, no hobnailed brogans?" muttered Kemble snidely.

"No, I suppose not," replied Elliot calmly. "Just polish up the old topboots as best you can. They'll do nicely."

Kemble nodded sagely, but Elliot could see the sarcasm flicker in his pale, expressive eyes. "In short, my lord, you wish to look like a common peasant?"

"Not quite as bad as all that, Kem!"

"And what about some coarse flannel drawers, my lord?" trilled the valet. "Nothing so stimulating as having homespun wrapped around one's ballocks!"

"Ouch!" Elliot felt a smile tug at the corner of his mouth. "Let's not get carried away with this ruse, old boy!"

Having dispensed with both his man of affairs and his valet, Elliot turned his attentions to his uncharacteristically choleric and still-indisposed uncle.

Sir Hugh had left orders for MacLeod to direct Elliot to his apartments upon his return, no matter the time. Elliot, who as a matter of principle took orders from no one, nonetheless paid this directive a moment of heed. Sir Hugh was about as prone to give a command as his obstinate nephew was to obey one; therefore, the fact that his uncle had troubled himself to leave such a message intrigued Elliot exceedingly. Though inordinately fond of each other and bound by any number of similarly bad habits, he and Hugh were not overtly close. Days, sometimes weeks, might pass without the two speaking, save for tripping over each other in a gaming hell or whorehouse.

Elliot sighed wearily. His uncle was most likely in trouble.

Sir Hugh, caustically referred to as the Blight of the Benhams by his socially rigid sister, sauntered through life with as much concern, and almost as much exertion, as one might give to an afternoon stroll around Hyde Park. As he had done with illustrious success for some eight and fifty years, Hugh Benham was resolved to enjoy a life of indolent debauchery until the precise moment at which he cocked up his toes, an event the dowager marchioness of Rannoch had often said could not possibly come too soon.

When not distempered by a gouty foot or bilious liver, Sir Hugh was a popular fellow, possessing charm and wit sufficient to offset his lack of income. As a result of Elliot's desire to aggravate his mother, Sir Hugh lived off the Rannoch coffers. Elliot paid his uncle's bills, settled his gaming debts, and even served as a second on those rare occasions when Sir Hugh managed to get caught in an ill-timed indiscretion. In such cases, however, the combination of Elliot's nasty reputation and Sir Hugh's willingness to blithely—and meaninglessly—apologize was usually enough to avoid an actual sword point.

Through these worthy efforts, Elliot earned the pleasure of thumbing his nose at his cold, supercilious mother. Lady Rannoch's father, she was ever fond of complaining, had been no more prudent than her brother. Long on the slippery slope to both moral and financial ruin, the entire Benham family had been dragged from the brink by her sacrifice on the marriage altar to a moody, pious Scot. The fact that the shame associated with her brother's ribald antics and her son's abhorrent reputation precluded—in her humble opinion—her appearance in polite society was but further fuel to the fires of the dowager's self-pity.

Tonight, however, Elliot was not in the mood for his uncle, however secretly fond he was of the old scoundrel. But there was no avoiding it. Hugh was the closest thing to a father Elliot had, and so he gave a peremptory knock upon the door to his uncle's sitting room and entered. He found Hugh much the same as he had been for the past four days, his inflamed foot elevated on a pouf, his *élan vital* drowned in misery and drink.

"Come in. Come in," muttered Hugh, jabbing impatiently toward the sofa. "Sit over there where I can see you. And rid us of that damnable footman."

Elliot strolled to his uncle's table for a whisky, motioned away the footman, and sprawled on the sofa, his long legs thrust casually in front of him. "I missed you, too, Uncle," he drawled.

Hugh stared at him down a long, bladelike nose that looked aristocratically becoming on him but huge and haughty on his similarly adorned sister. For all his age and dissipation, the baronet was still a good-looking man. "Reminds me, my boy," commented Hugh, "where in Hades did you hie off to? Still determined to run that fancy piece to ground?"

Elliot stifled a deliberate yawn, but inwardly he felt tense and restless. It had been thus since his return to Strath House earlier in the evening. He was anxious to resolve this business with Hugh, so that he might then retire to the solitude of his bedchamber and suffer his strange disquiet in privacy.

"No, Hugh," he responded dryly. "I did, however, manage to find her mother, and I left what I daresay is a clear indication of Antoinette's future, or lack thereof, with me."

"What do you mean?"

"I bought her a bracelet which, should she choose to sell it and live frugally, will keep her for several months. I left it, along with a note that plainly told her to make no mistake, this was the end. My words were a bit blunt, perhaps, but I wanted to be clear."

"Humph," grunted Hugh noncommittally. Cocking his head, one sharp gray eye squinting, the baronet scratched his ear. "Long trip, it was?"

"Suffice it to say that I became distracted along the way," responded Elliot flatly.

Hugh's face split in a knowing grin. "Aye, you're my blood and no doubt! Can't leave town without stumbling over a willing one on your way out."

"As it happens, she's not willing. Or perhaps I should say not available," answered Elliot, staring fixedly at his glass. Indeed, he ruefully considered, Hugh had one thing right. He was his uncle's blood. Again, one had only to look at the Benham nose, for despite the badly healed break in Elliot's, the similarity was unmistakable. For once, their similarities saddened him. Was this to be his fate, too? Living alone with chronic gout and all the companionship money could buy? Good Lord, life seemed unexpectedly bleak. "And in the country, this one was," Elliot murmured despondently, then tossed off the rest of his whisky in one swallow. "In Essex."

Arching his brows in surprise, Hugh pulled at his drink with a slurp. "A country gel, eh? I do wonder at that! Not your usual style, my boy."

"I should rather we not discuss it, Hugh," stated Elliot coolly, returning his emotionless gaze to his uncle. "What was it you wanted to talk about?"

"As you wish," agreed Hugh convivially, "for we assuredly have more pressing concerns than choosing your next light skirt."

The derogatory phrase struck a raw nerve with Elliot, and he suppressed a visceral urge to rise from his seat and throttle his uncle where he sat. Wrestling the foreign emotion under control, Elliot forced a neutral tone. "And those concerns would be—?"

"The new Baron Cranham—very interesting news. Winthrop and Linden dropped by last night. Seems Godfrey Moore is back from that rat hole he scuttled off to—India, was it? Perhaps he thinks you've forgotten your threat."

Elliot put down his glass with a sharp clatter. "Moore has returned? And has managed to snag the title? That I cannot comprehend."

"No other heirs, Elliot. The title would otherwise have gone into abeyance, no doubt about it." Hugh leaned forward to shift the weight of his foot, grimacing as he did so. "Moore quietly returned from Baipur weeks ago, claiming his mother's marriage lines were finally found. And under the circumstances, who would bother to argue? The estate is not a rich one, a small manor house near Nottingham and an income that barely keeps it up. Nonetheless, it was enough to bring him back to London and grant him entrée into a few drawing rooms."

"Bloody hell," muttered Elliot almost to himself. "Am I to be eternally tortured by the past? I vow, I am sick to death of it."

"What a new and touching sentiment, my boy," replied Hugh dryly, "but there's no help for it. Moore, Cranham—or whoever—the fellow has returned, and trouble shall follow, mark my very word."

"Undoubtedly, though I'm not sure what should be done."

"Kill him," grumbled Hugh, one brow crooked high. "Kill him now. Save yourself any future inconvenience, and finish what you started ten years ago. It shan't be too difficult. Trump up some vague excuse, and call him out again, or, better yet, just garrote the bastard in a dark alley."

Three days ago, Elliot considered, he would have had no compunction whatsoever about killing Baron Cranham, newly invested or no. Swords, pistols, or a good knife fight, it mattered not one whit. He would have had no need of a dark alley, nor would he have troubled himself to trump up a challenge. He had reason enough. Ten years changed nothing. Moreover, this time, he would have made damn sure that no one spirited Cranham onto a Bombay-bound merchantman in the dark of night.

But now? Had Elliot harbored any doubt that his meaningless life was God's idea of a sarcastic joke, this twist of fate would have confirmed it. Killing Cranham was just a matter of time. It would be unavoidable, and probably necessary. Elliot knew it with a sickening certainty.

May had turned to June when, true to his word, Elliot Roberts returned to Wrotham-upon-Lea. He came late one afternoon, riding the sturdy chestnut and carrying a fat saddlebag, evidencing his intent to stay. Evangeline was reluctant to acknowledge, even to herself, that she had spent the better part of the last three days puttering about in the front gardens, eagerly awaiting his arrival. The children, too, had been enthusiastic, asking for word of Elliot's return every night at dinner.

Evangeline, accompanied by the dog, was cutting fresh flowers when at last he did arrive. Impulsively, she wished that she had dressed in something a little finer or arranged her hair a bit more elegantly, but it was too late. Despite her doubts, Elliot had returned, and with him came her unsettled emotions. That now familiar, still disturbing warmth began to curl deep inside her stomach as she watched him drop the reins of his chestnut and stride across the drive with his easy masculine grace. In the sunshine, Elliot looked even larger than she remembered. Today he was dressed very simply, a fact that somehow added to his aura of power and strength.

"Miss Stone!" he greeted her warmly, walking toward her with both hands extended, the grim lines of his face suddenly softened by a gentle smile. Upon hearing Elliot's voice, Fritz bounded from the clump of shrubbery he had been desultorily sniffing and dashed into the drive to trot along at Elliot's heels, as if herding him toward her. Evangeline lifted up her skirt to step a shortcut over the floral border that edged the circular drive. As she did so, Elliot took her hand in his, lightly curled the other about her waist, and gently assisted her across to the graveled surface. His hands were huge and warm, hard but not rough, and for an unnecessary moment he held her. She sensed it and felt as giddy and foolish as a schoolgirl.

Evangeline could not bring herself to pull away, and then she remembered, with irrational disappointment, his solemn vow not to flirt with her. "Mr. Roberts," she managed to say breathlessly, "you did return, after all."

"Indeed, did you think I would not?" With what felt like measured reluctance, Elliot slowly let his arms drop to his sides.

Evangeline looked up at him and smiled, unable to hide her pleasure. "I thought it very likely you mightn't."

"Why?" His tone was blunt. "Did you think me so false as that?" He stared at her again with that sudden intensity that made her knees disconcertingly weak.

As if hoping to rid herself of the perplexing sensation, Evangeline brushed at a wisp of hair that had come loose to tease at her forehead. She studied his hard gray eyes, which always seemed to hold a firm resolve. "Indeed, I have no notion why . . ." she explained weakly, letting her words trail away. "Come, let me take you in."

He offered her his arm, and they trailed back along the drive and up the wide front steps. "Bolton will show you to the Tower Room," she continued to chatter nervously, "if you found it to your liking when last you were here at Chatham?"

"Oh, yes, Miss Stone. I found everything here at Chatham very much to my liking," he answered softly as they crossed the threshold into the cool shadows of the hall. "This is a most agreeable place in every respect."

Evangeline parted her lips uncertainly, not quite sure of his meaning. He was looking at her with a sharp, sidelong gaze. "Thank you, Mr. Roberts. The tower rooms have always been my favorite. So quiet and private, with an exceedingly fine view."

"Quiet and private, Miss Stone?" One dark, slashing brow tilted up very slightly, then gave way to a puzzled frown. "I wonder, then, that you do not occupy them yourself?"

Evangeline smiled graciously as she reached up to tug the bell pull. "Solitude is a luxury that is rare to me, sir. I must be near the children on the second-floor wing, which is more modern if somewhat less charming."

"Ah, yes! Your rooms are near the south alcove—by the window seat?" On the rug at Elliot's feet, Fritz began to roll on his back in a blatant request for a belly scratch, his tiny paws flailing aimlessly in the air. Elliot very graciously bent to oblige him.

"Yes, it is much newer than the tower rooms, which are stacked atop one another," she explained, watching in fascination as his fingertips stroked the dog's rough jet-black coat with slow, hypnotic motions. She wondered fleetingly what it would be like to be caressed just so by those long, elegant fingers. His hands were large and beautifully formed, his touch light but sure—

Bolton's slow, dignified footfalls ended her fanciful

daydreams. "Mr. Roberts, is it?" asked the butler with his usual level of polite ambivalence. "Welcome back to Chatham Lodge."

"Bolton, kindly show Mr. Roberts to—to his usual room." Evangeline turned to face Elliot again, praying that he did not notice her heightened color. "Dinner will be served at half past six. Since it is now very near four, I shall have Cook send up a light repast, then leave you to your own devices. Please ring for a bath if you wish it, or feel free to join Gus and the boys outside."

Elliot seemed pleased at the second suggestion. "Where might I find them?"

Evangeline tossed her hand and gave a little laugh. "In the rear gardens, Mr. Roberts, where they are engaged in something vile under the guise of what Theo and Michael call 'chemical experiments.' Go at your own risk, for it apparently involves a great deal of noise, smoke, and smell." With that warning, Evangeline strode back toward the garden, in hope of retrieving both her basket and her composure. Fritz, however, deserted her, springing deftly to his feet and bounding happily after Elliot. Turning to look over one shoulder, only to see them disappear into the depths of the hallway, Evangeline found herself keenly jealous of her own dog.

Elliot followed Bolton up the main staircase and down the corridor to the circular stairs of the ancient tower, the tap-tap of Fritz's claws echoing cheerfully behind. Elliot found that his step was light, and his mood rose incrementally with every tread of the turret stairs. Inwardly, he breathed a silent sigh of relief, not realizing until this moment that he had been holding his breath in anticipation.

But he need not have worried; it was still there. All was as he had hoped; it was unchanged. The mood. The magic. That mysterious feeling that all was right with the world. Ah, and Evangeline Stone! She was more exquisite than ever. Even as he had rounded Chatham's drive to see her standing ankle-deep in thick grass and spring flowers, some strange, soothing emotion had enveloped him. He had been almost tangibly encircled by feelings he could only vaguely put a name to.

Unfamiliar words tumbled about in his head and in his heart: *shelter, sustenance, redemption.* It was irrational, Elliot reminded himself as Bolton threw open the door to his comfortingly familiar bedchamber. But there it was. Evangeline's presence breathed a sense of utter peace and contentment into this house, filling it just as surely as did the June breeze that billowed in through the soft draperies of his open window.

With her usual intrepidity, Evangeline refereed the chaos that passed for dinner at Chatham Lodge. As the courses were served, then just as quickly consumed, the cheerful clamor rose and fell accordingly. Throughout the meal, Evangeline played Solomon, disposing of quarrels between children and remanding inappropriate topics for later discussion. Aside from the constant activity, however, she silently studied her guest.

What manner of man was Elliot Roberts? A handsome one, though not in the way of most Englishmen, which was to say blond, languid, and elegantly dressed. Elliot was dark, athletic, and simply attired. Moreover, if Winnie was correct, he was not English at all. That, perhaps, in some way accounted for his rugged good looks. Indeed, it had become obvious that Elliot was far too handsome for her peace of mind.

He was a man of means, but how ample those means might be, Evangeline could not guess, and in truth it mattered little. More importantly, what of his character?

Certainly, he seemed often introspective and somewhat obdurate. Yet in the twinkling of an eye, he could become flirtatious, then just as quickly compassionate. His good nature charmed all manner of people. The staff had easily accepted him, and her extended family had eagerly embraced him. Even the little *spitske*, a dog that rarely tolerated strangers, had taken to Elliot.

How all this had happened in so short a time was beyond her. Nevertheless, as she cast a sidelong glance at the dark man seated on her right, it surely seemed as if he belonged at Chatham Lodge. Even more disconcerting, everyone else seemed to agree. Elliot flirted lightly with Winnie, caroused good-naturedly with the boys, and listened attentively to Nicolette's girlish inanities. For little Frederica, however, Elliot seemed to reserve a special fondness. He made an obvious effort to include her in every conversation and watched her carefully from the corner of one attentive eye.

Elliot had fallen into Chatham's routine as if he participated in lectures and debates over dinner every day of his life, engaging in vigorous argument and fork pointing with the best of them. He laughed frequently and heartily, yet Evangeline was struck with the perplexing impression that Elliot was not a man to whom laughter came easily. A pervasive sadness, a sort of withdrawal, seemed often to cloud his eyes and harden the features of his harsh, aristocratic face.

Nonetheless, tonight he seemed very much at ease, though she tried not to stare at him. Given the incessant smoke and laughter that had emanated from the gardens earlier in the afternoon, and the bandaged finger Elliot now cheerfully sported, he must have demonstrated quite an enthusiasm for his afternoon chemical experiments with the boys. And only moments ago, after politely securing Winnie's permission, Elliot had promised to teach Theo the rudiments of hazard, then dutifully rummaged through his coat pocket to produce the requisite dice.

Was he a man with vices, then? Was he given to excessive drink or gaming? Such a virile, well-born man would undoubtedly have a mistress or at minimum acquaintances among the demimonde. This thought gave Evangeline pause. Indeed, it troubled her far more than it should have done, but she was not naïve. She had been raised, not in the stilted artificiality of English society, but in a more bohemian Continental environment. Marie van Artevalde, who had not suffered fools gladly, made certain that her eldest daughter was not one of them. Consequently, Evangeline well understood the world and all of its realities, and for that she was infinitely grateful.

What of Elliot—did he have a mother? A home in the Highlands? Who loved him, and had he ever been in love? Yes, he had once been very deeply in love, Evangeline realized with a little stab of discomfort. She remembered how she had seen anguish flare in his brilliant gray eyes when he told her that his betrothal was over. Why would any woman end her betrothal to such a man? These questions nagged at Evangeline unmercifully, and the intensity of her obsession frightened her. Heavens, the man was a client, a guest in her home! If he wished to become anything else, he was more than capable of making his interest known. Though occasionally withdrawn, Elliot was by no means shy. Moreover, he already knew that he could charm her; that much had been evident during his last visit.

Though drawn to him, she was very careful not to make any prolonged eye contact with Elliot, and she tried, with limited success, to hide her unease. Following the meal, Evangeline ordered Tess to fetch port and two glasses, then tactfully relinquished her guest's entertainment to an eager Gus, cautioning herself yet again that it would be prudent to keep a cordial, professional distance between herself and Elliot Roberts.

Elliot found that his second evening at Chatham began much as the first had done, passing in quiet familial harmony with the exception of the raucous hazard lessons. Much to his satisfaction, the charming inhabitants seemed even more welcoming than before, an effect that was enhanced by Wilson's timely report on James Hart.

Though never one to take pleasure in another man's misery, unless Elliot himself had deliberately set about to cause it, he had been nonetheless pleased to learn that Hart's betrothal had quickly come to naught. Hart's young fiancée, having fled a fortnight earlier to Gretna Green, was now wed to the youngest son of her local rector. It explained why Hart had failed to keep his appointment with Evangeline. Undoubtedly, a wedding portrait was the least of the poor fellow's concerns, a fact that lessened the probability of his somehow showing up on Evangeline's doorstep. Elliot's ruse was safe for now.

Elliot leaned back in his drawing-room chair, stretched out his long legs, and tried to relax as he surreptitiously watched Evangeline devote her attention to Frederica's playing. When that task was finished, she took up a basket of mending and moved to share the sofa with Winnie. Her companion sat, curled up with a newspaper, while the cats drowsed by the hearth at Mr. Stokely's feet. Fritz danced back and forth between the pianoforte, where Nicolette now played, and the card table, where the boys sat transfixed by Elliot and Gus as they demonstrated the nuances of gentlemanly gaming.

After a quiet hour had passed in such amiable pursuits, Elliot put away the dice and challenged Frederica and Nicolette to a hand of whist. Theo amicably agreed to partner him, so Gus and Michael surrendered their seats to the ladies. The foursome played happily for another half hour until, absently, Elliot found his eyes drawn from the cards to rest on his hostess. With a teasing grin, she was looking very pointedly at Mrs. Weyden.

"Are you reading the gossip rags again, Winnie?" admonished Evangeline, trying to peer around the newspaper her companion clutched somewhat awkwardly.

"Umm," denied Mrs. Weyden, rather absently. The widow's back was angled toward Elliot, and he could see her duck furtively behind the paper.

Evangeline and Gus exchanged humor-laden glances, and Evangeline began to tease her companion. "Are you not? Yet that is surely what you appear to have, tucked in behind that old copy of the *Times*," insisted Evangeline in a bemused tone. "Of course, I may be mistaken."

"Umph," came Winnie's ambiguous reply.

With a knowing wink, Gus joined the banter. "Why, Mama, that paper is a week old! What grand news does it convey that holds you so enthralled? More tales from Downing Street? Raffles' return to Singapore? Ah! I have it now, Evie! Mama must have a newfound concern for the price of corn on the 'change!"

From his chair by the fire, even Mr. Stokely was forced to suppress a discreet snort of laughter.

"Oh, plague take all of you!" muttered Mrs. Weyden at last, peeking from behind her paper. "If you must know, it is just a bit of gossip! There's no help for it—'tis my undying vice."

"Oh, no, no, Mama!" cried Theo dramatically. "I brought the afternoon post in for Bolton, and I noticed an exceedingly plump package bearing Lady Bland's seal. Confess it now—she's sent you the scandal sheets!"

Gus laughed, then addressed his mother in a hushed, conspiratorial tone. "Do read us all the news of society, Mama. And let us not miss one nasty rumor, not one scandalous *on dit!*"

Winnie snorted her indignation. Her subterfuge discovered, she held the *Times* lower now, and Elliot could see the pile of clippings and papers in her ample lap. "Really, now, Augustus!" she answered archly, still scanning her correspondence. "Is it your hope that we shall read of some other hapless mother whose son has been pitched out of Cambridge on his—er—oh, my, what's this?" Winnie began to softly mouth the words to herself.

"Oh, do read it to us, Mama," wheedled Theo again as he picked through his cards. "It must be something especially wicked!"

Gus, rising from his chair by the hearth, leaned across his mother's shoulder to kiss the top of her head. Then he cleared his throat with mock ceremony and began to read aloud from over her shoulder:

"What has become of the infamous Lord R_____?
Only his charming uncle remains in town. Rumor
holds that the handsome Scottish peer, who has not
been seen in his usual haunts, may have retired to the
country to court a bride. Can it at last be so?"

As Gus finished reading, he lifted his head to stare at Evie, his mouth open.

"Rannoch!" hissed his mother from behind her newspaper, lowering it into her lap with a vicious crush. "What drivel, Evie! That vile, sniffing hound. I cannot think what decent woman would have him—"

From his table across the room, Elliot suppressed a choking sound, mislaid his trump, and lost a critical trick to Frederica. "Drat you, Elliot!" grumbled Theo, tossing his hand down in disgust.

"Our game, sir," chortled Nicolette, fanning out the cards.

"Rannoch?" puzzled Mr. Stokely absently. "I cannot say as I've heard of him."

"Rannoch?" asked Gus, studying his mother's face. "Isn't he the blighter Lady Bland is always reporting on, Mama? She's forever mentioning him in her letters—the marquis who abandoned his fiancée whilst she was, ah, you know . . ." His words trailed away, and his face turned pink.

"Indeed," answered Winnie acidly. "The very same, and that's not the half of it."

"Winnie!" Evangeline's voice held a sharp note of warning.

Ignoring her, Gus absently rubbed his jaw. "Aye . . . but wasn't there something more about him, Evie? I recollect having heard the name bantered about elsewhere."

"To be sure, you have!" interjected Winnie, her voice dropping to a conspiratorial whisper. "Why, Rannoch is the one who became embroiled in that sordid affair with . . ." From his position across the room, Elliot could no longer make out her words, but he could see Evangeline's eyes flash with anger.

"Winnie! Gus! A blighter he no doubt is, but Lord Rannoch's business is none of ours. Please hush this instant!" Evangeline's voice was sharp. "And Gus, do stop hovering, and go stir up the fire. Winnie, I want you to look at this stitch, for I cannot seem to get it aright."

As Nicolette swept up the cards for the next round, the vile Lord Rannoch, sniffing hound that he was, seemed quickly forgotten. By almost everyone.

❧ 5 ❧

An affair with the moon, in which there was
neither sin nor shame.
—LAURENCE STERNE

ℱor the remainder of the evening, Elliot pondered Winnie's remarks and tried not to feel insulted by her words. After all, they were essentially true. Furthermore, he wondered which of his sordid affairs they might have been referring to. With an inward sigh, Elliot realized that it could be any one of two dozen. Did Winnie know, or could she learn, about all of them? The thought made Elliot sicken.

Elliot reminded himself that any decent family would look down upon a blackguard like the marquis of Rannoch. And while the Stones and the Weydens were more than decent, they seemed detached from society in general. He had sensed that much immediately upon his arrival. Yet they spoke his name as if it were regrettably familiar to them. Why would they know or care about the marquis of Rannoch? The Stones and the Weydens lived the kind of life Elliot thought he had long ago ceased to desire. Indeed, it was a lifestyle he had coldly and deliberately rejected, one he now could never have.

Yet in place of what he might have had, Elliot found himself living a lie of the heart. He found it painfully disconcerting to realize how a man's youthful desire for hearth, home, and family could so easily become an anathema and then, just as quickly, become an unattainable fantasy once again. But this fantasy into which he had so deceitfully ingratiated himself, were it anything more than just another illusion, was something Elliot Armstrong would never have the opportunity to enjoy. Oh, he could get a wife quite easily, despite Mrs. Weyden's pointed and somewhat accurate jibe. Nonetheless, it would not be a woman like Evangeline Stone. It would be a town-bred chit who was short on looks, low on fortune, and desperate for a title. Such a girl could not afford to be too selective about whom she wed.

Yet even more than his concerns about Mrs. Weyden and her gossip, something else troubled Elliot. Despite her obvious pleasure at his arrival, Evangeline had begun to withdraw from him. He had sensed it clearly throughout dinner, and it was that circumstance, more than any other, that hurt him tonight almost beyond bearing. In the short term, Mrs. Weyden's comment paled in significance.

Evangeline watched as the night grew late and one by one the children drifted off to bed. Elliot, who had grown very quiet during the evening, seemed to linger at first, then rose abruptly and said good night. Rising from her chair, Winnie put down her reading and went to make a final check of all the children, while Gus secured the door locks and Evangeline gave breakfast orders to the cook.

A quarter hour later, all tasks complete, she followed the others up the stairs to bed. It would, she was certain, be another restless night. She turned from the second-floor landing and went down the long, dim corridor to her bedchamber.

"Miss Stone?" The deep, soft voice slid from the night like a warm caress.

Evangeline felt her heart stop. "Mr. Roberts?"

"Yes," he answered quietly, rising from the darkened window seat just beyond her door.

"You have been waiting for me?" she asked uncertainly. "Is something amiss?"

Slowly, he approached her from the shadows, the width of his shoulders silhouetted in shimmering moonlight. "No. Indeed, your hospitality is all that a guest might wish for, with but one exception . . ."

Evangeline watched, transfixed, as he moved toward her and into the lamplight with his disquieting grace. "My apologies," she managed to answer politely. "You have only to tell me what is needed—"

Elliot came nearer until he stood looking down into her face. He was very tall, and Evangeline realized with a start that her head did not reach his shoulder. If she could put her arms about his waist and lean her head against his broad chest, her ear would rest very near his heart. She wanted that. She wanted to hear Elliot's heart beating, strong and steady, as she knew it would be.

Suddenly, his voice pulled her back from the edge of foolishness. "Miss Stone," he asked gently, "could you manage to stop avoiding me? It's rather obvious, you know."

"I meant no offense, Mr. Roberts," she stammered nervously.

Suddenly, Elliot looked uncertain. His silvery gaze broke away to stare down at the tops of his boots. Tentatively, he reached out to rest one hand lightly upon her shoulder. "Miss Stone, I should very much like us to be friends." He lifted his dark eyes to hold hers. "Please." His voice softened. "Just tell me what I need to do to accomplish that. To become more than a subject for your canvas. To earn your trust."

She felt the warmth of his hand burning through the muslin of her dress. "Mr. Roberts," Evie said, trying to keep her voice soft, "we are indeed friends, and of course I do trust—"

"No," he quietly interposed, dropping his hand abruptly. "You do not. I make you uncomfortable, and that was never my intent. Moreover, you scarcely looked at me during dinner. I think you deliberately sought to avoid my gaze."

He was entirely correct. She had meant to avoid him, but not for the reasons he had given. And there was no explanation she could give to justify her behavior. Elliot looked hurt, and she began to apologize further, but he quickly cut her off.

"Evie—forgive me—Miss Stone. I realize that we have not known each other for very long. Moreover, I have no right to trespass upon your good graces. But please do not shut me out as though I'm just another client."

"Indeed, Mr. Roberts, you are a good deal more than that."

"Am I?" he interrupted, studying her seriously. "Then I pray you will not ignore this fragile chance we have for . . . for friendship."

"Friendship?" she repeated, surprised to hear the breathlessness in her own voice.

Elliot's gaze drifted slowly over her face. "Yes," he answered softly.

At a loss for words, Evangeline merely nodded, watching as Elliot shifted uneasily.

"Walk with me, Miss Stone?" he asked abruptly. "Come, bear me company for a small part of this lonely evening?"

"Walk with you?" Her voice quivered as she tried to hide her astonishment. "Why, wherever would we go?"

Even in the flickering light of the wall sconce, Evangeline could see a mischievous smile tug at the corner of Elliot's full, sinfully handsome mouth. "In the gardens," he whispered, leaning into her. "Beneath the light of the moon. Where is your sense of romantic adventure, Miss Stone?"

"I do not think that we should—"

"Ah, Miss Stone! Do something wildly irresponsible for once." Without taking his eyes from hers, Elliot placed his hand on the doorknob of her bedchamber and flashed her a wicked grin. Slowly, he pushed the door open on silent hinges, his big hand splayed against the wood. A wave of desire and uncertainty shook her.

"Your cloak," he answered in response to her disquiet. Elliot gently tipped her chin up on his finger and looked down into her eyes. It should have been a sweet gesture, but in the darkened corridor it felt like something quite different. "You are safe with me, Miss Stone," he whispered. "The pleasure of your company is all I seek tonight. But do go in and fetch a cloak, for you shall find the night air far less benign than I."

With her heart pounding, Evangeline flew to the wardrobe and hastily pulled a woolen cape from its hook. Whatever was she thinking, running off to walk in the dark of night with a man whom, in truth, she hardly knew? It was reckless, for any number of reasons. Nonetheless, Evangeline was beginning to think that perhaps she had been far too prudent for one lifetime.

Elliot was right, she realized a few moments later. The night still held the faint chill of spring. Evangeline stood on the upper terrace of Chatham's rear gardens and pulled her cloak more securely about her. The gardens were beautiful, with moonbeams spearing through the trees to shimmer across the surface of the ornamental ponds. The shadows of the lush summer rosebushes snaked across the long, twisting path which dropped from terrace to terrace until it disappeared into an ancient wood beyond. Though charming by day, Chatham

Lodge was noted for the beauty of its gardens, and tonight they were enchanting in the pale, shimmering light.

Although she could not see him, Evangeline's every sense was acutely aware of Elliot standing above her on the steps. She could feel the heat radiate from his body, carrying with it the earthy, intoxicating aura that was uniquely his: subtle cologne, expensive tobacco, warm wool, and untamed sensuality. Drawing deep of the night air, Evangeline indulged in a rare moment of luxury, breathing in the seductive essence, basking in his warmth as he stood so near.

She suppressed a shudder of unexpected pleasure when, after a long, silent moment, Elliot bent to speak softly into her ear, placing his hands lightly upon her shoulders. "Where do we go from here, Miss Stone?" he asked in his deep, silky voice which seemed pitched to both seduce and soothe.

Turning quickly on the narrow step to face him, Evangeline almost lost her balance, but Elliot merely tightened his grip and gently turned her to him.

"What do you mean?" she asked uncertainly, sliding one hand up to steady herself by grasping his elbow.

The soft light only served to emphasize the strong angles and planes of his face as his mouth curled in a quizzical smile. "Where shall we walk, Miss Stone? You must lead the way."

"Oh!" Evangeline felt her face go warm. She wanted him to kiss her. The realization was disconcerting.

Elliot saved her from further embarrassment. "For example, this terrace path—where does it go? Shall we follow all the way?"

"No, I shouldn't think—not all the way." Struggling to retain far more than her footing, Evangeline raised her hand to point toward the trees just beyond the last terrace. "The path continues through that narrow strip of wood and through our meadows. Beyond them lies the River Lea. It would be unwise to risk it in the dark."

Elliot nodded as he pulled a cigar case from his pocket. "Then we shall circle the gardens only," he answered, casting her a sidelong glance, then returning the case, unopened, to his pocket.

Evangeline looked up at him and smiled. "If you would care to smoke, Mr. Roberts, pray do so."

Despite the dim light, she could see his teasing grin. "It would be exceedingly wicked to smoke in the presence of a lady. Are you certain?"

"Yes, indeed," she responded, greatly relieved to have his attention focused elsewhere. She watched as Elliot's graceful fingers drew a cheroot from the elaborate case. "Light it from the hall lamp," she suggested, pointing toward the door from which they had come.

In the pale light, Elliot nodded. He was gone but a moment, his movements silent and lithe. When he returned to the steps, he boldly took her hand and led her down the steps and onto the path. They strolled through the dark, Elliot silently smoking and Evangeline acutely aware that he had not released her hand. She felt foolish, almost young and giddy, as they continued thus around the back terraces, along a stone path past the kitchen orchard and through the front gardens. Silently they wandered, hand in hand, for about a quarter hour, until Elliot gently urged her north along the tower.

"There is great beauty in this place, Miss Stone," he whispered as he looked up at the ancient and imposing tower walls. He paused to stare at the nearly full moon through the spreading branches of a young oak. "I find such an ethereal peace here, yet I cannot quite find the words to explain how I feel." A heavy stone bench sat just beneath the tree, and Elliot pulled her down toward it.

"Yes, the tranquility is most welcome. Certainly, I found it so when first I came here," agreed Evangeline softly. "It is said to have been a royal hunting lodge, you know. The Epping Forest is very near." She deftly arranged her skirts, then settled into the curve of the seat. Though Elliot did not touch her, she could sense his arm, warm and strangely comforting, stretched across the back of the bench.

Elliot regarded her in silence, exhaling an agonizingly slow stream of smoke that appeared soft and white against the restless night air. "How long?" he finally asked. "How long have you been at Chatham?"

Evangeline watched the smoke curl and melt into the tender spring leaves of a low-hanging limb and tried not to think of Elliot's masculine heat and seductive scent which drifted on the evening's chill to tease at her senses. She tried not to recall how suggestively his powerful thighs had flexed when he sank onto the bench beside her. She tried not to think about his lean hips and narrow waist, his hard, flat stomach, which rose up to a broad, muscular chest. Nevertheless, with every breath, she became increasingly aware of him in a way that was new and disturbing.

Elliot cleared his throat softly, and Evangeline recalled his question. "Many years," she answered abruptly. "Since we came from Flanders."

"Why did you leave, Miss Stone, if I might ask? Did your father's English background make it prudent to evade Napoleon's boot heel?"

Evangeline gave a brittle laugh. "In some small part, I suppose. But mostly we were just fleeing memories."

"Why did your parents decide—"

"I decided, Mr. Roberts," she interrupted. "My mother was dead, and God help us if I chose wrongly . . ."

Elliot paused for a long moment. "I see," he responded at last, his voice but a whisper in the dark.

In the silence, Evangeline hesitated as the old pain and fear washed over her. "I did what I thought was best," she added quietly, "but coming to England seemed a far wiser thing to do when my father was still alive." Evangeline could sense the muscles of Elliot's arm go taut as he pitched the cigar onto the path beneath their feet, then ground it hard beneath the heel of his boot.

"You seem eminently wise to me, Miss Stone," he replied. Evangeline shifted on the bench uncomfortably. Almost absently, it seemed, Elliot leaned into her, tenderly pulling her cloak more securely about her neck. "Evangeline?"

"Yes?"

"Will you tell me what it is that troubles you?" He asked the question softly, his mouth so close that Evangeline could feel the warmth of his breath caress her cheek. She did not miss the significance of his use of her given name. Evangeline squeezed her eyes shut and froze. His was more than an offer of comfort; it was a subtle invitation as well. If she turned to face him now, her lips would almost certainly brush against his. A man's strength and compassion would be so welcome, yet she dared not accept it. The wait was agonizing, but at last she sensed that Elliot had drawn back. Only then did she trust herself to turn on the bench to face him.

In the shadows, she held his gaze, still yearning to lean into his powerful arms, into the warm male strength of him, but she could not. "Perhaps you would care to tell me the same," she countered softly. "For example, what still-tender scar lies just beneath that most agreeable veneer of yours, Mr. Roberts? Was it the ending of your betrothal? Did you love her so very much?"

Beside her, she felt Elliot go perfectly still. Mortified at her own words, Evangeline opened her mouth to apologize, but, to her surprise, he answered her question. "Yes," he answered in a soft, distant voice. "I did. I suppose I loved her almost beyond reason. And if you do not mind, I should rather we did not discuss it."

"Forgive me," she responded, disappointment knifing through her heart. "My question was inexcusable, but, despite the warmth of your smile, I sometimes see an abiding sadness in your eyes." She sighed deeply. "I suspect that neither of us wants to reveal our inner demons tonight, so perhaps we should simply enjoy the evening."

"But of course," he responded smoothly, leaning away almost imperceptibly.

Evangeline drew a nervous breath and tried valiantly to lighten her tone. "Tell me of yourself, Mr. Roberts. What are your interests? What of your family?"

She watched as unease and uncertainty flitted across his handsome face. In that moment, she was exceedingly glad that she had not surrendered to her desire to kiss him. There was an undeniable physical attraction between them, but his wounds were as raw as her fears were real. To set her lips to his would be the height of recklessness. Her feelings for Elliot Roberts were potent and disturbing, yet Evangeline knew herself so well. Were she ever foolish enough to touch this man, a consuming fire might well be lit inside her heart, and she would want far more from him than the mere friendship he had offered outside her bedchamber. She could so very easily love him, and yet it would have been an emotion destined for disappointment. An aching, unrequited love for a man who had loved and lost another. Such sentiments could only hurt her and interfere with her demanding responsibilities.

In the darkness, Elliot slowly turned to face her. She had almost forgotten her question, but he apparently had not. "There is little to tell, Miss Stone. I lead an exceedingly dull life."

"That is a tale I cannot countenance," she stated flatly. "And I have already noticed your faint Scottish burr."

Elliot's brows went up in apparent surprise. "Such a great many questions, Miss Stone."

"Am I to have answers to accompany them, Mr. Roberts? After all, it was you who suggested we might be friends."

Elliot rose abruptly from the bench and drew her up beside him. Almost possessively, he curled her hand just above his elbow, then laid his long, slender fingers across hers. Slowly, they stepped back onto the path that circled the house. As they set off, Elliot gave an almost resigned sigh, then he began to speak softly. "I was raised in Scotland, Miss Stone, on an estate not far from Ayr. My mother, however, was very much English. When she was quite young, she wed my father, a dour Presbyterian who was much older than she, in an arranged marriage. I am an only child. That is all there is to tell."

Evangeline gave a gentle tug on his arm and glanced up into his shadowed eyes. "Oh, no. You shan't get off with so little as that! Are your parents still living? What other family do you have?"

"Family is exceedingly important to you, isn't it, Miss Stone?" His tone was grave.

"Yes. Will you answer my questions?"

Elliot drew a slow, deep breath, as if debating what he should say. "My mother remains in Scotland. My father died when I was a young man."

"Oh," she responded in a solemn whisper. "I am so sorry, Mr. Roberts. It must have been very sad."

"Yes, I suppose that it was, although we . . . we were not close." He shrugged abruptly, then altered the subject. "Tell me, Miss Stone, how did your father die? You must miss him terribly."

Evangeline looked up at him, still very much aware of his long, strong fingers lying across hers. "My father died slowly, Mr. Roberts, from his heart outward," she answered softly. "Oh, it was just a mild fever that finally carried him off, and the doctor said he could easily have recovered, had he but possessed the will to live. . . . How maudlin I must seem! Pray tell me of your father, Mr. Roberts. May I hope he lived to a ripe old age?"

Elliot looked down at her sharply. "Aye, tough as an old boot, he was. Consumption had him in its grip, yet he fought it for over a year."

Evangeline sighed. "Were . . . were you much affected by his passing, Mr. Roberts?"

Elliot's voice was an uncharacteristic whisper in the darkness. "More than you can ever know, Miss Stone. It was, you see, the beginning of the end of my innocence." Then, abruptly, he seemed to stiffen, and Evangeline felt his grip tighten incrementally. Yet when he spoke, his voice was stronger, as if he were willing away the past. "But he left sisters, so I have two rather eccentric spinster aunts who dote on me. And I have a maternal uncle who resides in town. As for the rest of my family, well, that is a long story, and I should prefer to speak of it another time and in greater detail, if that is acceptable?"

His words, though gently spoken, left her with no alternative. She could hardly be rude enough to insist. Especially when he had not pressed his questions to her. "But of course," she answered softly, returning the response he had given earlier.

Elliot must have sensed her disquiet, for he tightened his grip on her hand and then tilted his head to look down at her. "I live the life of an English gentleman, Miss Stone. I belong to very fine clubs, which I rarely visit, and receive a great many invitations, which I summarily ignore. I have an ancient Scottish butler, a fine French chef, and a tempestuous, epicene valet to whom I am greatly attached—not in any unnatural way, I can assure you. But I am exceedingly fond of him nonetheless. My mischievous uncle resides in Richmond with me but is rarely home due to his extreme, er, popularity. I, on the other hand, no longer go about in what is inexplicably called polite society."

"Are you a recluse, then, Mr. Roberts?" Her question sounded sharper than she had intended.

"No." The single word hung heavily in the air, yet he made no attempt to explain further. Instead, he pulled her to a stop on the path and turned to face her. "It was never my intent to sound reticent. Does my explanation ease your mind?" Even in the dark, she could see that the expression on his face was intense, almost anxious.

"Yes." Evangeline nodded, looking up at him from the shadows of the terrace. She took comfort in the fact that Elliot could sense her mood and had taken pains to soothe her curiosity. Slowly, his hand slid from hers, rising up to almost brush her cheek. This time, Evangeline was certain that he intended to lace his long fingers around the nape of her neck and kiss her, but at the last moment his hand stilled. Then, gracefully, he leaned close and gently tucked a lock of hair behind her ear.

It was another sweet gesture. Evangeline felt awash in conflicting emotions; overwhelmed with relief and crushed by disappointment. Deliberately, she straightened her shoulders and pulled open the rear door. "We should go in now, Mr. Roberts. We must both be in the studio early in order to catch the best light."

"Yes," he agreed quietly, still holding her gaze. He made no move to enter.

"Very well, then," she said with artificial brightness. "I

shall see you early tomorrow." Then, before she could do something foolish, Evangeline entered the rear hallway and started toward the back stairs. When she turned to mount the staircase, however, she saw Elliot in the corridor, bent low across the lamp, lighting another cheroot. The flame flared then danced inside the glass chamber, casting the harsh angles of his face into grim relief. Slowly, he rose, exhaled sharply, and spun on his heel to return to the terrace.

It was well over an hour before Evangeline heard the echo of his soft tread ascending the main staircase and striding down the hall toward the narrow tower stairs. Only then did Morpheus take her, dragging her deep beneath the shadows and into fitful, troubled slumber.

Pushing aside her disconcerting thoughts of Elliot Roberts, Evangeline drifted through the next two days with a serene ease. When she worked, her painting was inspired. When she spent time with her family, and consequently with Elliot, her laughter was lighthearted, her disposition cheerful. It was unavoidable. His presence made her happy.

She saw a great deal of her handsome guest, who was forever smiling in that gentle, tolerant way that had so quickly become his—eyes glinting silver, the corners crinkling softly. Such days of bliss, Evangeline often thought, must soon end, but they would leave her with wonderful memories.

She and Elliot spent the second morning as they had the first, sequestered in the studio. In truth, another few days could easily see the completion of Elliot's portrait. Yet he seemed in no rush and asked no questions; therefore, Evangeline found it easy to dawdle. Just as she dropped the last brush into its jar, Michael and Theo dashed in unannounced, in hopes of persuading Elliot to

ride with them. Gus, eager to put a newly purchased
gelding through its paces, had proposed a ramble
through the Epping Forest and back across the southern
edge of Chatham's modest estate.

Elliot laughed at their unbridled enthusiasm. "Do you
mind, Miss Stone?" he asked, turning his gaze upon her
as she carried her materials back to the big worktable.

"Not at all." Evangeline smiled. "I rather wish I might
join you."

"Nothing would better please me," he responded quietly.

Evangeline sighed and tossed a glance at the messy
table. "I cannot. The four of you must go, and have
enough fun for five. The day is so warm, almost hot, in
fact. You shall enjoy it."

An hour later, the mess tidied, Evangeline regretted
her diligence. Elliot's departure left a dark, silent void in
house. She missed his presence far more than she wished
to admit. Winnie and Frederica had gone for a walk.
Nicolette was engaged with Stokely in a history lesson.
Impulsively, Evangeline grabbed her bonnet and exchanged her kid slippers for sturdy half-boots.

The day was brilliant, and in no time at all she could
catch up with Winnie along the river path. Evangeline set
off in fine spirits, but halfway to the Lea she was drawn
to the bridle path which cut south toward the tenant
farms. Perhaps if she walked in that direction, she would
meet Elliot returning with the boys. Impetuously, Evangeline turned from the walking path and onto the
rougher trail which cut through the wood and into the
vast, rolling meadows of the estate.

After half a mile, the wood ended near the point at
which a cool brook snaked out of the forest from the
east. Though she rarely came this way, Evangeline remembered that a few yards farther on, the stream fed

into Chatham's great farm pond before continuing its journey to the River Lea. Grateful for her boots, Evangeline stuck to the path, looking for the tall willows that marked the far edge of the water. Slowly, the trees of the forest thinned, the last stand of beech not a stone's throw from the farm pond. Beyond them lay a low tangle of hawthorn.

Unexpectedly, laughter and shouting rent the hot summer air. Peering through the thicket, Evangeline could see that four horses had been tethered beside the willows across the water. In the soft grass that edged the pond lay a telltale heap of clothing and a jumbled pile of boots. The juvenile whooping and cheering grew louder still, and, leaning forward hesitantly to part the branches, Evangeline saw the four bare-chested males cavorting like schoolboys. Amid the turbulent splashing and dunking, it was impossible to identify anyone, until at last she saw Elliot leap up to plunge deep beneath the surface in an obvious attempt to escape the skirmish.

Lud, not one of them was wearing a stitch!

She should leave. She knew she should, but the temptation was overpowering. Had she not helped to bathe and diaper Theo and Michael when they were babes? And she had seen Gus half-naked on a dozen different occasions. Indeed, Evangeline further rationalized, she was an artist, trained to see artistic beauty in the human form. There could be no harm in looking, and no one would be the wiser.

Suddenly, Elliot surfaced in an erupting splash at the near edge of the pond. He stood, laughing good-naturedly, in water that was not quite waist-deep. Evangeline's gaze was riveted. Never in her life had she seen such a stunning man, and certainly not in such a state of undress. The power and beauty of his lean, muscled form would have made Donatello seize his chisel and pray for divine guidance.

It made Evangeline simply stop breathing.

The surface of the water lapped teasingly just below the taut muscles of Elliot's lower back. He was so close now, Evangeline could see the rivulets of water glisten as they ran down to hint at the slight curve of his buttocks. Awestruck, she watched as Elliot turned to almost face the copse of beech and hawthorn. He paused and, with an almost agonizing indolence, lifted his hands to wipe the water from his face, then raked his long fingers back through the unruly mass of too-long hair. The water skimmed low across his pelvis, accentuating the flat plane of his stomach and the dark line of damp, curling hair that ran from his chest and down his belly to disappear beneath the surface. To watch him was slow torture of the sweetest kind.

Then, just when she thought she might be able to breathe again, Elliot closed his eyes, tilted his head back, and lifted his elbows to wring the dampness from his hair. Hard chest muscles flexed as water ran down the taut cords of his neck, some of it trickling through the nest of dark chest hair, and lower still. Under the warm June sun, Elliot's well-muscled arms glistened and rippled, sending something hot, urgent, and long dormant surging through her belly.

Fingertips pressed hard against her lips, Evangeline sank to her knees in the tender spring grass beneath the beeches. It was then, in that endless moment of heat and sun and water, that she fully acknowledged the magnitude of her desire for Elliot.

From the corner of one eye, Elliot caught a glimpse of dark blue fabric in the copse of trees beside the pond. He almost turned to stare, then froze in shock as he realized who it must be. *Evangeline*. Was it? Surely not. She was hardly the type of woman to spy on a group of naked men. Was she?

He saw the color again, a hint of dark blue fabric all but hidden in the lush foliage. It was Evangeline; he could feel her heated stare. Suddenly, Elliot felt possessed by the very demons he had thus far managed to keep leashed. *Miss Stone wants to watch,* whispered a dark, seductive voice. Slowly, he lifted his arms to run his fingers through his hair. With deliberate, leisurely motions, Elliot wrung the water from his hair, intentionally flexing the muscles of his chest and shoulders.

If it was her curiosity the lady sought to ease, Elliot was more than willing to oblige. Indeed, he would gladly show her anything she found to her liking; he only hoped he sent her scurrying away with a problem far more frustrating than simple curiosity. Perhaps she would then need him to oblige an urge of a different sort . . .

Suddenly, Elliot was horrified to realize that he had become a victim of his own seduction. At the mere thought of enticing Evangeline, of awakening her virginal ardor, an insidious, melting warmth had begun to uncoil low in his abdomen. In mortification, Elliot felt his shaft thicken and begin to rise up in the water. Good God, how humiliating! Flushing with embarrassment, he turned his back to the beech trees and waded deeper into the chilly pond, fervently hoping that Gus and the boys would keep their distance for a time.

For many days after returning to Richmond, the thought of how Evangeline had watched him haunted Elliot, making him feel confused and restless. When he slept, and it was difficult, she haunted his tempestuous dreams—wild imaginings of butter-yellow hair and eyes that burned him like a hot blue flame. Evangeline clung to him in these nocturnal fantasies, eager and yielding, her bare thighs slender and silken. Between the sheets of his imagination, they tumbled, wild and insatiable, hands and mouths pressed heatedly against each other until he awoke, often gasping for breath, in a tangle of linen.

"For heaven's sake, hold still," hissed Kemble in apparent aggravation. "One would think you wished to cease wearing cravats altogether." With what felt like deliberate maliciousness, the valet drew the fine fabric another quarter inch tighter, then fashioned it into an elaborate, slightly embellished version of the *sentimentale*.

The final bow rested high beneath Elliot's chin. "Feel like a bloody trussed-up Christmas goose," muttered the marquis, thrusting out his arms for his embroidered waistcoat.

"What twaddle, my lord," replied Kemble smugly as he slid the garment up over the marquis's shoulders. "Indeed, that full effect would require corsets. Shall I oblige? Maurice can whip up something brutally painful in a trice." The valet strolled around and began to fasten the buttons.

Elliot ran one long finger around his collar in an attempt to mitigate the damage. "With all due respect to Maurice's skills, Kem, I sincerely hope I do not as yet require such artifice."

Kemble swept an appraising glance over him. "No, indeed, my lord. Far from it," he answered, his voice smooth and serious. He paused for a few seconds. "Who is she, my lord?" The question was interposed like a casual afterthought.

Elliot peered down at the smaller man, one brow crooked in deliberate arrogance. "Who is who?" he asked noncommittally.

"*Cherchez la femme*," muttered Kemble, eyeing his employer suspiciously while giving a final tug on the waistcoat. "Is that not what the French advise? And in this case, I am sure they must be quite right! You are always from home. You smoke like a bad chimney. You insist on wearing dreadful clothing and twitch as if you've contracted Saint Vitus's dance on those rare occasions when I try to dress you properly—"

"Kem!" Elliot's voice held a warning, but the valet was on a tear, pointing his elegant finger at the bed, its sheets a hopeless tangle.

"You sleep fitfully and at odd hours when you are here, and you almost never go to town. Moreover, Scotland cannot ferment that vile whisky fast enough to suit you." Kemble drew a deep breath and concluded, "Only a lover can be the cause of such disruption to a well-ordered life."

"Humph," grunted Elliot, abruptly shoving his arms into the sleeves of the coat Kemble held open. He turned around for another set of buttons, absently thinking that his valet was too damn smart by half. "If you must know, Kem, *la femme* in question is an exceedingly nice young woman. She is beautiful, sensitive, and gifted. An artist, in fact."

"And this goddess has deigned to keep company with *you?*" The valet looked up from his work, pausing in mid-button, his tone arch.

"Yes."

"Of her own volition? Or have you locked her in the attic?" Kemble stared at him in all seriousness.

The question stung, and Elliot chose to ignore it. He knew that Kem did not mean to hurt him, and so he changed the subject. "What of your new tailor friend? Maurice, did you say?"

Kemble nodded, cheerful for once. "Ah, he's in good looks these days, my lord! Busy, too, what with the season upon us. All the new fashions! Maurice says breeches are completely *démodé*, and trousers are now *de rigueur* in town. That is very good for business, of course."

Elliot nodded, still tugging at his collar. His eyes flicked down at the valet in sympathy. "Why not take the evening off, Kem?" he suggested softly. "I imagine I can get myself out of this rig when the time comes. Besides, Hugh and I are off to the club. We're to play a hand with Winthrop and Linden, and I shall doubtless be quite late."

Kemble did not wait for a second offer. Elliot's coat now fully buttoned, the valet darted through the room gathering up the marquis's stick, hat, and gloves, then dashed out the door with nary another quip or question. Elliot was left standing alone in the center of his vast bedchamber. He cast another glance at the tousled bedcovers, then threw down his hat and gloves in despair. He was glad to be rid of Kem. He did not want to go to the club. Not with Hugh. Not with anyone. He did not want to play cards. Nor did he want to be alone in this desolate house.

What he wanted, damn it all, was Evangeline Stone. Yes, he wanted her with an agonizing desperation that was almost tangible.

But it just was not possible. Moreover, it was foolish. Had he not learned his lesson at an early age? It was not worth it. Far better he should simply rip his heart from his chest and toss it to Winthrop's pack of rabid hounds. It would be quicker, and far less painful, than losing himself in another woman, for Elliot knew that despite his hardened resolve, were he to fall in love again, he would fall blindly, hopelessly, and irretrievably. It was his way, and he could not seem to alter the course. Already, he felt frighteningly near the precipice, mooning over another lost love as if the devastation of it might bring the spinning earth to a halt.

His first night back from Chatham, in an effort to dispel Evangeline's tantalizing memory, Elliot had forced himself to go drinking and whoring with Lord Linden, telling himself that his problem was, simply put, the deleterious consequence of self-imposed celibacy. Since Antoinette's last ugly tantrum, Elliot had been without a woman. It was perverse. Toward the end of their relationship, Elliot had found himself sick to death of his paramour's increasingly heavy drinking and volatile moods. Yet Lily, the young actress whom Antoinette had quite accurately assumed was to become her replacement, had also ceased to hold his interest. Regrettably, upon careful consideration, the alternatives seemed no more appealing.

The cloying ways of the demimonde had grown tiresome, while the manipulations and machinations of the *ton's* bored wives and widows were downright dangerous. He was tired of creeping in and out of assorted French windows, back doors, and service entrances just before cock crow. Moreover, on those rare occasions when his hearing failed him or he was otherwise too distracted, the aftermath was equally unpleasant. He had a scar on his arse to remind him. During the last ten years, Elliot had grown excessively weary of riding out at dawn to shoot and be shot at, over women who were, all too frequently, inadequate between the sheets.

Furthermore, he knew perfectly well what such women were about. These paragons of the *beau monde,* while all too willing to bed him in some vain attempt to lessen their ennui, ease their curiosity, or spite their husbands, would later arise—his scent, no doubt, lingering on their sheets—and very nearly trot across Bond Street to avoid having to cross his path and greet him in public. Some, like Jeanette, were worse. Contrary to all her feigned passion, she had sought nothing more than his seed. Jeanette had been anxious for a child, and any virile man, she had finally explained, would have done just as well.

Elliot suppressed a snort of disgust and rubbed the old wound. The manipulative vixen had used him, and perhaps that had been just as he deserved, for he had not cared for Jeanette. Indeed, he had not even liked her. But she had been beautiful, willing, and seemingly desperate for him. Unfortunately, her elderly husband, arriving home very early and very inebriated from White's one evening, had not appreciated Elliot's assistance in getting an heir on his young wife. Worse still, the man had not bothered to issue a challenge, which Elliot could have handled. Instead, he had taken a rather shaky but moderately successful aim out Jeanette's bedchamber window, lodging a ball of lead somewhat south of Elliot's black heart.

It was a sennight before Elliot could sit down with any measure of comfort. Since Lord Stephen was known to be an aging pantywaist, as well as a notoriously bad shot, the entire affair had been widely whispered about as something of a joke. The powerful family matriarch had not, however, seen any humor in the situation. Come hell, high water, or, in this case, lascivious scandal, her unwavering plan required Lord Stephen to carry on the family tradition of wielding parliamentary clout and leverage among the most resolute members of the Tory aristocracy. In retaliation for their antics, Lord Stephen's stepmother had suspended Jeanette's allowance and forced the hapless couple into rustication, as if they were nothing more than recalcitrant children. Wisely, however, the old lady had stopped short of maligning the marquis of Rannoch, who was both richer and meaner. Elliot had been almost disappointed.

It should have come as no surprise, therefore, that last

night's sinful foray with Linden had been an unmitigated disaster. The women had been forward and fawning, and the drinking, rather than serving as his consolation, had instead left him despondent. There would be, it seemed, no peace for Elliot Armstrong. Hell, maybe he didn't deserve any. Maybe Evangeline Stone was nothing more than a just punishment for his worldly sins, a celestial enchantress sent down to inflict his remaining days on earth with regret and torment. What, then, would perdition be like, he wondered?

Slowly, he inhaled a deep, ragged breath and walked to the tray holding his whisky decanter to try again. He jerked out the stopper with a scrape, sloshed three fingers into a glass, then pressed the chilly crystal surface to his temple. It felt cool and soothing against his throbbing pulse. Holding it thus, he walked to the window and stared down at the Thames, still visible in the dying light of the summer's evening.

He stared across the water toward Houndslow, watching mindlessly as, up and down the river, the last of the day's boats put to shore on the north bank, leaving the river empty and forlorn. Vast. Desolate. Pensively, he sipped at the whisky, rolling it over his tongue and trying to take some pleasure from the smooth, woody burn as it washed down his throat.

It was no use. Absently, he set the glass down inside the deep windowsill and leaned his head forward until it rested against a cool pane of glass. Yes, he would go to Brooks's to gamble and to drink and to look for trouble if he could find it. Yet trouble, like satisfaction, seemed ever more elusive these days. Indeed, even trouble seemed to stare suspiciously over its shoulder and walk a wide, cautious circle around him.

Nevertheless, he would go, and he would look, because it was all he had ever done. It was his life, such as his life was. And when Evangeline, along with the fleeting sense of contentment that her presence brought him, was gone, his miserable life would be all that he had left. It was, he supposed, better than nothing. After all, he had managed to sustain himself reasonably well on gambling, drinking, and trouble for any number of years.

He knocked back half his whisky, fighting down the urge to pack his bags and return to Essex that very night. It could be easily done; the moon was nearly full, and the sky was clear. But he could not do it, for he had left her only two days earlier. He could not justify staying at Chatham any longer than he had done. As it was, both he and Evangeline were fooling no one about the reasons for his protracted visits, save maybe themselves. Winnie Weyden merely cast him sidelong glances and curled her mouth into a mischievous half smile every time she saw him. Hell, the servants were beginning to behave as if they worked for him. The children persisted in acting as though he were a permanent fixture in their lives.

That hurt. And it worried him.

Slowly, he dropped his forehead to the glass once more. In three days, he was due to return. Immediately upon his arrival, he wanted to tell Evangeline the truth. She deserved to know. There was only one ugly alternative, and it was dreadfully ugly indeed. He could seduce her before she learned his identity.

Elliot was certain he could seduce an innocent. He had the expertise and notoriety, but perhaps not the heart, for just such a role. And, oh God, yes! Evangeline was ripe for his seduction! He had seen raw desire shimmer in her fiery blue eyes. He had recognized her passion in the way her soft, full lips parted invitingly when she tilted her head to look up at him. At first, he had been shocked that such a woman could want him. Him! But her incipient need was unmistakable.

This time, he would have to do a little more than simply hold her hand in the dark or flaunt himself in all his wet, naked glory. Elliot weighed his strategy carefully. Evangeline was strong and willful, but her unleashed passion would fast overrule her less carnal qualities. He felt sure of it. And it was a vision Elliot had conjured up in his mind time and time again. Evie, her thick blond hair spread across his pillow, her lithe, slender form reclining in his bed. Her small breasts were high and full, her hips elegantly flared. Elliot knew it instinctively and felt himself harden at the image. He would tempt her, and she would take him. With his consummate skill, he would please her, and with her innocent heart, she would give him the ultimate peace. And once the deed was done, she would be his, and the truth would matter a little less.

Evangeline would be left with no alternative. No alternative at all.

Good God, what was he thinking? Elliot raised his head from the glass, nausea roiling in his stomach. What had he been contemplating? Was he truly capable of defiling an honorable woman and forcing her into marriage? For that was most assuredly what it would come to. Restrained temptation was one thing, but he was well past sexual fantasy and fast crossing the bridge to outright wickedness. He was painfully aware that Evangeline did not deserve to be tainted by his touch, and yet the obsession would not leave him. Was he really that desperate to have her? Or was the evil just deeply and indelibly ingrained in his character?

No! In two days, he would leave for Wrotham-upon-Lea, and within five minutes of his arrival he would tell her everything. It was resolved. He was going to hurt her, had already hurt her, did she but know it. Elliot was many bad things, but he was not by his nature a liar. He would tell her.

Tell her what? That the object of her growing affection was none other than that *vile, sniffing hound,* Elliot Armstrong, marquis of Rannoch? Oh, that would get her attention, no doubt about it. Moreover, he already had some inkling of the low esteem in which her family held the marquis of Rannoch and those of his ilk. Given their seemingly deliberate reclusion, Elliot had been surprised to find that the denizens of Chatham had any knowledge of or interest in the antics of society; nonetheless, Mrs. Weyden had made their feelings about Rannoch quite plain.

And Elliot would make no apologies for what he was. Indeed, what would be the point? He was not some callow youth led into a life of debauchery out of ignorance. No, he had chosen his path with great deliberation and reaped the fruits of his lifestyle with abandon. It was his means of protection; it was his prudently chosen defense against the harsh truths of this ugly world. He had no need to search his soul. Elliot always knew precisely what he was about, even when it was not very nice.

His reputation was well earned. There was nothing malicious in what was said about him; much of it was true, and in time the remainder would no doubt come to be fact. Yes, he was on that slippery slope that had so disturbed his mother and tempted generations of Benhams. However, in his case, it was not the slope to ruin, though he had indeed sent many a man down it. No, Rannoch himself was on the slippery slope to hell, and heretofore he had not much cared.

Impetuously, he turned from the window and strode from the room, turning left into the corridor and bounding up another level of the sweeping circular staircase. When he arrived at the third-floor landing, Elliot took up the hall lamp and turned right. Quickly, before he could change his mind, he walked past the schoolroom and opened the door just beyond. Stealthily, he eased inside and put down the lamp beside his daughter's bed.

❦ 6 ❦

It is the end that crowns us, not the fight.
—Robert Herrick

Zoë looked unusually peaceful in her sleep. By the light of day, the child occasionally looked apprehensive, and far older than her seven and a half years. Pretty little Frederica d'Avillez was, what, eight or nine? Certainly no more. Yet they were altogether different children, and Elliot again suffered the sickening suspicion that the difference was his error, that he had in some essential way failed his daughter, his own flesh and blood.

Settling himself carefully onto the small half-tester bed, Elliot looked about Zoë's well-appointed bedchamber. Tastefully decorated in pink and gold, the room was filled with soft white furniture imported from France. Books and toys lined the walls, fine silk slippers sat heel to toe in Zoë's wardrobe, and all manner of lacy little-girl things filled her chiffonier. Miss Smith, Zoë's governess, slept in an adjoining room, and Elliot had been assured that the woman provided the best education money could buy. All this, however, was not enough. After his time at Chatham Lodge, Elliot was slowly beginning to understand what Zoë needed from him, but often the knowledge brought him little hope and even less comfort. In truth, Elliot sometimes feared that he had nothing more to give, that it had already been wrung out of him. Shut off. Forever disconnected. He was trying, but he needed help.

Evangeline. Evangeline would know what to do, and suddenly he wished that she were with him. He needed her. God, he needed her for so many things. Impulsively, he leaned down to kiss Zoë's plump, pink cheek, and as he righted himself, Elliot was dismayed to see that her eyes were flickering open.

"Papa?" In the darkness, her whisper seemed as uncertain and ephemeral as Zoë herself.

"Go back to sleep, Zoë." He patted the blankets reassuringly. "I did not mean to wake you."

"Is anything wrong, Papa?" Her huge brown eyes blinked in confusion as she pulled herself up onto one elbow. One dark, bouncing ringlet fell from her nightcap and tumbled over her face.

Elliot smiled. "Oh, no, sweet. I just came up to kiss you good night and to tell you that I love you." He watched Zoë nod and smile, as if nightly, or even daily, visits from her father were the norm. They should have been, but they were not, and both of them knew it. Slowly, she rubbed one eye with the back of her pudgy hand, then settled herself back into her pillow, pulling the covers up to her dimpled chin. Big, innocent eyes, unblinking now, stared up at him.

"Zoë," he blurted out uncertainly, "are you happy here?" Elliot wanted to bite back the words at once, but it was too late.

The little girl looked up at him a little anxiously and said nothing.

"It is perfectly all right to tell me, Zoë," Elliot whispered reassuringly. "Strath is a big, empty house. Sometimes I get lonely, and I just wondered if, perhaps, you did, too."

"Miss Smith tells me I must be grateful that I have a

home," answered Zoë reluctantly. "And because I am allowed to stay here, she says I must work very hard on my studies and be very good. I should not complain or cause trouble."

Elliot made a mental note to discharge Miss Smith directly after breakfast. "Zoë," he whispered, chucking her softly under the chin with his knuckle. "I love you, and your home will always be with me, regardless of whether you are bad or good, silly or smart. Did you not understand that?"

Mutely, the little girl shook her head, her chestnut curls tumbling loose to glint in the candlelight. Elliot looked at her and felt true shame. Despite his belated determination to be a better father, fear and insecurity, two emotions no child should suffer, still tormented his child. And it was his fault. Awkwardly, Elliot leaned forward and pulled her tiny frame to his chest, wrapping his arms around her as if he feared she might vanish in the night. It was often thus with Zoë. To Elliot, it was as if she did not belong on this earth, let alone in this house, and now he feared that she might feel it, too.

She was like a delicate feather, this daughter of his. "I love you, Zoë," he whispered again, this time into her curls. *And I wish I could be a better papa. But I am afraid and ignorant and frozen inside.* Those words he did not say. Instead, Elliot held his tongue and after a long moment forced himself to lessen his grip and pull away. It was too much; he did not wish to frighten her. Or himself.

The Great Subscription Room of Brooks's was awash in the *haut monde*. Tonight, England's nobility and gentry mingled, shoulder to shoulder, about the gaming tables and throughout the adjoining card room, as they did almost every evening, in season and out. Elliot arrived

late, and in an exceedingly ill humor. He did not want to
drink and gamble; he wanted to stay at Strath House and
wallow in the misery of what his life might have been
like.

Nonetheless, he could not do so. He had given his
word to Winthrop, in a vain attempt to end last night's
mind-numbing barrage of questions about where and
with whom he had been keeping himself. Evangeline did
not deserve the kind of mischievous havoc Major
Winthrop, Lord Linden, and Sir Hugh were capable of
wreaking, and he knew perfectly well that his cronies
would not hesitate to have him followed should their curiosity get the better of them.

Pray God they had not already done so. Elliot had not
missed the significance of society's interest in his antics.
Winnie Weyden's little scandal rag had taken a year or
two off his life, and he knew perfectly well that either
Hugh or Linden had been responsible for the printing of
such drivel.

With a weary sigh, Elliot strode through the rooms
searching for his uncle. As they invariably did, everyone
stepped quickly from his path, even those few who, according to the strictures of English society, outranked
him. It had always been thus; men either averted their
eyes or nodded reverently, depending upon their prefer-
ences, but no one looked him in the eye. No one sat
down with him absent an invitation. No one challenged
him to play or duel without great forethought. And no
one ever, ever laughed at him to his face.

Not anymore.

Just inside the card room, Hugh and the others had already taken a table, as well as a bottle, and sat in impatient readiness. Elliot slipped into his seat without
comment, and Hugh filled his glass. Slowly, Elliot eased
into the rhythms of the game. This one was for sport, not

money. Elliot never took advantage of his friends, and Winthrop and Linden were the best of friends, steadfast and true, despite their incessant efforts to appear otherwise. The play was fast, and the conversation desultory, for the better part of an hour.

"Well, well!" boomed an obnoxiously jovial voice. Lord Barton, a club regular, approached their table. "Here's a nasty pit of vipers, indeed! Huddled all together tonight, gentlemen?" He paused just inside the salon, his florid face split in a wide grin, a nearly empty wine glass in hand. "Have you no innocent victims as yet?"

Elliot lifted his gaze from the table to eye the newcomer grimly. "There is no such thing as an innocent victim in this sport, Barton. You know it well."

"Nonetheless, the night is young," drawled the dandified Linden enticingly as he finished dealing with a sharp snap. The blond viscount cut a shrewd glance up at the visitor. "Care to join us, Barton?"

"Hah! I'm hardly such a dotard as all that, Linden. The four of you can sell your souls for someone else's gold this evening."

"Have you a suggestion, my lord?" asked Major Winthrop dryly, never bothering to lift his gaze from his hand. "Who among us looks plump in the purse tonight?"

Casually, Lord Barton raised a bejeweled quizzing glass to survey the busy room, then gestured with his wine glass through the doorway toward the gaming salon. "Yonder stands young Carstairs. He is eager, rich, and I daresay rather ignorant. Try your luck at—" Barton paused to narrow his gaze, grunting disdainfully. "No, never mind, gentlemen. Poor lad has just become carrion to the new Baron Cranham. They've fallen in together even as I speak."

"Cranham, eh?" Sir Hugh's voice was gruff. "What the

devil is this club about, I should like to know? Letting such a one slip through the doors! Why, the very purpose of this club is undermined by permitting the likes of him to crawl in off the street and taint—"

"Good God, Hugh!" Elliot barked as Lord Barton drifted away. "You sound as supercilious and sanctimonious as Mother. I marvel that you don't sprout angel wings right on the spot."

Major Winthrop looked at Elliot strangely, then lowered his gaze to his hand. "None of us has more cause to hate Cranham than do you, Rannoch," he murmured speculatively. "What I wonder is why you haven't called him out already."

Elliot regarded his dark-haired companion in silence for a long moment. "I want no quarrel with Cranham, Winthrop. I challenged him ten years ago, and he fled. He knows his own shame. 'Tis done."

Sir Hugh snorted derisively, then just as quickly hushed when he noted Elliot's hard glare. "I plan to mind my own business," added Elliot, the cold finality unmistakable in his tone, "and I suggest, gentlemen, that the rest of you do the same."

And so he did. For the better part of two hours, Elliot minded his own business. He was not, however, fool enough to take his eyes from Cranham. With a discreet vigilance, Elliot watched the enemy. The new baron seemed unaware of Elliot's presence in the room, but Elliot sensed that it was not so.

Cranham and Carstairs had drifted nearer and now stood only a few feet away, observing a heated game of hazard. Cranham was already known to be under the hatches financially, and the pair had been drinking prodigiously since midnight, a combination that, in Elliot's opinion, inevitably bode ill for someone. Both gentlemen were now well in their cups, but Cranham was showing signs of serious intoxication. With any luck at all, Elliot ruefully considered, his old adversary might just drink himself to death and save someone else the trouble of killing him.

Suddenly, Hugh flung his cards onto the table. "Well, that's it, gentlemen. Much afraid I'm all in."

"Agreed," said Lord Linden, sweeping up the table. "Call for your carriage, Winthrop. Let us all go down to Madame Claire's and get a private room and some champagne! She has a brace of buxom new lasses, one of whom can reputedly suck the brass off a cheap candlestick."

"Aye, well, I've a cheap enough one for her right here," suggested Hugh with a leer, waggling his grizzled brows enthusiastically.

Major Winthrop lifted one dark eyebrow skeptically. "I don't know, old chaps. Perhaps we might try—"

Elliot shoved his chair back with a harsh scrape. "I do not share women," he said irritably, his voice a low growl.

From the table just inside the adjoining salon, someone cleared his throat with apparent deliberation. "One does not always have a say in such matters, Lord Rannoch." The tone was contemptuous but unsteady. "For example, you shared Antoinette Fontaine, and quite generously, too. But, then, perhaps you were unaware of your hospitality?"

Elliot heard the unmistakable voice, rose calmly from the table, then crossed the narrow space between them. Cranham's insult had not been unexpected. In fact, it had been almost anticlimactic, and Elliot was glad to have done with the opening salvo. As he had known all along, it was inevitable that he would have to kill the bastard. He was not happy about it, but Cranham would insist.

Beside him, his friends and his uncle shifted uneasily in their chairs, but they did not rise. Elliot was more than capable of handling the new baron, and they knew it.

Elliot eyed Cranham derisively. "As it happens, Moore," he answered dryly, deliberately omitting his title, "I want no quarrel with you, and I hope you enjoyed Miss Fontaine. She is a far better class of whore than the last one we very nearly shared."

Behind him, Lord Linden burst out into a snicker. The crowd around Cranham nervously dispersed, leaving the gentlemen to their argument. Cranham's face flamed with rage. "How dare you insult my—my—"

"Your what?" asked Elliot silkily. "Your taste in women?"

Cranham brandished his fist in Elliot's face. "You weren't fit to lick the ground Cicely Forsythe trod upon, you ignorant Scot! I'll not stand by whilst you impugn her, damn you!"

Elliot widened his eyes and arched his brows deliberately. "Lick the ground she trod upon? Come, come, now, Cranham! That's doing it a bit too brown! I may be an inveterate blackguard, I'll grant you that, but as I recollect, the only ground Cicely was about to tread upon was the path to the altar. On my arm, with your bastard in her belly."

"You're a damned liar, Rannoch! You took her innocence, then abandoned her. I loved her, and she loved me."

"Aye, and some believe fairy folk roam the Highlands," muttered Elliot with a toss of his hand. Slowly, he turned to walk away.

"I would have wed her," rasped Cranham.

"Would you have, indeed?" asked Elliot softly. He spun back around to face Cranham. "How regrettable that there was not merely one but two social obligations forestalled by your untimely departure for Bombay."

Cranham, red-faced and almost slavering now, took a step toward Elliot and began to jab one finger at his chest. "She wanted to marry me, damn you to hell! Her uncle forbade it because I was poor and untitled! My father had me bound, gagged, and shipped off, just to spare his family the embarrassment. You bloody well know that's true."

Elliot felt a flicker of sympathy for the drunken, irate man who stood before him. "The latter may possibly be true, Cranham, but I pray you will not lie to yourself about what Cicely wanted. Her desperate uncle would have cheerfully wed her to a Covent Garden costermonger. It was Cicely who made a coldly calculated gamble on my goodwill and lost."

"She gambled, and she died, Rannoch," hissed Cranham. He was standing on his toes, staring into Elliot's face now. "She died because you ruined her and turned her away. And sooner or later, so help me God, you will pay for it!"

"Go home, Cranham," replied Elliot sadly, having lost what little enthusiasm he had had for the argument. "Go home and sober up and get on with your life, as I have had to do. Leave me in peace." He turned his back on Cranham, crossed back into the card room, and slid into his chair.

"Damn your impudence, Rannoch!" rasped Cranham, following him to his seat. "I shall not be so easily dismissed."

"Nonetheless, you are," replied Elliot, absently shuffling the cards. "Dismissed, that is."

In an apparent rage, Cranham grabbed the cards from his hand and sprayed them across the table. "Go ahead, you hulking Scots bastard! Call me out again—and this time I shall kill you."

"No," said Elliot quietly. Methodically, he began to gather up the deck. Major Winthrop and Lord Linden shot discreet, bewildered glances across the table and began to shove the strewn cards toward him. Sir Hugh merely tilted his chair backward on its rear legs to better view the fray.

"Go ahead," snarled Cranham. "I insist."

"Upon what?" asked Elliot, suddenly intent upon the cards. "Why should I trouble myself to challenge you when I cannot expect that you will keep your dawn appointments?"

"Go to hell," hissed Cranham, struggling to peel away his glove, then whipping it in Elliot's face. "I issue the challenge, Rannoch! My seconds will wait upon you tomorrow." He spun on one heel and began to walk away, but Elliot rose from the table and grabbed him by the shoulder.

"Drop it, Cranham! Perhaps we were both ill used. Most assuredly, I have no lingering urge to fight you." Elliot bit out the words coldly. "Withdraw your challenge now, and I shall gladly accept."

"No," replied Cranham quietly, sounding suddenly sober.

"As you wish." Elliot nodded brusquely, then unclamped his hand from Cranham's shoulder. "Send your seconds to Major Winthrop now. 'Tis half past one. As the challenged, I would have this deal done at first light. One shot, with pistols. Have you any objection?"

"None whatsoever," snapped his adversary.

Evangeline rose from her bed and pulled on her wrapper in the dark. Sleep had been slow to come and, when it had arrived, had lingered but briefly. This time, her restlessness had little to do with Elliot. It was a problem far more dire.

From her bedside table, she grabbed the letter that had arrived by afternoon post and shoved it into her pocket. Slowly, she made her way down the stairs and into the library, pausing to light a candle in the corridor as she went. The hallway lamp reminded her yet again of Elliot's harsh, handsome face as he bent down to light his cheroot only a few days earlier.

No! It simply would not do. She could not think of him. Not now. Not when Michael's happiness might well depend upon her. Quietly, she stole into the library and pushed shut the door. Taking her usual chair, she read the note once more, searching for some measure of hope, but the words were as clear by candlelight as they had been by the light of day.

Her grandfather was dying. In Peter Weyden's absence, her solicitor had written to warn her that Lord Trent's death was imminent. The doctors had left Cambert Hall some three days past, sending for the bishop himself as they went. It was consumption, and it was believed that this time he would surely die.

Her grandfather had always been a weak man, in every way save the physical. Was he now to fail his grandchildren in this way, too? Wearily, Evangeline sighed and pushed back her long rope of hair. Perhaps she attached far too much emphasis to her grandfather's passing. In truth, he had been almost powerless for years and therefore as good as dead to his domineering second wife. Why should his actual demise make any difference? But it would. Evangeline knew it. There was such finality to death; one could not help but think of those who had gone before, of what would never be, and of those who remained to constitute the future.

And her fatuous uncle would be the next earl! Certainly, she could not depend upon him for support. Indeed, he would be cajoled and browbeaten into playing the puppet for his stepmother, for without him Lady Trent would be no more than a dowager. Yes, after her husband's death, her power base would be at risk, and she was astute enough to know it. But good God, Evangeline's uncle was as weak and ineffectual as her grandfather had been. Was the whole lot of Stone men both spineless and complaisant? Evangeline felt a wave of guilt and bit her lip until she tasted the metallic tang of blood. Her hands shook as she leaned forward to lay the letter on the desk.

No, that was certainly not the case. The younger son, her uncle Frederick, had given his life for his king and country. Nor had her father been a coward. He had been sensitive. Yes, and resolute enough to give up everything to wed the woman he loved. Yet if her father had been the vivacity of their family, her mother had been its strength, and without it they had very nearly collapsed. Maxwell Stone had been a gifted artist who had loved his wife so deeply that he had been unable to recover from her loss. It had not been weakness; it had been uncontrollable grief. Evangeline refused to see it any other way, and she had never begrudged her father the peace death had finally brought him or resented the promise she had given to her mother. By example, Marie van Artevalde had taught Evangeline that it was the woman's duty to hold the family together no matter the cost.

Evangeline had inherited whatever artistic skill she possessed from both of her brilliant parents, but from her mother she had received her blond elegance and something far more valuable: a healthy dose of rock-solid Flemish pragmatism. She set about using it now. The danger posed by Lady Trent was not imminent. This was England. One could hardly be kidnapped from one's bed in the dark of night. Evangeline knew that she could stall for time, for weeks, probably months. On the morrow, she would write to her solicitor and instruct him to begin considering the legal arguments that would inevitably be needed. Only after all options were approaching exhaustion would she take Michael back to their homeland, where they would remain, in hiding if necessary, until her step-grandmother joined her husband in the family tomb.

Her mind raced through the plan she had repeated over and over in her head. She and Michael could flee on a moment's notice. Winnie and the remaining children could follow at their leisure, for no one would bother to hinder them. The wars were over at last, and Evangeline knew a dozen ways to get in and out of France and Flanders. Moreover, her parents had had friends in every province. She spoke six languages fluently, and Michael spoke four. They could easily pass for French, Swiss, or Austrian. Among the throng of Continental émigrés driven into England by Napoleon, she and Peter Weyden could count many friends and business contacts. It would not be difficult to hide and, ultimately, to escape.

It would, however, be painful. Once again, Evangeline knew that she must keep her promise to her mother, but this time it would hurt all the more. This time, she would be leaving her heart behind in England. After judiciously avoiding one potential suitor after another, she had unwittingly succumbed to the charms of Elliot Roberts, a man about whom she knew almost nothing. She had fallen hopelessly in love with him, a fact she admitted only to herself. Despite the short time she had known him, her desire had already become a private hell which melted to a sweet, exquisite torment whenever he was near. Although she was uncertain about Elliot's feelings for her, to be alone in Europe, never to see him again, would still be pure agony.

Leaving England was not an issue, for as much as she loved Chatham Lodge, she loved Flanders equally well. Chatham had been carefully entailed to Michael, and a generous marriage portion had been set aside for Nicolette, but the house in Ghent was Evangeline's. It was her home, and despite her family's constant travels across Europe, her mother had borne five children there. Situated on a picturesque canal, the fine old house had witnessed the births and deaths of her van Artevalde ancestors for three hundred years.

Despite the comfort of a return to her home, however, nothing could ease the loss of the one man she had ever been capable of loving. Evangeline had racked her brain to find a way to have it all. She could send Michael away to friends, then throw herself shamelessly at Elliot, but she knew she could bring herself to do neither of those things. She could beg Elliot to go with her, but that was both improper and foolish. Moreover, she felt far too inexperienced in the ways of men to understand his feelings for her. Elliot had recently suffered a broken engagement and had been deeply scarred by the loss. They had become dear friends, yes. And although he did not love her, Evangeline believed that he desired her. Nevertheless, men frequently desired women, and quite often it meant little more than that. In her situation, she could hardly afford to make assumptions.

Evangeline considered telling him everything, but she feared that result almost as much as she feared her stepgrandmother. Elliot, like most men, was stubborn and prideful. If by chance he felt any deep emotion for her, he might think it his duty to intervene in the coming battle with Lady Trent. That simply would not do. He could not win and by his efforts might well cause considerable damage. Her parents had shown her that waging war against Lady Trent was like a protracted game of chess; it could last eons, and one's survival often depended upon a series of carefully considered strategic moves. Bludgeoning her with a sharp ax, tempting though it might be, was foolhardy. The woman was Medusa personified.

Moreover, her family's estrangement from her father's

venerable lineage made his children all but social out-
casts according to the unyielding strictures of the socially
conscious *beau monde*. That fact alone might well dis-
suade Elliot from any further relationship with her.

Shockingly, her logic kept returning her to the one remaining alternative, and a sinfully tempting one at that.
She could take Elliot as a lover and enjoy him for whatever time was left to them. It would not be difficult; Winnie was a sweetly inept companion, and in truth they had
both lived far too long on the Continent to be overly
concerned with England's rigid social mores. Nonetheless, there were risks. The intensity of physical love could
be overwhelming. Would it make the leaving harder?
Without a doubt. Could it weaken her resolve to protect
Michael? Never.

Unfortunately, the risk of pregnancy was a far greater
concern. In England, Frederica was a social outcast
because of her heritage. In Flanders, it would be marginally easier, particularly within the artistic community.
Nonetheless, an illegitimate child was a risk that bore
careful consideration. Elliot's babe in her arms—the
thought rocked her to the very core of her soul. Until her
father's death seven years earlier, Evangeline had always
dreamed of a husband and a family. Then as now, visitors
from the Continent often filled their home, and Evangeline had never lacked for complaisant suitors. Her arms
ached to hold her very own child, for as much as she
loved Nicolette and Michael, it was not the same. That
she might love a man like Elliot Roberts, a gentle but
strong man, and be loved by him in return, perhaps even
bear his children, had become a fantasy, not an assumption.

Harshly, Evangeline shut away her impetuous dreams.
She would not consider such things. Not now. Not when
so much was at stake. There would be time enough for

pity, and for foolish daydreaming as well, when she was alone in her house in Ghent. Swiftly, she leaned forward and blew out the candle, then made her way back upstairs in the dark. En route to her bedchamber, she passed Michael's door, paused, and pushed it open.

Her brother lay sprawled atop his sheets, the coverlet and blanket long since shoved onto the floor. His window was open wide, casting a shaft of watery moonlight across the bed. In the weak illumination, Michael's pale hair gleamed, and even in sleep his expression was sweet and untroubled. Evangeline was ruthlessly determined that it would ever be so.

Life could be cruel, and Evangeline suffered no illusions about her inability to shield Michael from its harsh realities when he became a young man. Nevertheless, the sweet boy who slept so peacefully—the babe she had raised as her very own because she had loved him and had promised to care for him—yes, that child would not be taught to manipulate. He would not be told that he was better than another because of the blood in his veins, and he would not be allowed to learn how to wield power injudiciously. And he would not be torn from his family. Evangeline had given her word, and she would keep it, no matter the cost. Moreover, she loved him, and she would bleed to death from the loss were he to be taken from her now.

Godfrey Moore, Baron Cranham, sensed the angel of death draw nigh; its cold shadow cast a damp chill over his soul. There was no doubt in his mind. This was the end. With a sickening sense of doom, he hefted one heavily engraved pistol from its velvet swathing, testing its weight in the palm of his hand. Weakly, he passed it to Lord Henry Carstairs, his second, for examination and loading. Across the field, his other second, Edwin Wilkins, stood beside the elegantly dressed Lord Linden, negotiating the distance. Indeed, Cranham had been hard pressed to find seconds for this morning's duel. Very few men were willing, he had belatedly discovered, to stand on the wrong side of a challenge to Rannoch.

And it was his challenge against Rannoch. In front of him, Major Matthew Winthrop, smiling grimly, let the carved mahogany box thump shut to reveal the ornate Armstrong crest, bringing the horror ever more clear. Cranham's damnable, inexcusably stupid error merely served to make his present situation even more appalling. What in God's name had possessed him to get sufficiently inebriated, and sufficiently enraged, to deviate from his well-laid plans?

It had never been his intent to come out into the open with his plan to avenge Cicely's death. At first, Cranham had tried more subtle tactics. Attempting to enlist the support of Cicely's uncle had netted absolutely nothing; Howell had repeatedly refused to meet with him. Eventually, however, Cranham had succeeded in cornering the baron at their club, but the man had turned deathly pale and adamantly cut him off, insisting that he feared Rannoch's wrath.

Repeatedly seducing Rannoch's whore had been a waste of time; three weeks and six hundred pounds later, Cranham had spent damn near every sou he had and learned nothing that might advance his quest for vengeance. Far more dangerous than she had first appeared, Antoinette Fontaine prattled on about nothing more specific than the sexual positions Rannoch preferred and the enormous size of his cock, two topics that had quickly grown tiresome. However, it was her vile temperament, deranged rambling, and incessant drinking that had truly taken a toll on his nerves.

And then Rannoch had disappeared altogether. Night

after night, Cranham had lurked about in the hells and brothels of London awaiting the arrival of his nemesis. Rannoch had not come. Where the son of a bitch had been keeping himself, no one seemed to know or care, for he was not a well-liked man. The marquis had not even bothered to appear with his dissolute cohorts in Brooks's, where Cranham had been exceedingly fortunate to obtain a membership. Had his late grandfather, the preceding Baron Cranham, not been a member, Godfrey Moore would almost certainly have been refused. Nevertheless, despite the fact that his haughty, blue-blooded grandsire had never so much as acknowledged Cranham's presence at a soiree, let alone hung his name on the family tree, the exclusive gentlemen's club had granted him admittance because Cranham had snared the title. Remarkable what a mangowood chest of untaxed Indian opium could do when dropped on the right doorstep.

The crunch of gravel beneath carriage wheels signaled the belated arrival of the attending surgeon. Carstairs had rounded up some hapless sawbones at the last minute, and the man was almost half an hour late. The unexpected delay had very nearly unstrung Cranham, whilst Rannoch and his cronies had merely tossed out a blanket beneath an oak and commenced another leisurely game of whist. That in and of itself was enough to make Cranham want to kill him.

He saw Carstairs nod to Major Winthrop. It was time. Perhaps he could kill him. Hell, he had to kill him. Cranham felt the cold, dead weight of the gun pressed into his hand. Weakly, he curled his fingers about the butt as Wilkins urged him into place. Cranham began to fear the humiliation of casting up his accounts on the field, which only served to heighten his animosity. Despite his indignation, however, he could not seem to choke down his raging panic. It was irrational.

No. It was not.

His heart hammered in his chest as he watched Rannoch stroll almost languidly toward him. They turned, and he felt the soft superfine of Rannoch's coat brush against his. Christ, the man was tall. Beneath Cranham's boots, the ground seemed to dip, then tilt backward uncertainly, like the prow of a boat. From the corner of one eye, he saw an arm rise up. He tried to focus ahead, but the horizon blurred before him. When he tried to breathe, he drew in nothing but the scent of Rannoch's tobacco and cologne; he smelled no fear whatsoever. He heard the order to pace off, and miraculously his feet began to move.

Rannoch was quite possibly the best marksman in all the kingdom, having never lost a duel in his life. Moreover, when pressed, he had reputedly shot one particularly impudent Irishman clean through the heart. Rannoch clearly welcomed the opportunity to shoot *him* through the heart. There was no hope.

There was only one hope. *Do not wait.*

Turn and fire now.

Yes, now!

With meticulous timing, Cranham spun his heel hard into the turf, coming about just as Rannoch began to turn. Focusing fast on the widening angle of Rannoch's shoulder, Cranham leveled his pistol and fired without hesitation. The weapon thundered, then bucked hard against his hand, almost shattering the bones of his wrist. Tufts of black superfine tore through the air. He'd hit him! Damn it, he knew he had. Still, Rannoch stood, unmoved.

The enemy faced him solidly now, his pistol held high but falling. Cranham watched in abject horror as Rannoch lowered his weapon with an agonizing indolence until at last it was pointed squarely at his heart. Rannoch's aim did not waver. Slowly, his mouth curved in a bitter smile. A sheen of early sun reflected dully off the barrel as Cranham watched it drop just a fraction of an inch further. Cranham could almost hear the trigger hit home. The roar of the pistol filled his ears, louder and more abrupt than his own had been.

"Oh, God!" Cranham heard himself scream. He collapsed to the ground in a writhing heap as Wilkins and the surgeon rushed to his side. "I'm hit! I'm hit!"

Edwin Wilkins dropped to the grass beside him, scowling. Savagely, he jerked Cranham's wounded leg straight out before him. "Shut up, Cranham, you idiot! What possessed you to do such a dishonorable thing? By rights, he could have killed you!" Lord Henry Carstairs bent low to pull off his boot.

Cranham looked at Wilkins in amazement. "He *was* going to kill me, you imbecile! He damn near shot my ballocks off!" Wilkins merely deepened his scowl, stood up, and walked away. The surgeon had already pulled forth a pair of surgical scissors and was deftly slicing away the fabric of Cranham's trousers. A long, nasty scratch was oozing blood high on his inner thigh.

"Do you see?" whimpered Cranham, repeatedly jabbing his finger at the wound. "That bastard meant to geld me!" The surgeon brought forth a bit of flannel and liberally saturated it with the odiferous contents of a brown bottle.

Lord Henry, bending low on one knee, spoke softly into Cranham's ear. "Do shut up, old boy. If Rannoch had meant to kill you, you most assuredly would be dead by now. If he'd meant to unman you, I'd be raking your testicles out of the grass."

Wordlessly, the surgeon pressed the moistened cloth to the wound, and Cranham came off the ground with a piercing howl of agony. "What—is—it—you're—try-ing—to—say?" he asked between clenched teeth.

"Count your blessings," murmured the young lord, looking back over his shoulder at Rannoch. The marquis stood under the oak, legs spread wide, casually wiping his gun. Someone, Major Winthrop perhaps, had knotted a now bloodstained handkerchief about Rannoch's tattered coat sleeve, but otherwise he seemed wholly unaware of his wound.

Lord Henry shook his head in obvious amazement and returned his attention to the man sprawled beside him. "That was naught but a warning shot across your bow, Cranham, pardon the lamentable analogy. Indeed, one cannot help but wonder what accounts for such unexpected benevolence from Rannoch."

Suddenly, Major Winthrop squatted on the grass beside Cranham. His dark coat and broad shoulders seemed to obliterate every ray of morning sun. "Send your surgeon's bill to me, Cranham," he instructed in his grim, commanding voice, "and I shall see it paid on Rannoch's behalf. His lordship is leaving immediately on an extended trip to the country."

The following Wednesday afternoon, Elliot was invited to accompany Mr. Stokely and the younger children on an afternoon walk to the River Lea. Mrs. Weyden had compelled Gus to accompany her to the vicarage for the afternoon, a fate Elliot had very narrowly escaped. And Evangeline, with what Elliot hoped was reluctance, had sequestered herself in the studio to draft a letter to Peter Weyden. The perfect June day was warm, and Elliot, left with time on his hands, was suddenly glad for the invitation.

And so it was, oddly enough, that Elliot soon found himself pleasantly and industriously engaged in the procurement of materiel for the manufacture of daisy chains. Seated cross-legged upon one of two old blankets the group had brought along, Frederica and Michael worked fiendishly, chiding him for his sluggardly pace.

Laughing, Elliot swooped down to place a flower behind Frederica's ear. It hung rather whimsically, dipping down toward her chin. "Miss d'Avillez," said Elliot with a formal bow, "you are exceedingly lovely. As a single gentleman, I must beg you to tell me—have you come out?"

Frederica beamed, then giggled. "Oh, no, indeed, sir. We're none of us out here at Chatham."

"Are you not?" Elliot pressed his fingertips to his chest in feigned shock.

"No, sir. We're—" She searched for the word. "We're *recluses.*"

"That's right, Mr. Roberts," chimed Michael. "And Evangeline says that as there are so many of us, we needn't go out at all unless we want to!"

"I see," mused Elliot, dropping down to sit alongside Frederica on the blanket. "Is that why your sister never . . . goes out?"

"Oh, but she does," interjected Nicolette. "Last year, she went to Paris, and the year before that to Ghent. And she often goes down to London to see Uncle Peter."

"Uncle Peter?"

"Peter Weyden, Papa's brother," explained Theo. "I thought you knew him. He's ever so nice. Did you not know that he's Evie's . . . Evie's business partner?"

Nicolette frowned and pitched another daisy into the Lea. "Trustee, silly. Mr. Weyden's our trustee to keep us safe from trouble."

"What sort of trouble?" asked Elliot curiously.

"I don't precisely know." Nicolette shrugged. "That's just what Evie said. She said that Father knew he could count on Uncle Peter to look after us while we were here in England."

"While you are here?" It sounded so temporary. Elliot felt a rush of alarm. Did Evangeline plan someday to leave England? What sort of trouble could require such drastic action? "You've been here several years, have you not? Do you not mean to stay?"

Nicolette shot him a veiled look. "Evie says it is advisable to keep one's options open."

"Yes," agreed Frederica. "But we're to stay here as long as we can and get a proper English education."

"I've a capital idea!" Michael shouted. "If we have to return to Ghent, we shall just take Mr. Stokely with us. You'd go along, wouldn't you, Mr. Stokely?"

Harlan Stokely cleared his throat sonorously and pressed his glasses firmly back up on his nose. "Indeed, Michael, I might do. I have always wanted to see the world—"

"Whoa, team! Slow down!" exclaimed Elliot, forcing a smile. "It was not my intent to send all of you packing. And whyever would one go to Ghent, of all places?"

"Evie's got a house there," explained Michael with a sly smile. "A big one, so you could come as well, Mr. Roberts."

Frederica tossed a daisy at her cousin Michael. "But we cannot go there yet, silly, 'cause it's got tenants." The flower bounced off his thick blond hair and toppled onto the blanket.

"Tenants?" Elliot felt exceedingly confused.

Frederica shrugged. "You know, like mice or something."

Michael snorted. "Frederica, you goose! Tenants are leaseholders, like Farmer Moreton. Not rodents, for heaven's sake!" Michael and Nicolette burst into peals of laughter, toppling backward into the warm meadow grass.

Frederica's lower lip began to quiver. "I didn't know! How should *I* know? I have never been to Ghent—or—or to Paris or to Florence—or to anywhere but Figueira, and I cannot even remember that . . ." Her choked voice began to break into a wail as Elliot rose, lifting her up from the blanket in a smooth, fluid motion. Two big tears began to slide from her wide brown eyes.

"There now, Frederica! Come for a walk with me along the riverbank," said Elliot, widening his eyes at her. "Why, I was in Ghent once, and I saw tenants big enough to chew a man's arm off!"

"Did you?" Frederica looked amazed.

"Indeed, I did," insisted Elliot, speaking deliberately over his shoulder. "Great, fierce, hairy things they were, too. And d'you know what they like to eat best of all?"

Frederica shook her head solemnly. "No, sir," she whispered in awe.

"Wicked boys and girls who pick on their younger cousins!"

Frederica shrieked with laughter and began to squirm to be set down. "Do they really, Mr. Roberts?"

Elliot lowered her gently to her feet, keeping one eye on Michael. "Aye, they come out at night to roam about in search of bad children to eat for supper! If I were such a one, I should take great care to lock my door tonight!" Elliot lunged at Frederica and pretended to grab at her. Playfully, she squealed and danced away down the river path, Elliot trailing slowly behind.

"Ho! What's this, Mr. Roberts?" Evangeline's voice rang out across the meadow. "Did I hear aright? Are some of my charges about to be eaten?"

"Not me!" shrieked Frederica gleefully.

Elliot turned to see Evangeline standing above them on the hillock, her slender frame silhouetted against a brilliant backdrop of cerulean sky and emerald pasture.

She held a letter in one hand and wore a simple yellow walking dress which billowed gently in the breeze. Her silky butter-yellow hair spilled from beneath a plain chip bonnet, which she promptly removed. The sight made him wish, yet again, that he could paint.

Instead, he grinned. "Generally speaking, Miss Stone, only the wicked get eaten."

Evangeline's eyebrows arched up elegantly. "Indeed, Mr. Roberts?" she calmly replied. "That being the case, there may be a great many of us in need of locking our doors tonight."

Elliot's gaze fixed on the letter Evie suddenly thrust into her pocket. With a sick feeling, he wondered if Evie had somehow discovered the truth about him. But the fleeting fear passed as her face broke into a smile and she started down the embankment to join them. He caught her hand as she stepped gingerly down the last few steps of the steep slope, feeling a surge of possessiveness as her slender fingers folded tightly into his.

Evie was breathless, as if she had walked briskly across the meadows from Chatham. Bright, china-blue eyes smiled at him from beneath wisps of fine hair which now tossed gently in the wind.

"I was lonely," she explained without preamble. "I confess, I could not tolerate being stuck indoors whilst all of you were out having such fun."

Reluctantly, Elliot released her hand and gestured toward the blanket adjacent to Nicolette and Theo, who were spreading out their sketchpads under the auspices of Mr. Stokely. The three of them smiled up at her in greeting as she dropped to the ground. Farther down the path, Michael was busy making amends with Frederica by way of a frantic search for skipping stones.

"Have you no sketchpad, Miss Stone?" Elliot kept his voice low as he sank onto the blanket beside her.

"Indeed not," she replied crisply, turning her gaze back toward him. "That would constitute work, and I am playing the truant this afternoon."

"Are you?" he said softly, leaning onto one elbow and letting his eyes play slowly down her length. "And what does the proper Miss Stone do, I wonder, when she plays the truant?"

Evie smiled blandly. "Nothing very interesting, I'm afraid."

"No?" Elliot rose as swiftly as he'd just sat down and offered her his hand. "Come, Miss Stone, walk up the river with me," he invited. Surprisingly, Evangeline took his hand and allowed him to pull her smoothly to her feet.

§7§

Tempt not a desperate man.
—WILLIAM SHAKESPEARE

As they left Mr. Stokely and his pupils behind to make their way up the river path, the shrill voices of the younger children faded in the distance. The rush of current across a stretch of rocks, which ran the width of the Lea, soon replaced the happy sounds. Nearby, an ancient copse of hornbeams appeared to all but topple into the flowing river.

Without warning, Elliot stepped off the path, pulling Evangeline down to the water's edge. Catching her toe on a stiff tuft of grass, Evangeline stumbled, then promptly regained her footing. Nonetheless, it was sufficient excuse for Elliot. He seized the opportunity to haul her unceremoniously into his arms and spin her about.

Evangeline's eyes caught his, and he watched as a certain knowledge flamed deep within their rich blue depths.

She wanted him. The emotion was plainly writ upon her face. Perhaps she had even come there hoping to tempt him to do this very thing, drag her into the trees and ravage her mouth. Perhaps the reality of his hunger would frighten her; it would be just as well if it did. Almost roughly, he urged her back against the tree and leaned against her. He felt his breath catch, then grow rapid and shallow.

Neither had spoken a single word since leaving the blanket; it was almost as if their mutual need was understood. Yet Elliot was certain that Evangeline had no clue about just how desperate he had become. Such an innocent could not begin to comprehend the depraved imaginings that floated up from his dark subconscious. His pulse beat wildly in his temples as he lowered his lips toward hers. Already, he was growing hot and hard.

Just once, he promised himself. He had to kiss Evangeline just once. Before she learned the inevitable truth of who and what he really was. Elliot persuaded himself that every lovely woman deserved—and wanted—to be kissed.

No, hissed his tattered, crumpled conscience in response. *It is wrong. It is wicked. She doesn't even know your name.*

Just one kiss, argued the devil in his loins. *One innocent kiss.*

But Elliot, who had folded up most of his morals and stuffed them into the back of a deep, dark cupboard years ago, was now shocked indeed to hear them pounding at the door. He fought to ignore the mental cacophony and focus only on the physical pleasure. Eyes closed, Evangeline tilted her face knowingly upward to meet his lips, her cheeks still pink from the exertion of her walk, her lashes soft and thick against her cheeks.

Elliot was amazed at her blind complacence. Surely, she meant to protest? Then he remembered with a painful clarity that Evangeline did not know who he was. Plain, ordinary Mr. Roberts—did not innocent women twist and turn away when he attempted to kiss them? Elliot wanted to know. Gently, he touched his lips to the corner of her mouth, kissing first the right dimple, then sliding lightly across her full bottom lip to kiss the left. Reining himself under command, Elliot pulled away slightly to brush his cheek against her hair. Despite the roar of the water, Elliot realized that his breathing had become as ragged as his self-control.

Wrapped in his embrace, Evangeline moaned very insistently, and Elliot could not restrain himself from answering by opening his mouth over hers, melting it softly against her lips, slanting back and forth over and over. Evangeline's lips were firm yet pliant, her breath soft and quick. She wanted him. The realization surged hotly into his loins.

Their kiss was endlessly intoxicating in its innocence. Gently, Elliot leaned her fully against the broad tree trunk which slanted back toward the water, never lifting his lips from hers. Evangeline followed his lead, allowing him to urge her backward until Elliot had her firmly pinned between himself and the tree.

So innocent. So sweet. So wrong. Elliot deflected the annoying stab of morality by deepening his kiss. He was seized by the urgency of the moment. *Inside her mouth— just once,* whispered the devil again. At that precise moment, Evangeline sighed softly, and he felt her lips part invitingly. With practiced skill, Elliot seized the opportunity, sliding his tongue into the corner of her mouth and drawing it hard across her lips. Sweetly, Evangeline's opened as if in answer. Her blue eyes flew open wide, however, as Elliot's tongue surged into the moist, spicy warmth of her mouth.

Sensing her surprise, Elliot instinctively pressed himself more firmly against her and slipped one hand down to the small of her back to gentle her motions. As he continued to move his mouth on hers, he became dimly aware of Evangeline's fingers digging greedily into the fabric of his shirtfront. Her breath came faster as his tongue plunged again and again into her innocent depths.

The sweet kiss evolved into an urgent ritual, an emboldened assault against Evangeline's mouth. Elliot's kiss drove her head back against the tree, effectively countering Evangeline's fleeting attempt to move away. And it was a fleeting attempt, for Elliot vaguely realized that she was returning his kiss measure for measure. A soft groan of pleasure caught in his throat as Evangeline's breasts seemed to swell against his shirtfront.

Though he had fantasized repeatedly about this moment, his expectations vaporized in the explosive heat of Evangeline's reaction. Impatiently, she began to meet his tongue with little forays of her own, an offer of pleasure that felt like his for the asking. Her mouth hot against his, Evangeline's hands slid enticingly down his shirt and around to steal seductively up the quivering muscles of his back as she leaned into him, urging him closer still. The hot pulse still beat in his temples, and was spreading lower.

More. Now. Oh, Lord, no. Elliot's knees began to shake. The seducer was fast becoming the seduced, for even as he tried weakly to pull away from the kiss, Evangeline continued to respond, curling one arm around his neck, refusing to take her lips from his. As if possessed, his hand slid up to caress her breast, the weight cradled gently in his broad palm, his thumb sliding back and forth across the swell until her nipple drew into a taut little bud.

Ah, yes, she wanted him. He could feel it. She pressed herself urgently against his hard manhood, her delicate nostrils flaring as her breath came faster and faster. Surely, she knew what she was doing to him?

"Stop, Evangeline," he finally managed to whisper against her mouth. "Good Lord—stop—"

Not far downstream, a burst of childish laughter rang through the warm summer air, suddenly breaking the spell between them. Elliot was jerked harshly back to reality and let his hand slide from her breast. Still held loosely in his arms, Evangeline stiffened, then slowly brushed her mouth against his one last time and pulled away, her eyes lowered modestly, her arm sliding slowly from around his neck.

Irrationally, nausea began to churn in Elliot's stomach even as blood continued to settle hotly in his groin. The knowledge that, given half a chance, he would have taken an innocent in broad daylight by shoving her skirts up against a tree trunk was sickening. The suspicion that she might have let him did not help matters in the least.

In his heart, something vaguely akin to shame had begun to stir. But then again, Elliot had so little recent experience with shame that he had lost confidence in his ability to recognize that evasive emotion.

"Oh, my God," he heard Evangeline finally whisper as she sank weakly back against the tree. She lifted one trembling hand to her forehead and looked up at him with what appeared to be pure reverence.

Elliot forced himself to take another step backward. What he had done was horribly wrong. Yes, she was an innocent, and he was a knave of the worst sort. "Evie— Miss Stone." His voice came out thick and hoarse. "I—I cannot think what came over me. Such an inexcusable liberty. Please—I do beg your pardon!"

After a long moment, Evangeline truly focused on

him, eyes narrowing in the brilliant sunlight. After a moment, she came away from the tree, brushing at her skirts as if that would somehow set matters to rights. "I'm sorry," she said breathlessly. "I was, you know, a participant—"

"An unwilling one—"

"No," she interrupted with a nervous laugh, smoothing back her falling hair. "Hardly that!"

"Come, Miss Stone." Elliot forced a smile. "I cannot use your innocent curiosity as an excuse for my shabby behavior. I am not to be trusted. Allow me to return you to your family." He stood slightly uphill from her, extending his hand.

Evangeline made no attempt to take it. Instead, she swallowed hard and held his gaze intently. "Mr. Roberts, have you a great deal of experience in—in kissing women?"

Lord, what a question! Elliot hoped he could answer it with a straight face. "I suppose—some, yes. I have kissed a few ladies in my day."

"Oh, I just wondered," she murmured weakly. "Indeed, you seem—well, certainly, you are exceedingly good at it. And I have so little experience—almost none, in fact. None which can compare to . . . oh, drat." Abruptly, Evie lifted her skirt with one hand, took his with the other, and stepped uphill onto the path. "Never mind. You are right; we should return."

But strangely enough, Elliot now wanted to linger, reluctant to return to the gaiety of the children he had so enjoyed only minutes earlier. He stood on the path, still holding Evie's hand. It felt warm and gentle. Small yet strong and so right. As Elliot looked down to study their fingers clasped tightly together, he realized again how diminutive she was in comparison to his great size. Indeed, her hand quite disappeared in his, and her head did not reach his shoulder. With no trouble at all, Elliot could easily have carried her off into the tall grass and forced her to love him.

Forced? His stomach lurched again in disgust, yet he could not help but wonder again at Evangeline's willingness. Perhaps she would indeed welcome him to her bed. It was a shocking thought; nevertheless, she had seemed so enthralled, so eager. Though Evangeline was nothing like his usual mistresses, her Continental ways and unconventional attitudes seemed wholly divergent from those of a proper English miss. Moreover, she was too open, too trusting.

Suddenly, Elliot wanted to rail at her, to growl a warning at her. Decent women did not wisely go about kissing the marquis of Rannoch. Did she not know that? But of course she didn't. How should she? He had come back to Chatham to explain, to confess his sins, yet had thus far been unable to do so. Therefore, the innocent Miss Stone believed, with every good reason, that she was kissing the charming and uncorrupted Elliot Roberts.

As Elliot had so recently recollected, most of the women who so eagerly warmed his bed would rather not be seen with him in public. Yet here stood Evangeline, clinging to his hand and smiling up at his scowling face. She was warm and soft in all the right places, Elliot was sure of it. And he now knew that her mouth was spicy, her skin smelled of lavender, and her hair felt like silk. Damnation. These were things he did not want to know. Should not know. Wanted to know again and again.

"Mr. Roberts?" she asked, still standing on the path facing him. "May I ask a favor? If you think it not too forward, could you call me by my given name when we are alone?"

When we are alone. The words were significant. Dumbly, Elliot simply nodded. Then, realizing that some other response was called for, he swiftly brushed his lips across her forehead.

"Certainly, Evangeline," he answered with a sudden decisiveness, "and I shall be just plain Elliot."

Elliot had long ceased to be amazed at the educational methods employed in the schoolroom of Chatham Lodge. Lessons seemed to be a bizarre melange of candid discussions, informal lectures, nature hikes, and lively arguments. Maps of every nation, some of which were unknown to Elliot, hung randomly across walls and doors. Thick, richly bound tomes with titles like *An Analysis of Applied Trigonometry, Illustrated Comparison of Etruscan and Roman Architecture,* and *A Detailed Study of Byzantine Culture and Literature* lined the walls. And those were just the titles he could read. The foreign books looked far more intimidating yet just as worn. This, indeed, was a household of bluestockings and intellectuals. Elliot, whose father had not permitted his son what he called the "corrupting influence" of a university education, found it intriguing.

Along with the boys, Harlan Stokely cheerfully tutored the two girls in mathematics, Greek, Latin, and the sciences. When Elliot had expressed surprise at such an unconventional arrangement, Evangeline had sharply retorted that "an intelligent woman can be ignorant enough when required by circumstance and society, but an ignorant woman is simply ignorant." Elliot was quite certain she had meant it as a rebuke but found a frightening amount of logic in her statement.

During his second visit, he had learned that Mrs. Weyden was, in fact, Evangeline's former governess, who had ventured to Flanders to provide Maxwell Stone's eldest daughter with the training required of a proper Englishwoman. This education was broadened, however, by

Evangeline's mother's insistence upon extensive travel in the study of art, architecture, and languages. The traditional education apparently got short shrift, however, when the vivacious Winnie quickly caught the eye of Stone's youngest business associate, Hans Weyden. Winnie's duties as governess were short-lived, to be replaced by her role as family friend and confidante.

Not surprisingly, Harlan Stokely was Winnie's well-educated but impoverished second cousin, once removed. Elliot supposed that this distant kinship explained Stokely's family inclusion at Chatham. He was not, however, entirely convinced of this reasoning, since he had come to believe that the exuberant Stone-Weyden clan would likely throw their home open to strangers off the street. Had that not been the precise method of his own entrée?

In the hour allotted before Friday dinner, Mr. Stokely traditionally opened the connecting door between the schoolroom and the studio. Under Evangeline's tutelage, each student kept some painting or sketch in progress, and this period was devoted to such work. Though asked to stay and observe their studies, Elliot instead invited Stokely to give him a game of chess in the small drawing room and was pleasantly surprised when the retiring schoolmaster agreed. The hour passed without incident, and without excitement.

Eagerly awaiting Evangeline like a lovesick pup, Elliot kept one eye fixed across the hall on the schoolroom door. When Theo at last burst forth and dashed down the hall toward the gardens, Elliot excused himself and rose from the game. He entered the studio to see the girls gathered around Evangeline's worktable, debating some final aspect of Nicolette's painting. Just as Elliot stuck his head through the doorway, Frederica leaned forward to point to the far corner at the piece in question, inadvertently catching her sleeve on what appeared to be a nearly full pot of dark blue paint. The pigment gushed forth, trailing across the table and puddling on the floor.

Frederica began to screw up her face for a torrent of tears, but Evangeline quickly shushed her, dropping to her knees to better soothe the child. "Don't regard it, Frederica. No harm is done. 'Twas a dreadful shade of blue, mixed too dark, and I was going to throw it out."

Frederica's tears forestalled, Evangeline rose from the floor. She still had not noticed Elliot framed in the doorway to the schoolroom. "Nicolette," she said gently, "put your work away, then take Frederica upstairs to change for dinner. I shall fetch Polly and Tess to clean this spill from the floor."

In a trice, the room was empty, and Elliot retreated into the schoolroom to await Evangeline's return. He had every hope of persuading her to walk in the gardens with him before dinner. Although Evangeline had seemed perfectly at ease with what had transpired between them earlier in the afternoon, Elliot was anxious to reassure himself that this was indeed the case. Would she by now be experiencing guilt and regret? Or had their impulsive kiss merely served to embolden her passion?

In either case, Elliot was determined to do whatever was necessary to assuage her emotions. Thus far, his carefully considered options ranged from promising faithfully never to touch her again to dragging her into the rhododendron to make love on the spot. Elliot was fast coming to understand that he would do whatever was necessary to remain a part of Evangeline's life, for as long as possible.

The heavy clunk of metal on flagstone inside the studio disrupted his thoughts. Strolling back to the open door, Elliot saw Tess, one of the maids, straighten up from a bucket of soapy water. Diligently, she pulled a rag from her apron pocket, leaned across the table, and began to wipe the spilled paint from the surface. Polly, whom Elliot had already noted to be the most quarrelsome of Evie's servants, came in behind Tess, then dropped to her knees to plunk a scrub brush violently down in the bucket of suds.

"Bloody black-eyed imp!" she hissed from beneath the table. The scrub brush hit the flagstone with a thwack. "An' a bleedin' foreigner, at that! Can't credit that a good English housemaid ought'er be put to the trouble of cleaning up after—"

"Hush up, Poll!" interrupted Tess with a harsh whisper. "You're just arstin' for trouble, you are! The child don't mean no harm. Still just a babe, that one."

"Oh, aye," fumed Polly, slopping the brush carelessly back and forth across the floor, "and wot else is she, I should like to know? Naught but some nobleman's byblow, that's what! A war orphan, and a damned Portuguese bastard!"

Elliot felt a flash of red-hot rage as he stepped into the open doorway. "Polly?" He watched in cold satisfaction as the plump housemaid almost jumped out of her skin.

Still on her knees beneath the table, Polly flushed three shades of pink, finishing with a shade that was closely akin to a sickly vermilion. "Oh, Mr. Roberts! Beg pardon, sir. I didn't see you."

"Indeed, I hope you did not." Elliot lifted his thick black brows with a deliberately calculated arrogance. "But pray tell us, Polly, since when have you become an authority on Miss d'Avillez's parentage?"

"I—er—I . . ." Rising awkwardly from her knees, the maid stammered uncertainly. Tess took the bucket and darted from the room.

Elliot picked a bit of imaginary lint from his coat sleeve, then flicked his cold gaze up at her. "Polly, you are dismissed."

"I'm wot?" The maid's mouth gaped incredulously.

"Dismissed." Elliot's words were crisp and clear. He jerked his head toward the rear cottages. "Collect your things from the servants' quarters and be gone by half past the hour."

"Or wot would you be doin' about it, sir?" she challenged, a belligerent gleam in her narrow eyes. The maid set her hands upon her hips and tilted back on one heel.

"Or I shall make it my life's ambition to ensure that you never find gainful employment again," answered Elliot softly.

The buxom maid stood firm, still sputtering indignantly. "Why, you—! You can't turn me off without no more'n a by-your-leave! You don't—you're naught—you're just a—"

"Guest?" Elliot finished sharply, letting his anger burn like a cool blue flame. It was a comfortingly familiar, if not altogether pleasant, sensation.

"Aye," agreed the maid with a saucy toss of her mobcap. "An' you got no call wheresoever to go about dismissin' servants. Not in this house, nor any other, I should think." With a derisive snort, the insolent maid let her eyes wonder over his simple clothing.

"Indeed, do you think not?" Elliot reclined casually against the doorframe, crossed his arms stubbornly over his chest, and let his cold gaze rake over her. "Pray watch me while I do so."

Polly did watch him. Very carefully. And as she watched, Elliot let his lips thin deliberately into a tight, cruel line. His countenance darkened, from years of practice, into a glower so evil that it had been known to send servants scurrying for cover with regularity.

Polly was not immune to this effect, and as Elliot began to stir his great height from his position against the doorframe, the plump little maid finally capitulated, darting from the room in a jiggling whirlwind of black and white cotton.

Elliot listened as the rear door slammed behind her, and as the burning anger eased, he began to wonder what had possessed him. Well, a bit late now. He bounded up the two flights of stairs to the Tower Room to dress hurriedly. Before he joined the family for dinner, he knew he must make some explanation to Evangeline. Far sooner than he had expected, however, a sharp rap rang against his door. His cravat still loose about his neck and his shirt not fully closed, Elliot yanked open the door, expecting to see Gus bringing an acrimonious summons from Evangeline.

He was very much mistaken. It was his hostess who stood upon his threshold. She drew a deep breath and stepped inside the room without invitation.

"Mr. Roberts!" she began without preamble, then came to an abrupt halt as she stared fixedly at the open throat of his shirt. Suddenly, her face suffused with color. "Oh, I say—please excuse me."

"Oh, come on in," answered Elliot with a resigned shrug. He quietly pushed shut the door, motioning toward one of two wing chairs beneath the narrow tower window, then pulled his shirtfront together.

Looking almost grateful, Evangeline crossed the room and sank down into one of them. "Mr. Rob—Elliot, I pray that you will disabuse me of this notion that . . ." Evangeline paused, pressing her fingertips hard into her temples as if suffering from a severe headache. She drew a deep breath. "Indeed, I must confess that I cannot quite fathom . . ."

Elliot cleared his throat softly. "Why a guest in your home would be so presumptuous as to dismiss one of your servants?" he completed, folding himself into the other chair.

"Ah, yes," she agreed, staring pointedly at him. "That would be it. But surely you did not—that is to say, certainly there must be some misunderstanding?"

Elliot drew a deep breath and leaned forward in his chair to hold her gaze intently. "None on my part, Evangeline. A measure of high-handed arrogance, perhaps. But no misunderstanding. I very plainly heard your servant insult the parentage of your young cousin."

"Parentage?"

"To be blunt, Polly expressed her extreme resentment at being expected to clean up this afternoon's paint spill, and very callously referred to Miss d'Avillez as a bastard."

"Well, I am sad to say that it is true—"

"I long ago surmised as much, Evangeline," he agreed, with more asperity than he had intended. "I'm hardly stupid."

"Forgive me," Evangeline said stiffly. "I did not mean to imply that you were."

Elliot felt his rising ire abate. "No, I am sure you did not. I am in the wrong here. I forgot myself; I should have come to you at once. I might have explained the incident and allowed you and Mrs. Penworthy to handle the matter. But I am, I suppose, too much accustomed to, ah, to—"

"To seizing command in a crisis?" She shot him a wry grin.

"I was going to say having my own way, Miss Stone." Elliot smiled back, chagrined. "You are most kind. My actions are nonetheless inexcusable, yet it pained me so greatly to hear an innocent child spoken of in such vile terms, I could not help but feel that punishment should be swift."

"And just?"

"Indeed, I believe it was just, Miss Stone."

Evangeline pursed her lips and rested one slender arm

gracefully across the pie-crust table between them. As if in deep thought, she drummed her fingers on the smooth, polished surface. "I am inclined to agree with you," she said slowly. "In any event, Polly shall be leaving shortly."

Elliot could not hide his mild surprise. "Have you agreed to send her packing, then?"

Evangeline sighed. "Yes, though I came here immediately thereafter. I do trust your judgment, Elliot. You are an honored guest at Chatham, a situation that I hope shall continue, and I saw no way to rescind your directive without"—she paused as if searching for just the right word—"without weakening your position here."

Having fired countless servants, often arbitrarily and occasionally even justifiably, Elliot felt nonetheless warmed by her concern. "I thank you," he said simply.

Evangeline slid forward as if to rise from her seat, then suddenly slumped backward. He could see that she was tired, a realization that was followed by a wave of guilt for having burdened her with such a problem.

When she spoke, it was with a weary resignation. "I have long suspected, Elliot, that Polly was not all that she should be and that she was not always kind to Frederica. Unfortunately, there was nothing specific, just a disquieting impression. And Frederica—well, she is so quiet and so very grateful for every kindness."

"Indeed, she is a wonderful child," agreed Elliot softly.

"Yes," replied Evangeline quietly, her gaze far away and unfocused.

Elliot took a deep breath. "Do you not think, Evie, that given our—our friendship, you should confide in me about a few things? You might begin by telling me a little more about Frederica's background."

Evangeline's blue eyes sharpened and flicked up at him. A look of regret, or perhaps it was sadness, drifted across her delicate features. "Yes, to be sure," she answered softly. "It is no particular secret. Frederica is my uncle's child. He was in the allied forces during the Peninsular Campaign and was stationed at Figueira for a time."

Elliot nodded, and Evangeline continued. "It was there that he met Frederica's mother. She was the widow of an attaché to the Council of Regency, and she was sent to a village near Figueira for her safety. She befriended my uncle, and over time they fell in love." She looked up at Elliot as if she dared him to dispute the fact, but he remained silent.

"During the war, they saw each other when possible, but always they corresponded. I have many letters which, along with Frederica, were eventually brought out of Portugal by a family friend, an army captain. His wife followed the drum, and they believed it best that Frederica be brought to us in England."

"Your uncle died?"

"Yes, he was wounded at Busaco and died within two days. Some months following, Frederica was born. He and her mother had meant to marry, but fate decreed otherwise."

"What happened to her mother?" asked Elliot quietly.

"It was a difficult birth, and she was not a young woman. She lingered for several months."

"And was there no one else to care for the babe?"

Evangeline shrugged. "Frederica remained with her maternal cousins until Uncle's friends were able to leave Portugal. By that time, however, Papa was dead, and no one else was willing to take her. It was left to me, and I thought it best she come to us at Chatham."

"A very sad story, but one with a happy ending," Elliot reassured her. "You shall see to that, I am quite confident."

Evangeline smiled weakly. "Thank you for your faith, Elliot. I wish I could fully share it, but life in England is difficult for anyone who is foreign-born, doubly so if one has the great misfortune to be illegitimate."

Elliot gave a harsh crack of laugher. "Aye, 'tis trouble enough for a Scot, so I fear you may be entirely right." He leaned forward in his chair and took her hand in his. Gently, he lifted it to his mouth, barely brushing his lips against her skin. "I thank you, Evangeline, for confiding in me. It seems I find myself required to apologize for my reprehensible conduct today, on not one but two occasions."

Evangeline studied Elliot's face intently, her earlier aggravation long forgotten in the face of his concern for Frederica and his forthright apologies. She did not pull her hand from his. "For the second offense, sir, your apology is accepted. For the first offense, well, I was not particularly offended."

"You should have been," he replied brusquely, staring past her shoulder and out the tower window. "Evie, I must return to London tomorrow."

"Must you?" Evangeline could not suppress the disappointment in her voice.

Elliot laughed softly. "Evangeline, you flatter me. Regrettably, I have pressing business in town."

Evangeline looked at Elliot intently, watching as something very like uncertainty clouded his dark gray eyes. "Can—will you return for the weekend?" she asked softly.

"Is that an invitation?" He tightened his grip on her hand and narrowed his silvery gaze.

"Elliot, I do not play games. I think you know what it is."

"Evangeline," he interrupted her, "listen to me. I have something important to tell you. Something that I want you to consider whilst we are apart."

Evangeline felt suddenly ill. Elliot was going to tell her something that she did not wish to hear, she knew it. She could sense the reluctance in his voice. Was this it, then? Was this to be the secret? The bitterness? The barrier between them which she felt but did not understand? Anxiously, she swallowed. "Of course. I am listening."

"I—I must confess that I have not been entirely honest with you about—well, about some things, one thing in particular that is very important to me." He paused, as if he could not find the words to express all that he wanted to say.

"I know," she said softly, and watched as Elliot winced. "I know you have secrets."

Taking her hand into his lap, Elliot slowly began to trace the lines in her palm, refusing to meet her eyes. "Someday, Evie, I would like to talk to you about a great many things. Regrettably, I am a slow and stubborn Scot who takes but one fence at a time. Can you understand?"

Evangeline wanted to understand, but the secrets between them frightened her. "I am trying, Elliot."

He nodded. "When we spoke of Frederica, and of the obligation you feel toward her, I was reminded again of your commitment to your family."

"Family is everything," she agreed with a calm she did not feel. Her mind raced frantically. Had he learned about Lady Trent? Or had this something to do with his former fiancée? Did he have some hope of resuming his betrothal? Surely not, not after what they had just done . . .

Elliot interrupted her panic with a resigned sigh. "Evie, like most men, I am no saint. I never have been. Most certainly, I have done some things in my life of which I should be ashamed. I cannot claim to be ashamed of all of them, mind you. But I probably should be."

Evangeline could not suppress a nervous laugh. "At least, sir, you are honest."

"Aye, well, as to that, you'd best reserve comment," said Elliot dryly. His head was lowered now, and his eyes flicked up at her from beneath heavy lids with sinfully long lashes. "But there is one thing that, well, things being as they are between us—"

And precisely how are things between us, Elliot? Evangeline wanted to ask. She bit back the words. It was a question to which there could be no good answer. "Yes, go on," she replied instead.

"Evie, I have a daughter. Zoë." Suddenly, words began to tumble from his mouth. "Aye, her name is Zoë. She is beautiful, bright, and as shy as a mouse. Her only friend is my ancient Scottish butler. She looks pretty in violet, she loves to read, and she adores raspberries and kittens, and—well, dash it, I am ashamed to say that's essentially all I know of her." Elliot had resumed his study of Evangeline's palm and refused to meet her gaze. "But I am learning."

Evangeline caught her breath. "Does this have something to do with your broken betrothal?"

Elliot gave a harsh laugh and pulled himself stiffly upright in his chair. He looked at her very steadily then. "No, Evie. Believe me when I say that I never, ever compromised the woman to whom I was betrothed, and I have no wish to discuss her."

"I did not mean to suggest that you *compromised* anyone!" choked Evangeline. She felt her face suffuse with color.

Finally, Elliot blinked. "No, you did not, did you? Forgive me, but it is an ever open wound." He drew a deep breath. "The plain truth is that Zoë's mother was a dancer, and not a particularly good one. Like many women I have . . . known, they aspired to be something quite different, really."

"A mistress."

"Yes."

"And was she?" Evangeline forced herself to hold his gaze. "Your mistress?"

Elliot exhaled. "For a time."

"And then came Zoë?"

"Yes. Eight years ago. I should have been glad, but I was enraged. At first, I did not want a child." He gave another bitter laugh. "Neither did Zoë's mother, for that matter."

"What did you do?"

"We came to an amicable settlement, a settlement that enabled—no, make that required—Zoë's mother to reside abroad. Permanently."

Evangeline sucked in her breath harshly. "And so you do not see your daughter?"

Elliot looked at her sharply, and when he spoke, his voice was cold and firm. "I take what is mine, Evie. Make no mistake about it."

Despite her confusion, Evangeline did not miss the ominous tone of his words. "Who cares for her?" she managed to ask.

"I take care of her. To the best of my ability," he answered crisply. "Which is to say, I pay for nursemaids and music teachers and governesses, but even I am not stupid enough to think that it is the same. Not the same as . . . as what Frederica has, for example."

"No, perhaps not. Certainly not. But it is far better than most—"

"Better than most men treat their bastards?" Elliot bit out sarcastically, shaking his head. "I do not know, Evie. I just do not know. God knows I have tried to do the right thing by her, but in the end it seems like so very little."

"What, precisely, do you mean?"

Elliot released Evangeline's hand, rose from his chair, and began pacing across the room. "The child hardly knows me. Certainly, I am a little late in trying to know her. She is, I think, a little frightened of me. And I am scared of her, too."

"Scared?"

"Aye, Evie. *Scared* is the right word. I was never a child. I did not have a childhood. I had responsibilities. Duties. Expectations." Suddenly, he whirled to face her. "You can have no idea what that is like."

Evangeline reached up to him and held out her hands to take his. Slowly, he walked toward her and slipped his hands into hers. "But I do, Elliot," she answered softly. "I do have some idea. Not the same way, perhaps, but I understand what you mean."

"Tell me," he said simply, coming back down onto the chair across from hers, still holding both Evangeline's hands in his.

"When my mother died, I was but seventeen, and already I had helped to raise my brothers and my sisters."

"Brothers and sisters?"

"Yes, we were once a much larger family. It was cholera, you see. There was so much illness and disease on the Continent during the war. Mama was weak from her confinement with Michael, and she fell ill first. Then Amelia; she was fourteen. Harold . . . he was ten."

"I'm sorry, Evie. I did not know."

"But the worst thing, Elliot, the worst thing of all was what it did to my father. For nearly a year, he scarcely left his bedchamber. He ceased to sleep. He ceased to paint. I became frantic. I did not know what to do. Michael was just a baby. Finally, I decided that we should come home. To England. Although it was not a home to me, I thought perhaps—"

"That it would feel like home to your father?"

"Yes, but there were problems here, too, so it was no small risk. Nonetheless, I decided that we would remove to Chatham Lodge and isolate ourselves from the memories of our happier times in Flanders. We avoided Papa's family altogether. It was not difficult—his stepmother made it plain that my mother's death changed nothing—and we tried to be a family, just the four of us."

"You tried to keep the family together, Evie," Elliot added softly. "And you have done an admirable job."

"I have no need of your sympathy, Elliot. I just want you to see that I know what it is like to have your childhood limited by responsibility and expectation. But more importantly, I want you to consider how critical it is that children have security and love. Nicolette and I were fortunate to have that much. Perhaps you did not, but it is nonetheless within your power to give to your daughter."

Elliot nodded. "As you have done for your family."

"Yes. And as I shall continue to do, especially for Michael."

"You worry constantly about Michael, Evie. Do not deny it, for I know that you do. Why?"

Evangeline felt emotionally drained, and she had no wish to explain her fears about Michael's future. Instead, she deliberately changed the subject. "Why, Elliot, did you choose this time to tell me about your daughter?"

"Because," he said softly, tearing his gaze from hers and staring out the window into the distance, "I wanted you to know. It is time, well past time, in fact, that I began to explain myself to you." She noticed the suddenly rigid line of his jaw as he held some inscrutable emotion at bay.

"Oh?" Evangeline did not know how to respond. What did he mean?

Elliot continued to speak. "Zoë is in need of a new governess, and interviews have been scheduled for the day after tomorrow. That is why I must leave so soon, Evangeline. It is time I began attending to such matters personally rather than simply deferring the job to someone else." Suddenly, Elliot exhaled slowly. As if a dreaded task were over, his face broke into that brilliant, heart-stopping smile which never ceased to take Evangeline's breath away.

"You are entirely correct," she managed to reply. "I thank you, Elliot, for explaining. Come, now, let's go down to the dining room before one of the children discovers me in your bedchamber." She forced a cheerful expression and dragged him up from his chair.

What followed in the next moment felt sweet and true. As if sealing a promise, Elliot pulled her smoothly into his arms, slid his hands to her back, then dropped his head to kiss her. Evangeline did not struggle. As his mouth moved on hers, tender but sure, she felt her desire strengthen, then melt to submerge her in gentle warmth. His was not a kiss of heated passion but an unhurried acknowledgment of pleasure deferred. She sensed it, and answered it, until at last he pulled back.

Slowly, he leaned away, smiled charmingly, then lowered his brow to rest on hers. "Come along, Evangeline." He laughed softly. "I should very much enjoy the pleasure of your company at dinner."

§8§

Latet anguis in herba; there's a snake hidden
in the grass.

—VIRGIL

The following morning, Elliot remained stoic throughout his portrait sitting, leaving Evangeline's nascent emotions in turmoil. Throughout the sitting, the minimal conversation that passed between them was superficial and tinged with that awkwardness that inevitably follows when friends become something more and inherently sense that their bond has been suddenly and irrevocably altered in some significant, unsettling way.

Neither made any mention of the preceding afternoon, yet Evangeline was acutely aware that the memory of all they had shared loomed large over them both. Elliot seemed alternately distant, then amicable, but invariably introspective, and Evangeline began to wonder if something far more serious than a furtive, impassioned kiss was responsible for his disquiet.

As was their custom, Evangeline saw him to the door alone in the midafternoon. After a surreptitious glance down the long hall, Elliot bent to brush his lips across her forehead, then jerked open the door and moved with long, quick strides toward his waiting horse. As Evangeline watched him ride away, she realized that his brief parting kiss had been the only real gesture of intimacy between them all day.

Nonetheless, Elliot's brief visit to Chatham Lodge had been eventful. They had shared so much, not the least of which had been what many would term an inappropriate degree of physical intimacy. Yet Evangeline could not find it within her heart to regret her response to Elliot's overtures. In truth, the rush of feminine passion she had experienced in his arms had only served to heighten her determination to have him, if only briefly. Though her life was committed to her work and her family, Evangeline was newly resolved to steal a few moments of happiness for herself. And Elliot, she had come to realize, made her happy.

Nonetheless, Elliot gave rise to many other unsettling emotions as well, and they troubled Evangeline throughout the afternoon and evening. Upon careful consideration, Evangeline still found his dismissal of her servant

disconcerting. In light of Elliot's explanation about his
daughter, however, she was inclined to view his impetuous, almost visceral reaction as understandable. There
was no doubt that Elliot had acted to protect Frederica,
much as he would have done for his own child. That was
oddly reassuring.

Nevertheless, to dismiss another's servant required unmitigated gall. Without a doubt, Elliot had a quick temper and a healthy measure of arrogance. Neither, she
inwardly considered, was altogether a bad thing. But even
more obvious was the fact that he was well accustomed
to having his way in most matters. His control of Zoë's
mother was yet another example.

By bedtime, an uncomfortable and insidious notion
had begun to worm its way into Evangeline's train of
thought. Had Elliot assumed that the physical liberties she
had granted him gave him license to take similar liberties
in the management of her household? And if that was
what he believed, to what extent did he presume such
rights might extend? His kiss last night had felt so tender;
so sweet and full of promise . . . *Good Lord!* Did he think
perhaps to wed her? It was preposterous, yet when she
considered it, Elliot had made several statements that
leaned toward that unworkable course of action.

In three days, Elliot had promised to return. As dusk
settled over Essex, and Chatham Lodge began to fall
quiet, Evangeline realized that it was time to make clear
her intentions to Elliot. Moreover, she must soon gather
enough presence of mind to make her proposal—not of
marriage but of something far less permanent.

She went to bed early, her heart filled with joy but her
mind filled with doubt.

In the darkened streets of London's East End, there
were a great many who did not enjoy an untroubled

evening in the quietude of their homes. Indeed, more than a few laid claim to no home at all. The day having been uncommonly hot and humid, the night air now lay close and fetid, edging the pervasive mood ever closer toward hostility. In the dirty, narrow streets of Whitechapel, the boisterous crowds of lower-class London poured in from sweat shops and dockyards to mill about the corners and make their way from one pub to the next.

Amidst all this drunken revelry, no one noticed as Lord Cranham, in a deliberately shabby coat and unfashionably broad-brimmed hat, dropped stealthily from the step of a passing carriage. By the light of a sputtering lamp, which swung just outside a narrow doorway, Cranham melted away from the swelling throngs and into the adjacent wall, pausing just long enough to pull a note from the folds of his coat. Slowly, he flicked it open and reread the roughly scribbled sentences. After hours of study, one word—*Rannoch*—kept tormenting him, leaping off the page like a red-hot flame, licking at his eyes and singeing his skin.

But this time, after ten years of waiting, Cranham was very, very close to his means of revenge. He was certain of it now. He could feel the incipient satisfaction thrumming through him. Ruthlessly, he shoved the note back into the pocket, then, without withdrawing his hand, meticulously recounted the coins he had carried with him, letting them slip coldly through his fingers, one by one.

Reassured that the amount was correct, the baron straightened his coat, stepped back into the passing throng, and strode briskly down the lane toward a crooked street sign marking the right turn into Pig Path Alley. Looking first behind and then before him, Cranham stepped off the marginally cobbled street and onto the packed dirt surface of the darkened alleyway. As he walked, he counted off the doors to his right, doors that served as rear exits for the crumbling shops and pubs that fronted the cobbled lane.

He soon saw, however, that he need not have counted with any measure of diligence, for the rear exit of his appointed destination, the Sleeping Hound, was clearly marked by empty barrels, splintered crates, and the sour, pervasive stench of human waste. Even the reek of India's worst slum could not compare to this, Cranham dryly considered, sliding into the shadow of a collapsing stoop and lifting a linen handkerchief to cover his nose and mouth. The motion, which briefly obscured his vision, was a dreadful mistake.

The ice-cold garrote was about his throat before Cranham's eyes could blink against the pain. As his handkerchief fluttered to the ground to be trampled into the filth of the alley, Cranham's hands came up to claw impotently at his throat. His attacker held a great advantage, for he was much taller, and far heavier, than Cranham. The struggle went on and on, Cranham's boots flailing frantically amidst the broken slats and barrels, until at last the clamor in the cobblestoned street beyond roared into silence, and his vision began to narrow, then fail. As the dimness of the alley became the darkness of approaching death, Cranham felt himself being swallowed up by the gloom and stench and utter lack of rationality.

Suddenly, with the clarity of a lightning strike, he realized one thing with an astonishing certainty. The message in his pocket had been nothing but a lure. Rannoch had set him up, enticed him with the ultimate temptation, trapped him like a rabbit to be throttled, then left to rot in the mire and excrement of an East End alley.

That grim realization alone was impetus enough to drive Cranham to renew the fight with what little strength he still possessed. Madly, the baron thrashed, and, catching his attacker off guard, he dropped his hands and pitched back an elbow, which miraculously connected solidly beneath an already heaving ribcage. The big man emitted a guttural, choking grunt directly into Cranham's ear, and the garrote slackened incrementally. Ruthlessly, Cranham rammed his elbow backward, again and again, until finally his attacker faltered ever so slightly.

In desperation, Cranham flailed backward with one hand, ripping away a handful of expensive brown superfine, and the wire at last fell free, only to be replaced by a muscular arm lashed high about his throat. Yet as Cranham wrestled to pull the arm away, he did not hear the knife slide from its sheath or see its glittering reflection as it sliced upward and into his belly, with a sickening, sucking sound.

The following morning, the marquis of Rannoch found himself staring across his wide mahogany desk at a dour, pinch-faced woman who sat stiffly in a chair before him. By some miracle, the feeble afternoon sunlight had wedged its way through London's perpetual haze to seep through the library windows of Strath House and illuminate the woman's deathly sallow skin, drawn taut over harsh, angular cheekbones. The pale light had no effect, improving or otherwise, on the dull black bombazine that swathed her from tiptoe to pointed chin.

Aye, and a hideous protuberance that was, Elliot inwardly acknowledged. Miss Hildegarde Harshbarger's jutting chin wanted only a wart. That, and a judiciously placed hook in her bladelike nose, would surely be sufficient to send Zoë screaming into MacLeod's sitting room, where she would inevitably be discovered cowering behind the draperies. Elliot sighed. It was not an altogether unfounded fear; she had behaved just so on more than one occasion.

Elliot cleared his throat and forced himself to be civil, absently fiddling with the quill on his desk. "Thank you, Miss Harshbarger, for spending this past quarter hour with us today. I believe that I have no further questions." Turning his attentions to Gerald Wilson, he lifted his one brow in a deliberately calculated gesture. "Have you anything further for this candidate, Mr. Wilson?"

Seated adjacent to Miss Harshbarger, Wilson twisted uneasily in his chair, then flipped open a thin leather notebook. After consulting his notes, he raised his eyes to the marquis. "We did not, my lord, discuss needlework," replied Wilson uncertainly, clearly out of his depth. "I daresay that is a skill at which young ladies are expected to excel, is it not?"

Elliot pressed his lips tightly together in aggravation. *Sewing?* Bloody hell! Harlan Stokely taught exciting things—Greek classics, Byzantine sculpture, astronomy. Why, there wasn't a sewing basket to be found in Chatham's schoolroom! And Zoë was a brilliant child, more than capable of learning both arts and sciences. Was it not far better to give a young lady the advantage of a rounded education, as Evangeline believed? Certainly, Zoë would need every advantage. She might not have, and might not want, a conventional life filled with childbirth and embroidery. It was a novel concept.

Amazingly, Miss Harshbarger lifted her sharp chin a notch higher. "Indeed," she answered in her sharp, supercilious voice, her jawbone rigidly locked. "I am an accomplished needlewoman, my lord. And my charge shall be one as well, you may depend upon it." Her ominous tone made it plain that she would brook little opposition to her training methods.

"Indeed! Yes! Yes, I am quite sure," murmured Wilson

anxiously. He consulted his notes again. "And dancing, ma'am? Miss Armstrong shall soon require simple dancing lessons. Would you be able to begin? Or would you recommend a dancing master?"

"Dancing?" Miss Harshbarger's tone was arch. She turned her narrow gaze on Elliot. "Do you really think it wise, my lord, under such unfortunate circumstances?"

From the corner of one eye, Elliot saw Wilson quite literally flinch. "Precisely what are these unfortunate circumstances to which you refer, ma'am?" Elliot's tone was deliberately cool and silky.

Miss Harshbarger drew herself up to an alarming degree of rigidity, folding one gloved hand primly across the other. "Why, the circumstances of her birth, Lord Rannoch. That is to say, such a vigorous physical activity, combined with a probable predisposition toward frivolity, might inflame the humors, and that would undoubtedly lead to—"

Elliot snapped, literally splintering his quill into two sharp pieces. "Out!" he roared, flying to his feet and tossing the mangled feather into the air. "Out! Out! Remove yourself from my library this instant, madam!"

An expression of wide-eyed fear chased the haughtiness from the would-be governess's face, and it was clear that Hildegarde Harshbarger had unexpectedly met her match. Amid a veritable snowstorm of flying feathers, shuffling papers, and swishing bombazine, the woman yanked herself out of the chair and bolted from the room, Wilson on her heels like a pointer flushing quail. Elliot was fairly convinced that he caught a glimpse of Prussian jackboots beneath her flapping skirt hems as she rounded the corner.

Choking down his rage, Elliot fell back into his chair and slowly gathered his composure. *Insufferable bitch!* Each potential governess had been worse than the last.

Were these the sort of people in whose care he had unwittingly—no, indifferently—left poor Zoë? Well, it damn sure would never happen again. The very thought made him ill.

In a few moments, he heard the resounding thump of the front door echo through the house. An abject Wilson soon reappeared in the library door. Elliot forced a sardonic smile and waved the man inside. "Have we any more pompous, hatchet-faced old crones waiting, Wilson?"

"Er, no, my lord. That one seems to have been the last. Of the hatchet-faced crones, in any event." Wilson grinned nervously.

Elliot tried to reassure him with a warmer smile. "Aye, then. And good riddance to the lot of them! Is there something else, Wilson?"

"Indeed, my lord. MacLeod begs me to inform you that Viscount Linden has called. MacLeod put him in the drawing room to await your pleasure."

"Humph," muttered Elliot thoughtfully.

"My lord?" Wilson still stood before the desk, clinging to his notebook with a white-knuckled grip. "What would you have me do? About Miss Armstrong's governess, I mean."

Elliot stared at the earnest man and carefully considered his question. "Nothing at present, Wilson. None of today's candidates was satisfactory, but you cannot be blamed for that misfortune. Perhaps something else will work out."

Even as Wilson sighed his relief, his ruddy brows knitted together. "Something else, my lord?"

Absently, Elliot flipped open the top file from the stack on his desk. "Never mind, Wilson. My daughter certainly shan't expire for lack of a governess. Please speak with Mrs. Woody. Ask that she assign one of the housemaids to see to Zoë's needs for the nonce. A sort of abigail. Trudy, perhaps?"

Wilson bowed. "Yes, my lord. Trudy it is."

From the hallway, someone cleared his throat. " 'Twas a fair bird indeed, Rannoch, who just flew your coop." Elliot and Wilson turned to see Lord Linden reclining indolently against the doorframe.

"Come in, Aidan, if you must," answered Elliot dryly, even as Linden strolled toward the desk.

As Wilson made a hasty exit, the elegant viscount flopped down into his vacant chair. "Interviewing replacements for Antoinette, old man?" teased Linden, tugging off his tight kidskin glove to draw a jewel-encrusted snuff box from his snug coat pocket.

Rannoch looked up absently from the stack of files on his desk. "Go bugger yourself, Linden," he replied coolly.

"Indeed! Better myself than your lady in black," chortled the dandified Linden, deftly flicking open the bejeweled lid and dropping a pinch onto the back of his hand. "Daresay I couldn't stir myself to poke at that old buzzard with Winthrop's diseased rod."

Elliot snapped shut the file and darkened his glower. There was a sad truth to Linden's jest, for their friend Matthew Winthrop, despite all his solid strength and military bearing, whored like there was no tomorrow. "Good Lord, Linden. Have you indeed risen at the crack of, oh, what?" Elliot tossed a glance toward the mantle clock. "Four in the afternoon? And just to regale me with poor Winthrop's sexual misadventures? I am indeed honored."

Linden looked upward with a broad grin and inhaled his poison. "Ah, I see the way of this. Now that you are keeping country hours—"

"Linden!" Elliot darkened his glower again with immediate effect.

"Oh, very well!" replied Linden dismissively. "As it

happens, I did not come to talk of Winthrop's ill luck. However entertaining such a topic might be, I come bearing tales of another's misery." Linden paused to sneeze emphatically into his handkerchief

"Oh, God, what now?" Elliot rolled his eyes.

"Cranham," answered Linden with a toss of his manicured hand. "Someone, it would appear, very nearly murdered him yesterday."

A deadly still silence fell across the room. "Murder?" asked Elliot sharply. "When?"

Linden smiled and narrowed his gaze. "I wondered if you mightn't ask that. Happened just after dusk, as I heard the story. Poor man was found behind a Whitechapel alehouse with a shiv in his gut. Wicked work, that."

"Good Lord! Cranham knifed in the East End? What, pray, was he about?"

Linden shrugged equivocally. "No one seems to know, but rumor has it that a missive of some sort was found in his coat pocket. Something to do with you, Rannoch."

"Me?" A cold, sickening sensation was wrapping itself around Elliot's lungs. He willed himself to breathe. "Why, I have no notion . . . What did it say?"

Linden shrugged again. "That I don't know, old boy. Thing to do, ring for that limp-wristed valet of yours. What that sly devil can't tell us ain't worth knowing!"

Elliot nodded, rose, and pulled the bell. Like a stealthy ghost, MacLeod floated in through the doorway, then just as quietly floated out in search of Kemble.

"Is he expected to survive?" asked Elliot as he strode across the room. He poured a whisky and a brandy, then dropped down onto the sofa near Linden's chair.

Linden took the outstretched brandy. "Not likely. I daresay a fever will likely do him in, or so Winthrop tells me. Saw a good deal of that sort of thing in the war, old Matt did."

"What do you think happened, Aidan?" asked Elliot uncertainly. He lifted his glass, stared across it at the viscount, then set the glass down again. "Some minor embarrassment with the money lenders?"

Linden shook his head. "Oh, Cranham's under the hatches, all right, but not far enough to make the cents-per-cents cry foul! No, Cranham seems to believe it was you who tried to do him in, Elliot. In fact, your name and an ensuing string of rather creative blasphemies are the only coherent words he has managed to mumble."

Elliot froze. "*I* tried to do him in? *Me?* Bloody hell, I passed up my opportunity to kill him. A clear shot, it was."

"Much as I might relish a good scandalbroth, Rannoch, I am inclined to agree with you."

"Inclined?" Elliot felt his anger flare. "Bloody well right you'll be agreeing with me. Most assuredly, had I wanted Cranham dead, 'tis dead he'd now be!"

Languidly, Linden raised one elegant hand as if to forestall him. "Good God, Elliot. Pray leave off the enraged Highlander routine! It becomes you very ill. Certainly, I believe you, and Wilkins and Carstairs will bear witness to your gentlemanly restraint at the duel."

"Bloody well right," grumbled Elliot.

Linden dropped his hand. "But aside from my good opinion, unless Cranham regains the mental wherewithal to do something other than curse your name with his dying breath, I daresay one must agree that there might be some question."

Elliot drained half his glass in one swallow. "I do not," he replied stubbornly.

"Where were you yesterday at dusk, Elliot?"

Elliot scowled and narrowed his gaze at his companion. "Are you the damned watch now, Linden? I was out."

"Out where?" asked Linden softly.

"Returning from . . . returning from a social engagement in the country. It is my business where. Certainly, I did not stop in the East End, of that you may be assured." Elliot set down his glass with a clatter. "Damn it, Linden, a back-alley knifing is hardly my style."

"I know it, Elliot. You are notorious for exacting your revenge in broad daylight. But I also know you'd been from home for three days. Were you in the Armstrong equipage with your coachman?"

"I rode," barked Elliot. "I was on horseback."

Linden's brows went up in surprise. "Really? No witnesses to—"

A sharp rap sounded upon the library door, and Kemble entered upon Elliot's command.

"Kem," began Elliot bluntly, "what, if anything, have you heard about this knifing incident with Lord Cranham?"

"Very little until about an hour ago, my lord," replied Kemble crisply. Then the willowy valet began to rattle off the details. "Mrs. Woody and Mrs. Nettles—she's housekeeper to Lord Wainright—use the same coal porter, who is a brother to the butcher in Arch Street, near the chandler's, and he met Cranham's—"

Elliot waved his hand in surrender. "Stop, please, Kem! I am sure you prefer to keep your sources confidential. Just give us the particulars of the missive that was found in his pocket."

"Ahem! Yes, the note. Reportedly, the author was anonymous. The note was delivered to Cranham's rooms off Fitzroy Square at three o'clock yesterday afternoon by the crossing sweep, who was given it by another urchin. The document instructed Cranham to meet the writer behind this particular alehouse, whereupon, for a certain sum of money—twenty pounds—Cranham would be given information that would prove ruinous to you."

Linden fell backward into his chair and began to laugh. "My God, Rannoch! You were to be given up cheaply enough. Judas cut a better deal than that!"

"Twenty pounds was likely all the poor bastard had," mumbled Elliot.

"A very astute comment, my lord," remarked Kemble, nodding sagaciously.

Linden ceased his laughter at once. "What's that?"

"It tells us something about the sender of the note, does it not?" answered Kemble. "I daresay the perpetrator was well aware Lord Cranham hadn't a feather to fly with and set the amount accordingly. Ergo, one might assume that expediency, not money, was his real concern."

"By damn, you're right," agreed Linden, his elegant blond brows drawing together. "Whom do you suspect, Kemble?"

The valet exhaled sharply and gave a theatrical roll of his limpid green eyes. "Well, I cannot possibly know, my lord! Nonetheless, it is probable that the attacker was, if you will pardon the irony, a man of Quality. Servants, shopkeepers, even bankers rarely suspect the financial straits in which the aristocracy often live. An ignorant man would have asked a hundred pounds!"

"A bit blunt, ain't he?" asked Linden, turning to Elliot.

Elliot, however, was studying Kemble through narrowed eyes. "The goal was murder, was it not?" replied Elliot thoughtfully. "There was no information, and even if there had been, I daresay it could hardly have been worse than that which is already believed of me. Someone simply wanted Cranham conveniently and discreetly dead."

"No surprise there," muttered Linden, rising to refresh his drink. "Man's a dashed nuisance."

"Most probably," agreed Kemble, ignoring Linden. "However, there remains a slight possibility that someone wished merely to cast blame upon you, my lord. If you'll pardon my plain speaking, how came your coat and shirt to be torn and bloodied a few days past?"

"Aye, I was wondering when you would come around to that, Kem," commented Elliot dryly.

"A duel, my lord?"

"Aye, with Cranham." Elliot snorted derisively, absently rubbing his injured shoulder. "I all but shot into the air, even after the bastard wounded me."

"Is it common knowledge?"

Elliot shot a questioning glance at Linden, who was settling back into his chair.

"No, I shouldn't think so," answered Linden thoughtfully. "Several people witnessed the argument, but they slipped away before Cranham's challenge. Certainly, Winthrop and I have said nothing, dawn appointments being so ill received nowadays."

Elliot nodded slowly. "And you may be sure Cranham's seconds kept it quiet. Wilkins was humiliated by Cranham's cheating. Young Carstairs, too, I daresay."

Kemble nodded. "It is then possible, my lord, that the attacker was unaware your quarrel with Cranham had been settled and merely wished to make it appear that you lured him to his death."

Elliot rubbed his hands up and down over his face. "Bloody hell. Can matters get worse?"

Kemble threaded his fingers and stared down at them studiously.

"Well?" demanded Elliot, looking at him.

The valet's head came up. "Since you mention it, my lord, there is one thing. Your mistress reappeared in town, setting herself up in exceedingly fine rooms in Marylebone and reportedly taking on both a butler and a lady's maid."

Elliot's brows shot up in surprise. "Did she indeed? I think I hardly care."

"I am sure, my lord, that you do not," responded Kemble. "But regrettably, Miss Fontaine has again vanished. The butler, who does not live in, discovered her rooms in a shambles and no sign of the woman."

"Who had her so well set up?" asked Linden, clearly stunned.

"That's the odd thing, my lord," replied the valet. "Apparently, no one. Miss Fontaine somehow discovered the wherewithal to maintain herself."

"And in a rather grand style, too," mumbled Linden. "Tell you what, Kemble. Best keep an ear open. Let us know what grist the rumor mill grinds."

"Yes, my lord."

"And Rannoch," Linden continued stiffly, "I need not tell you that something wicked is afoot. Can you remain in town for a time?"

Elliot clasped his hands stiffly behind his back. "No, Linden, I cannot. I must return to the country."

"A great pity," murmured Linden, looking uncharacteristically grave. "I think you should not do so. I am worried."

"My remaining here is out of the question," answered Elliot dismissively.

Evangeline sat in the sunny rear gardens of Chatham Lodge, diligently sketching a patch of wildflowers. With an exasperated sigh, she put down her pencil. Who, indeed, was she trying to fool? The entire household knew that she was already awaiting Elliot, who was not expected until late in the afternoon. No one, save perhaps Evangeline herself, still bothered to pretend that he was coming to have his portrait painted.

Oh, Evangeline was slowly painting him, of that there

was no doubt, but the majority of his time at Chatham was spent not seated obediently before her easel but walking, reading, or just laughing with her. Moreover, when Evangeline was otherwise engaged, as was often the case, Elliot seemed content to chatter aimlessly with Winnie or to turn pages for Frederica whilst she played the pianoforte, whispering suggestions and compliments into her ear. Evangeline was gratified to see that in Elliot's company, Frederica lost the uncertainty and shyness that had plagued her since coming to Chatham. Their quiet camaraderie was comforting to Evangeline.

Quiet camaraderie was not, however, an element of Elliot's relationship with Gus, Theo, or even Michael. In fact, Elliot's attentions had something of an unsettling effect on her brother, for in his presence, eleven-year-old Michael seemed intent on being one of the men. Whatever mishaps and mayhem the Weyden boys instigated, be it gaming, shooting, or riding hell for leather across the countryside, Elliot seemed to enjoy cavorting like a boy whilst Michael did his best to swagger like a man. It was perverse, but, to Elliot's credit, he did not permit the older boys to exclude Michael from any sport. Such gracious championing, of course, had the predictable result of instilling a mild case of hero worship in Michael's youthful breast.

Nicolette generally admired Elliot from afar, seizing every opportunity to tease Evangeline unmercifully. "April and May, April and May," she had chanted when at last Evangeline had acceded to Winnie's wishes and called upon the dressmaker for new gowns. Nonetheless, Nicolette, too, unfailingly wore her very best frock to dinner when Elliot was present. Indeed, the man's presence intensified every pleasure associated with life at Chatham Lodge, which had been an exceedingly fine place before that.

Uneasily, Evangeline shifted positions on the garden bench. There was something nagging at her, however. A troubling sense that all was not quite right with Elliot Roberts. Try as she might, Evangeline could never be more specific, but she felt it. Despite their many shared confidences, something still hung unresolved between them. No, not precisely between them, Evangeline reminded herself. They had made no spoken pledge to each other, nor would they.

Since that magical day by the Lea when Elliot had kissed her in the tangle of hornbeams, he had outwardly shown her no real passion. Though they had shared a kiss in his bedchamber, it had been one of promise but not desire. It was true that he often held her hand on those rare occasions when they were alone and sometimes brushed it gently across his lips. And although Evangeline was inexperienced in the ways of courting, she knew passion with an artist's heart, and she recognized what she saw when Elliot glanced at her with that subtle, hungry look in his smoke-colored eyes.

Elliot did not speak to her of such things, but Evangeline was convinced of his lust for her. His other emotions, however, were less apparent. As for her own sentiments, Evangeline was uncharacteristically confused. Her feelings for Elliot were an intricate knot, and from it she could unravel only one lucid truth. She felt a pure, heated desire when Elliot touched her. Never one to engage in foolish self-deception, Evangeline admitted that she wanted him, and she believed that he was well aware of that fact. Now she must wait to see what, if anything, Elliot would do about it.

"Miss Stone?" Mrs. Penworthy's voice abruptly pierced her introspection. "Begging your pardon, miss, but a messenger's just come with a letter. Bolton left it with today's post. 'Tis on your desk in the studio."

Evangeline was instantly alert. "A messenger? From town?"

The cheerful housekeeper bowed slightly, her ponderous key ring jingling as she did so. "Aye, miss, to be sure. And the letter bears Mr. Weyden's seal."

Two days after his disquieting visit from Viscount Linden, Elliot sent word around to his well-appointed stable instructing his staff to prepare his curricle and put to his best blacks. It was time, he decided, to travel up to Wrotham-upon-Lea in a better style. Forgoing the services of his tiger, Elliot set out from Richmond early and alone. The unsettling events of the preceding week had left him with much to consider, and careful deliberation was not one of Elliot's strong suits. Nonetheless, he crossed the Thames into London and headed north, already lost in thought.

Today, Cranham lay near death in his London apartments. Kemble had discovered that, true to Winthrop's prediction, a raging fever had taken hold of the baron, and he was not expected to last the night. Yet, other than Linden's pointed barbs, no one had questioned Elliot about the stabbing, nor was anyone likely to do so. Elliot took no comfort in the fact that absent some damning evidence, the authorities would not dare to imply culpability on the part of a nobleman, even a disreputable one. In this case, however, they would not need to trouble themselves. Assumptions alone would do almost as much damage. Assumptions could shatter a man's dreams, as well as his reputation, provided, of course, the gentleman in question still had one.

Ten years ago, Elliot had persuaded himself that what society believed mattered little. Then, during the agonizing months that had followed his betrothal to Cicely Forsythe, he had proceeded to live his life in a fashion that made his disdain apparent to all. Elliot had simply hardened his heart and stopped caring. There had been no other choice, for the pain and humiliation had very nearly consumed him. He now understood that a nebulous yet damning cloud of evidence was not easily dispelled. Whispered insinuation could not be stopped. Sometimes Elliot wondered if it was not easier to be tried, convicted, and hanged for your alleged crimes, rather than suffer the prolonged agony of being pricked to death by the pointed barbs of innuendo.

Worse still, Elliot was only now beginning to face the fact that he had sown the seeds of his own discontent along with his wild oats. Perhaps with time, society might have forgotten Cicely, for he understood now what he had been too naïve to see ten years ago: that Cicely had been neither liked nor respected by the *ton*. In his righteous indignation and youthful anguish, however, Elliot had created something they were not likely to forget: a rake and a reprobate who cheerfully bankrupted his peers, then bedded their wives. A man who whored and drank and gambled his way toward something that might, on a good night, pass for satisfaction if one did not look too closely. By the time his anguish had numbed and his indignation had turned to arrogance, the *ton* knew him for what he was: a wealthy, well-dressed pariah.

Now the situation was quite different, and things that had mattered little ten years ago mattered a great deal. What would Evangeline Stone say when he told her the truth? And he would tell her. Soon. Slowly. Thus far, slowly had made for a successful approach. In tolerable increments, he was revealing himself to Evangeline. But how much time did he have until she discovered the whole truth by her own means? Or by accident? It was fortunate indeed that Evangeline was in many ways a foreigner, having minimal interaction with or interest in English society. But Evangeline's disinterest did not obviate the danger of Winnie Weyden, and Elliot feared that behind her riot of gold-brown ringlets, frivolous laughter, and lush bosom, there lurked a worldly woman with the social contacts to find him out. In fact, it was insanity to think otherwise. It was insanity to hope.

Insanity? Hope? How had he allowed himself to come to this? Hope was a sentiment for fools and children. His life was what he had made it, and it would never be otherwise. One could not go back in time to recoup an innocence lost, to revive a dream long ago withered.

Aye, and it didn't do to go to bed fully sober. For years, shrouded dreams of Cicely had haunted him, haunted him still with an increasing frequency. In them, Elliot would be transported home, to see his enduring vision, her dark silk skirts still sweeping quietly through the stone passageways of Castle Kilkerran, a half dozen laughing children in tow.

But the old dream had become slightly altered. The smell of freshly cut flowers now blended with the scents of oil and beeswax. Fat black puppies rolled across the ancient carpets. The movement of his beloved had become graceful and smooth; her laughter had become throaty and gentle. The pale Scottish sunlight still spilled through the high stone arches to reflect, not off raven tresses, but against a soft sweep of blond hair. And when his fantasy turned to smile at him through the haze of his slumber, the visage did not turn harrowing. The mocking laughter did not ring out into the blackness of his night. Instead, the clear light held steady, and the face that smiled back at him had become serene, oval, and perfect. Evangeline's.

Had it ever been anyone else's? Truly?

But it was naught, after all, but a dream. Elliot held the

reins loosely in his right hand and scrubbed his other palm down his face as if willing the vision to disappear. He prayed that Evangeline did not discover the truth too soon, not before he could convince her. Convince her of what? And how? God almighty, he had very nearly seduced her by the river at Chatham, and it had taken every tattered scrap of his willpower to maintain a decent distance until his departure. Now he was returning to Evangeline, and in an even less stable state of mind.

As his justification for leaving during his last visit, Elliot had used the pretext of pressing business, and that had been true enough. In reality, however, his weakening self-control had driven his departure as much as Zoë's need for a new governess had done. Somewhere in this convoluted mental process, he must have subconsciously convinced himself that he could explain the truth gradually, and Evangeline would then fall into his arms and forgive his deceit. Now, however, his need for her was growing in proportion to his fear, and Elliot felt caught in his own trap.

And Zoë, too, was very much on his mind. Today, he had uncharacteristically resented leaving her alone. Servants, even good ones, were hardly sufficient comfort. A child needed more. Perhaps fathers did, too. Elliot thought again of Frederica and how similar, in both temperament and circumstance, the two children were. And what was it about Frederica that plagued his subconscious?

Despite the adversity of the last three days, Elliot had found his thoughts turning repeatedly to Evangeline's young cousin and, consequently, to the appalling housemaid whom he had felt compelled to discharge. What had Polly said that fateful afternoon? There had been a significant implication in her words, yet in that moment the word *bastard* had unleashed Elliot's blistering rage, blinding him to all meaning.

Mentally weary, Elliot stopped briefly at a wayside tavern for a light repast, washing it down with a tankard of ale so dreadful it must have been made from leftover pickle brine. He quaffed the last of it in spite of its vile taste. He could not find it in his heart to blame the tapster. Neither food nor drink held any special appeal to him of late, and much to Kemble's disapprobation, Elliot's trousers were starting to slide off his already narrow hips.

Upon command, the ostler brought forth the sleek team of blacks, and Elliot took up the ribbons to continue on his way, quickly crossing into Essex. Soon he passed through the Wrotham crossroads, noting that at last the signpost had been repaired and restored to its mound of earth. The sun shone brightly upon the narrow, dry roads, and within the hour, Elliot's curricle spun merrily through the tiny village of Wrotham-upon-Lea, past the crumbling church, and down the lane toward Chatham Lodge. It felt, Elliot suddenly realized, like coming home.

Filled with a restless energy, Antoinette Fontaine hopped down from her hired carriage and glanced anxiously back up the length of Meeting House Lane. "Wait at the end of this street," she abruptly ordered the driver, tossing him a couple of coins. "I'll be a quarter hour, no more."

After carefully tucking the money into a greasy leather waistcoat, the old man gave Antoinette one last leer, nodded, then busied himself by spitting energetically into the narrow, cobbled street. Suppressing her disgust, Antoinette lifted her skirts and resumed her journey on foot, making her way along the rubble-strewn path which cut down to the Thames above Wapping New Stairs. Descending toward the river, Antoinette thanked

God it was a Sunday and that very few people were about their business. Only a scattering of dockhands and steve-dores stirred, ogling her as she passed.

Ignoring the occasional vulgar comment, Antoinette steeled her expression and pulled close the drab woolen cloak that thoroughly concealed her jewels and clothing. While she was far from the sort who intimidated easily, not even the most hardened of whores would dare enter the environs below the dockyards at night. Even in the light of a Sunday afternoon, she did not wish to be there. But she feared the consequences of ignoring Rannoch's summons far more than she feared a Sunday stroll through Wapping.

Nonetheless, it greatly angered her that Rannoch would expect her to travel alone to such a place. Why there? She had heard the rumors that Rannoch might be courting a bride. It was almost laughable, and yet per-haps the tales were true, and now he merely sought to avoid the embarrassment of meeting his mistress in pub-lic. But here, in this godforsaken place? Apparently, the high-handed bastard spared no thought for her safety, while showing every concern for his damnable privacy.

But there was nothing else for it. Antoinette was not fool enough to believe she could avoid the marquis in-definitely, not with his vicious nature and his notorious cohorts, chief amongst them that sly, all-seeing valet of his. Nor could she afford to anger Rannoch beyond any hope of reconciliation. Oh, she had a few cards tucked up her sleeve, cards that would make her forever free of Rannoch and his ilk. But the time to play them had not yet arrived.

Far better to come out of hiding now and attempt some semblance of peace with Rannoch. Far better to do what he asked without argument. Indeed, what choice had she? Somehow, the devil had ferreted her out and

demanded that she come there. He would never again be
her ally, but under no circumstances did she want him as
an enemy.

As the footpath intersected with Wapping, Antoinette
made her decision. Yes, she would keep the peace, but
sooner or later, she hoped the self-serving pig would get
what was due him. Looking up and down the street that
edged the waterside, she lifted her chin to sniff the fetid
air, fully alert to any portent of danger. Antoinette
Fontaine would be no man's fool. Carefully, she patted
the six-inch blade tucked discreetly into her pocket. Antoinette saw no sign of her former lover, nor had she expected to. Rannoch had always had the disquieting
ability to slide through both daylight and dark like a nebulous, malevolent mist.

Suddenly, Antoinette found herself wondering if the
marquis were now regretting his impulsiveness in casting
her so quickly aside. Could that be the reason for this
veiled summons? Antoinette tossed back her head, resist-
ing the urge to cackle with delight at that hopeful
thought, then just as quickly sobered again.

No, Rannoch did not want her back. She had well and
truly burned that bridge. Nor was it Rannoch's style to
summon her there for something so simple and, to Rannoch, so meaningless. The marquis chose women the
way most men bought horses. He would simply have set
that bloodhound Kemble on her trail, then ordered his
man of affairs to pay her an unambiguous visit. Antoinette shivered with sudden unease, then forced her attention back to her path. Beyond, she saw Gun Wharf,
and, after striding past, she turned right onto yet another
footpath. Carefully, Antoinette picked her way down,
skirting broken bottles and filthy rags as she approached
the river's edge.

The appointed meeting place looked just as the mes-

sage had described it. Again, she shuddered, staring at the
bleak plank walls, now warped and weathered, spotted
with black from the incessant damp. *Why here?* The decrepit shack looked as if it would smell and look even
worse from the inside, and Antoinette was hardly the
most fastidious of women. Along the water, the wind
kicked up, blowing in the odor of mud flats and fish guts.
Disturbed by her intrusion, the gulls overhead began to
shriek and wheel, their white wings held at stiff, odd angles, like frosted door hinges, until at last she reached the
squalid shack.

Gingerly, Antoinette pulled open the makeshift door
and stepped inside, slowly allowing her eyes to adjust to
the darkness. It smelled miserable, dark and dank with
the stench of things Antoinette preferred not to think
about. Repressing the urge to gag, Antoinette spun
about and thrust the door back open, just enough to let
in a little light and air. She stared across the Thames,
watching as a barge passed, riding high in the water, her
cargo apparently disgorged somewhere upriver. With a
somewhat clairvoyant desperation, Antoinette found
herself wishing that she, too, were on the barge, sailing
far and forever away from the squalor of London and
her life. At that unsettling thought, she drew in a deep,
unsteady breath.

It was to be her last.

A cold, determined hand whipped around her neck.
Powerful fingers seized the heavy strand of rubies, yanking it taut, choking off her breath. Antoinette's arm
dropped. The rickety door clattered shut. Her bloodcurdling scream weakened to a hacking, garbled cough. She
swam in darkness. Instinctively, she arched backward.
She clawed wildly at her throat, then grappled for her
knife. It was useless. With a burst of desperation, Antoinette flailed, then kicked, almost catching her attacker

in the groin, only to find that another arm lashed about her waist and jerked her off her feet.

Snared in her attacker's ruthless grasp, the necklace bit into her neck, digging into the soft, tender flesh of her throat. Dimly, she heard the silk of her gown rip as she fought to free her arms. It was hopeless. Weakly, she kicked once more, but the black, stinking depths of the river were rising up around her.

The remaining struggle was brief. Antoinette weighed but eight stone, her assailant significantly more. Yanking the chain tighter still, he strengthened his grip about her frail ribs until she felt two of them crack in rapid succession. The sound was a deep, disembodied sensation, as if her body no longer belonged to her. Soon, there was no pain. Antoinette fell limp and gave herself up to the dark, swirling waters, allowing them to take her deep beneath the surface.

§9§

Thou tyrant, tyrant Jealousy, thou tyrant of the mind!
—JOHN DRYDEN

Elliot turned his sleek black geldings deftly into the sweep of the circular drive, arriving at Chatham in time to observe a pleasantly familiar, if somewhat laughable sight just inside the front gardens. Michael and Theo, shovels in hand, stood ankle-deep in a freshly turned flowerbed. Their shoes and stockings had been discarded in a heap, and streaks of mud stained their clothing. On the ground alongside them sat a battered tin pail filled with soft dirt. A plump brown worm was already snaking its escape down one side.

After stopping to exchange pleasantries, Elliot was immediately and enthusiastically assailed by alternating pleas to drive his "bang-up" curricle, supervise an afternoon fishing expedition, and then escort them to a clandestine prize fight in Tottenham on Saturday. Elliot's good humor now fully restored, he agreed to consider the first request, consented readily to the second, and refused the third out of hand. Then, waving good-bye, he snapped the horses forward.

Evangeline's lugubrious, stoop-shouldered butler greeted Elliot at the portals of Chatham Lodge and informed him, in his perpetually gloomy voice, that the young mistress was sequestered in the studio. After exchanging mindless remarks about the weather and depositing his bag at Bolton's feet, Elliot convinced the old retainer that he need not bestir himself for a formal announcement, then he eagerly made his way toward the studio. Unaccountably happy to be back at Chatham, Elliot strode quickly down the long hall in hope of surprising Evangeline with his early arrival. It was he, however, who was to be surprised.

Evangeline unthinkingly ignored the soft knock at her door. Only when the creaking protests of an ancient hinge betrayed her visitor did she lift her chin to see Elliot standing in the doorway. For a moment, his presence did not fully register, and she must have stared dumbly at him.

"Evangeline?" His inquiry was solicitous and soft. "I apologize for interrupting. I knocked . . . but perhaps you did not hear?"

With the back of her hand, Evangeline discreetly wiped away the traces of her tears and refolded Peter Weyden's short missive. "No, indeed, Elliot. You are not interrupting. Do come in. How pleasant that you are early. I was just—just—"

"—reading some bad news, I should say," he finished softly, quickly closing the short distance between them. He stood looking down at her with frank concern. "At least, the look of your eyes would indicate as much."

Evangeline inhaled deeply, trying unsuccessfully to suppress the ragged hitch in her breath. "No, not the best of news, I suppose. But I am well. Or soon shall be, in any event." She forced a more cheerful expression and rose to her feet. "Have you just arrived? I own, I'm exceedingly glad to see you."

"You have not the look of a happy woman, Evie." Elliot smiled warily, shifting his feet somewhat anxiously. "And yes, I have just arrived. Moreover, I have been entreated to tell you that Michael and Theo propose that we all make an afternoon of fishing. They are poking about for worms in your newly turned flowerbed even now."

"By all means, Elliot," she agreed, hiding her disappointment. "You must join them."

"We both know that I came to see you, Evie," he responded quietly. "Will you not come, too? It might be just the thing." He extended his large, well-manicured hand across the desk in invitation.

Evangeline tried to smile up at him. "I thank you, Elliot, but I cannot. I have something I must do, and I fancy that I would not make for the best of company just now."

With a silent nod, Elliot turned and slipped from the room. Reluctantly, Evangeline turned her attentions back to Peter's letter, trying to suppress the unexpected surge of isolation left behind in Elliot's wake.

She was skimming the letter for a third time when Elliot returned. Lifting her eyes to his, she watched him stride across the room to take, without invitation, the seat across from her desk. As usual, he looked exceedingly large and elegantly masculine as he leaned forward in the delicately carved chair. Elliot propped his elbows up on the edge of her desk and touched his fingertips together, one by one, with purposeful deliberation. Then he touched his lips tentatively to the steeple of his index fingers and stared intently into her eyes.

"I have sent the others on with Gus," he said softly. "Now, what is it, Evangeline? What pains you so greatly that you refuse to speak of it—even to me?"

Evangeline pulled open the top drawer of her desk and dropped Peter's missive summarily inside. "It is nothing," she replied. Then, as she placed one hand on the desktop as if to rise, Elliot reached swiftly out to cover it with his own.

"Evie." His voice held a gentle caution. "You'll not put me off. It is time we were honest with each other."

Suddenly, Evangeline wanted to confide in him. Moreover, she wanted to take comfort from him. The shadowy presence of her father's family had turned to a darkly ominous cloud, and in the face of it Evangeline desired nothing more than to be pulled into Elliot's arms and comforted. In compromise, she gave in to only half her desires. "It is my grandfather," she answered softly. "He is dead. Last night."

Elliot's confusion was plain, but he tightened his grip on her hand. "I'm so sorry, Evie. I thought—that is to say, I suppose that I had assumed you and your siblings were now alone in the world, save Mr. Weyden?"

"True enough. As you already know, Papa was estranged from his family. Yet one cannot help but be sad for—for what might have been. For what will never be." *And for what might come to pass,* she added silently.

"Then it was his great loss, Evie," replied Elliot softly. He rose from his chair, still holding her hand, and pulled her from behind the desk. "Come with me into the gardens? No one will disturb us."

Evangeline nodded, then looked up at him in gratitude. Suddenly, Elliot pulled her lightly into his arms and pressed his lips hard against her forehead. Almost immediately, he released her, then, taking her by the hand, urged her toward the studio window and pushed it open. Together they walked out into the quiet of the sundappled gardens.

Arm in arm, they silently strolled past the arbors and shrubbery until at last Elliot urged her down beside him onto a secluded bench. "Come here," he said, almost roughly, then dragged her back into his arms, burying his face in her hair. "Ah, Evie, I cannot resist. I have missed you. No, far worse! I've counted the minutes until I could return. And to see you now, with tears in your eyes, and to be unable to make things right . . ."

She said nothing and felt his warm lips brush her temple as she tucked safely into the crook of his arm. He felt so good, solid and comforting. How long had it been, Evangeline wondered, since she had enjoyed such a luxury? Too long, she decided. For far too many years, she had struggled alone, aided only by Winnie and Peter. It was not enough. Elliot, however, with his warm, innate strength, felt like more than enough. That fact should have concerned her, but for the moment she resolved only to savor his closeness.

"Now that I am here," he continued, "I cannot bear to see you unhappy."

"I am not, precisely, unhappy," she countered, letting herself relax against him.

"But you are distraught," he added gently. Letting his hand slip down her shoulder, Elliot began to rub her upper arm in gentle, soothing motions. "Did you miss your grandfather a great deal?"

"I—no, I did not," she heard herself admit. "I did not know him."

"And yet you cry for him?" His tone was soft and non-judgmental.

"Yes," she answered uncertainly, tilting her chin to look up into the unfathomable depths of his silvery gaze. "But I cannot explain . . ." She let her voice trail off uncertainly. "He was weak, I suppose, standing aside whilst my step-grandmother forced his children to choose between duty and dreams."

"Like your father and his work?"

"Yes, and his love for my mother. And other things, too, but oh, Elliot! Please let us talk of something else."

Evangeline saw a flash of guilt play across Elliot's face. "Very well, Evie," he answered quietly, pulling her closer. "We shall say no more." Instead, he lifted his hand to cup her jaw and tenderly brush the swell of her lower lip with his thumb. Slowly, he dipped his head to meet her mouth with his.

It was a sweet gesture of consolation, but the moment Elliot's breath brushed her cheek, Evangeline's need flared hot inside her, and she willed the kiss to be something more. She wanted to taste him, to draw comfort from him, to take him inside her again. When he pulled away, his luxuriant lashes feathered darkly against his cheeks, and, with a sound of protest, Evangeline slipped her arm up and around the taut muscles of his shoulder to draw him nearer.

His eyes flickered open, a flash of quicksilver beneath sensuous, hooded lids, then Elliot answered her by kissing her again, deeply this time, parting her lips expertly, then surging inside in a smooth, intimate act of possession. Evangeline stroked her hand across the breadth of his shoulder, then slid it up to caress the silken hair at the nape of his neck. Sinuously sliding his tongue back and forth against hers, Elliot moaned low into her mouth and let his hand slide from the curve of her jaw, along her arm, and down to cup her breast.

When her nipple hardened against his urgent touch, Evangeline felt no shame, just perfect, pure desire. She understood that she wanted this man in the most intimate way a woman could want a man, and when he gradually pulled his mouth away again, his palm still resting against her swollen breast, Evangeline wanted to cry out at the loss.

"Evie," he rasped, his breath shallow. "Darling, we have to talk."

"Talk?" Suddenly alert, Evangeline slid upright from her position in his arm and blinked, barely noticing that his hand dropped from her breast to rest lightly at her waist. "About what?" she managed to say. She felt panic begin to ease its cold grip about her heart.

Elliot pulled his hand from her waist and speared his fingers through his thick, dark hair. "I'm not sure," he muttered vaguely, staring at the ground now. "Things— us—damn it, I just don't know."

Behind them, a honeybee droned industriously, hovering through the humid air from one blossom to the next. The brilliant sun had shifted and now cast a shaft of pure afternoon light across the garden path along the bench. Elliot still stared into it as Evangeline inhaled deeply and repeatedly, drawing in the thick, familiar smell of moist earth and coming rain, until she felt both her panic and her passion subside. Then, slowly, Evangeline pulled away from him, mumbling some vague excuse about being needed inside the house. She walked toward the rear entrance, all the while feeling Elliot's heated glare upon her, until she pulled open the door and entered the hall.

It was a difficult job, yet it had to be done. As did most things, therefore, it fell to him, thought MacLeod with a resigned shrug. Such had been his opinion last week, at any rate. Now, however, his hostess poured the tea with an artless grace, dribbling it across the saucer and onto the knee of his breeches. With a patient sigh, the old man tugged a square of linen from his pocket. Fortunately for MacLeod, the tea had long since cooled.

"Verra gude, Miss Zoë," the butler encouraged. "Howiver, when ye guest asks tae have more tea, ye should take the cup frae his hand intae your ain. 'Twill work a wee bit better than thrusting the pot o'er the table tae pour at a moving target."

From across the table, Zoë giggled and put down the child-sized porcelain pot with an inattentive thump. "Sorry, MacLeod," she answered, wriggling in the tiny chair he kept on hand for her frequent visits to his sitting room. She beamed sweetly at him from beneath a riot of curls, then sighed. "Do you think my papa will ever let me pour for him?"

MacLeod nodded solemnly. "Aye, miss. I'm verra sure he'll do. Ye want only a bit o' practice."

And Rannoch might do just that, the old man decided, taking a delicate sip from a china cup scarcely bigger than the end of his thumb. The butler was secretly pleased that his lordship's attitude toward Miss Zoë had undergone a remarkable change of late. The child was showing a newfound confidence, and that was a good thing indeed.

Zoë smiled and leaned forward to lift a plate carefully. "Now I must pass you these tea cakes, MacLeod. But take only one or two," she instructed. "More than two is considered bad *ton!*" She giggled again, took three, and passed the plate.

MacLeod made his best effort at a frown. "Och, now! Guests first, Miss Zoë," he admonished. He took one cake, then bit into it. "Umm, 'tis a fine, fair cake, ma'am. Ye maun ask your cook tae give me the recipe."

"By all means, Mr. MacLeod," she answered primly, tossing her thick hair back across her shoulder. "It would be an honor."

A discreet cough at the door to MacLeod's sitting room forestalled any response. A powdered footman, looking very ill at ease, held an outstretched salver bearing a calling card. "Beg pardon, sir. There be a caller abovestairs asking for his lordship."

MacLeod looked at him sharply. "Didna ye tell him that Lord Rannoch is no at home and is no expected?"

The footman nodded effusively. "Aye, sir. I did. He wants to see someone in authority. Someone besides meself, sir, is what he meant—but he did ask particular-like if the marquis had a secretary. I put him in the yellow salon."

MacLeod sighed and beckoned the man into the room. The footman's choice of salons was telling; the yellow room was reserved for visitors who were less than quality but more than servants. He lifted the card from the salver and peered at it, then flicked a glance at Zoë. "Didna he state his business, man?" asked MacLeod, bristling.

The footman shook his head. "No, sir. But we 'eard some ter'ble rumors belowstairs this morning." MacLeod looked uneasily down at Zoë's chestnut curls and saw that the child was humming softly and nibbling on her cake. "Mayhap 'tis about that," concluded the footman.

"Perhaps," agreed MacLeod with a blunt nod, "but idle jabber it is, to be sure. Show young miss back up tae Trudy. And fetch Gerald Wilson at once."

Zoë initiated a long wail of disappointment, then, apparently catching the look on MacLeod's somber face, ceased abruptly.

"Hie off wi'ye now," he said affectionately, standing up and lifting her out of her chair. " 'Tis wearing late, lass, and time tea was o'er."

Gerald Wilson had bolted up the stairs to answer MacLeod's rather extraordinary command. It was not every day that the second footman came hurrying into the study with a message ordering him to report directly to the butler, but given MacLeod's standing in the Armstrong household, Wilson proffered no argument.

"A Bow Street runner?" he echoed, still gasping for breath. "I say, MacLeod! I cannot think that—what I mean to say is—do you think we ought? I mean, what if his lordship doesn't appreciate our intrusion?"

MacLeod looked at Rannoch's man of affairs and pulled a scowling face. "Gude Lord, man. Just take yerself aboon and see what he knows—and tell him naught! 'Tis no aften a runner comes calling, and he'll no be leaving 'til someone sees tae him, ye may be sure."

Wilson slumped in his chair and nodded. Dejectedly, he studied the calling card. What now, he wondered? His duties on behalf of the marquis of Rannoch had seemed far less sordid of late, but a murder! That must be what brought the runners down upon Strath House. Wilson felt his palms begin to sweat. For days, the servants had been whispering about the death of Lord Cranham, but that spurious rascal still clung tenaciously to life. The news of a death, when at last it had come, was instead a shock.

"And you are sure that Miss Fontaine is dead?" Wilson asked, dropping the card back onto the tray.

"Aye," answered the old butler grimly. "Nigh the dock-yards the poor lass was. Strangled—'tis what the tweeny heard. Kemble's off tae see what he may learn, but a run-ner, och! And here sae quick . . ." MacLeod shook his silver head, and the weariness suddenly showed. "I dinna quite know what tae do."

"I'll get rid of him," answered Wilson abruptly, with a confidence he did not feel.

He left the butler's sitting room and moved swiftly back downstairs to the formal rooms of Strath House. He entered the yellow salon to see a fair-haired man standing by the window that overlooked the rear gardens. Mr. Albert Jones, still holding his hat in his hands, turned to face him. Jones was a stocky, broad-shouldered man with a flattened nose—evidence, no doubt, of a hard life. His face, however, was otherwise pleasant, and he looked almost as hesitant as Wilson felt.

After brief introductions, Wilson invited him to take a seat, explaining that his master was traveling in the country and that the date of his return was unknown. In carefully measured tones, the runner confirmed that he was pursuing routine inquiries regarding the death of Antoinette Fontaine, a well-known actress. Miss Fontaine, or Miss Tanner, as she was legally known, had been found four days earlier in an abandoned shed near the dockyards.

When the details were complete, Wilson inhaled a long, deep breath and adjusted his pince-nez a little higher on his nose. "Mr. Jones," he began calmly, "I can assure you, sir, that we were all greatly disturbed by this vicious murder, but I cannot see how I may be of help."

The caller cleared his throat. "Mr. Wilson, we know that your employer had a past relationship with Miss Fontaine. Could you tell us if he remained on—er—good terms with her?"

Wilson looked at him archly. "Yes, so far as I know. I cannot think why he would not have done, but that is a question you must ask of his lordship."

A smile played at Mr. Jones's mouth, but his eyes were

impenetrable. "As it happens, that was my intent, but it seems he is often in the country of late." When Wilson made no reply, he continued in a blunter tone of voice. "Your employer no longer supported Miss Fontaine, I believe?"

Wilson crooked one brow stiffly. "I could not say, sir."

Jones sighed. "I understand. Though I suspect you handle most of his funds and know perfectly well that he had not done so for some time." Wilson merely looked at him for a long, expectant moment, and Jones was compelled to continue. "Yet Miss Fontaine continued to live affluently. Indeed, her financial circumstances seemed much improved."

"I would not know, sir. We are all, however, exceedingly sorry that she is dead."

"Yes, indeed. As is her family."

"Family?"

"Yes, her father died in the spring, and the mother just closed their tavern in Essex. There's a sister in Mayfair, a quiet woman in service as a housekeeper, I collect."

Wilson could not help but smile. "Nothing like her sister, I daresay?"

The runner shook his head ruefully. "No, nothing like, I'm afraid." He reached deep inside his coat pocket and pulled forth a bundle of black velvet. Gently, he laid it across his knee and unrolled the fabric to reveal an ornate gold necklace set with flaming rubies. Wilson felt sick as the runner spoke. "Sir, I must ask, have you seen this before?"

Wilson swallowed hard again and felt the blood drain from his face. Fleetingly, he considered lying, but this particular bit of jewelry was far too easily identified. And this—well, damn it, this was *murder*. Not even for Rannoch, as much as he was beginning to like the man, would he lie. He drew a deep breath. "Yes, I believe that belonged to Miss Fontaine."

The runner looked at him with polite curiosity. "You knew her well, I take it?"

Wilson licked his lips uncertainly. "Ah, no. I had not the pleasure."

"Yet you recognize her jewelry?"

Wilson nodded stiffly. "That particular piece was a Christmas gift from his lordship. I, er, picked it up from the jeweler's myself. Of course, I might be mistaken."

"Are you mistaken?" Jones's voice was crisp.

"No," said Wilson weakly. "No, I fancy not." He paused for a moment, very much aware that the runner's eyes were watching his every twitch. "As it happens, the necklace was part of a set. There should have been . . . that is to say, did you find a matching bracelet?"

"No." The runner shook his head slowly. "No, there was no bracelet."

Wilson looked at him hopefully. "I daresay it was stolen. The thief—the murderer—he must have taken it."

"I don't believe that was the case, Mr. Wilson. Robbery was not a motive. After all, the killer left this necklace behind."

Wilson's hope for an easy answer began to fade, but he grasped at a straw. "Perhaps he—he missed it. Perhaps it was late at night and very dark. He may have been overheard and forced to flee before . . ."

Wilson's words trailed away as Albert Jones gently shook his head. "No, Mr. Wilson. The killer definitely did not overlook this necklace. Quite to the contrary, he wrapped it very deliberately around her throat, then choked her to death with it."

A wave of nausea came out of nowhere, making the room swim unsteadily before Wilson's eyes. His face was suffused with heat, and the air seemed suddenly close.

Strangled. With the very necklace he had bought. And the marquis had given her. It was too horrible. What was worse still, he, Gerald Wilson, had just helped to incriminate his employer, the all-powerful and unforgiving Lord Rannoch.

"I—I am sorry," he stammered uncertainly, "but you have made an erroneous assumption, Mr. Jones. The marquis of Rannoch would never harm anyone."

The runner looked bemused. "I daresay you are leaping to conclusions I have not yet drawn, Mr. Wilson. Nevertheless, your employer's reputation, I regret to say, does precede him." Wilson began to protest vehemently, but Jones held up his palm. "Say no more, sir. Bow Street is hardly stupid enough to accuse a peer of murder without ironclad evidence. But his lordship is sometimes known to be, shall we say, vindictive."

Wilson shook his head firmly. "No, I could not agree. He isn't like that. Not now. I cannot say what he may have been like in his youth, but he is a good and generous employer. And fair. Yes, more than fair." That, Wilson decided, was essentially true. He had been good, generous, and fair. Lately.

Jones made no response as Wilson wrestled with his conscience. Instead, he reached into his coat pocket again and withdrew a folded card of heavy vellum which had once been sealed with black wax. "Mr. Wilson, do you by chance recognize this paper or this seal?"

Wilson took the card and examined it. Though the wax had been slit, there was no mistaking the Armstrong crest. He returned it to Jones, noticing as he did so that his hand was shaking. The sick feeling grew stronger. "Yes, that is his lordship's seal. I cannot be certain of the writing paper."

Jones flicked the vellum open with one deft motion of his fingers and held it before Wilson's eyes. "And would you say, sir, that this is your employer's handwriting?"

Wilson scanned the note and swallowed. Rannoch's bold, heavy-handed scrawl was unique, especially when his lordship was in a temper, as he no doubt had been when he penned the eight little words that now danced before Wilson's eyes:

Make no mistake, Antoinette, this is the end.

Wilson dropped his gaze from the note and stared at his feet, stalling for time, trying to think of something that might mitigate the damage.

"Well?"

"It would appear to be his penmanship, yes."

"Thank you, Mr. Wilson." The runner rose from his chair. With a troubled mind, Wilson stood up and followed him through the door.

"Please tell his lordship that I may need to speak with him personally," added Jones as they started down the stairs. "And tell him something else, if you would?"

"Certainly," agreed Wilson, turning to glance at him.

"Tell him that his friend Lord Cranham has made a miraculous recovery. It seems the devil does indeed look after his own."

They had arrived at the front door, which Wilson held open as the runner took his leave. "Certainly, Mr. Jones," he replied, now having regained a little of his aplomb. "But if you don't mind my giving you a word of advice?"

"No, not at all," answered the runner, looking rather intrigued. "We can always use a little help in Bow Street."

Wilson forced down his nausea and dredged up what little haughtiness he possessed. "Try barking up Lord Cranham's tree, sir, and see what comes crawling down. You might be surprised to find that there are others with a motive for murder. He and Miss Fontaine had been keeping company of late, I believe."

Albert Jones merely nodded, shoved his hat down hard on his head, and stepped out onto the marble steps. He turned back to face Wilson. "I can assure you, sir," he answered with perfect calm, "that the fact had not been lost on me. Of course, there is a question about the timing, Lord Cranham having been somewhat indisposed. Unfortunately for me, the uncertainty about precisely when the murder occurred makes almost anyone suspect."

Wilson nodded stiffly. "Thank you, at least, for keeping an open mind."

"You are quite welcome," replied the runner. Then he turned and went down the sweeping marble steps at a fast clip.

Elliot prepared for dinner in great haste. He was anxious to speak with Evangeline again, to reassure himself that all was well, though they had parted company less than two hours earlier. The memory of her kiss still burned on his lips. Something, he realized, had to give. Something had to be resolved, or he would soon go mad with fear. Or worry. Or unslaked lust. At this point, Elliot hardly knew which volatile emotion was most apt to drive him over the edge first. But for the moment, simply seeing Evie might suffice, and so he dressed with great care in another simple but serviceable coat and trousers, which Kemble had reluctantly provided, then tied his own cravat in an ordinary style. There was nothing, he later realized, to portend the discomfort his manner of dress would shortly bring.

Dashing down the steps and past the drawing room, he caught sight of Evangeline standing by the pianoforte. She was formally dressed in a stunning new gown of sapphire silk shot with gold, cut fashionably low. It looked as though Winnie Weyden had been conspiring with the dressmaker on Evie's behalf. Elliot moved toward the wide double doors and was taken aback to see that she was not alone.

"Ah, Mr. Roberts!" she cried out, sounding far more strident than usual. "Do come in. There is someone here I should like you to meet."

Struggling to remember that only hours earlier she had felt warm and pliant in his arms, Elliot watched in the tense silence as Evangeline moved toward him with constrained, prim motions. He stepped fully into Chatham's drawing room to take in the elegant, almost foppish gentleman, dressed in Continental fashion, who stood by the cold hearth, one expensively shod foot set high on the brass fender. Elliot knew instinctively that the man was not English. Tall, lithe, and exceedingly handsome, the foreigner put Elliot very much in mind of Linden, though even the dandified viscount had never dressed so well. Uncomfortably aware of his own plain attire, Elliot could not but despise the newcomer on sight.

"Mr. Roberts?" repeated Evangeline smoothly. "Please allow me to introduce Etienne LeNotre, the comte de Chalons, a friend who has just surprised us with a visit. Etienne, this is Mr. Elliot Roberts, the houseguest I mentioned."

Elliot could not help but notice that he had swiftly become the milksop *Mr. Roberts* once more, while the visitor was *Etienne*. The polished nobleman let his foot slip gracefully from the fender and bowed civilly, one elegant blond eyebrow crooked in polite curiosity. Despite de Chalons's faultless manners, Elliot could sense that the visitor regarded him with veiled suspicion.

"Ah, yes, indeed. From London, I believe?" de Chalons asked in a coolly expectant tone. "You are to be my Evangeline's latest masterpiece, *n'est-ce pas?*"

Elliot forced a rigid smile and managed to hide his

surge of panic at de Chalons's choice of words. *His* Evangeline? In a flash, Elliot's unexpected anxiety escalated from a vague concern that he might be asked to relinquish his seat of honor at dinner to a chilling fear that some more significant position had already been usurped. He realized that the comte was still staring at him expectantly.

"Certainly, we hope that it is so," Elliot agreed, forcing a low, even tone. "You are a friend of Miss Stone's family?" The question was somewhat forward, yet Elliot swiftly decided that two could play the role of suspicious protector.

The comte seemed to take no offense. "*Mais oui!* Of many years." Suddenly, his gaze slid smoothly toward the door, and what might have been bitterness quickly flared in de Chalons's vivid blue eyes. "Ah! Here is the merry widow now!" he said evenly, his chiseled features returning to a mirror of impassivity.

Elliot turned to see Mrs. Weyden sailing into the room, attired in her becoming red dress. It was scandalously cut, displaying her voluptuous figure to its best effect. Certainly, it affected the comte, whose face drained of all color. "Winnie, *ma jeune femme!*" he exclaimed, striding smoothly across the room with outstretched arms.

Mrs. Weyden laughed dryly. "Etienne, *mon jeune amour!*" she answered, turning her flawless cheek into the Frenchman's kiss. "But, darling, perhaps we both lie? I am not young, nor should I speak to you of love."

"Ah, *mon coeur!*" De Chalons pressed his fingers to his heart melodramatically. "You do wound me to the quick. To be treated thus, when I have come all the way from Soissons just to dine with you."

"Bah." Mrs. Weyden laughed, flicking an unexpected glance toward Evangeline, then eyeing the comte appraisingly. "I know what brings you here, Etienne. You have come to see Evangeline." She fixed her lush lips in a pout. "You would take her away from me, would you not?"

"*Mais non*, Winnie. I shall take you both!" answered the comte, laughing with a seemingly specious gaiety which Elliot sensed hid a far less pleasant emotion. De Chalons spun a neat quarter turn and gracefully offered his arms to the ladies. "*Allons*, pretty jewels. I shall take you in to dinner."

Winnie slipped her arm through de Chalons's and continued to chatter amiably as they walked. Evangeline, however, smoothly dropped back to join Elliot, seizing his arm with a possessiveness Elliot found suddenly reassuring. He turned slightly to look at her from the corner of his eye, noting that she seemed far paler than she had earlier in the day. He allowed his hungry eyes to sweep from her face down across the deep décolletage of her rich sapphire dress, and the words *brittle* and *cold* came swiftly to mind. Almost simultaneously came a somewhat reassuring suspicion that Evangeline was not altogether pleased to see Etienne LeNotre.

Much to Elliot's relief, his seat of honor was not expropriated. The comte sat to Winnie's left, his distance from Evie constituting the only bright spot in an otherwise miserable meal. Much of the dinner conversation ensued in French, after Elliot politely agreed that, yes, he did indeed speak the language. That statement, he soon realized, was questionable at best. Everyone else, including Frederica, babbled vivaciously in a rapid stream of cosmopolitan chatter. Many of the words were unfamiliar to him—partly Flemish, he began to suspect. Elliot looked down at his ordinary clothing, listened to the urbane discourse all about him, and realized that he had never felt so out of place in his life. Right between his recently discovered feelings of *guilt* and *shame*, Elliot wedged *artlessness* and *stupidity* into his emotional repertoire.

The only topic he distinctly understood was Nicolette's proposal that the family organize a presentation of *Much Ado about Nothing*, to be performed on the garden terrace within the fortnight. Coquettishly batting her eyes, she solicited Elliot's participation as Benedick to her Beatrice, then arbitrarily assigned the remaining roles. None too soon, the seemingly interminable meal was over, and the family began to disperse toward the drawing room.

De Chalons declined his hostess's offer to savor a bottle of port with Gus and Elliot. "*Merci, mais non,* Evangeline. I have something I must discuss with you, my dear."

Evangeline stiffened, her gaze flitting somewhat anxiously from Gus to Elliot, then back to the comte. "By all means, Etienne," she finally agreed. "Shall we go into the drawing room?"

De Chalons smiled blandly. "Let us go into the studio, if you please. I feel the need to view your father's work once again. It has been some time since I have seen it, and to do so would bring me great joy. Afterward, perhaps you would be so gracious as to walk with me in the garden?"

Evangeline nodded. Just then, Tess entered with a heavy salver bearing a bottle of port and three glasses. Gus nodded invitingly toward the tray, and Elliot slid back into his chair as Evangeline and de Chalons departed. "Friend of the family," repeated Gus sympathetically, as if an explanation to Elliot was obviously in order.

Suddenly, Elliot wondered what the Weydens thought of his growing relationship with Evangeline. Were his proprietary feelings for her so apparent? And did Gus believe the Frenchman to be Elliot's rival? Slowly, Elliot sipped at his glass. "Do you know de Chalons well?"

Gus shook his head, yet a knowing light flickered in his eyes. "Not well. As it happens, he stayed here awhile during the war, but I was at school during much of that time. Apparently, Peter saw Etienne in Vienna last month and asked him to return to London with him. Perhaps that has something to do with Etienne's sudden arrival here."

"Why?" asked Elliot bluntly, raking his eyes over the younger man. He perceived that Gus, who was uncharacteristically restrained tonight, did not fully trust de Chalons. Suddenly, Elliot realized that they were keeping some dark secrets in this house. He could sense it. Tonight, for the first time, he felt like nothing more than a guest at Chatham, and he was shocked at how greatly the realization pained him.

Gus tossed off his port with a flourish and put down the empty glass with a maladroit clatter. "Can't say, Roberts. Just a suspicion." He shoved his chair away to rise abruptly from the table. "Whist?"

Elliot shook his head. "No, Weyden, but thank you. I think I shall stroll through the studio if de Chalons has finished, then take myself off to bed."

"Suit yourself," agreed Gus, nodding amiably. Tonight, he seemed almost relieved to be rid of Elliot.

The studio was indeed vacant when he strolled into the vast room. The sound of his boot heels echoed hauntingly through the emptiness as he roamed idly over the flagstones. The painting of Leopold still stood turned against the wall, an open crate in the floor beside it. At first light, Peter Weyden's men were to haul it away to London. Fleetingly, Elliot wondered if Evangeline was agonizing over her decision to part with such an obvious masterpiece. How would she feel when she learned that Elliot had bought it? Or would she ever know? With that bleak thought, Elliot wedged himself into the corner to admire the massive canvas's stunning beauty, but once positioned, he hardly saw it, quickly losing himself in a maelstrom of worry.

Who was Etienne LeNotre? The reaction of the family members at dinner had been surprisingly mixed. Michael seemed to regard him with the sort of distant enthusiasm one might reserve for a favored but rarely seen uncle. Nicolette and the older boys were almost wary in the comte's presence. Frederica, however, remembered him not at all, and Evangeline had explained that Frederica had been but a toddler at the time of de Chalons's last visit. Though Evangeline had not seemed to dislike the comte, she had been decidedly ill at ease throughout the meal. What did that signify? The air inside the studio felt suddenly thick and hot, and, impatiently, Elliot pulled at the throat of his shirt, loosening his cravat.

Suddenly, the scrape of the French windows pulling open from the terrace dragged Elliot forcibly from his disquiet. Given his awkward position behind Evangeline's massive easel, he saw no tactful means of escape. Elliot could see only one end of the southerly wall, but he knew instinctively that Evangeline had entered the room. Furthermore, the strident sound of de Chalons's voice soon made it plain that he had returned with her.

They spoke in rapid French, and Elliot understood even less now than he had during dinner. Clearly, the two were arguing, but there was no discernible fear in Evangeline's responses to de Chalons's rapid barrage of questions.

Elliot strained both his ears and his vocabulary. Michael's name was frequently mentioned, but in an unclear context. Given the resonance in the vaulted chamber, it sounded as if Evangeline and the comte were slowly strolling along the south wall. At last, they came

into Elliot's view so that he was able to observe their lips
and gestures.

It quickly became apparent that de Chalons was insisting that Evangeline go away with him. Elliot was
stunned. Earlier in the evening, he had supposed that
Winnie was merely jesting, but now de Chalons seemed
quite serious. His entreaties became more vehement as
they moved through the room, and Evangeline appeared
to grow increasingly distraught with each step. Suddenly,
de Chalons stopped and slowed his voice to speak more
emphatically. Now Elliot could understand most of what
was said.

"Evangeline, my darling," the comte insisted, "you
must come with me to my chateau now. Stay with me in
Soissons until the New Year. You must."

"No, not yet, Etienne." Evangeline was almost crying
now. "Please, not yet."

"Shush, Evangeline. It is not so bad as all that! I want
to keep you under my protection. I promise you will be
happy in France." He pulled her into his arms.

At that gesture, Elliot barely suppressed a vicious urge
to go for de Chalons's throat. How dare that pompous
fop barge into Chatham and force his attentions on an
innocent young woman? Elliot was already weighing his
odds against the Frenchman—he had a good three inches and at least two stone on the man—when it occurred
to him that what LeNotre was about did not greatly dif-
fer from his own actions toward Evangeline. The shame
of it shocked him.

No, it was not the same at all, Elliot argued with himself. This arrogant, polished Frenchman apparently
sought a mistress. Elliot wanted a wife.

A wife? The realization sobered him. But it was true,
he realized. Somewhere along the way, marriage to Evangeline had become as necessary as it was hopeless. Absent

something very drastic, she would never have him. And why should she? Clearly, Evangeline did not lack for wealthy suitors.

She spoke almost inaudibly into the comte's shirtfront. "I cannot do that to Michael, Etienne. Besides, we are so happy here at Chatham."

"Evangeline." He pushed her away from him, then gently shook her by the shoulders. "You might have no better alternative. Who else can you trust in this way?"

"Please, Etienne. You cannot ask that I leave Winnie and the children!"

"Winnie can meet you next year in Ghent," he persisted softly.

Mutely, Evangeline shook her head. Tears were indeed spilling down her ivory cheeks now, and it required every inch of Elliot's rather limited self-control to remain hidden. He wanted desperately to leap from behind the canvas and throttle the Gallic bastard until his piercing blue eyes glazed over and rolled heavenward. How had such a man come to have power over Evangeline? He said she might not have an alternative. What a lie! Undoubtedly, there were hundreds of honorably intentioned men who would willingly hurl themselves at her feet, had they any chance of winning her affection. How could de Chalons force Evangeline to act against her wishes?

Evangeline's voice dropped to a whisper. "No, Etienne, I—I cannot go with you. If you care for me, you will not insist. Perhaps when I have no other choice, if it comes to that. Perhaps then I shall be grateful for what you so generously offer me now." Through her tears, she was smiling sweetly, and Elliot felt himself grow sick with disgust and fear.

Surely, it was not a matter of money? Chatham Lodge was a gracious home, and Evangeline's extended family lived in apparent comfort, but perhaps all was not as it appeared. Indeed, she had once spoken of their finances in general terms and expressed a vague concern about the preservation of capital, but that was no more than a sensible business practice. Was the estate in debt? Perhaps Chatham was unentailed and had been mortgaged? No, that made no sense.

Suddenly, de Chalons bowed low over Evangeline's hand and murmured something Elliot could not hear, then took his leave in haste. Her back turned to Elliot, Evangeline remained standing by her desk for a moment, then abruptly fled through the window into the garden.

In the dark recesses of Elliot's mind, a seed fertilized by fear took root and began to grow. There was at least one obvious solution. Quietly, he made his way out of the cramped corner and followed Evangeline.

❧10❧

Pains of love be sweeter far, than all the other
pleasures are.

—JOHN DRYDEN

Earlier in the evening, a warm northeasterly wind had swathed Essex in a blanket of low clouds which now shrouded a thin sliver of moon. The night air was growing heavy with the promise of a coming storm as the surrounding trees shivered in the faint breeze. Straining his eyes in the near darkness, Elliot could barely make out Evangeline as she stood, staring out across the gardens. She leaned almost weakly against the stone barrier that flanked the upper terrace. A low rumble of distant thunder penetrated the stillness, rolling across from

East Anglia and echoing ominously through the nearer hills.

"Evangeline?"

At the sound of his voice, Evangeline's head whipped around. Blankly, she stared at him. In silence, Elliot drew nearer until he stood beside her at the edge of the flagged terrace. She turned her gaze once more toward the distant forest.

Resolutely, Elliot braced his arms wide on the low stone wall, feeling his fingers involuntarily dig into the rock and mortar. He dropped his head and prayed for strength. "Evangeline, tell me truthfully." His words came out in a tormented rasp. "What is your relationship with the comte de Chalons?"

"Did you overhear?" she asked in a soft, emotionless tone.

"Some of it, yes." He turned his head to look down at her, awaiting what he knew might be a scathing reply, but none came. "Damn it, Evangeline, tell me! Whatever is between the two of you, for God's sake, tell me. Don't make me imagine the worst."

Evangeline answered him with a bitter laugh which pierced the gloom. "The worst? What is the worst, Elliot? I wonder."

And suddenly, he had her by the shoulders, pulling her toward him far more roughly than he had intended. Even in the weak lamplight that trickled from the studio, she looked pale and shaken. "The worst, Evie? The worst would be that you do not care for me at all. That you care for—for him, that man, LeNotre. A stranger whose name I have never heard before tonight, whose presence in this house takes me by complete surprise . . ."

"Elliot," she replied in an almost inaudible whisper, "de Chalons was a student of my father. A friend to Peter. He is dear to me, yes, but nothing more."

"Pardon me for noting that his feelings for you seem somewhat less platonic," insisted Elliot bitterly, slamming his fist down onto the stone wall, a flicker of distant lightning punctuating his angry gesture. "Damn it, Evangeline! I cannot bear it. Let me understand. He proposes to *keep* you—I think that is a fair translation of what the man suggested. An insufferable insult! And from a man who arrives here uninvited, then behaves as if he belongs in this house."

Evangeline lifted her chin to look straight into his eyes, and Elliot sensed her animosity flare. "I care for you, Elliot," she whispered hoarsely, her voice never wavering, "but you are not my keeper, nor need I apprise you of who comes and goes from my home."

Elliot raked one hand through his hair in agitation, realizing that he had overstepped himself. "That's not the point, Evie. I only meant—"

"I know what you meant," she coolly interposed, "and the point is, there is much you cannot begin to understand, many people in my life of whom you know nothing. The converse is undoubtedly true. I do not delve into your past, and I would prefer that you extend to me the same courtesy."

Elliot nodded stiffly. "Very well," he replied, sensing that he was on the crumbling edge of a crisis. Even worse, Evangeline's argument held far more truth than she knew, and he was ashamed yet again. He watched as she shook her head almost indiscernibly, blinking back another tear.

She was angry, and she hurt in some inexplicable way that Elliot could not begin to assuage. In the near silence, he listened to her breathing calm, then he set one arm reassuringly about her narrow waist. "Forgive me, Evie. I forgot myself."

In apparent resignation, Evangeline exhaled a deep

sigh into the warm night air. "Elliot," she began in a soft, tentative voice, "because I care for you, because I want you to understand what Etienne meant, I will explain—"

Elliot interrupted her gently, tightening his grip around her waist and pulling her to him. In that gesture, which was meant only to console, as he leaned close and inhaled her warm, feminine fragrance, his jealous rage rekindled into pure desire, flaring low and hot in his belly, burning away all logic. His gaze drifted down the perfect turn of her face, taking in the sadness in her crystal-blue eyes, the elegant curve of her jaw, and her tremulous, delicately ripe mouth.

De Chalons, he abruptly decided, could burn in hell.

"No, Evie," he rasped, sliding his free hand up along her spine to wrap it surely about the nape of her neck, "you mustn't say anything." Elliot's voice came out in a tortured whisper as he dipped his head to brush his lips against the soft skin below her earlobe. "You owe me nothing," he continued, moving his lips across the lovely turn of her jaw to take her mouth.

With total surrender, Evangeline let Elliot capture her lips in a kiss that was fierce, unrelenting, and almost savage in its intensity. His crushing mouth tasted of warm wine and honeyed silk, and this time, when his tongue slid seductively against her lips, she opened eagerly, taking him deep inside to stroke and explore. Reacting purely on feminine instinct, Evangeline moved urgently against him, sliding her tongue smoothly against his and returning his passion with growing confidence. A soft moan began deep in her throat as she allowed one hand to slide around his waist and up beneath the warm wool of his coat to feel the solid muscles of his back. Despite her flash of anger at Elliot, this felt real. This felt safe. Elliot's embrace felt like the only thing that could give her even the briefest illusion of security.

Dimly, Evangeline sensed the growing recklessness in Elliot's motions as she felt his hand slip down to stroke across the swell of her hip, then lift her roughly against him. The flame heightened instantaneously when he pressed himself into her, and she felt his arousal, hard and erect, against her feminine mound. An urgent, driving hunger pierced her belly, and in response she moaned again and felt her fingernails claw into the fabric of his waistcoat as she begged for something she wanted but did not fully comprehend. Warmth and heat and need surged through her as she arched against him instinctively and wantonly.

Her sweet, throaty moan of passion sent hunger slicing through Elliot's gut like a sharp blade. God, how he wanted Evangeline, would do anything to have her. Sensing that he was rapidly losing himself, Elliot at last managed to dredge up enough self-control to pull incrementally away from Evangeline's inviting hips and mouth. She whimpered softly in protest as his lips parted from hers. Almost blindly, it seemed, she slid her hands down the small of his back and lower still to urge him against her in a gesture that was the very definition of sweet, guileless seduction.

"No," he rasped harshly, and watched as hurt, then humiliation, played across the gentle features of her face. "Oh, God, Evie—"

"Don't you want me, Elliot?" she whispered. Her upturned face was innocent despite her full, inviting lips. "I had hoped that you found me desirable."

Elliot let himself slump hard against the stone wall at his back, then dropped his forehead to touch hers lightly. "Good Lord, yes, Evie. I want you. So much so that I very nearly—" Abruptly, Elliot checked himself.

"Good," interrupted Evangeline breathlessly. Across the garden wall, a spear of lightning threw the distant forest into harsh relief, and thunder, much nearer now, rumbled through the clouds again.

Elliot jerked his head upright and pulled her hard against his chest. With great concentration, he disciplined the movements of his hands, rubbing them lightly up and down the delicate curve of her narrow back. "Evangeline," he spoke into her hair in a heated rush, "will you marry me?"

The unexpected proposal had scarcely burst from his mouth when he felt her stiffen in his arms. "Marry you?" Her voice came out as a whisper against his chest as the full import of his own words struck Elliot. Slowly, she lifted her head, and Elliot let his grip go slack. Evangeline deliberately tilted her chin to stare up at him. Was he serious? She was as stunned by his proposal as she was by her unexpected desire to say yes. "I—I hardly know what to say," she hedged, unexpectedly faced with both her most cherished daydream and her most haunting nightmare.

Deep inside, temptation and regret welled up into an aching knot. Oh, she wanted Elliot Roberts, more than she had ever desired anything in her life! But how could she be so selfish as to commit herself to another, when Michael might need her total devotion? Indeed, how could any English gentleman want her when he learned the truth: that she and her siblings had been coldly disowned by her aristocratic relatives and that anyone who befriended them could expect to suffer the wrath of that all-powerful family. Moreover, Elliot's heart belonged to another. His proposal had been spoken on impulse, driven by nothing more than absurd masculine jealousy and heated desire. Evangeline recognized the emotion that now lit his eyes; it was shock. Indeed, it was plain that Elliot had been taken aback by his own words, which had been spoken in the heat of possessiveness and passion.

"Say yes," answered Elliot with a confidence that was growing in spite of his better judgment. After all, he should marry, should he not? Though he was, perhaps, too jaded and too scarred to love, did that totally preclude marriage? Indeed, his mother often reminded him that he needed an heir and that he could be an adequate husband if he tried. Evangeline was a beautiful, passionate woman who desired him. Him! And he needed her desperately; only with her could he find any measure of peace. He knew that now. Surely, despite all the odds, a marriage between them could be good. Surely, he could find the words to explain his inadvertent deception and somehow make her understand how he felt.

"Yes," he repeated firmly. "Just say yes, Evie. Say yes, and everything will work out. I promise."

Mutely, she shook her head. On the horizon, lightning flickered again, brighter now, and Elliot could see her soft glow of passion draining from her face. "No, I cannot. Elliot, I'm so sorry. I thought—I thought that we might—that is to say . . ."

Elliot shoved her away another inch and shook her gently. "Damn it, Evangeline, why not? I'm a wealthy man. More so, quite probably, than your fine French count. I can afford to care for you, all of you. And most assuredly, I can resolve whatever it is that troubles you far better than he may."

Evangeline shook her head resolutely. "No," she whispered, her voice hollow and uncertain. "No, I cannot, Elliot. Please. Please do not insist that I explain myself. I just have too many pressures right now. Too many responsibilities. But I had hoped . . . that is to say, I thought that we might . . ." Slowly, her words trailed away, and she dropped her eyes to stare fixedly at the folds of his disordered cravat.

Elliot felt a burst of impatience, then just as quickly

suppressed it, realizing that he had little experience in dealing with women like Evangeline. And she did, indeed, have a great many responsibilities. He felt ashamed for pressuring her, particularly given that his request came on the heels of de Chalons's demands. "You thought what?" he asked, as gently as he could manage, deftly tilting her chin up with one finger, then dropping his head to nuzzle her lightly along her delicate jawbone.

"Elliot, I have something I must confess—"

Elliot lifted his mouth from the warm angle of her throat and stared into her eyes. "Good Lord. What?" he whispered hoarsely, wondering what new crisis fate might next hurl his way.

Evangeline's gaze lowered to focus on the soft tangle of hair now visible at the throat of his shirt. "I have never taken a lover before," she answered hesitantly, "but I want you. So much." She watched, entranced, as his hands slid to her shoulders to push her away fractionally.

"So that's what you are about now?" Elliot's harsh gray eyes studied her none too gently. "Taking a lover?"

Evangeline could not mistake the tinge of annoyance in his voice. "Yes," she answered honestly, her voice still thick with need.

Tearing his eyes from hers, Elliot's gaze seemed to harden on a point somewhere in the distance. "I thought it rather more than that, Evangeline. I cannot like your phrase. It feels too cold a description for . . ." But Elliot, too, had run out of words and was looking unexpectedly hurt and angry.

"Too cold?" Evangeline slowly shook her head. "I want you, Elliot. I think you know that. I care for you, far more than I ought. But I'll not mislead you. I do not seek a husband. Nor, I think, do you really seek a wife."

Elliot nodded, his lips drawn into a thin line. "No, perhaps I have not the makings of a suitable husband."

The torment in his voice tore at her heart. "Elliot, you mistake my meaning. My wishes have nothing to do with you. I truly need you, but I have obligations, most of which I cannot begin to explain," she answered, but her reasons slipped away, because suddenly, Elliot was kissing her again, and Evangeline found herself slipping back into the warmth of uncertainty and temptation.

As his mouth, gentle but sure now, moved on hers, she found herself regretting her words, her reluctance, and virtually every decision that had formed the basis of her life for the last ten years. When his hands slid from her shoulders to splay across her back, gathering her gently against him for a kiss that was exquisite in its sweetness, Evangeline experienced the agony of true need. She felt her muscles weaken against the hardened length of his body as his kiss and his touch became ever more coaxing. More tempting. Yes, it was that. Dangerous. A bit like strong ratafia, rich and intoxicating.

Elliot's mouth, spicy and sweet, held the promise of pleasure. She was warm with the scent of him: smoke, soap, and man. Filled with the rumble of thunder, which was closer now, the air was thick and hot, redolent of summer flowers. Evangeline wanted him to take her. Now. In the soft, fragrant grass of the garden. Before she returned to reason. This was the very dream that had so disturbed her sleep of late. She wanted this and could not let it end.

"Now," she begged. Her plea was no more than a whisper of breath against his mouth.

Elliot elevated simple seduction to a high art. Evangeline knew that she would never have the strength to resist him, to fight the unleashed urge to have him, or to ignore the way her body begged him for pleasure. And because she was a victim of her own uncontrollable need, God only knew what else she might be persuaded to do, by him, this man she had come to cherish beyond reason. She pressed away the thought, and as her hands opened against the warm wool of his coat, his fingers came up to tangle in her hair, forcing her head to still.

She felt his control slip suddenly. His tongue, hot and aggressive, plunged, drew back, then surged deeply into her again and again, the rhythm compelling her to want more. All. In the darkness, she felt his hand skim down and drag up her skirts in a smooth, forceful motion. A warm breeze of silk and lawn whispered up her thighs, and then his hand was sliding between them, touching her flesh intimately, in a way that felt both persuasive and treacherous. Warm and smooth, his fingers slipped into the folds of her womanhood, probing, coaxing, then stroking, until they were slick. Slick with her passion. It was all so new, yet Evangeline understood.

Through it all, Elliot's mouth never ceased in ruthless invasion of her mouth. Evangeline clutched at him for balance, her legs melting beneath her. She wanted it, yes, wanted everything he had to offer. Whatever the price, no matter the complications. Abruptly, she pulled her mouth from his and tilted back her head to stare into his eyes, which seemed black and impenetrable in the darkness. "Please, Elliot," she begged. Involuntarily, her body trembled against his hand, and she gasped for breath. "Please." She felt like a wild thing caught in his snare, left at his mercy, and begging for release.

Elliot stared down into her eyes, held her gaze, and continued his torment until her body began to respond by arching against him, aching for more. Then, slowly, his mouth came down on hers again, even as his hand stilled. Evangeline wanted to scream in protest when the demanding pressure of his hands and mouth relented, then pulled slowly away, leaving her wanting and desperate.

Elliot loosened his grip and held her in his arms. Tenderly, he dipped his head to press hot kisses along her cheekbone. The light touch of his tongue against her earlobe sent fire coursing through her body to the emptiness between her thighs. She felt his breath against the dampness of her temple, and she realized that he had deliberately tormented her into near madness.

"Come to me tonight, then, Evangeline," he whispered silkily into her ear. "If you want to take a lover—if you truly believe that is all you need—come to me, and I shall oblige you well. Then we shall see who does the begging. And for what." With that, his arms dropped away, and he was gone, striding across the terrace and through the back door.

The clock struck ten as Elliot stormed across the hall to climb the central staircase that led to Chatham's family bedchambers. On the landing, he paused to listen uncertainly. Despite the painful throbbing between his legs, his ears still worked sufficiently well for him to discern an indistinct noise in the corridor. He froze. In the distance, he heard the sound again, the faint hiss of silk, he guessed. Confusion shifted to rage when he saw Etienne LeNotre treading softly down the older tower stairs that entered the corridor further down its length. LeNotre paused to duck beneath the low stone beam before stepping out into the candlelight of a wall sconce. Fully expecting the comte to turn right toward Evangeline's room, Elliot felt the blood rush to his head as he prepared to step into his path and threaten him.

Attired in a long dressing gown of dark silk, the comte instead turned left, then all but vanished in the dark beyond. Quietly, he drew up before the last door on the right and entered without pausing to knock.

Good Lord! So that was the way of things. The comte de Chalons was having an affair with Winnie Weyden!

Little wonder, then, why Gus held the man in some suspicion. Despite his own libidinous frustrations, Elliot was forced to suppress a snort of amazement. Yet he had to admit that Winnie Weyden was a beauty, if a man preferred his women bold, voluptuous, and a dozen years older. Elliot, however, did not. Moreover, his relief at discovering the true direction of de Chalons's desire did nothing to mitigate his own lust.

The dank smell of London closed in around Godfrey Moore, Baron Cranham, as he made his way through the dark streets between Fitzroy Square and St. Marylebone. The rain had now slowed to a steady drizzle, and his journey was not overlong. Despite the damp chill, a carriage, Cranham cautioned himself, would have been too indiscreet. Indeed, he had often made this surreptitious trek on foot, but tonight the distance seemed inordinately difficult. Weakened by his recent illness, Cranham could nonetheless summon breath enough to curse Elliot Armstrong deep into the bowels of hell.

A passing chaise rolled briskly through a deep puddle in the center of Portland Place, churning back a spray of filthy water which drenched Cranham's long coat from hip to hem. Muttering a string of curses, he mentally renewed his vow of vengeance and leaned weakly into his cane. Cranham continued thus for a half mile, then turned down the alley which would eventually take him to the rear entrance of Antoinette Fontaine's residence. Although the authorities had searched her rooms, it was entirely possible that they had missed something. Something that Cranham might now find useful in his quest for retribution.

It was fortunate indeed that in her increasingly desperate, drunken rages, Antoinette had so often been less than circumspect. Initially, he had believed her mad, but then her standard of living had abruptly and dramatically improved. No great exertion of logic had been required to surmise the means of her newfound wealth. She was blackmailing someone, and it could only be Rannoch. One could only imagine what ugly secrets the man's lover had been privy to. It pleased him to know that the marquis would continue to pay for his sins. Antoinette's little cache of sordid secrets, if he could but find it, would ensure it.

The rear steps loomed up in the dim light, and Cranham paused just long enough to allow the burning ache in his belly to subside, then gingerly made his way up to the second floor. Reaching deep into his pocket, Cranham withdrew a key and chuckled at his duplicity in having stolen it weeks earlier. As he touched the metal to the ancient lock, however, the soft sound of a man clearing his throat caused Cranham's hand to still.

A low, rich chuckle arose from the darkened stairs below. "Well, they do say the criminal always returns to the scene of the crime," drawled a languid voice. Smoothly, Viscount Linden slid from the shadows at the foot of the steps to stand in the feeble lamplight. Cranham dropped the key back into his pocket, his eyes darting up and down in desperate search for a means of escape.

"Oh, I shouldn't bother to run, dear boy," responded Linden silkily, propping one elegantly shod foot on the bottom step. "After all, you're in a weakened state, and I rather think I could take you down without muddying my evening slippers." Arrogantly, the man dipped his head to light a thin, dark cheroot. Drawing deeply, Linden clamped down on the cigar, then returned his gaze upward, a lazy, glittering smile working its way across his face. "Do come down, old sport, or my neck shall surely crick in this infernal damp."

"Rot in hell, Linden," hissed Cranham. "Don't you

think you and your cohort Rannoch have done me enough harm?"

"Ah! Well. As to that, Cranham, it begs pointing out that you are yet alive. And Miss Fontaine, regrettably, is not. I wonder how that happened?"

Cranham snorted in outrage. "Rannoch killed her, you imbecile. What's more, everyone knows it."

Linden merely shrugged and withdrew a pistol from deep within the folds of his greatcoat. In the shadows, Cranham watched as the viscount motioned him downward with the barrel. "I don't think so, Cranham." He chuckled softly. "Come down now, if you please, sir. I've a snug little barouche just around the corner. Let's get out of this rain and trundle down to Brooks's. We shall have a drink, just you and me, eh?"

"You must be mad, Linden. I shall go nowhere with you."

Linden merely laughed again. "Ah, perhaps! But your life is in danger, Cranham. Mayhap you cannot be too selective in your choice of allies, hmm?" The glittering smile returned as Cranham walked slowly back down the stairway to join him.

For two hours, Elliot stormed back and forth across the floor of his bedchamber, waiting for Evangeline. Outside, another sort of storm raged, whipping rain across the window with a driving fury. She would come, damn it. Her body had answered his just as he had known it would. She would come to him, and then what? He wanted her, but what was worse, he needed her. He needed her a great deal more than she, apparently, needed him. And he had proposed marriage to her. The reality of it stunned him.

Good God, what did the woman want from him? He had never known a more disturbing female. Would she have him beg for her love? He would not do so, for he had nothing true enough to give in return. For her hand? He would willingly continue to plead for that, if she would have him. Or did she indeed want nothing more than the pleasure and comfort his body could provide? What a vengeful twist of fate that would be.

In aggravation, Elliot ripped a cheroot from the case in his coat pocket, strode to the deep, mullioned window, and shoved open the casement. For the most part, the rain came straight down now, rushing through the gutters and only occasionally lashing back in an angry spatter against the stone walls. Elliot ignored it. He drew hard on the cigar, using the lamp from his side table as a light, then settled himself sideways into the deep windowsill. A split of lightning forked down from the heavens, illuminating the gardens below with a clean white light, only to be followed by a rolling crash of thunder that resonated off the tower.

The brilliance of the lightning seemed to reflect his unease, throwing it back at him like the quick flash of a mirror. The problem was not Evangeline, he realized, exhaling a harsh stream of smoke out into the turbulent Essex night. It was him, his anger and his fear and this damnable, inextricable mess he had created out of a foolish impulse. Moreover, his misery was heightened by the knowledge that, even with his sordid history safely hidden, he could tempt her to nothing more than a clandestine affair. And she, an inexperienced virgin! Had he suffered any doubt on that score, Evangeline had erased it with her sweet, breathless confession.

What did he want? To wed her, yes. The uncomfortable truth was driving him mad. What he had felt upon seeing LeNotre touch Evangeline had been a harsh realization, not a passing fancy. He wanted Evangeline Stone to be his marchioness, to give him children, and to do all those sweet, traditional things such as comfort him in sickness and in health. Moreover, Elliot wanted to give the very same to her, for without a doubt, she was deserving of his best. Nevertheless, it was well worth recollecting that this was not the first time he had allowed himself to yearn for, and to offer, such things. Elliot forced himself to remember that painful truth. The gardens sprang to life again as a bolt of lightning split the sky, but Elliot scarcely heard the resultant thunderclap.

Did he love Evangeline? No, he believed that he had lost that ability long ago. In youthful naïveté and ignorance, he had loved Cicely, and the ripping away of that love had torn out some essential part of his humanity. The last ten years of his life had clearly evidenced the loss in the ugliest of ways. He thought about Evangeline, recalled how she had felt in his arms, so soft and yet so strong, and he wondered how on earth they had come to this. Why, despite all his wickedness and dissolution, had he been inextricably drawn to this woman to the point that his judgment weakened?

What pathetic human fragility made him willing to ruthlessly deceive her, over and over, impelled by a fear that far exceeded any remorse he might ever have been capable of? Like the wicked Tarquin, tempted beyond his feeble resistance by the virtuous Lucrece, Elliot had used deceit and cunning in an attempt to have his way with an honorable woman. And now, did not his false heart bleed? Yes, it did, but like Tarquin, he had been unable to alter his path, to do the right thing.

Now, out of what felt like desperation, he would gladly take her innocence, knowing full well that it was all she was likely to give him. Such a willingness was not love; it was something worse. What he felt for Evangeline was wholly divergent from any feeling he had harbored for his long-dead fiancée.

Had that been love? That painful ache he had felt for Cicely?

Perhaps not. The doubt rose from his subconscious mind to rock the foundations of everything he had come to be. Without question, her calculated deception had stripped him of his youthful dreams and left him dead inside. Then, just as quickly, the residual agony had made him hunger for revenge, not only on her lover but on the *beau monde* that had first laughed at him, then whispered behind his back, and ultimately heaped him with scorn.

No one—not even Hugh, who should have seen what was coming—had bothered to explain that Cicely Forsythe was little better than a shameless coquette. She had courted ruin in a determined effort to snare a rich husband, until at last she was forced to settle her expectations on Lord Cranham's bastard. Elliot now knew that by the time he had arrived in town, naïve and unenlightened, Cicely was barely tolerated in polite society. Only the *ton's* respect for her plain but highborn aunt, whose ample dowry had shackled her to nothing more than a disreputable, debt-ridden baron, had allowed Cicely to cling to the edge of respectability. Moreover, it was obvious to many that Lady Howell had cared far less for her husband's niece than did the *ton*.

However, if the end of his engagement had been a bad dream, Cicely's death had been a nightmare. Following Elliot's refusal to honor the betrothal, the gossips had whispered that Lord Howell's niece had removed to the country to nurse her broken heart, which had been so cruelly ravaged by the overly proud, newly invested marquis of Rannoch. Of course, London society loved to relish and embellish a scandal, and Elliot knew that his determined efforts to kill Godfrey Moore had only fanned the flames.

The obvious fact that by the time Elliot had returned from his father's funeral, Cicely's condition had been readily apparent had not kept the *ton* from blaming him for abandoning his pregnant fiancée. Precisely how she had come to die less than a month later, Elliot did not know. Nonetheless, she had purportedly been found in a squalid flat, dead of blood loss. It was widely rumored that Cicely had tried without success to rid herself of the child, and Elliot had little doubt that it was true.

Sir Hugh had merely stamped his foot in rage, insisting that it must be plain to anyone who could count that Elliot had scarcely been in town long enough to leave any chit that far gone with child. Nonetheless, after her death, the vile rumors had persisted, driven as much by Elliot's refusal to renounce them as by his newfound arrogance and treacherous moods.

The rain had changed directions again to spatter back against the tower wall, and Elliot was dismayed to see that his coat sleeve was now soaked. With a soft hiss, he pitched his cheroot into the night and pulled shut the window. It rasped against the casement with a dull scrape of ancient metal. Ah, the past. His heart had been young and foolish then. He had hurt, and he had lashed out. But what was done was done, he knew. Questioning the past could not undo the damage.

He was suddenly quite weary, his unslaked lust all but forgotten. He pulled his watch from his waistcoat and glanced at it. Evangeline was not coming. He had hoped he had tempted her beyond resistance. That perhaps he had given her cause to regret her hasty rejection of his proposal or, at the very least, cause to come to his bed. But it was half past eleven, quite some time since they had stood in a tangled embrace on the terrace, and the household was long since abed. What would he have done, he bitterly considered, had Evangeline accepted his offer of marriage? Simply prayed she would not notice his full name on the marriage license?

Damn it, it was time he went to bed himself. With a sigh of resignation and regret, Elliot shrugged off his damp coat and began to undress.

From her position in the narrow stone corridor, Evangeline heard the window scraping shut. Three times she had lifted her hand to knock, and three times let it drop to her side. Beneath her bare feet, the stone was cold, and she shivered despite her nightdress and wrapper. She had been so certain of what she was about mere hours ago, yet now she was not sure. Not sure at all.

She had put off ascending the curving tower stairs until she was confident that Etienne and Winnie were asleep, or at least otherwise occupied. The time had seemed interminable, and as it passed, her resolve had weakened. It was an irreversible step, this uncertain thing she so desperately contemplated, and it would forever alter her friendship with Elliot. Yet at the memory of his touch, and the deep ache of longing it stirred inside her, Evangeline lifted her hand again, and this time she rapped softly on the thick planking of the ancient door.

Elliot opened the door to see Evangeline standing in the shaft of weak lamplight that shone from his bedchamber. Bare feet peeked from beneath her nightclothes, and though her expression was uncertain, the purpose of her visit was obvious.

Wordlessly, Elliot pulled her inside the room and into his arms, pushing shut the door with the heel of his boot. "Evie." His hand molded to the small of her back and stroked up and down as his mouth sought hers. There seemed to be no need for conversation. For better or worse, all that needed to be said had been said on the terrace, and Elliot put aside his hurt and let desire take hold once more.

Her lips trembled against his as he kissed her with his eyes and his mouth open, devouring her. His shirt billowed loose from the waist of his trousers, and as he pulled her hard against him, he felt Evangeline twine one arm around his neck. Her tongue felt like warm satin as it slid willingly into his mouth, and Elliot thought he knew, and was prepared for, his body's response. But when her free hand slid beneath the linen of his shirt to touch his naked flesh, he quivered. Raw need fisted in his stomach like a sharp, sweet pain.

Any doubt Evangeline might have felt seemed to have dissolved in the wake of their passion. Her hands were on him, certain and needful, and Elliot reveled in her touch. He pulled her across the room, through the pool of lamplight, and onto the bed. At the adjacent window, a hard rain beat a strong cadence against the whorled glass. Without taking his lips from hers, Elliot urged her backward into the bedcovers, his right knee bent to the mattress.

Slowly, he pulled back from her, trailing fervent kisses down her throat. He walked to the side table, lowered the lamplight to a mere flicker, then returned to sit on the edge of the bed. *Too fast,* he thought. He was pushing her too fast. *Too slow,* argued the hungry voice in his head. Elliot pulled in a ragged breath and leaned forward to rest his forearms across his thighs. He stared at the floor. "Evangeline—are you sure?"

She answered by coming up onto her knees behind him and sliding her hands beneath his shirt once more. Her palms were cool and strong against his fevered flesh. With surprising ease, she dragged the fabric up and over his head, then set her mouth to the curve of his collarbone. "Elliot," she whispered against his skin, "I'm sure."

It was the touch of her hand and the sound of his name that did it, evoking in him the same ache that had seized him that first day he had come to Chatham, desperate and angry, in the cold, driving rain. In the hall, she had laid her hand against his arm, and he had looked down into her gentle eyes, and the painful yearning had gripped his heart and reached down into the pit of his belly. Sweet, sweet agony. It had to be right to make love to her now.

Swiftly, he undressed and turned to press Evangeline down into the softness of his bed. He stretched his length out along hers, feeling the curve of her hip against his. Almost reverently, he lifted his hand to the close of her wrapper and opened it, pushing away the fabric to reveal the sheer lawn of her nightrail. In the near darkness, Elliot imagined he could see the firm, dark areolas of her full breasts. He reached out and found them, already hard with nascent desire.

Beneath his touch, Evangeline trembled, then moaned. "Make love to me, Elliot," she whispered in the darkness. "Now, please."

"Ah—yes, Evie," he answered, moving his hand to the other breast. "I will. But slowly. You are special. Something to be savored." He lowered his mouth to suckle her, drawing both fabric and nipple greedily into his mouth, and was thrilled to feel Evangeline arch with sudden pleasure. He laved each breast in turn, over and over, finding himself strangely humbled by her soft sighs of delight. She was so passionate and eager. Unlike any other woman he had known, her emotions felt pure and uncomplicated. When he felt her hips begin to move, he impatiently pulled up her gown and slid his hand along the inside of her thigh.

Slowly, he took his mouth from her breast and drew back to look into her eyes. His vision had adjusted to the darkness, and he gazed at her as he slid his hand higher, to the joining of her thighs. Evangeline's head was tilted back, and already one hand was fisted with pleasure in the bedcovers.

"Evie, look at me," Elliot whispered, and her chin came down, and her eyes opened wide to meet his. "I want to watch you when I touch you, sweet." Propped beside her on his elbow, he pulled deliberately closer and speared his fingers into the nest of curls between her legs. "Mine, Evie?" He gave a gentle tug, watching in the darkness as she nodded almost imperceptibly.

"Remember what I said then, Evie? I take what's mine." So saying, he plunged one finger into her and felt the sudden tightening of her feminine sheath. She cried out softly, already warm and ready. But not yet, Elliot cautioned himself. He drew back and heard her whimper, then slid two fingers deep inside. Again, she arched off the mattress, and Elliot began to move inside her. Slowly he began to brush the ball of his thumb up and across her sweet nub, already hard with need. She whimpered again, and Elliot felt the pull of her muscles against his fingers.

Gently he moved his hand on her and returned his mouth to hers, repeating with his tongue every stroke of his fingers until Evangeline writhed beside him. He swallowed up her little cries of pleasure as she pressed against him, instinctively seeking a release he knew she did not yet comprehend. Pulling back to watch her face as she neared the edge, Elliot could sense the growing tautness of her body, tight as a bowstring. Finally, he felt her tension snap, and Evangeline began to convulse in his embrace.

Watching her come was infinitely satisfying, more so than his own release would have been. The thought surprised him as he saw her head tilt back and felt her insides pull and pulse around his fingers. It was a new experience for him, this unselfish giving of pleasure. He had thought only to prepare her for his body, but in so doing had found immense satisfaction. In the past, if a woman took pleasure in coupling with him, it had been incidental, not intentional. A woman's satisfaction had never been high on his list of priorities. The need to give pleasure, this perplexing wish to give of himself, was disturbing in its intensity. But any fear was forgotten when Evangeline's eyes fluttered open and she sighed.

Even as the sense of utter calm washed over her, Evangeline felt Elliot pulling away her robe and then lifting her as if she were no more than a child, to peel away her nightgown. Within moments, she was completely naked, and he was staring at her in a way that was raw and urgent. But not frightening. Or embarrassing. Not after what he had just given her.

Evangeline had not understood that the man brought that sort of pleasure to the woman. And certainly not in that sort of way. Suddenly, she was eager to learn more, and why not? She was with Elliot. She could give herself over to him. She could trust him. It was a joyous acknowledgment which made her desperate to please him as he had pleased her. She rolled toward him, slid one arm beneath him to embrace his narrow waist, and pulled herself closer to his warmth.

When fully nude, even in the dim lamplight, Elliot's beauty far exceeded the near perfection she had seen while watching him at the pond. He was a big man, but beautifully formed, with wide shoulders and a lean stomach which plainly revealed that his clothing owed little to a tailor's expertise. It was this glorious body that filled and shaped Elliot's plain coats and ordinary trousers. His chest was broad and nearly smooth, with just the lightest dusting of dark, curling hair which trickled between his breasts, across his abdomen, and down his belly.

Suddenly, Evangeline wanted to caress him. In the near dark, she watched Elliot smile at the touch of her hand laid flat against his chest. With slow deliberation, she skimmed it downward over his midriff, across his taut stomach, then lower still. And then she touched him. His manhood lay hard and erect against his belly, and Elliot gasped as her fingers brushed the hot flesh.

"Ah!" he gasped. "Evie, so sweet!"

Evangeline understood. "Can I touch you? There?"

In the pale lamplight, she saw Elliot bite hard on his lower lip for a moment. "God, I don't know," he replied hoarsely. "Yes, I think so."

Tentatively, Evie slid her hand back against his belly, feeling his flesh quiver now at her touch. Taking the weight of his shaft in her hand, she held him and felt the blood pulse hot and strong beneath the taut skin. His flesh was like velvet. Drawn tight over iron. She slid her hand back and forth again, reveling in the feel of power that lay just beneath the surface.

"Evie—stop!" His voice was an indistinct rasp. She pulled back her hand as if bitten, and Elliot came off his side and rolled on top of her, wedging himself between her thighs. She embraced him, sliding her palms down the taut, smooth length of his back and onto his lean buttocks, only vaguely aware of the deep, puckering scar on one hip.

"Evie, I have to have you," he moaned. His hands came up to cradle her face even as he lowered his open mouth to hers in a kiss that was savage and unyielding. Roughly, he plundered her with his tongue, his shaft pressed hard against her belly, his powerful legs urging hers apart, his pelvis grinding her down into the mattress.

The weight of him alone was enticing. Instinctively,

Evangeline urged her breasts and belly hard and higher against him until she felt his heavy manhood slide down between her legs to push against her entrance. And then his hands were beneath her hips, cradling her buttocks and easing them higher and apart. Suddenly, she felt him begin to sheath himself inside her, and she gasped.

In the dimness, she watched his eyes fly open wide. "Evie, sweet, I'm sorry. I don't want to hurt you." But he did, sliding deep inside her with one smooth motion. A fast, sharp pain knifed inside her, and she must have cried out, because Elliot froze, then lifted himself incrementally away to look at her.

"Ah, God, Evangeline! I'm so sorry. I can't—can't help it." He stilled himself inside her and dropped his head to whisper against her temple. "There—better?"

"Yes," she whispered uncertainly, then more confidently. "Yes, better."

Elliot uttered something that sounded like a visceral groan and withdrew almost fully. There was no real pain, just a deep, aching void where he had been. The worst was over, she knew. She was ready for him and wanted to give him pleasure as he had given her.

"Oh, Elliot," she whispered, wrapping her arms tight about his waist, "come back to me." With her womanly instinct, Evangeline angled her hips enticingly, and Elliot answered by sliding fully inside her again. His loving had made her slick and silky with wetness, and she savored the feel of him, hard and warm inside her. Evangeline listened as he drew a slow, ragged breath and moved again, then she let herself tighten against him, and relax, as they began an ancient rhythm. Beautiful. Evangeline thought it was beautiful.

Elliot lifted his head to watch her expressive face as she moved beneath him. Evangeline's passion was innate; her timing and grace as she arched against him were almost

feral in their beauty. Each time he drove into her, his
control almost slipped. Evangeline moved with him in
smooth, perfect motions which belied her inexperience.
But she was inexperienced; the undeniable barrier of her
maidenhood, now torn asunder, confirmed her virginity.

Yet Evangeline knew precisely what she was doing.
Doing to him. She pivoted her hips and urged herself
against him, drawing him into her with all the skill of a
practiced courtesan. God, no. Elliot had taken many
courtesans, and it was nothing like this. This was better.
This was give and take. A sense of togetherness that Elliot
had never before known. Making love. Yes. Therein lay
his inexperience, yet it felt like lovemaking to him.

He sensed, even if Evangeline did not, the growing
tension in her body and prayed that he could hold himself in check long enough to pleasure her once more. Biting his lip again, Elliot tried to focus on matching his
rhythm to hers, on instinctively sensing the need within
her every sigh and movement. Ah, she had twined her
legs about his waist now. Each stroke was exquisite beyond description. It felt pure and good to love her.

Relying on a male intuition that had not been much
used, Elliot paced and deepened his rhythms, hoping to
bring her over the edge with him. He did not know what
else to do. He had so little experience to guide him.
Blindly, he relied on Evangeline to show him what she
needed, leaning close to whisper against her hair. "Yes,
Evie, yes," he encouraged. "Come with me."

When she came, it was with an explosion of force. She
seemed literally to shatter against him, to splinter in his
arms, seized by a deep, shuddering climax that drew him
down with her into an abyss of hot, pulling need. Evangeline trembled uncontrollably in his arms, and he heard
himself rasp out her name. And then blessed relief; he
was coming apart with her, within her, spilling his seed

into her womb and crying out as if he had never before
spent himself inside a woman.

He collapsed against her and felt her, still trembling
beneath him. She cradled his face in her hands and
sought his mouth with hers, waiting for his breathing to
calm. Her heart beat hard against his. Or was it his heart
that pounded so wildly? As she pulled her mouth from
his, he felt her reach up to spear her fingers through his
hair, now damp with sweat. For a long, timeless moment,
they remained thus, and he felt the remaining tension
slip from their still-joined bodies.

"Elliot, my love," she whispered at last, her tone reverent. He froze, then lifted his face from hers and stared at
her. "Ah, yes. My love ... for I do love you," she murmured drowsily. Evie's eyes were closed, her lashes lush
against her skin. She was drifting very near sleep now.
Only a smear of dampness marred her perfect thigh, and
Elliot was struck with the realization of what it represented: innocence lost. Slowly, Elliot rolled to her side to
let his heart still, keeping one leg hooked possessively
over her.

She loved him? He did not believe it. Not really. Her
goodness and purity were astonishing. He, an irre-
deemable blackguard, had dared to defile her, a woman
he could not begin to deserve, and in response, she had
whispered love words to him. Elliot knew that he should
be ashamed, yet he thrust away the ugliness of what he
had just done and clung greedily to those very words.
With a newfound urgency, Elliot pulled her closer still
and settled her into the crook of his arm. What had just
passed between them had surely felt true and beautiful.
More than a mating, more than just a gratification of
sexual need. But love? How could she love him? She did
not know him. And yet she had said the words. He closed
his eyes and savored their sweetness and magic. Such

words were a rare gift, and he would forever treasure them, whether or not she meant them tomorrow.

Against his ribs, Evangeline stirred, only half awake. She slid one hand up the length of his chest, letting her fingers play across the skin, taking comfort in the smell of him and in the taut strength of his muscles. Slowly, she let her eyes come open and tilted her chin to look up at him. In the darkness, he was watching her.

She had said that she loved him, Evangeline realized with a start. And the vow had been prompted by something more than the beauty of his loving. But she would think about that tomorrow. Snuggling closer, Evangeline skimmed her hand higher to caress his harsh jaw, and then down his neck and across the top of his shoulder.

High on his shoulder, she felt a second scar. No, not exactly a scar. Just a superficial wound. She felt him flinch ever so slightly and let her hand slide away. "Elliot," she mumbled sleepily, "you must be more careful."

His words sounded strained. " 'Tis naught, Evie. A flesh wound," he answered, threading the fingers of one hand gently through her hair. "Sleep, sweet. I want to love you again before I have to let you slip from my bed."

"Umm," she answered, snuggling deeper into the covers. And then she did sleep, deeply and dreamlessly, beside him. When she awoke, the storm had ended and the lamp was out. Elliot, still awake, feathered his mouth across her face, then made love to her again with his mouth, his hands, and his body, filling her with an aching sweetness and bringing her to blessed release.

Afterward, they remained entangled in each other until it was time for her to slip away to her own bed.

§11§

By the pricking of my thumbs, something wicked
this way comes . . .
—WILLIAM SHAKESPEARE

$\mathcal{E}$vangeline had come to believe that happiness was often short-lived. Nonetheless, the maelstrom of trouble that descended upon Chatham Lodge came far more quickly than even she might have guessed. After a night of pure bliss in Elliot's arms, Evangeline had crept quietly back to her own bedchamber in the hours just before dawn. After seeing *Leopold* packed and shipped, she breakfasted alone with a taciturn Etienne, who hung over his coffee like a dejected dog. The comte, undoubtedly frustrated by his rather ephemeral and inconstant *affaire de coeur* with Winnie, made no further mention of France. He and Winnie had argued again, it was clear. With a little stab of annoyance at Winnie, Evangeline pretended not to notice his disappointment, then kissed Etienne's cheek good-bye and saw him on his way to London.

After her guest's departure, it was time to retire to her studio for a period of solitude before the children arose. She wanted to be alone with her thoughts of Elliot. She wanted to sit quietly and relive every moment of the previous night—except, perhaps, for one. Would he be the same this morning? Would her impulsive, artless vow have changed anything between them? She and Elliot were lovers now. Did not lovers share words of love, even when they did not entirely mean them? Elliot, though, had not said them. Evangeline had. And she was a little bit afraid that she had meant them. Nonetheless, she did not regret having said it. She had known intuitively that he needed to hear it, even if he did not.

In her discomfiture, she reminded herself that Elliot had asked her to marry him. But Evangeline had the impression that that was something a proper English gentleman felt compelled to say when he wanted a woman physically and did not wish to content himself with a mistress or a common prostitute. And although he never willingly discussed the ending of his betrothal, Evangeline understood that no one could easily recover from the loss of someone so obviously beloved. Yet she was not fool enough to believe that a man like Elliot did not have physical needs.

That was it, almost certainly. Elliot had lost the woman he truly loved. He had offered for Evangeline because he was fond of her and found her physically desirable, and, most likely, he would have obligingly married her. But Evangeline, with her blatant invitation, had made such a sacrifice wholly unnecessary. Perplexingly, however, Elliot had not looked relieved at her refusal. In fact, he had seemed quite angry, but as Winnie so often said, men were prideful creatures. Moreover, Elliot had quickly recovered from any disappointment he might have felt. That much had been obvious from the moment she had slipped into his room, into his arms, into his bed.

His bed. Oh, Lord. Evangeline had never known such pleasure. Already she was planning ways to be with him. Until she was forced by her step-grandmother to return to Flanders or her life took some other unexpected turn, Evangeline desperately hoped to keep Elliot as her friend and her lover. Squeezing her eyes shut, Evangeline refused even to consider the possibility that she might lose him. It was too painful to think about. Other than her family and her work, Elliot was her only need. She had a promise to keep, and she would do so, no matter the cost, but she needed Elliot. Oh, yes, she needed him very much.

For the remainder of the morning, Evangeline forced herself to work, busying herself by stretching canvases and touching up Elliot's portrait. It was essentially finished now, and could have been done weeks ago, but she was loath to part with it. After an hour had passed, the rest of the household began to wake and ramble down into the dining room for breakfast. Eventually, Nicolette drifted in to say good morning, then sauntered out into the sunshine of the terrace, leaving the doors open at Evangeline's request. The morning after a storm always seemed glorious, and she wanted to take full advantage of the sun, the breeze, and the extraordinary clear light.

Michael and Elliot soon followed, and the moment Michael's attention drifted away, Elliot planted a discreet kiss on her forehead. "Mmm," he said softly. "Sleep well, Evie?" His wicked, knowing smile warmed her in a way the sun never had.

"Indeed, Mr. Roberts," she replied nonchalantly as Michael rejoined them. "And I hope that you slept well, too?"

Elliot agreed that he had slept exceedingly well, then cheerfully acquiesced to Michael's plan that they join Nicolette on the terrace to sort out costumes for their Shakespearean comedy. Evangeline watched them go with a measure of disappointment, for she would have liked to have kept Elliot to herself for that special morning. But he was good for Michael, and that was important.

Elliot, she had come to realize, was a complex man. Evangeline had never ventured out into society, and that decision had been hers, not Maxwell Stone's. Winnie's girlhood friend, Lady Bland, had twice offered to bring

Evangeline out, but Evangeline had graciously declined. Until she had met Elliot, Evangeline had considered all gentlemen of the English aristocracy to be shallow, vain, and, in most cases, profligate. Elliot, however, was different, and Evangeline now felt a tinge of guilt for having mentally painted every Englishman with the same brush.

For the remainder of the morning, Evangeline continued to work in her studio. The children dashed in and out of the house, asking all manner of questions and lugging out mysterious books and boxes, but on the whole, the day seemed pleasant and ordinary. At about half past eleven, Evangeline thought she heard the rumble of carriage wheels rounding the circular drive but paid it little heed. Bolton by no means elevated butlering to any glorious height; however, one duty he unfailingly accomplished was the discreet but thorough interrogation of unknown visitors. Moreover, the elderly retainer was careful to announce all callers formally before allowing them admittance to the drawing room or studio.

Other than she and Winnie, who had not deigned to participate in Nicolette's theatrical production, the entire household had assembled on the lower terrace, where play practice was now in session. Aside from the occasional shouts of raucous laughter that floated up from the gardens, the house was serene.

Given all this, it was with great surprise that Evangeline heard the clamor of agitated voices erupt in the corridor outside her studio. The sharp, cultivated tone that carried most distinctly was rapidly approaching her door, even as Winnie's polite protestations ensued from further down the hall.

"Miss Stone most assuredly will see me, Mrs. Weyden," insisted the imperious voice, "or she shall see my attorneys. And we none of us want that, I should hope."

Winnie's polite rejoinder faded as a clatter of ladies'

heels arrived at Evangeline's open door. Stunned, she looked up to see an elderly lady standing, proud and ramrod-straight, upon her threshold. A cold, appraising gleam sparked in the lady's eyes as her gaze swept the room, and Evangeline was struck with the fleeting thought that the Conqueror himself must have looked just so as he sailed into Pevensey.

The woman was tall, slender, and elegantly attired in a black carriage dress which made a perfect foil for the silver of her elegantly coiffed hair. She possessed an icy sort of beauty which seemed to have faded very little, though Evangeline estimated her age at just over three score. An obviously disconcerted Winnie stood just to the lady's left. Behind them stood a couple: a beautiful raven-haired woman, exquisitely dressed in dark gray silk, and an older gentleman whom she held lightly by the elbow. A sick, sinking sensation hit Evangeline as she forced herself to rise from her desk chair. After almost ten years of relative peace, it seemed that her family had at last come to call.

Winnie pursed her lips in an angry gesture, then waltzed boldly forward into the room. "Pardon the interruption, Miss Stone," she began, reverting to their rarely used formalities. "May I present Honoria Stone, the dowager countess of Trent?"

As Winnie moved to stand beside the desk, Evangeline dropped into a stiffly elegant curtsy. "Your ladyship," she murmured coolly, returning her gaze to defiantly hold that of her visitor. "To what do we owe this unexpected pleasure?"

The dowager came forward into the room in a rustle of black silk, followed by her companions who trotted behind like dutiful hounds. At her quick, almost indiscernible motion, the couple obediently moved to flank the elderly dowager, and Evangeline could almost imagine her ordering them both to "sit" and "stay."

"I come on business, Miss Stone," the dowager began crisply. "May I introduce your uncle, Lord Trent, and his wife, Lady Trent?"

Evangeline eyed the gentleman appraisingly, taking some small measure of satisfaction when he paled visibly under her direct gaze. "My uncle is known to me, my lady," she replied with a cool nod in his direction, "and I am, of course, pleased to make the belated acquaintance of my aunt."

"You have a foreign accent," snipped the dowager unexpectedly.

Evangeline forced a wry smile. "That would depend, my lady, on one's definition of foreign. I can assure you that my Flemish is flawless, should it please you to converse in another language."

"Impudent wench! But of course, I expected no less." The dowager scowled, but Evangeline held her firmly frozen smile. "Well, girl? Will you ask us to be seated?"

Evangeline waved her hand, palm up, toward the sofa. "By all means. Would anyone care for coffee?"

Lord and Lady Trent murmured their refusals and dutifully took seats on the sofa on either side of the dowager as if they were the king's personal guard. Evangeline watched as the elderly woman settled stiffly onto the edge of her seat, then straightened her skirts. Beside her, Stephen Stone, the new earl of Trent, looked almost older than his stepmother, and Evangeline seemed to recall that the dowager was but a few years his elder. The younger Lady Trent, however, was no more than five and thirty and possessed of the same selfish eyes and brittle beauty as graced the dowager, a circumstance that was not surprising, since Evangeline knew that they were aunt and niece, as well as in-laws.

The marriage had been yet another tribute to Honoria Stone's power. When her son-in-law's first wife died childless, a new bride was imperative. Evangeline could easily guess Honoria's requirements: the second wife must be biddable, fertile, and possessed of excellent bloodlines. Who better, then, than Honoria's seventeen-year-old niece, a lovely girl who had just made her come-out? As soon as the minimal period of mourning had passed, the new bride was expediently ensconced at the ancient family seat, Cambert Hall.

It was strange, Evangeline thought as she surveyed her three callers. She felt very little fear or unease at their effrontery, just a calm sense of outrage and a strong willingness to fight. Paradoxically, though Evangeline had dreaded this battle, she now welcomed the opening salvo. There would be a certain relief in drawing the battle lines and engaging the enemy. The sooner the matter was resolved, the sooner Evangeline could get on with her life, wherever it might take her. She only hoped that the children—and Elliot—remained ignorant of the visitors.

Evangeline motioned Winnie toward one of the carved armchairs, then seated herself in the other. "Very well, then," she began crisply. "I can see that this business must be dire indeed, since it has brought you to Chatham after all these years. Pray begin."

Evangeline watched as the dowager narrowed her eyes and looked her up and down suspiciously. Finally, she spoke. "As you are obviously unaware, Miss Stone, your grandfather recently passed away."

Evangeline nodded curtly. "Indeed, I was aware, my lady. Our condolences on your loss." Winnie murmured her agreement.

The dowager frowned, displeased, perhaps, by their cool composure and good manners. "I assumed you had not heard," she answered acidly, "since you have not seen fit to put on your mourning."

"I have nothing to mourn, ma'am. I did not know him."

The dowager's gaze sharpened as she folded her gloved hands neatly in her lap. "So that is how it is to be, Miss Stone? I own, I should not be surprised at your attitude."

"Indeed, you should not. With all due respect, my lady, it was you who determined how things were to be—which is to say, nonexistent—between my grandfather and my father." Evangeline deliberately kept her voice polite but otherwise emotionless. "You must now excuse me if I cannot mourn the death of a man whose affection I was denied during his life."

"I see. Your disrespect is born of resentment."

Evangeline shook her head and smiled wanly. "No, indeed, my lady. You mistake me. I cannot think that we grandchildren have suffered greatly by the loss of our grandparents' regard, though we would have welcomed you—indeed, do welcome you—into our home at any time. And as you can see, you are here today, and with our every felicitation."

The dowager pulled a skeptical face, clearly nonplussed by Evangeline's equanimity, and stared pointedly at Winnie. "Mrs. Weyden, you are her guardian, are you not? Have you taught her no respect for her betters?"

Following Evangeline's example, Winnie smoothly refused the bait with her most simpering smile. "I daresay Miss Stone's manners are all that they should be, my lady. However, I am merely her companion. Evangeline is now of age, and my brother-in-law is their trustee."

"Bah! Naught but another foreigner," challenged the dowager.

"Perhaps you were unaware that Peter is half English," interjected Evangeline, "his mother having been a cousin to the earl of Fothereigh?"

"Indeed?" conceded the dowager with a stiff little tilt

of her head. "Nonetheless, it will be of no consequence. He is in trade. Moreover, the matter of his nationality pales in significance to the problem we must discuss today."

"Ah, yes. The problem. I pray you will explain it to us, ma'am," suggested Evangeline with exceeding politeness.

"Indeed, Miss Stone. Your grandfather is dead, and, as a family, we must now address the issue of primogeniture. Your uncle"—she wrinkled her nose and stared almost distastefully at the gray-haired man at her elbow—"has no heirs, and it appears highly unlikely that he will get any."

At this remark, which was made in the coldest of tones, the new Lady Trent dropped her chin and blushed effusively.

The dowager continued. "And since your Uncle Frederick died childless—"

"I beg to correct you, your ladyship," interposed Evangeline softly. "He left a beautiful child. That same daughter whose upbringing you refused five years ago."

The countess drew herself up sharply on the sofa. "Very well, Miss Stone. A daughter. A Portuguese bastard at that." She sniffed disdainfully. "Nonetheless, that is not what I meant, and well you know it. Frederick left no one to inherit. Your father, Maxwell, was the youngest son, therefore your brother, Michael, is now heir presumptive."

"I understand that," agreed Evangeline smoothly.

"Indeed? But what you must also understand is that as the heir to the Trent fortune and title, the boy must be brought up to do his family duty. He must be taught his social obligations and our political objectives. Furthermore, he must be properly educated in a fashion befitting the future earl of Trent. And eventually, he must marry in accordance with his station."

"What, precisely, are you suggesting, my lady?" asked Evangeline evenly.

"With the boy under my tutelage, I daresay society will soon forget that his mother was a foreigner and a commoner. The Trent heir cannot be left running wild in some heathen artist's colony where he is exposed to—to libertines and Continentals with revolutionary political ideals." The dowager sneered, letting her eyes drift with slow deliberation across the paintings and easels that lined the walls and littered the workspaces. "And I am sure that you want what is best for your impressionable young brother," she added caustically.

Evangeline struggled for composure now. It was exactly as she had feared, and in her growing unease Evangeline was only dimly attuned to the rising clamor of shrieking laughter and pounding footfalls which rang across the garden terrace.

"My lady," she began, forcing her breathing to calm, "I can assure you that under this roof Michael will learn all that is required of a future peer of the realm. And I can further assure you that we harbor no revolutionaries or libertines in our closets, nor does Michael *in any way run wild*—"

Unfortunately, the heir presumptive chose that very moment to do precisely that. He burst with a bloodcurdling scream through the open window, a wooden sword in hand. He stabbed madly at the draperies, then spun on his heel to bolt for the narrow staircase leading to the upper gallery. The boy wore Nicolette's lavender cloak, slung casually across his narrow shoulders, with a tattered wig of long blond ringlets askew atop his head, tilted rakishly forward over one eye. Apparently oblivious to the trio seated stiffly upon the distant sofa, Elliot and Theo bounded in on Michael's heels, their makeshift swords frantically flailing, their colorful capes flying out behind. In a swirl of lavender, Michael turned to face his pursuers, very nearly losing his mop of yellow curls.

"O God, Don Pedro!" shouted Elliot over his shoulder to Theo as they neatly pinned Michael against the steps with their wooden blades. "Here is a dish that I love not! I cannot endure this harping Lady Beatrice and shall run her through with my—"

His mangled oratory was cut short by an agonizing female scream. The sound tore through the room, reverberating off the vaulted ceiling. In that instant, Evangeline saw the new Lady Trent staggering to her feet. "Good God! Elliot!" She choked, clawing spasmodically at the black collar encircling her throat.

Her husband sprang from the sofa, his face suddenly florid. "Rannoch! You son of a bitch!" he added. "What the devil are you doing here?"

"Oh, dear Lord!" prayed his countess, still weaving unsteadily on her feet. Her voice dropped to a whisper as she slid into a dead faint on Evangeline's rug.

The dowager glared at her stepson. "Get her up, Stephen, you dolt!" she snapped, rising smoothly from the center of the sofa and stepping neatly over her daughter-in-law's body. The elderly woman stared through narrowed eyes at Elliot, whose gaze was firmly fixed on the comatose woman in the floor.

"*Jeanette?*" he croaked, lifting his eyes to survey the crowd one by one. His normally handsome face was swiftly losing all color as his eyes finally settled upon Evangeline. "*Evie?*"

"Ah-ha!" answered the dowager, striding into the center of the melee, her face already swollen with anger. Her long, bony finger pointed unwaveringly at Elliot, but her eyes held Evangeline's with heated anger. "I see the way of this now, Miss Stone. Did you think to surprise us with a protector? If so, you chose well. Very well indeed, but this battle is not over—not nearly over."

Winnie now knelt alongside the earl of Trent, anxiously fanning a deathly white Jeanette Stone. Gus, whom Evangeline had not seen enter the room, had joined his mother on the floor. The dowager spun to face them. "Pick her up, Stephen! For God's sake, stop that infernal fanning. Just put her in my carriage."

Still on his knees, the earl of Trent faced the dowager, his mouth gaping open. He shut it, then opened it again, but no sound came out.

Gus shot a sidelong glance at his anxious mother. Upon Winnie's curt nod of approval, Gus smoothly scooped up Jeanette's limp body and rose from the floor. Her mind very nearly unhinged, Evangeline choked on a hysterical burst of laughter at the sight, for Gus wore a makeshift leather jerkin, paired with puce tights and belted with a length of rope. At his side, another rough-hewn sword dangled loosely, and on his head, he sported a pointy green cap with a feather so enormous that it arced neatly around to tickle the nose of the woman whose head lay limply against his shoulder.

Winnie rose to stand beside her son, looking almost as drawn and pale as Lady Trent. The pervasive feeling of hysteria was growing. The entire scene felt unreal, at once absurdly funny and horribly frightening. Suddenly, Evangeline could not breathe. Reality began to sink in, and something felt horribly wrong. In a split second, her life seemed to have changed, resulting in wild panic edged with an aching sense of loss. It cut Evangeline to the heart. Fighting to subdue a rolling wave of anxiety, Evangeline let her eyes flit across the room, trying to make sense of the appalling farce.

Who was here? Elliot. Jeanette. Uncle Stephen. *Rannoch?*

Gus strode across the carpet, Lady Trent's gray silk skirts draped elegantly across his right arm. Uncle Stephen followed behind with his head held low. Nicolette and Frederica had entered the room at some point and now stood looking anxious and contrite along the bank of French windows. Appearing even more repentant, Michael and Theo hovered in the corner as if awaiting punishment for a crime they did not quite comprehend but felt nonetheless accountable for.

The dowager countess of Trent finished a low, curt exchange with Elliot, whose visage had turned into a dark, threatening glower. The dowager then swept out the studio door followed by Stephen. Gus trailed behind, carrying Lady Trent, who had begun to stir. Her sweep of gray silk was the last thing to vanish out the studio door.

They were gone, Evangeline realized as an expectant hush fell over the studio.

"Well, Evie," murmured Winnie, breaking the uncertain silence, "look on the bright side. Maybe Jeanette Stone is *enceinte* at last! After all, that was an exceedingly impressive swoon!"

Within five minutes, the studio was desolate and empty, save Evangeline and Elliot, who stood on opposite sides of her imposing desk. Even as the Trent equipage was rolling away down Chatham's drive, Winnie was shooing the children out of the room and pulling shut the offending French windows as she departed for the gardens, leaving them alone, faced off like enemies.

Inside, the vast chamber was so silent that Elliot imagined he could hear the freshly stretched canvases creaking. The mingled odors of solvent and oil permeated the air, which seemed suddenly thick and still. Outside, the sun was still shining, and it was, Elliot supposed, entirely possible that the fluffy white clouds were still merrily scuttling and the birds were still happily singing. In Elliot's heart, however, all joy had come to an agonizing halt and now hung suspended, awaiting Evangeline's next words.

"Who are you?" Her voice was soft, but it nonetheless managed to pierce the silence, as well as Elliot's soul. Absently shuffling the papers on her desktop, Evangeline did not look at him.

Elliot carefully considered his answer and realized that he did not have one. Not a good one.

"Who are you?" she repeated weakly, this time lifting her eyes to his. Her expression was flat and emotionless, but her voice was a haunted whisper. "You're the marquis of Rannoch, are you not? But I should like to hear the admission from your own lips."

For the first time in his life, Elliot had to stay himself from literally wringing his hands. "Miss Stone—Evie—I can explain . . ."

"Explain?" she asked quizzically. "Explain what? That you lied to me? That you lied to my family? Is this your idea of a joke? Or is it just some mean-spirited betting-book wager?"

Elliot saw the familiar blue fire flash in her eyes, but this time it had nothing to do with passion. "Evie, forgive me. I never said—"

"Why did you come here, Lord Rannoch, and ingratiate yourself into my household?" The calm had splintered now, and her rising tone began to take on a shrill, almost hysterical edge. "Explain that, if you can, though I daresay I have some idea of what revenge you hoped to gain."

Elliot felt himself begin to tremble weakly. Good God, she thought he had done it maliciously. On purpose. "Evie, darling," he began to plead, "it was an accident. Please believe me when I say—"

"Believe you? A deceitful blackguard?" She almost screamed the words, and Elliot suddenly realized just how incredible his story would sound. Especially now, following the appearance of Stephen and Jeanette Stone. Indeed, he was forced to admit that the truth would seem laughable. Who would believe that the wicked marquis of Rannoch had sought nothing more than shelter, then friendship, and finally peace, within the walls of a pretty house filled with pleasant people?

How could he explain to Evangeline the emotional hunger—indeed, he could think of no better description for that compelling force—that had driven him to deviously misrepresent his identity and his purpose? He had wanted—no, needed—to tell her. Now, too late, his mind was scrambling for the right words.

This was madness. He had known it all along. And he had known that it would someday end. But never had he dreamed that by the time the farce was over, he would have come to rely upon these people for friendship and comfort. And far more than that, where Evangeline was concerned. Oh, God, much, much more. With a visceral agony, Elliot remembered her soft affirmations of love, passionate words borne on her warm breath and whispered against his ear at the height of her sweet feminine arousal. Yes, mere hours ago.

Damn it, who would have known that he would come to need Evangeline like this? With an aching desperation that cut through him like a knife? That he might need her in a way he had never before needed anyone? Or worse still, that he might actually hurt her? Oh, God! Perhaps he *did* love her. He did not know, and it hardly mattered. Not any longer. These people meant more to him than weak, inadequate words like friendship, comfort, or even love could define. They had come to constitute his reason for living, his very identity, or at least the identity of the person he wanted to be. Elliot Roberts.

Not Elliot Robert Armstrong, the false-hearted marquis of Rannoch, who scarcely gave a damn for anyone or anything. And in that moment, given the choice, Elliot realized that he would have traded his name, his power, his estates, and indeed his very last sou, if only he could have become Elliot Roberts and severed himself from the marquis of Rannoch forever. But he did not have that choice. Fate and his own perfidy had destined that he would forever live on the edge of emptiness, forever be an outsider who merely looked in upon something that was pure and beautiful.

Evangeline was still staring at him as if he were the very embodiment of evil. "Good God, Elliot," she whispered hoarsely, "you were my aunt's lover! What's worse, everyone knows it."

"That was another mistake," Elliot bit out. "I have made a great many, and if you will just give me a—"

"I shall give you nothing, sir! And you have made your last mistake here." The words were uttered with a chilling confidence. Evangeline was beautiful in her fury. And frightening, too. In truth, she was beginning to look quite dangerous. Stepping away from the chair, she began to circle slowly from behind her desk.

Not only were her eyes flaming, but her hands had begun to tremble with barely suppressed rage. Suddenly, Elliot had a horrific vision of her artist's temperament unleashed in the worst sort of way. Angry women disconcerted him. No, that was not entirely true. In the past, angry women had *inconvenienced* him. And the marquis of Rannoch quickly rid himself of all inconveniences.

In this case, however, expediency was not an option. This woman he must somehow keep. "Evangeline, darling, if you will just give me a chance to explain—"

"Explain?" She shrieked the word, throwing her hands in the air and waving them madly about. "*Explain?* Given any choice in the matter, my lord, I have just heard you utter your last filthy lie! I shall thank you to leave this house. The sooner your dust settles, the better off we shall all be."

Elliot was stunned to realize that she had no intention of hearing his explanations. Her anger was potent. And contagious. It leapt toward him like a spark from a raging fire. "Evie, please! You cannot think . . . I never said—"

"Now see here, Elliot Armstrong—Lord Rannoch—or whoever you are—"

"Just *Elliot,* damn it!" he rasped, one hand clutched in an angry fist at his side.

"Whatever." Scorn laced her rage. "You led us to believe that you—you—you allowed us to accept you into our home as an honored guest, as a friend, as a—"

Elliot felt his lips turn up into a cold smile. "Aye, say it, Evangeline," he hissed venomously. "As your *lover.*"

Despite his hard-earned experience in evading irate women, Elliot never saw the blow coming. Evangeline's hand contacted his jaw with a resounding crack that echoed through the vaulted room.

After a long, silent pause, Elliot tentatively touched his stinging flesh with the tips of his fingers. "I deserved that, I suppose."

"You lying bastard!" she screamed. "What you deserve is to be hanged!"

That was just too damn much, even for Elliot Roberts. "Oh? And were you truthful with me, Evie?" challenged Elliot, deliberately keeping his voice soft. He began to edge carefully toward her.

"I have no notion what you mean," she insisted, her eyes flashing blue fire.

"Perhaps I mean many things," he whispered, taking one more step toward her. "But let's start with your identity, shall we? Why did you not identify yourself as the earl of Trent's granddaughter?"

Evangeline took a step backward, as if she knew she'd gone too far. "Why, how dare you try to turn the tables on me, you dissolute rakehell, you—you *despoiler of women!*"

Elliot felt red-hot anger explode in his chest. "Aye, you've taken the viper to your breast, quite literally, have you not, Miss Stone? And now you are ashamed. Embarrassed, in fact. That's a big part of this little farce, isn't it?"

"You're bloody right," she bit back at him.

Elliot deliberately dropped his voice to a dark, silky whisper and took another step closer. "Are you embarrassed about us, Evie?" He watched in satisfaction as her eyes opened wide with shock. "Are you embarrassed about how you respond to me? How you grow wet to my touch? How you writhe beneath me?" He reached out to grasp her trembling chin in his hand.

Evie, beginning to blink back tears, tried to jerk away. "Get away from me, you devil." Her voice was a soft hiss.

"Oh, aye, Evie. I'm the devil, all right. And last night, you were begging to step into the fire." In his anger, Elliot had now backed her up against the wall behind her desk. He wanted to stop, tried to stop, yet as he watched Evangeline's tears of anger, he could not. How dare she refuse to hear his explanations? Didn't she know that he loved her?

Oh, Jesus. *He loved her.* Beyond reason. And she hated him now with her blue-flame eyes and her burning artist's heart.

Trapped between the wall and Elliot's chest, Evangeline began to squirm, shoving hard against his shoulders with the heels of her hands. "Get away from me, Elliot," she whispered. "Get out of this house. Out of my life."

Nevertheless, she was no match for Elliot's sheer size, and as she writhed against him, his rage and pain flared, then melded into something uncontrollable. He wanted to make her feel it, too. To make her see the truth of what was between them. Lashing one arm firmly around her waist, he forced Evangeline's hips hard against his. Bending his head low, he took her mouth, still cupping her jaw hard in his hand. When she refused to open for him and tried to turn her face away, Elliot tightened his grip and slipped his thumb up to coax open her mouth.

Elliot felt rather than heard her little whimper of surrender as Evangeline's lips gave way to his ravaging. Slowly, deliberately, he slid into the warm recesses of her mouth, pleading and coaxing her with his tongue. *Want me. Take me. Give to me,* he begged her with his every thrust, slipping his hand lower to cup her soft, round bottom.

When the force of Evangeline's palms against his shoulders finally weakened, Elliot growled his satisfaction and slid his hand from her jaw and around to the nape of her neck. He felt hope when her hands began to skim lightly down his torso to rest low on his hips, and he caught a glimpse of victory when her arms went around his waist. Then Elliot, his rage and pain now little more than blind, hungry need, made a tactical error. When Evangeline surrendered completely and entered his mouth, he slowly lifted his lips from hers and slid them around to brush the warm, silky flesh beneath her ear. "Evangeline," he begged, his voice a hoarse whisper, "say you still love me. *Please.*"

In a flash, she had twisted away from him and was backing toward the door. "Oh, you just couldn't resist, could you?" she shrieked, her face devoid of all color, her hands thrust forward in an irrationally defensive gesture.

"I have never been able to resist you, Evie," he answered honestly, his palms turned up in supplication.

"You really are the devil incarnate!" Evangeline screamed, backing toward the door. "You could not resist the opportunity to humiliate me once more, could you? To make me feel like the whore you want me to be. A whore like Jeanette and the hundreds of others you've no doubt had." Her expression had contorted into a caricature of pain and anger. Her eyes darted about wildly, as if searching for something to throw.

"Evie, you are wrong!" Elliot made a move toward her, but she jerked open the door.

He took one more step, and Evangeline's eyes settled on a cast-iron doorstop near her feet. "Take your sweet words of seduction, Rannoch, and get the hell out of my house!" She seized the heavy chunk of metal, spitting out his title as if it were an insult to her lips. "I'll not be one of your filthy diversions, so do not ever come here again. It sickens me to know how I trusted you!"

As Elliot opened his mouth to plead with her, Evangeline heaved the chunk of metal at his head. It fell blessedly short, goring out a chunk of the ancient stone floor and sending it flying through the air. And then, in a whirl of blue muslin, Evangeline was gone, banging the door shut behind her. Through it, Elliot had caught a fleeting glance of Gus Weyden standing in the hall beyond, an expression of loathing indelibly etched onto his face.

Bloody, bloody hell! Gus had overheard everything. Not only was Evie gone from his life, but the people whose respect and friendship he had come to treasure now knew the truth of what he was, and they were disgusted by it. Elliot felt weak, as if the heavy oak door had just swung shut on his heart, slamming both blood and breath from his chest. For a timeless moment, he stood, staring at the door, until slowly, inexorably, he fell to his knees on the thick Oriental carpet beneath the desk. Evangeline was gone.

She meant it. She hated him. Any love, any desire she had felt had not been for him at all; it had been a gift from God, to a man who did not exist. Just a deception he had ruthlessly crafted, a man who could never be. Elliot felt an unfamiliar ache wrap itself around his heart, and then the sobs took hold, choking and sucking the air from his lungs. He was alone. Time stood still. Elliot remained on his knees, his arms still outstretched, until numbness set in and there were no more tears to shed.

"Evangeline," he whispered into the stillness, "I'm sorry. I'm sorry. I love you."

Morning did come at last to Chatham Lodge, yet it mattered very little to Evangeline. From her seated position in bed, she pulled the heavy covers high against her chest and shivered uncontrollably. She was cold, so cold. Inside and out. Chilled to the core of her soul.

Throughout the evening and endless night, Evangeline had remained closeted in her room, pacing the floor, awaiting the tears that would not come. Now she sat slumped in surrender, her anger incinerated, her heart hollow. There was no grief, she told herself insistently. Grief insinuated loss, and she simply could not allow herself to believe that Elliot had been hers to lose. The implication would be too profound, the pain too much to bear. Already, sweet dreams of all they had shared tormented her fitful sleep.

Oh, but she did grieve! Evangeline suppressed a wretched sob. She grieved for the loss of a dream. The loss not just of a lover but of a deep and abiding friendship. She had trusted Elliot with her secrets, her hopes, and her heart, sharing with him in the most intimate things a woman could share with a man. How lowering it was to realize that his feelings for her had been a sham, undoubtedly a part of Rannoch's vengeful scheme.

And then, when he had been caught out in his machinations, the marquis had proposed marriage. The audacity of it! She almost wished she *had* hit him with the damned doorstop. Oh, Rannoch must have something vile up his sleeve! Why else would he have made her such an offer? Evangeline simply could not allow herself the indulgence of hoping that his had been an honorable proposal.

Roused by the force of sheer indignation, Evangeline heaved the bedcovers onto the floor and began to strip off her nightclothes. A slow burn of anger subdued her sorrow. By God, what she wanted now was revenge—of any sort—for the pain and embarrassment Rannoch had caused her. And it was not just her pain for which she sought vengeance. The faces of the children last night had been agonizing.

At that memory, Evangeline began ripping the clothing from her wardrobe in search of a gown and some slippers. Finding both, she tugged them on with a ruthless energy. She thanked heaven for Gus, who had risen to the occasion with a maturity Evangeline had not known the young man possessed. Initially, she had been horrified to see him standing outside her studio following her ugly altercation with Elliot. Clearly, Gus had overheard every vile word that had passed between them. And yet Gus had quietly and understandingly stepped in to smooth over the dreadful events of the afternoon.

For once, Evangeline had been too absorbed in her own pain, and Winnie too choked with rage, to manage the near crisis. It hurt to think of how Gus had tried to console the children by murmuring some vague explanation for the three visitors, as well as an excuse for Elliot's sudden departure. When he elaborated, however, by saying that Elliot would be too busy in London to return to Chatham, Frederica had sobbed wretchedly.

It was all too dreadful to think about. In frustration, Evangeline tore a smock from the hook inside her wardrobe and yanked it over her head. Carelessly, she wrestled her hair into some semblance of an arrangement and stormed out the door.

Perhaps she could not wreak Rannoch's sort of vengeance, but she could certainly vent her ire in her own way. He was cruel—barbaric, even. Yes, that's what he was, and that is what the world should see him as. Dear God, how had they been fooled by him? Worse, how could she hunger for such a man? How could she have given herself up to him with such reckless abandon? She felt her face grow hot with embarrassment at how she had behaved, willingly, breathlessly spreading her legs for Rannoch like a common strumpet, with less than a moment's hesitation.

And she had enjoyed it. Yes, damn it, she had. At the thought of his heavy hands on her, Evangeline felt her traitorous nipples grow hard and eager beneath her paint-spattered smock. She tried to will away the memory of how his strong, long-fingered hands had teased and entranced her, how they had wrapped about her waist, then slid down, to effortlessly ease her bottom up against him so that he might fill her with pleasure. The sudden rush of arousal was hot and real; Evangeline wanted to feel him thrusting into her again.

Almost missing a step, Evangeline tried to focus on the twisting staircase beneath her feet. She all but flew around the next turn. *He's a devil,* her inner voice shouted, further goading her wrath. She forced away her baser urges and concentrated on hate, not lust. What a vile, deceitful, depraved bastard! How amusing he must have found her family's artless, provincial ways. How he must have laughed at her easy surrender to his expert seduction. She burst through the doors of her studio, realizing that the *whats* and the *hows* came freely enough, but the *whys* still evaded all logic.

Why would the marquis of Rannoch come to Chatham Lodge, she wondered as she dragged his portrait off the wall and shoved the frame onto an empty easel. Why would he ingratiate himself, charm her family, then seduce her? Why would someone she loved—no, *thought* she had loved—hurt her so profoundly when there had been so little to gain? Was it really retaliation? It was true that finding Rannoch at Chatham had incensed her step-grandmother, but the dowager had not been publicly humiliated, and she was far from defeated.

Evangeline went to her worktable, scrabbled through her pigment trays, and jerked out an assortment of brushes. Ruthlessly, she ground and scraped and stirred, slamming containers as she went, all the while wondering if the marquis truly wanted nothing more than revenge. For a moment, she paused just long enough to look at the mess she had made, ignored it, and went on. Certainly, Rannoch was known to be vengeful, yet that theory made no sense. Perhaps he had hoped to parlay their relationship into something far uglier. Something that would enable him to wield influence over Michael? At that thought, a bottle of oil slipped from her grasp and thudded onto the rug. *Michael?*

Perhaps her brother was the means to an end, and Rannoch sought vengeance, pure and simple. The blood was undeniably bad between the marquis and the Stone family. Because of the Stones, society had had a rare laugh at Rannoch's expense, and undoubtedly he had not forgotten. Though Jeanette Stone had reputedly taken many lovers in her desperate attempt to beget an heir, Rannoch was the first to be caught—and in a very painful, very public way. By Jeanette's half-witted husband, no less. The humiliation of being effectively treated like a standing stud could only have been surpassed by a ball of lead in the buttocks.

But that Evangeline should have been used as the instrument of his revenge, that she—and potentially Michael—could have been so cruelly manipulated, yes, that hurt almost as much as the loss itself.

By the time Winnie found Evangeline, hours later, the air reeked with the smell of solvent. In the center of the chaos, Evangeline sat on a stool, leaning intently into the portrait, steadily at work. Winnie knocked softly on the open door and slipped inside, almost unnoticed. Standing beside the artist and the canvas, Winnie stared at the portrait and shot Evangeline a look of grim sarcasm.

Muttering something that sounded suspiciously like "Satan in a kilt, eh?" Winnie shrugged, then crossed the room to the bank of windows and began to neaten the draperies. Outside, another brilliant morning was unfolding.

"Evie, my dear," she sighed, finally turning from the windows to face her. "We must talk. I refuse to pretend that he has not hurt you very badly. I am sorry."

Evangeline stiffened her spine and pulled herself erect on her stool. "Thank you, Winnie. So am I. I did not need this. Not right now. None of us did."

Gracefully, Winnie came toward her and gathered her into a warm embrace. "Oh, Evie," she murmured, "to think that I encouraged you! You must believe me a worthless chaperone!"

"Nonsense, Winnie," she answered, pushing her gently away to hold her at arm's length. "You did nothing to make matters worse. It was I who—who—"

"Fell in love?" Winnie asked, staring down and absently scooting her toe through a glop of white paint on the flagstone. "You did, I know. And I let it happen. Do not deny it."

Evangeline turned her head away, resolutely biting at her lip. She would not cry. She would not, for once the tears began, Evangeline was not entirely convinced that they would ever stop. Or that she would ever be able to see things clearly again.

She turned back to see Winnie's hands fisting in the fabric of her skirt. "Why, Evie? Why do you think Elliot misled us? I have wracked my brain all night for an answer. To deliberately do something so—so odious . . . it just makes no sense!"

"It was all a ruse, Winnie," she answered bitterly, staring at the Scottish barbarian who was rapidly taking shape on the canvas before her. "Perhaps it was his idea of a joke on Uncle Stephen. But I rather suspect it was far more malicious than that."

Winnie looked doubtful. "But how could he know of us?"

Evangeline's expression hardened as she laid her knife against the canvas, peeling away one of Rannoch's ears with a ruthless scrape of the blade. She would bloody well like to use it on another part of his anatomy altogether. "We're hardly hermits, Winnie. I'll own we're reclusive, but we've not hidden from the world."

"But you *have*," protested Winnie. "You've deliberately avoided society. You insist on painting under your mother's surname. Other than your trips to see Peter, you never go into London."

"Merely to avoid Father's family—"

"Indeed, and it has worked perfectly! Society scarcely knows of your existence, let alone your association with the earldom of Trent." She leaned closer toward the painting, a bit of color draining from her face. "My God, Evie . . . what have you done to his eyes?"

"And just what is wrong with them?" snapped Evangeline.

"Well . . ." Winnie shuddered. "Even Rannoch never looked quite *that* wicked . . . and what the devil is he doing with that big sword thing?"

"It's called a claymore, Winnie." Evangeline shot her a dark, narrow look. "And when did you begin to fancy yourself an art critic?"

"Fine! A claymore, then. Nonetheless, I must tell you, that is the most dreadful painting I've ever seen." Then, with another equivocal shrug, Winnie returned to her original argument. "And anyway, how could Rannoch seek you out? If his plan were so preconceived, how would he find you? Or know that you were lovely? And of age? How would he know about Michael?"

"What are you implying, Winnie?" Evangeline's voice was cold. "Rannoch is licentious and treacherous, a cold-hearted gamester, a cruelly vindictive man who ruins innocent young girls—and those are among his finer qualities."

Her companion paused, then pensively caught her lower lip between her teeth. She began to pace back and forth across the studio, her kid slippers swishing softly over the flagstone. "I just do not know, Evie," she finally answered. "Do you remember the day Ell—Rannoch came to Chatham?"

Did she remember? Evangeline put down her knife with a clatter and pressed the palm of her hand into her throbbing forehead. Good God—how could she forget? "Yes, I remember," she quietly answered. "It was raining."

"Well, I remember, too," replied Winnie with a distant look in her eyes. "There was something so exceedingly odd about it all. He seemed most unsure of himself. Do you recollect how apprehensive he looked when I called him by the wrong name?"

Evangeline's brow furrowed. "Yes—I suppose I'd forgotten."

Winnie nodded, her eyes narrowing perceptively. "He remarked upon having other business in the area. And then the next day, you said he turned toward Wrotham Ford?"

Evangeline exhaled irritably. "And your point is . . . ?"

With a crooked smile, Winnie opened her hands in plaintive exasperation. "Well, there is just something odd about it all, is there not? A man comes to a portrait sitting—five hours late, mind you—in a drenching rain. And then just happens to have business in Wrotham Ford? What sort of business? There's nothing there."

"Indeed," whispered Evangeline slowly. "And he looked surprised when I mentioned Wrotham-upon-Lea, as if he'd never heard of it. He seemed quite unacquainted with the local villages."

"Yes!" replied Winnie, walking quickly toward the easel. "And I must tell you something else. I looked in my peerage this morning. The full name of the marquis of Rannoch is Elliot Robert Armstrong. Is that not odd?"

"Odd in what way?" asked Evangeline resistantly. She took up her brush and slapped a dollop of gray paint on what had once been a cloudless blue sky.

"Well, if a man wanted to be taken for someone else, why would he use the better part of his own name?"

"Because he's insane," retorted Evangeline.

"Moreover, you said he knew nothing of portraits," persisted Winnie. "Indeed, you said that he did not even know what he wanted! It merely occurs to me that if it was all some sort of ruse, he did a most unsatisfactory job of thinking it through."

Evangeline whirled about on her stool to stare pointedly at her companion. "But what else could it be, Winnie? There is no other explanation, particularly in light of—in light of his later behavior."

"Toward you?"

Evangeline felt her face grow warm. "Yes," she admitted softly.

"What, precisely, are you confessing here, Evangeline?" Winnie's voice dropped to a whisper. "No—never mind. I suppose I do not wish to be sure. Perhaps I have no wish to recognize just how badly I have failed in my duties."

"As to duty, Winnie, any failure on that score has been entirely mine," Evangeline replied. She choked back the hot press of tears. "I know my duty, too, yet I foolishly allowed myself to be blinded by things I should never have contemplated."

Unexpectedly, Winnie reached down to lay a cool, smooth hand against Evangeline's cheek. "Is it so hard to imagine, Evie, that the man might have been charmed by you? That his affection might have been genuine? Oh, I know he is wicked, but perhaps he came under false pretenses and found himself falling—"

"That's enough romantic drivel, Winnie," interrupted Evangeline, spinning back to her work. "Whatever he was about, 'tis over and done. And we now have the perfidy of Honoria Stone to deal with."

"Why, you cannot imagine she would dare to return here?" asked Winnie, aghast.

"Before the week is out," snapped Evangeline. "Depend upon it."

"Hmm . . . you may be right," mused Winnie, turning toward the door. "I'd best warn Bolton to keep a sharp eye out."

"Bolton?" muttered Evangeline absently. "Yes, pray do so."

As Winnie stepped across the threshold, she suddenly whirled about to face Evangeline. "Oh, and Evie?"

"Yes?" Evangeline's tone was impatient.

"About that claymore thing you've painted there ... isn't that a Highlander's weapon?"

Rather annoyed at her companion's teasing tone, Evangeline looked up from her work. Winnie went on, her eyes twinkling. "I mean—I do seem to recall that being the case ... and the Armstrongs are, after all, more of a Lowlands clan."

"Artistic license," hissed Evangeline, slapping on another blop of gray paint. "Symbolism."

"Oh! *Symbolism!*" Brows arched high, Winnie shot her a knowing grin. "Why, my dear, you quite put me to the blush!" Then, with a speed that belied her mature years, Winnie darted through the door, expertly dodging the paintbrush Evangeline hurled at her head.

§12§

Much drinking, and little thinking.
—JONATHAN SWIFT

*T*wo whole days had passed, had Elliot been fully cognizant of time, when Old Scratch rose up from the pits of perdition to whip open his heinous toolbox. In the frightful, suffocating darkness, however, Elliot could discern only one sure thing. The devil's minions had forcibly wedged his head in a vise and were proceeding to beat him senseless with a sledgehammer. Whilst they were at their handiwork, another determined crew set about hacking out his temples with a brace of rusty wood chisels; and down below, a third malicious little rogue poked holes in his bowels with a hot iron rod.

Bam! Bam! Bam! The devil's chosen instrument pounded upon his skull, then relented, but briefly. *Bam! Bam! Bam!* Each blow to his forehead made his brain rattle like shattering glass, and the ensuing pain made him want to retch. Yet the incessant pounding was nothing when compared to the slicing shaft of light that suddenly caught him full in the face, piercing his eyes like a sharp knife intent on laying open his cranium.

"Get up, you laggard!" grumbled Sir Hugh, drawing back another heavy velvet bed hanging with a vicious yank. "And roll over, for pity's sake. You're so snared up in those damn sheets, 'tis a wonder you've not smothered."

Bam! Bam! Bam! The infernal pounding jarred his very bed now.

Elliot forced one eye back open. Just a crack.

It was too far. He saw Matthew Winthrop standing at the foot of his bed, rapping energetically against the mahogany footboard with one massive fist. He appeared to be upside down, too.

"Up and at 'em, Sleeping Beauty!" Winthrop howled joyously. "Had to let ourselves in, don'cha know," he added with mock solemnity, "since you ignored our polite knocking."

Like magic, a small silver tray holding a delicate teacup materialized out of the depths of hell and appeared in his unfocused field of view. Elliot was further mystified to see that it, too, was upside down. However, the tea, or whatever it held, did not spill. With a manful grunt, Elliot rolled over.

Ah. Better. But not much. The bed took a couple of turns about the room, then spun slowly to a stop.

"What have you there, Kem?" he heard Winthrop ask. "Hair of the dog?"

"Hardly, Major," Elliot heard his valet trill. "This is my secret hangover remedy." The salver, now right-side up, edged measurably closer. "Now, drink it down, my lord. There's a good fellow."

Bravely, Elliot heaved himself up onto one wobbly elbow, lifted the teacup, and swilled courageously. The result was almost instantaneous. Fortunately for all, Kemble was equally swift with the chamber pot.

"Christ, Kem!" yelped Winthrop, jumping back from the paroxysm of spewing, gagging, and hacking. "Call that a remedy? He looks damn near dead now."

"Ugh," grunted Sir Hugh, peering at the mess from the opposite side of Elliot's bed. He shook his gray head as if in puzzlement. "Ain't a chit in England worth this, my boy." With one smooth yank, he stripped back the covers. "Come on, Kemble. Let us get 'im up and into that wing chair. Ought not be able to fall out of that, I daresay."

"Nooooo!" Elliot heard himself wail, even as his toes slid off the bed to trail limply through the thick pile of his opulent bedroom carpet. "Out of my house, Hugh, you worthless son of a bitch! You are dismissed, Kem! Get away from me! Bugger you both, damn it!"

"Ooh!" squealed Kem in mock delight. "What an invitation! And you're *sooo* attractive this morning!"

As Major Winthrop chuckled sympathetically, Elliot found himself summarily dropped into the aforementioned chair. Smoothly, Winthrop shoved a sturdy ottoman beneath his feet.

Elliot instinctively recoiled. "Don't bloody touch me, Matt! You ungrateful bastard."

"Man can curse like that must be on the way to recovery," he heard Hugh reverently whisper.

"Coffee, anyone?" chirped Kemble.

A quarter hour later, Elliot was fairly well convinced he was going to live, and none too gladdened by the knowledge. Having spent the better part of the previous two days trying to kill himself, he found his failure to do so more than a little discouraging, especially when one considered the consequent agony. Liveried footmen were, however, pouring a bath before his very eyes. Winthrop had managed to force two cups of strong coffee down his gullet, and Kem was laying out his clothes. It was therefore obvious to Elliot that he was expected not only to live but to bathe and to dress as well. He found it a disheartening prospect.

Behind him, a housemaid was resolutely clearing the remnants of last night's suicide attempt. The clink and clatter of the bottles as she gathered them up felt like more of Satan's handiwork to Elliot's aching head. In short order, however, the maid was done, and Kemble was shooing the servants away from the huge copper tub. Steam now roiled ominously from its surface. Elliot did not even bother to whimper or curse when Kemble and Hugh forcibly divested him of his day-old shirt and drawers, then plopped him into the hot water.

Matthew Winthrop stood to one side, his hands set stubbornly at his waist, and studied his friend. "I swear, Elliot! Drunk for two days—not your style. What you need, old boy, is a good tumble—and please tell me you're not still grieving over your actress?"

Elliot gave a harsh bark of bitter laughter and managed to sluice his face with a handful of scalding water. "Hardly that, Winthrop."

The major lifted one brow questioningly and waved eloquently about the disorderly room. "Well, there's a petticoat involved here—God knows I've seen that pathetic expression often enough to know. Though, admittedly, not on you."

Elliot merely shook his head and slipped deeper into his bath.

"Have it your way, Rannoch," insisted Winthrop with a slow shake of his head. "But I'll be hanged if you ain't a man nursing a broken heart. Comes as quite a shock, too, considering that we none of us thought you had one."

"Faith, Matt!" muttered Elliot, letting his head go limp against the rim of the copper tub. He squeezed shut his eyes and forced a grim smile. "I have it on the best of authority that I want not only for a heart but for decency, morality, and honesty as well."

"Well, I'm damned," muttered Sir Hugh, amiably tossing off the remainder of his coffee. "Been messing with that country gel up in Essex again, ain't you, boy?"

"Ah! Your mystery lover," said Winthrop softly. "Who is she, Elliot?"

"*Oui, oui!*" Kemble sang out cheerfully from the adjoining dressing room. "*Cherchez la femme!* Naught but trouble! I've said it for weeks!"

Elliot ignored Kem, dunked himself face first into the tub, and came up spewing. The shock of the hot water made his next words bearable. "Trent's niece," he managed to rasp through the water streaming down his face. "Can you believe my damnable luck?"

"Truly, Elliot?" Winthrop's mouth gaped in shock. "Old Trent had a granddaughter? And you've been trifling with her? A well-bred lady, too! Not at all the thing, my old fellow!"

"Didn't think there was anyone left in that line," muttered Sir Hugh, "save that mama's boy, Stephen."

"Oh, yes," sighed Elliot morosely. "Two granddaughters and a grandson. The heir presumptive, no less. Children of the old lord's youngest son, Maxwell."

"Maxwell?" Winthrop mused. "Hmm . . . I only remember Frederick. But I recollect he died at Busaco. And a brave fellow he was."

Frederick. The name hit Elliot like a brickbat. *Frederi-*

ca. Portugal. Naught but a nobleman's by-blow. Suddenly, Elliot realized that the trail of truth had been there all along, had he but followed it. How many families named Stone were there amongst England's gentry, anyway? No more than two dozen, in all probability, yet the thought had never occurred to him to put the pieces together.

Sir Hugh grunted again and scratched his ear. "Aye, I remember Max Stone—the fellow liked art or some such tomfoolery, I recollect. All the talk thirty years ago. Seems his step-mama scotched his admission to that—what d'ye call it—Royal Academy? Fellow flew up in the boughs, ran off to Italy or some damn place. Thought he died."

"He did," said Elliot dryly. "But in Essex, just a few years ago."

Now it was Winthrop's turn to sigh. "Lud, Elliot, what took hold of your brain? Jeanette's niece, no less! I must admit, you do amaze me."

Sir Hugh slapped his knee cheerfully. "That's my boy, Elliot. Keep 'em on their toes. Wish I could have seen that old bitch Honoria's face when she caught up with your ruse."

"Indeed, Uncle, I *did* see it. Moreover, I can assure you it was not a pleasant sight. And there was no ruse." Elliot sluiced his face brutally with hot water, squinting through the rivulets. "I just didn't realize who the young lady was."

"Good story, my boy!" Sir Hugh thumped his chair arm jovially. "Stick to it."

Elliot turned to glare at his uncle. "Listen to me, Hugh! *I—did—not—know,*" he repeated, coldly enunciating each word.

"But why did she—?" Winthrop paused when he noted Elliot's glare.

Elliot looked away and stared into the depths of his

tub. "I do not know. Suffice it to say that I failed to make my identify fully known to her."

"Jesus, Rannoch! Surely you did not—you didn't . . ." Winthrop's words ground to a halt, and his mouth fell open. "And then, you didn't . . . ?"

"Oh, hell, yes," answered Elliot bitterly. "I did. Of course I did. What else would a licentious reprobate like me do, Matt? Of course, I couldn't stop myself."

"Good Lord," murmured Winthrop solemnly. "What happens now? Or need I ask?"

"Apparently, nothing happens now," answered Elliot bitterly. "And I'll tell you truly, gentlemen, the fool who labeled women the weaker sex never met this one. I'm lucky I survived when she found out who I was."

"Found out?" shrieked Hugh, bouncing out of his chair. "My God, she knows who you are?"

"Indeed," muttered Elliot. "But don't trouble yourself, Uncle. She has no interest in furthering her relationship with the marquis of Rannoch. I collect that her family considers me—ah, yes, I have it now—*a vile, sniffing hound.*"

"Enough of this matutinal *tête-à-tête*, gentlemen," interjected Kemble firmly from across the huge room. "Haul his maimed and jug-bitten buttocks out of there, and I'll have him shaved, dressed, and ready to go in a trice."

"*Go?*" moaned Elliot, but it was too late. He was being heaved unceremoniously from the tub.

"Go," affirmed Winthrop stubbornly. "We'll not stand aside whilst you drink yourself to death over a woman, Elliot."

"Aye," added Sir Hugh cheerfully. "The betting books at the club are flush with wagers on today's match between O'Connell and Jennings. A bit of bloodthirsty sport and a spot o' fresh air—'tis just the thing, m'boy!"

* * *

If Sir Hugh's disparaging comment had set Honoria Stone's ears to burning, her upright posture and zealous eyes gave no indication of it, for even as Hugh impugned her character, the "old bitch" herself sat in the middle of Evangeline's library, her demeanor giving every impression of a self-satisfied, morally superior gentlewoman who was confident of having the whip hand on lesser mortals, her errant granddaughter included.

The dowager countess carefully smoothed the already neat folds of her black bombazine skirt, then dropped her matching reticule neatly into her lap. "I thank you, Miss Stone, for agreeing to see me today," she asserted from her chair by the cold hearth. "I am vastly reassured to learn that you feel as I do, which is to say that we both want what is best for Michael."

Evangeline eyed her step-grandmother with carefully veiled suspicion. The woman had returned as predicted this morning, without her minions and with a dangerously uncharacteristic deference which was belied by her eyes. Today, the dowager countess was civil, almost cordial, and Evangeline could not but wonder at the price such a performance extracted from the woman.

"Make no mistake about my beliefs, Lady Trent," interposed Evangeline coolly as she bent forward to pour coffee. "I am persuaded that what is best for Michael is that his life remain unchanged. Be so obliging as not to press me further on that point."

The dowager's thin mouth curled into a stiff smile. "I daresay you are quite determined, my dear. But pray think of Michael and the many advantages your uncle and I are in a position to provide."

Evangeline let her gaze drift slowly across the taut, almost haggard lines of Lady Trent's face. "Had you wished to provide for my brother, my lady, you would have done so ere now," she softly challenged. "Moreover, I fear what

Michael's life would be like under your tutelage, for he is a gently reared child, possessed of artistic leanings."

Lady Trent's eyes narrowed as she folded her slender, gloved hands tightly into her lap. "I am all astonishment, Miss Stone, if you imply that you desire only what is best for your brother. For I would ask you about your relationship with the marquis of Rannoch. I cannot think him fit company for a boy of Michael's gentle nature." Something that might have been desperation flared in her eyes but was quickly hidden.

Suddenly, Evangeline's thoughts began to fall into place. This visit had little to do with Michael. This was about Elliot. Lady Trent was anxious; that much was becoming clear. Evangeline could sense that barely suppressed rage lurked just below the dowager's restrained courtesy. Evangeline lifted her chin and forced a look of cool disinterest. "I thank you, my lady, for your concern. You may be sure that my acquaintance with Lord Rannoch will have no effect whatsoever on Michael."

"I must say, Miss Stone, that I am exceedingly pleased to hear it. His use of your given name two days ago implied an unseemly degree of familiarity." The dowager sipped delicately at her coffee.

"Have a care, my lady," cautioned Evangeline gently. "You are welcome under this roof whenever you deign to call upon us; nevertheless, I will brook no slur upon my character—nor upon his lordship's," she added as an afterthought.

Lady Trent's dark, angular brows shot up. "My dear girl, you may be perfectly sure that nothing I may say can cast further aspersions upon Rannoch's character! Indeed, he quite rejoices in his ill repute."

Evangeline's eyes held her step-grandmother's as she boldly lied. "I have no real knowledge of his lordship's character, my lady. Be assured, however, that I am not one of his conquests."

Lady Trent's face turned pallid as she set down her cup with a clatter, and Evangeline could see that her hands shook as she did so. "If you think to use him against us, Miss Stone, you will quickly discover exactly who is using whom. He will never wed you."

"Do you fancy not, my lady?" asked Evangeline, feigning naïveté. "After all, he has asked me. More than once, I might add." As she watched the dowager turn from white to flaming pink, Evangeline assuaged her conscience. He had asked, had he not? Though doubtless he had not meant it, her claim was not a total fabrication.

"Come now, Miss Stone! Surely, you cannot have believed him serious. The man is a debaucher of innocence. What else could he want from you?"

Evangeline deliberately let her brows rise in apparent ignorance. "Why, I cannot think, my lady! I can assure you that his deportment has been all that it should be. Quite gentlemanly, in fact."

The horror-stricken look on the dowager's face confirmed Evangeline's suspicions, and she watched as Lady Trent drew a steadying breath. "Miss Stone, if he has seriously offered for you, there can be only one reason, and you must acknowledge it. Rannoch seeks control of my, er, of my stepson's heir."

"I do not recollect, my lady, that he was aware of my full identity when first we met," Evangeline answered sweetly. Her conscience rankled at the almost certain lie, but it was necessary.

Lady Trent almost snorted her incredulity. "My dear girl, you cannot be witless enough to believe such nonsense as all that! Do you really imagine that despite your withdrawal to this village, naught but twenty-odd miles from town, Rannoch could not have easily discovered your existence? Why, Max Stone's dismissal from this family was the talk of the *ton*."

"Indeed, but that was thirty years ago. My father is now remembered only for his work, while his connection to the earldom of Trent has been long forgotten."

"Hmph," snorted the dowager dismissively. "I fancy you are not acquainted with Rannoch's uncle, Sir Hugh Benham. Come, Miss Stone, give the devil his due! Rannoch comes by his lax morals honestly, for that vulgar makebate uncle of his has been hanging about since Jezebel—probably bedded her, too."

Evangeline hedged. Elliot had said something about an uncle, but she knew nothing of the man. "Indeed? Then he must be an exceedingly entertaining character."

The dowager sniffed disdainfully. "They are both dissolute rakes, Miss Stone, and are rarely received in polite society." A malicious look flashed in her eyes. "Surely Mrs. Weyden has warned you about the terrible fate of the young lady Rannoch seduced and abandoned? She died, you know."

Evangeline swiftly lowered her eyes. She did not want Lady Trent to see the pain that suddenly flared there. The story was, she knew, perfectly true. Lady Bland's gossipy letters had recounted that old and sordid tale, shortly after Rannoch was shot while exiting Lady Jeanette's bedchamber. Inwardly, she sighed. How in heaven had she been taken in by such a man? And given her heart to him as well? But she had, and as Lady Trent continued her diatribe against Elliot, Evangeline steeled herself.

"Rannoch has no conscience, Miss Stone," the dowager continued. "I pray you will be mindful of how he seduced and humiliated your foolish aunt. Indeed, he has been known to bankrupt young gentlemen for sport, only to take their mistresses out of spite."

"However do you come by such vast and certain

knowledge, my lady?" asked Evangeline flatly, staring into her coffee.

"Indeed, he does not trouble himself to hide it, Miss Stone. The man has no honor, and even less shame. He flaunts his bastard daughter—the child of a dancer, no less. 'Tis said that he often drinks all night, then duels without compunction the next morning."

"Those are old stories, my lady," answered Evangeline softly. "Perhaps his lordship has resolved to change his ways."

The dowager snorted her incredulity. "Old stories? Oh, my dear child, you are shockingly green! Why, hardly a fortnight past, he took a wound in the shoulder! Lord Cranham challenged him over a woman."

The wound across Elliot's shoulder! Shot over a woman? Evangeline tried to quell her gasp of horror, but it was too late. Her step-grandmother had heard it. "Indeed, you may well be shocked, Miss Stone, but matters are much worse than that for the marquis of Rannoch. Last week, his mistress was found murdered."

Pain sliced through Evangeline's heart like a red-hot knife. "*Mis—mistress?*" she stuttered weakly.

"Ah, indeed! A Drury Lane actress. He bought her last year from under Lord Clivington's nose, then flaunted her all over town. And she was hardly an actress in truth, just a flame-haired tavern wench. But several weeks ago, she was foolish enough to quibble with him in public, and now she has been found dead. Choked to death, if rumors are to be believed, and with the very necklace Rannoch had given her."

Evangeline had learned long ago that there were two sides to every tale, but the angle from which she viewed Rannoch's scandals seemed to make little difference. The marquis looked hopelessly wicked from every vantage point. She resolved, however, not to give the dowager the satisfaction of her uncertainty. "I am sorry, madam, but I cannot believe you," she answered, but the words came out far weaker than she had intended.

"Do you not?" asked Lady Trent with growing self-confidence. "Then you must simply ask him! Knowing Rannoch, he'll not deny it. Better still, write to your trustee, Mr. Weyden. I can assure you, the talk is all over London."

"Uncle Peter does not much concern himself with gossip," answered Evangeline coldly.

"Indeed?" retorted the dowager. "Well, perhaps he will have a little more concern about your legal problems, Miss Stone. I give you fair warning. If I do not soon have the Trent heir living under my roof, where his morals and his upbringing can be properly attended to, then you and Peter Weyden shall have the devil to pay. The law will be on my side, you may be sure. "

And leaving that dire suggestion hanging heavily in the air, and having done about as much damage as one malicious old crone could be reasonably expected to accomplish in a busy afternoon, the dowager countess pulled taut her gloves, took up her reticule, and bade her step-granddaughter a good day.

Elliot knew that although today's prize fight was almost certainly illegal, its location would be a poorly kept secret. Tradesmen, laborers, and gentlemen alike would undoubtedly flock to the event, hoping to make an afternoon's sport of drinking, wagering, and carousing. Under better circumstances, it would have been a pleasant excursion. Today, however, it was not. Nonetheless, Elliot found himself too weak to argue when Hugh gave the traveling orders to his coachman. Instead, he allowed himself to be shoved inside his carriage, where he summarily curled up against the velvet squabs and began to pray for a swift demise.

It was not to be. His only brush with the great here-after came four miles out of London, when he abruptly and violently parted company with his two cups of coffee. Otherwise, Elliot was compelled to endure, and so he set about ignoring his throbbing head, roiling stomach, and boisterous companions. Hours seemed to have passed when at last the rocking of the carriage ceased, heralding their arrival at the town where the match was set to begin. Though they had arrived well ahead of schedule, traffic choked the roadways. Every mode of transportation, from high-perch phaetons to foundering nags, encircled the field where Pat O'Connell—if one could believe the chanting, jostling crowd—would shortly meet his maker.

Elliot, however, was too close to meeting his own to expend much worry on Mr. O'Connell. Slowly, he trudged uphill to a nearby tree, slumping against it whilst Winthrop and Hugh pressed forward into the throng of men in hopes of attaining a better vantage point. The sun was warm, so Elliot made himself as comfortable as possible by sitting down, his back reclined against the broad trunk. He tipped his hat forward over his eyes, then settled back to wait out the fight, paying little heed to the hearty revelers. Soon Elliot began to drowse, and he passed the next hour in hazy awareness of the clamor that surrounded him.

The roar of the crowd finally disturbed his slumber, and Elliot came awake to find that the horde of men below were breaking apart into smaller brawls and fights around the periphery of the boxing match. "He's a cheat!" shouted an angry voice above the rumbling crowd. Already, Elliot could make out a couple of bleeding noses.

"Aye, bloody well right!" cried another voice. "Open 'is hand!"

In the makeshift ring below, Elliot could see that O'Connell had his opponent pinned and was trying to wrest open his clutched fist. "Open 'is hand!" the angry mob shouted, taking up the chant. In the rows of on-lookers nearest the ring, shoving and pushing had already broken out. Fists and hats were flying. Still slightly hung over, Elliot stumbled weakly to his feet and was relieved to see his uncle and Matt Winthrop burst from the crowd to clamber up the hill toward him.

"Come on, Elliot," panted Hugh breathlessly as he waved his hat. "To the Hart and Hare! 'Twill soon get ugly below."

Winthrop, being younger and fitter than Hugh, easily reached Elliot first and stood looking back down at the crowd, which was now brawling in earnest. "Aye, tempers are hot. I agree with Sir Hugh."

"Escape it is, then," agreed Elliot flatly, shoving his hat back into place. The three men strolled back down to the edge of town to find the nearest tavern. All but empty, the Hart and Hare was small, having only a narrow tap-room with a kitchen in back and little else to recommend it. It was, however, clean and quiet. Elliot and Hugh took a seat just opposite the door as Winthrop strolled forward to give their request to the huge, broad-shouldered tapster.

Elliot's head was still pounding, but his stomach was slowly returning to normal. Unfortunately, the bleak reality of his situation was also beginning to return as well. A dark ocean of sadness seemed to tug inexorably at him, and Elliot fought against the undertow. Yet he could not, he knew, remain drunk for the rest of his life. Some other solution was needed. Perhaps he might even think of one, if his damn head ever stopped hurting.

"What happened back there?" he muttered, absently rubbing one temple.

"Looked like Jennings mebbe had a slug of iron in his hand," replied Hugh as he lifted the glass of ale Major Winthrop had just set down.

Elliot merely stared at his drink and felt what little color he had recovered slowly drain away.

Winthrop tapped one finger against the glass. "Well, Rannoch, you know what they say," he cautioned. "If the horse throws you . . ."

"Hmph," replied Elliot noncommittally. His mouth still felt like warm, moldy wool. But maybe Winthrop was right. With measured caution, he hefted the glass, took a sip, and sighed with relief when his stomach did not instantly revolt. "Where are we, anyway?" he asked, wearily scanning the room, which was slowly filling with rambunctious revelers. Strath House, he absently mused, might be cold and lonely, but at least it was quiet.

"Tottenham," answered Winthrop nonchalantly, just as the bulk of the crowd began to stream into the pub.

In groups of twos and threes, the men made their way between rows of chairs and tables to join their cohorts in a glass of ale. The smell of stale beer began to mingle with body odor and tobacco smoke, and within five minutes it became obvious that tempers still raged. The debate about Jennings recommenced as a low rumble and was soon back in full swing. As the spectators settled throughout the narrow room, voices began to rise sharply. When a particularly tumultuous argument commenced in a rear corner, however, the broad-shouldered tapster stepped unhesitatingly from behind his post with what looked like an ax handle balanced casually in his huge fist. He moved toward the corner with a steady, even stride, whispered a few words, and almost immediately, the aggressors moved their quarrel outside.

Elliot drew a sigh of relief, but he had barely exhaled when the door swung open again to admit a shaft of sunlight. The silhouettes of three newcomers filled the narrow opening. Absorbed in his own misery, Elliot paid the customers no heed, until gradually he became aware of a burning gaze fixed upon him. The outsiders still stood frozen upon the threshold. Elliot flicked a disinterested glance upward.

Gus Weyden stared back at him, raw hatred burning in his light blue eyes. Behind Gus stood Crane, Evangeline's brawny footman, and just inside the door hovered Theo, staring at the floor, his hands shoved deep into his pockets.

Good Lord . . . *Tottenham!* "What day is it?" Elliot rasped sickly.

Hugh put his glass down with a thud. "Saturday. Why?"

Damnation! Elliot looked into Gus's blazing eyes and felt a horrific wave of guilt. Theo would not even meet his gaze. This, then, was the boxing match Theo had wanted to attend, the very diversion the boy had begged Elliot to arrange. Suddenly, Elliot's guilt was suffused with anger. This was no place for green boys; the crowd was very nearly a mob, with tempers barely tethered. Moreover, Crane was hardly an appropriate escort. Indeed, a lad of Theo's age had no business here at all, damn it. But if he was to have come, it should have been with Elliot, where he could have been properly supervised.

Unexpectedly, Gus started forward toward their table. Elliot tilted back his chair to look up at him, arching one brow in greeting. "Weyden," he said smoothly, in as gentle a tone as he could muster, "surprised to see you here."

"Oh, I'll just bet you are, Rannoch!" the young man bit out. There was no mistaking the frank hostility in his voice.

Suddenly, Hugh and Winthrop pulled themselves up

erect in their seats to survey the situation. "Are introductions in order, Elliot?" his uncle asked caustically, his gaze raking the newcomer.

"Apparently not," murmured Elliot softly, his eyes searching Gus's taut face for any sign of their former friendship. "Look, Gus, I can explain . . . explain everything. Can we go outside?"

"You can go to hell, you lecherous pig," replied Gus coolly. Then, like a bolt of lightning, the young man's booted leg shot out, kicking Elliot's chair from beneath him. Dulled by two days of incessant drinking, Elliot's reactions were pathetic, and he found himself sprawled on the floor amid a tangle of boots and chairs. A hushed murmur rippled through the crowd as necks craned to see the incipient brawl.

Winthrop was up in a flash, pulling a staggering Elliot to his feet. His eyes shot warning daggers into the grumbling crowd. Almost at once, the tapster was upon them, his hefty ax handle balanced loosely in his hand. "Take it outside, gents," he advised in a low, cool voice.

"Gladly," snarled Gus Weyden, spinning on one heel. As he approached the door, Elliot saw Crane touch him lightly on one arm, then murmur a few quiet words in Gus's ear. Gus responded by tossing a vitriolic glance back over his shoulder at Elliot, who still stood, weakly gripping the table edge.

Roughly, Gus shoved away the footman's hand. "I don't give a bloody damn who he is," Gus growled over his shoulder, his challenge unmistakable. "Outside is good enough for me." And with that, he turned and strode through the door.

"Outside!" shouted an eager voice from the rear of the tavern. "The two swells 're gonna fight!" Suddenly, half the room seemed to surge to their feet as Elliot dusted himself off, grabbed his hat, and headed for the door.

Heedless of Winthrop and the audience that followed on his heels, Elliot slapped on his hat, threw open the door, and strode out into the packed dirt yard. A flow of latecomers still trickled toward the tavern as a stream of horses moved from the road into the wayside. In the midst stood Gus Weyden, stripping off his coat. He hurled it into the hedgerow, then spun toward Elliot, his hands set resolutely upon his slender hips.

It should have been hilarious, but Elliot saw no humor in the matter. With the most determined stride he could muster, Elliot approached Gus, one hand elevated, palm outward. "Look, Weyden, be reasonable. I just want to talk ab—oof!"

Gus's first punch caught him squarely beneath the chin, snapping his head back and sending his hat tumbling into the dirt. Elliot staggered backward, catching himself just as Winthrop reached the fray.

The blow induced a stir of anticipation among the crowd as they realized the mill was in earnest. Shouts and cajoles mingled with hastily murmured wagers as the emotionally charged mob surrounded and sized up the two combatants. "Two quid on the big nob," Elliot heard a rough, uncultivated voice rasp from the edge of the growing throng.

A bitter, determined smile curved Gus's mouth as he waved Elliot toward him with one hand. "Come on, Rannoch," he taunted softly. "I don't give a bloody damn how big you are."

"I just want to talk, Gus. Not fight," said Elliot softly, bending down to scoop up his dusty hat. Angry jeers broke from the crowd just as his fingers touched the brim, and almost simultaneously, Gus's boot connected with his ribcage, sending him sprawling into the dirt.

The crowd roared.

"Three-to-two odds!" shouted an eager voice from the

back of the mob as Elliot hefted himself ungracefully from the ground.

"In whose favor?" quizzed Sir Hugh avariciously. Elliot's head pivoted backward in amazement just as Gus's next punch caught him evenly in the stomach, sending him reeling ignobly backward again.

"The youngster, I s'pect," came the stunned, uncertain response.

Elliot burned with righteous indignation. Damn it all, Gus was no more inclined to listen than Evangeline had been, and now his own uncle was taking odds on his fight. Lifting his chin to face his accuser, Elliot saw Gus's muscles bunch for the next blow and, summoning all his strength, effectively threw one arm high to block the punch, catching Gus squarely in the gut with the opposite fist.

"Nah," hedged the gamester again as Gus exhaled in a whoosh and staggered backward. "Odds on the big gent, I reckon."

Gus quickly regained his balance and wound up for the next punch. Tired of treading the high moral ground, Elliot stepped back, ripped off his coat, and hurled it at Hugh's face. Like a couple of enraged roosters, the pugilists began to circle each other, as if pulled by centrifugal force.

"Don't make me do this, Weyden," cautioned Elliot softly. "I may be coming off a two-day drunk, but I'm nearly twice your size."

"Aye, Elliot, brute strength?" jeered Gus. "Is that the way of it? Is that how you forced yourself on Ev—"

"Shut up, you fool!" roared Elliot, diving into the younger man.

He took Gus down with a forceful blow, sending them both tumbling to the dirt yard in a whirlwind of dust. Around them, the crowd skittered back from the fray as

Elliot pinned him hard against the ground and sprawled on top.

Gus tried to spit upward into Elliot's face. "Evie loved you, you unprincipled libertine!"

Elliot leaned deeper, forcing his opponent's shoulders into the dirt. "Damn you, watch your tongue!" he whispered, this time against Gus's ear. "Now, I understand you're angry, and mayhap you've every right, but this is neither the time nor the place to mention the names of—"

Suddenly, Gus's knee came up out of nowhere to catch Elliot almost square in the crotch. Elliot roared in pain, rolled to one side, then lay there panting as Gus scrambled to his feet.

"Get up, you son of a bitch," snarled Gus, waving him up invitingly. The knuckles of his hand were already dark and swollen.

"Oh, hell!" rasped Elliot. "Pound me to flinders, then, Weyden, if it'll make you feel any better." He spit out a mouthful of dust and launched himself at Gus again. In a matter of seconds, they were rolling through the tavern yard like a pair of snarling mongrels, first Elliot on top, then Gus. Fists and elbows flew as the world seemed to tumble about Elliot, pulling him into a whirling vortex of dizziness and nausea.

Both men were panting and covered in grime. At last, Elliot succeeded in getting the upper hand, pinning Gus firmly to the ground once more, and fighting to subdue his own flip-flopping stomach. Elliot's hair hung limply over one eye, partially obscuring his view of his opponent outstretched beneath him. Just then, Gus shifted, and Elliot looked down to see that the younger man's nose streamed with blood. It gushed down his face and throat, coloring Gus's once-white linen with a bright red stain.

The vision was just too much.

Elliot was undone, the sight overcoming his suddenly delicate sensibilities. With a groan of protest, he rolled off Gus and crawled onto his knees, clutching at his belly just as the glass of ale rebelled and came up ignominiously into the dirt of the tavern yard.

Suddenly, Gus, too, was on his knees, clutching his heaving stomach. But he, Elliot saw with outrage, was laughing. *Laughing!* A fair mill amongst friends was one thing, but dash it all, laughing at another fellow's hangover was not at all the thing. And a knee in the ballocks was just damned dirty fighting.

Instinctively, the crowd drew back. A couple of fellows scuffled off toward the taproom as the odds-makers scratched their heads. It was apparent to all that the row was over, at least for the nonce.

"Drat you, Weyden," Elliot grunted, staggering uncertainly to his feet, then spitting violently into the yard. He reached down and yanked Gus up with newfound strength, then dragged the young man in the general direction of the stables. "You and I are going to settle a few things, my friend." He glowered back over his shoulder at Crane and Sir Hugh and their coterie of spectators. *"Alone!"* he bellowed, and the crowd shrank back as if burnt.

In the shade of the stables, Elliot shoved Gus down into a pile of hay and collapsed wearily beside him. Much of the younger man's rage appeared to have been dissipated in the dirt. His bloodlust now reduced to a narrow-eyed scowl, Gus began mopping at his nose.

With a sigh of relief, Elliot dragged a filthy shirtsleeve across his brow and heaved a ragged breath. "Look here, Weyden," he slowly began. "I know this looks bad, but you have got to help me. Just listen to my side of the story . . ."

* * *

Evangeline had been in the front hall when Gus limped up the steps earlier that evening, Crane and Theo following in his wake. Now the erstwhile pugilist sat slumped in an ancient kitchen chair, his booted legs spread wide, his head tilted back against the topmost chair rung.

"Aye, miss! They do say boys will be boys," quoted Mrs. Penworthy as she cheerfully lifted a now-tepid compress from Gus's bloated face. Beneath it, his nose was engorged to twice its size, and one bruised eye was already swollen shut. Bracing her plump hands upon her knees, the housekeeper squatted down and peered appraisingly up into Gus's nostrils. "But I s'pect 'tis broken, more's the pity. And we'll be needin' a beefsteak for that right eye."

From a pot on the kitchen stove, the cook, Mrs. Crane, sniffed pitifully, then lifted another steaming cloth from a cast-iron pot containing a malodorous boiling concoction. Using tongs, she plopped it onto a porcelain tray and sighed morosely.

"Mr. Roberts—*the marquis of Rannoch*—is a grown man, Mrs. Penworthy," snapped Evangeline. "As is Gus, much as he likes to ignore that fact." She picked up the cloth by one corner, waited a moment as it cooled, then resolutely folded it and applied it to the worst of Gus's bruises.

Gus scowled beneath the steaming compress and tried to lift his head from the rung of the ladderback chair. "I'b well aware of my owd age, Evie," he groused nasally. "And I don'd think you're being fair to Elliod aboud this. Hear me oud, thad's all I ask."

"Fair? *Fair?*" Evangeline screeched. "You'll bloody well get fair, Gus Weyden, when your mama returns home and sees that you have been brawling in a tavern yard like common riffraff! And with an amoral reprobate like him, no less. I vow I cannot credit it! Have you no notion of propriety?"

"Eh?" interjected Mrs. Penworthy. "P'raps 'e likes a good mill well as the next 'un—but that nice Mr. Roberts, a reprobate? Don't seem quite the right word somehow."

From the steaming kitchen pot, Mrs. Crane gave a sharp, tragic sigh. " 'Tis Crane's fault, anyways," she moaned, rolling her eyes heavenward. "Sweet piety! What come over 'im, I arst you? Carryin' off them boys to a boxing brawl. And all the way to Tottenham! Lucky t'weren't worse."

"Oh, devil fly away wid Crane!" grumbled Gus, tossing the compress aside and staggering up from the chair. "I think I'b ode enough to know whad I'm aboud! And Elliod's nod a reprobade."

"You think not?" whispered Evangeline coldly, leaning forward to lock her gaze with his. "Then just what would you call a man who debauches, then abandons, innocent young ladies? A man who flaunts his mistresses, swindles naïve young men out of their inheritances like some conniving Captain Sharp, and engages in bloodthirsty duels for the casual entertainment of his friends?" Evangeline gave a sharp yank on Gus's collar.

"Lies!" retorted Gus nasally. "Bloody insulds! Who the devil said such things?"

"Lady Trent," hissed Evangeline, setting her hands stubbornly upon her hips. "And now that I think of it, calling that man a reprobate *is* a bloody insult—to the expression, not the man!"

Before Gus could respond any further to Evangeline's choleric invective, Frederica burst into the kitchen, came to a skidding halt just inside the threshold, and gave a horrified squeak. "Is it true?" she asked in a stricken voice, staring up at Gus's harrowing visage. Her face drew taut in an expression of terrified innocence, and she burst into tears. "Is it true what Theo says? That you and Mr. Roberts had a fight?" she sobbed. "That you *hit* each other?"

"Damnation," cursed Evangeline, pitching the next compress across the kitchen and whirling about in a rush of silk. She stalked toward the door. "That's it! That is the last tear to be shed at Chatham over that dissolute scoundrel! It is time I made it clear to him that he's not to come near any member of this household." She clambered up the ancient kitchen steps as Mrs. Crane and Frederica wailed miserably in her wake.

Elliot shouted out the address Gus had given him, and the elegant carriage lurched off toward the river to travel into Westminster. Tossing his hat onto the opposite seat, Elliot ran his hand down his face as if wiping away an unpleasant vision. Yesterday had indeed been a nightmare. The sight of Gus's bloodied shirt had truly sickened him, and the knowledge that, fully sober, he could have seriously injured the boy had left Elliot badly shaken. He had not, however, been sober and consequently had been very nearly bested by a lad almost half his weight and age. Somehow, despite the ribbing he had taken from Hugh and Winthrop, the fight's outcome seemed meaningless. It was still his heart, not his pride, that ached so unremittingly.

It had not helped matters much that afterward Gus had stood, cool and resolute, in the midst of the musty tavern stables as Elliot had literally begged his forgiveness. Dredging up every ounce of humility he could find, Elliot had tried to explain his honorable intentions and convince Gus of his unlikely tale. Elliot's utter humiliation had been such that he had sworn his love for Evangeline and pleaded with Gus for his help. Yet in the end, all Gus could do was look at Elliot sympathetically, clamp one filthy arm about his shoulders, and suggest that he call upon Peter Weyden.

Things had not improved on the way home. It was only then that Winthrop had broken the news about Antoinette. Admittedly, the necklace had been an ugly touch. Antoinette had deserved better. Elliot shivered despite the warmth of the day. Try as he might, his former mistress's visage haunted him, her pale, stark beauty contorted into a horrible death mask. Poor, poor girl. She had been greedy and desperate, yes, but not inherently wicked. Elliot was very much afraid the same could not be said of him.

Through the window, Elliot watched the passing scenery along Haymarket with cold indifference and wondered what his life was coming to. Down Jermyn Street, he could see throngs of well-dressed ladies and gentlemen darting in and out of carriages and shops, busying themselves with their final shopping of the season. Within a matter of weeks, much of polite society would remove to their country estates or head for the midlands in anticipation of hunting season.

Elliot turned from the window to stare blindly into the shadows of his carriage. He did not care about shopping or hunting, and he certainly did not care about the season's end. His carriage moved on through the swarming streets until at last they reached Peter Weyden's address. Set on a quiet lane just a few yards south of Great Marlboro, the four-story building was elegant and immaculately kept. A simple brass plaque identified the business.

Weeks ago, much to Elliot's relief, Gerald Wilson's investigation of Weyden had indicated that Evangeline's guardian was an honest man who could be depended upon to see to his ward's best interests. Elliot could only hope that Weyden would agree that those best interests ought now to be extended to include marriage. It was a long shot at best, but Elliot was a desperate man.

Elliot hurtled impatiently from the carriage without waiting for his footman to put down the steps. He leapt up the six wide stone stairs, and, almost immediately, the door swung inward and a powdered footman bade Elliot enter, graciously took his card, then disappeared up a wide staircase which circled the vaulted central hall. The room was not large, but it was tastefully decorated with landscapes and seascapes which had been strategically placed to draw the eye through the room. For a few moments, Elliot paced anxiously, alternately feigning interest in the paintings and then flicking open his watch, until the footman returned and asked Elliot to follow him upstairs.

Peter Weyden was a dapper gentleman of perhaps sixty years, with a face that was at once purposeful and pleasant. His immaculately cut hair was a brilliant shade of silver, as were his eyes and his spectacles. A coat of rich, russet superfine covered his elegant gray vest, from which a long watch chain looped down and across his ample belly. He looked, on the whole, like a cross between an ancient, sharp-eyed owl and a prosperous Zürich banker and seemed possessed of all the meticulousness and precision the latter might imply.

Four soaring Palladian windows cast a soft light across his imposing office-cum-sitting room, which was expensively furnished yet somehow spartan. At one end sat a broad mahogany desk, devoid of clutter save a stack of tooled-leather ledgers and a modern steel writing pen. As the footman ushered Elliot inside, Weyden rose from his chair in the sitting area opposite the desk and made a polite, precise bow. Seeming completely unfazed by the unexpected appearance of a marquis in his study, he bade Elliot to be seated, then offered a glass of sherry.

Elliot declined the drink. "Mr. Weyden," he began, folding himself into one of his host's small chairs, "since we have not the pleasure of an introduction, I am certain that you wonder what brings me here today."

From across his sparkling spectacles, Peter Weyden peered sharply at him. "On the contrary, Lord Rannoch. I strongly suspect that I know the reason for your call, having received by yesterday's post a rambling, penitent *mea culpa* from my sister-in-law, whom I daresay fears the worst." Weyden spoke in precise but heavily accented English and finished with a stiff, caustic smile. It was his only outward sign of emotion.

Elliot felt his brows rise involuntarily, then fought back the innate arrogance. Such an emotion had no place here. He was fully at fault and owed this man an apology. "It would seem, then," he commented softly, "that Mrs. Weyden has kindly saved me the humiliation of relaying the unfortunate details of my, ah, relationship with your ward."

Weyden simply shrugged and rose from his chair to take up a decanter of sherry. Elliot shook his head, and Weyden poured himself a glass. Drink in hand, the portly man strolled to one of the deep windows and stared out into the haze of what was still an unusually bright London day. When he spoke, his tone held a distinct edge of finality, and Elliot felt as though he were being effectively dismissed by a weary schoolmaster.

"Thank you for being honorable enough to come here today, my lord, but I think we need prolong neither your discomfort nor this visit." Weyden turned from the window to face him. "If indeed there has been, shall we say, an inappropriate degree of familiarity between the two of you, then I am well aware that many of your rank would not have troubled themselves to call upon me under such circumstances. Regrettably, Evangeline bears much of the burden, and very little of the benefit, of a daughter born into a noble family."

Uncomfortable with the calm resolve in Weyden's voice, Elliot rose and joined him at the window. "What is it, precisely, that you are saying, Weyden? Does this have anything to do with Etienne LeNotre?"

Weyden smiled wryly. "No, no, my lord. I merely suggested that Etienne shelter Michael and Evangeline in Soissons until Winnie could charter a schooner to transport their belongings to Ghent. Though he was astute enough to have some suspicion of your . . . interest in Evangeline, he hardly shares it. Indeed, he has trouble enough without the complications of an *affaire*. As do you, my lord, if the talk about town is to be believed."

The rumors about Antoinette's death had spread quickly, Elliot realized, choosing to ignore the subtle reminder. "Yet you must be aware that I have compromised your ward. Rather badly, I am afraid. Certainly, her grandmother must think so, and since Miss Stone is a lady of quality, I feel compelled to do the proper thing. However, she is inexperienced and does not fully comprehend the implications of what—what has occurred."

The elderly man turned to face him squarely. "On the contrary, my lord. It is you who do not understand." Weyden's words held no hint of anger. "We are not of this culture. We do not live and die by your English rules of conduct."

"Then you countenance her behavior?"

Weyden shook his head emphatically. "By no means, my lord. Nor do I condone yours. I shall, of course, speak sharply to Evangeline. However, she is not foolish by nature, and I am no longer her guardian. She is of age."

"I have asked her to marry me." Elliot could hear the hollow sadness in his own voice and was surprised to feel a hot, stinging pressure well up behind his eyes.

Weyden nodded once, then looked abruptly away to stare into the liquid he now swirled absently in his glass. "So Winnie has explained. And Evangeline has refused you. That was, perhaps, unwise." He glanced up appraisingly at Elliot. "Or perhaps not."

Elliot felt his anger flare. This situation was preposterous; these people were mad. In fact, Weyden should be demanding either a wedding or satisfaction, yet the man's voice was all but devoid of emotion. "Perhaps you do not understand, Mr. Weyden. I have ruined her."

"Ruined her for what, Lord Rannoch? Becoming a simpering, virginal wife for some pompous Englishman?" Weyden's keen, piercing eyes held a hint of humor. "A worthy enough goal, perhaps, for those who have none better. Nonetheless, Evangeline is an artist in the true Flemish tradition, with potential unlike anything I have seen in my lifetime. Furthermore, she is devoted to her family. I cannot believe that one indiscretion precludes her success in anything that greatly matters."

Weyden's unaffected words and casual dismissal of his relationship with Evangeline cut Elliot to the quick. Weyden obviously had no qualms about lumping him into the category of things that did not greatly matter. This time, his ire sprang to the surface. "Damn it, man! Do you not see? She has chosen to live in England, where she is a lady, granddaughter of a peer, sister to a future earl. Such a birth carries a heavy obligation."

Weyden quirked one thick gray eyebrow and stared at Elliot over the rim of his glass. "Evangeline may remove to the Continent at any time, should she find the strictures of English life not to her liking, my lord. Moreover, an heir presumptive is not the same as an heir apparent, is it? The new earl of Trent has a wife who is still, as I understand you are aware, of childbearing age. Perhaps there may yet be a son born to her?"

"Not without a miracle," muttered Elliot, crossing his arms over his chest.

To his surprise, Peter Weyden threw his head back and laughed richly. "Indeed, my lord. That may well be what it will take. Speaking with perfect frankness, if neither you nor any of the other libidinous gentlemen among the *ton* has accommodated her ladyship, I hold out small hope of success."

Elliot could not suppress a scowl at the mention of Jeanette Stone. "There is something else you should consider, Mr. Weyden. I can protect more than Evangeline's reputation. I can protect Michael from the machinations of his father's family. They would not dare cross me. For any reason. And indeed, Evangeline may already carry my child. I own, I had not thought of it until now, but it is something that must doubtless weigh heavily in your decision."

Peter Weyden's thick gray brows went up at that. "My decision? Indeed, Lord Rannoch, what is it that you would have me do? Did you harbor some belief that I would—or even could—force Evie into a marriage?" An almost sympathetic smile played at one corner of Weyden's mouth. "I cannot, you know," he added softly.

After a long moment of silence, Elliot nodded stiffly, realizing that the meeting was at an end. "Then I thank you for your time, Mr. Weyden, and shall waste your day no further. I shall see myself out." He strode toward the door through which he had come, but as he laid his hand upon the ornate brass doorknob, Weyden spoke again.

"Lord Rannoch?"

Elliot turned on his heel to face him. "Yes, sir?"

"Do you love Evangeline?"

After the briefest of hesitations, Elliot nodded and cast his pride to the wind. "Yes, Mr. Weyden, I do. Very deeply."

"Then perhaps you might try to win her heart? Perhaps you will succeed where others have failed. If you can, I shall gladly give you my blessing."

"I thank you, Mr. Weyden." Elliot felt his face grow hot. "But I fear that my ill-considered deception has forestalled any possibility of success with that method."

"A pity," murmured Peter Weyden, downing the remainder of his sherry. He paused thoughtfully. "Perhaps I should go up to Wrotham-upon-Lea to confer with my brother's widow. Though Winnie appears quite henwitted, in reality she is far from it. Yes, and I shall speak to Evangeline. I will strongly recommend that she reconsider your offer. That is all, my lord, that I can promise."

Elliot nodded in gratitude and pulled open the door. "Mr. Weyden?" he asked, turning back once more.

"Yes?"

"I want you to know that I asked Evangeline to marry me before we—I—compromised her," said Elliot humbly. "I will admit to you, sir, that I was stunned to hear myself ask, but I, er, well, damn it, I meant it. I still mean it."

🦢13🦢

Blasphemous fables, and dangerous deceits
—PRAYER BOOK

Lord Cranham waited for his jaunty new curricle to roll to a halt before the narrow town house in Maverton Square. As his tiger leapt down to take the heads of his well-matched bays, Cranham stared obliquely at the door that had slammed so firmly in his face—and on his life— ten long years ago. Indeed, he had no real reason to be-

lieve that it would open for him today, but the presumptuous Lord Linden was insistent that they carry out this
charade. Nervously, Cranham's stomach roiled with nausea, as it had done since the scheme's inception.

He felt like a sitting duck. No, it was far worse than
that. He felt like bear bait being dragged through the
streets and stews of London. The enemy could be anywhere. *Anywhere.* Resolutely, he swallowed down the bile
that threatened to choke him and tried to focus on his
personal quest. To hell with Linden. Cranham had his
own reasons for calling in Maverton Square, and they
had nothing to do with his promise of cooperation. And
next time, he assured himself, his complicity in Linden's
little intrigue would cost the arrogant viscount far more
than the price of a new curricle.

As he turned to instruct his tiger, Cranham's attention
was distracted by Major Winthrop, accompanied by an
equally brawny cohort, ambling around the corner just
opposite. The two men paused beneath a nearby lamppost, glanced casually up and down the square, then bent
their heads in soft conversation. Both wore nondescript
greatcoats and broad-brimmed hats pulled low on their
foreheads. Nonetheless, Winthrop's wide shoulders and
military posture were unmistakable. Despite Lord Linden's airy assurances, Cranham thought it rather unlikely
that the major would rush to his side, even if the killer
set upon him in broad daylight.

As the major leaned casually against the lamppost, the
right-hand side of his coat swung partway open, hanging
stiff and heavy from the pistol Cranham was certain he
carried deep within his pocket. Matt Winthrop was
renowned as a crack shot, perhaps even better than Rannoch himself. Well, another man's marksmanship was of
no use to Cranham, for he still believed that Rannoch
was his only enemy. Just then, Winthrop lifted his gaze to

hold Cranham's briefly, suspicion and hatred etched indelibly upon his face. Clearly, the major considered his task distasteful.

Cranham shrugged. Let them follow, day and night, as they had done for the last two days. There would be, he felt certain, nothing to interest them, unless they wanted to watch Rannoch slit his throat. Reluctantly, Cranham climbed the four steps to the town house and dropped the knocker. The door was answered immediately by a young, unpowdered footman in ill-fitting livery who nodded solemnly, dropped the baron's card onto a small salver, then disappeared.

He was back within two minutes. "I regret to inform you, Lord Cranham, that his lordship is indisposed. Lord Howell begs you will accept his apology, but he is quite unable to see you today."

Cranham snorted incredulously. "Nor any other day, I do not doubt."

The footman merely stared at him, unblinking.

Cranham whipped around as if to leave, then half turned back again. "Tell your employer," he muttered, jerking open the door himself, "that I believe his fear of Rannoch has thoroughly unmanned him." The young servant's mouth dropped open, but any response he might have made was forestalled as, farther down the hall, a door swung wide.

A tall, horse-faced woman stepped out into the corridor, jerking on riding gloves as she trod resolutely toward them. "Connors!" she called as she walked. "Has my groom come 'round with—"

Her step faltered almost imperceptibly when she noticed Cranham silhouetted just inside her front door. "Good afternoon, Mr. Moore," she murmured, giving him a stiff nod of acknowledgment. "Ah, but pray forgive me! Lord Cranham now, is it not?" she added sardonically.

Cranham bowed. "A pleasure to see you after so many years, Lady Howell."

"I had heard," she replied, her eyes narrowing, "that you had returned to town of late."

"Yes, my lady. One eventually comes to miss the hustle and bustle of London."

"Indeed?" Lady Howell answered, her ill-favored features forming a chilled expression. "Then I shan't keep you from it."

The dismissal could not have been more obvious. Cranham took up his hat, which the footman had set upon a hall table, then turned again to leave. From behind him, Lady Howell unexpectedly spoke again. "And Lord Cranham?"

"Yes?"

Lady Howell stepped incrementally closer. "If you are wise," she said quietly, "you will stop trying to speak with my husband. In fact, I strongly suggest you stay away from him altogether, since the past is best forgotten. Do I make myself clear?"

Cranham nodded curtly. "Abundantly, madam," he said stiffly, then turned to walk out the door. He noticed, however, as he trod back down the steps, that the major and his companion were now mounted on a pair of near-spavined hacks at opposite ends of the square. To the untrained eye, they could have been almost anyone, almost anyone save a wealthy gentleman accompanied by a hired thug.

For two days following his impulsive visit to Peter Weyden, Elliot did not stir from home, fervently watching for some word or signal from Chatham. When none was forthcoming, Elliot struggled to rally his spirits by keeping company with his daughter. Zoë, too, was at loose ends, having neither nurse nor governess to occupy her time, and so it seemed oddly logical and unexpectedly comforting to immerse themselves in each other.

Despite the fact that he had shut off his emotions for a very long time, Elliot was not a fool. The shift in his relationship with Zoë was no more than a change within himself, for his daughter was as constant, and yet as ephemeral, as ever. Elliot realized, too, that he should make some decision about her future, yet he could not bring himself to do so. He was waiting, he knew, for Evangeline. Though he had no intention of again abdicating his daughter's care, Elliot longed for Evangeline's advice. Making such a monumental decision without her counsel would feel the same, he inwardly acknowledged, as accepting that their families would never become one. It would be like acquiescing to the end of their love affair, admitting that there was no future. This he was not yet prepared to do.

Elliot had been surprised by Matthew Winthrop's unexpected, and apparently purposeless, call one afternoon. His day, Elliot had politely but assiduously explained, was promised to Zoë. Major Winthrop, amiable as always, seemed content merely to linger. Now, by that odd bit of happenstance, both Elliot and Winthrop found themselves seated before the low table in his library, watching as Zoë deftly balanced both dishes and tea pot in an eager demonstration of her budding social skills. The little girl poured with charming grace, then passed the first serving to their guest. Indeed, Elliot inwardly admitted, it had been quite sporting of Winthrop, who was ordinarily second only to Elliot in debauchery and vice, to join their family interlude.

As Elliot watched Zoë's eyes brighten with pleasure, the now familiar feeling of shame welled up inside his heart. How pathetically little joy his daughter had seen; how pleased she was by the smallest attention from anyone, and Winthrop seemed well on his way to becoming a particular favorite. However, despite the fact that Elliot now knew he could—and should—do better by the child, inside he could bestir little emotion save despair. Where boundless anger and seething resentment had once burned, nothing now seemed to exist. His soul felt suspended, as if it awaited—awaited what? Some word, some signal from Evangeline? Or did he perhaps hope that Weyden would appear on the steps of Strath House with a resolute parson and his recalcitrant ward in tow?

No, that would not do. As desperately as he needed Evangeline, Elliot was not sure he could bear to wed her under such circumstances. He briefly considered riding to Chatham and flinging himself at Evangeline's feet, but that would serve no better purpose. She was still angry. For the first time in more than a decade, Elliot felt attuned to the needs and emotions of someone other than himself, and despite their total absence of communication, Elliot felt Evangeline's anger as if it were a tangible thing. And so he waited and watched his daughter and wished for something better than the emotionally barren existence that had entrapped them both for far too long.

"That was very well done, sweetheart," Elliot murmured absently as she poured the remaining two cups.

"Do you think so, Papa?" she asked brightly. The heels of her violet slippers dangled and bounced haphazardly before her, and Elliot made a mental note to purchase a small ladies' chair for the library. Something pretty and delicate, he mused. Something like those carved armchairs in Evie's studio.

"Oh, exceedingly well, Miss Armstrong," commented the major, apparently noting that Elliot had not answered his daughter. "Why, I have taken tea with duchesses and such, don't you know! Never have I seen it poured with such aplomb and dash!"

"Oh!" she squeaked, her cheeks flushing with pink. "Thank you, sir!" Abruptly, she lifted the tray of tiny sandwiches and passed it across the table. "Will you have a nibble, Major Winthrop?"

"Oh, yes!" he answered, helping himself as Elliot inwardly thanked the Lord for old friends. For the next quarter hour, the three chatted aimlessly until it was time for Zoë to return to the schoolroom. Trudy departed with her charge just as MacLeod appeared to clear away the sandwich tray.

"My lord?" The elderly butler paused, his burden held aloft to one side, then inclined his head toward Elliot's rather disordered desk. "Dinna ye open the letter that came by messenger last night?"

Elliot lifted his distant gaze from the tea table and focused on the servant. He could feel Winthrop's piercing eyes staring at him intently. "Ah—no, MacLeod, I suppose I failed to see it." Smoothly, he rose and moved toward the desk as the butler departed, pulling shut the door.

Winthrop left his chair and approached the desk, his teacup still in hand. "What is it, old fellow? You seem lost in thought today. Are you worried that Linden's mad scheme will go awry? He's very sure he can find the real murderer, you know."

"I—no, it's not that," Elliot answered, flicking his friend a neutral look. "It is just fatigue, I daresay." Winthrop crooked one brow in silent disbelief but said no more. Willing his hand not to shake, Elliot picked up the envelope that lay in the center of his desk. His heart jumped to his throat when he saw the precisely slanted copperplate. It was Evie's. He would know her fine, angular penmanship anywhere. Nervously, he tore open the missive, and a single slip of paper floated down to the desktop. Elliot glanced at the letter and its five cutting words: *Stay away from my family.*

Feeling sick, Elliot picked up the slip of paper and stared fixedly at the numbers. Money. Evangeline was returning his money. The price of the portrait he had commissioned but never taken. No word of kindness or regret, nothing but five bitter words and a bank draft. In his aching heart, a banked anger kindled and began to burn. The blatant unfairness of it all cut him to the quick.

"I say, Elliot," commented Winthrop, abruptly setting down his dish. "Must be rather bad news indeed."

"In a manner of speaking," agreed Elliot coldly, tossing the letter down before his friend. "It would appear Miss Stone thinks to renege on our business arrangement, but she'd best think again. A deal with me may be a deal with the devil, but 'tis a deal just the same."

"Ah, yes! The object of your unrequited affections," answered the major knowingly. "I must confess, I've never seen such a case of the blue-devils. Tell me, old fellow, will the lady not have you?"

"Have me? She'll not even speak to me." He focused on the bank draft, feeling the hot, burning pressure behind his eyes again.

"Elliot, I am worried for you. Your luck has been bad of late." Winthrop's expression seemed carefully veiled, but his voice was unexpectedly compassionate. "Let me be blunt—have you asked for her hand?"

"Aye," he answered sadly, unable to meet his old friend's eyes. "I've asked."

"Then ask again," insisted the major. "Pack your bags and return to Essex this afternoon. Ah! I have it! My carriage is outside. Come with me now to fetch a special license, if it's a leg shackle you're after. Then beg her, kidnap her, do whatever it takes, Elliot, if you want her that badly. If you give up, you will forever regret it."

* * *

During the week that followed Elliot's unceremonious eviction from Chatham Lodge, Evangeline had hardly slept. The mood of the household seemed uncharacteristically surly, the children discontent. Other than her pathetic obsession with Elliot's portrait, Evangeline's work came to a near halt, and food held no temptation. Indeed, the dining room seemed always empty with Elliot's seat vacant. Her normally steadfast moods now swung wildly, alternating between a fear that she, like her father, would never work again and a raw, unremitting hatred of Elliot Armstrong.

Winnie was of little help, clucking incessantly and giving unwanted words to Evangeline's traitorous thoughts. Yes, he was handsome. Yes, the children missed him. Yes, she had been quite taken with him. *Yes, yes, and yes, damn it.* And she hated herself for all of it. She was weak, and what was worse, she had surrendered to the weakness of the flesh. Now, her nights were tormented by the memory of Elliot's body pressed urgently to hers, by the undeniable pleasure they had taken from each other.

How she had enjoyed those perfect summer days spent in quiet companionship with a man who had seemed like nothing more than a warm and considerate gentleman of moderate means and gentle nature. God, how she wished he had never come to Chatham, never stepped into her studio that fateful afternoon in his rain-soaked clothing, with his sensual gray eyes glinting, his long booted legs striding across her floor.

She had been alone for so long, yet she had been content. Then he had come to disturb her peace and make her want things she could not have. And just when she had begun to indulge in foolish fantasies, the ultimate betrayal had come. As a result, Evangeline had lost her focus, her drive, and, worse still, her serenity.

* * *

Elliot arrived at Chatham in record time, his black Arab having chewed up the ground between Richmond and Essex. The highly strung horse was now a foaming bundle of bare nerves, and Elliot felt little better. Nonetheless, he was a driven man. The portrait had become a symbol that represented the blossoming of his relationship with Evangeline. Beyond that, it was a representation of how Evangeline had once seen him, and despite his frayed nerves and smoldering wrath, Elliot realized that it was a vision he wanted to cling to.

Dropping the reins of the exhausted animal, Elliot pounded on the door, which was thrown open by the wide-eyed housekeeper. To her credit, she was as cordial as ever, though clearly stunned to see Elliot. His hat in hand, he strode into the long hall. "Good afternoon, Mrs. Penworthy." Elliot bowed neatly, shot her his brightest smile, and watching her instantly melt. "I wonder if I might have a word with Miss Stone?"

The housekeeper's warm eyes quickly reglazed. "Ooh! Well, now . . . as to that, I'm sure I couldn't say, Mr. Rob—er, I mean, my lord!"

"Mr. Roberts or Mr. Armstrong will do just fine, Mrs. Penworthy," he reassured her gently.

"Aye, p'rhaps!" answered the housekeeper, peering at him skeptically, "but I'm not a'tall sure miss will see any of you, by any name! Howsoever, it cannot hurt to ask, I dessay." She smiled weakly.

Elliot strode back and forth across the width of the hall until an agitated Mrs. Penworthy returned, her keys bouncing merrily against one ample hip. Her expression, however, was anything but cheerful. "Very sorry, Mr. Roberts—I mean, *my lord!* Miss says—I mean, Miss Stone is not at home, I'm to tell you."

"Oh? Wishes me at Jericho, does she?" Elliot answered, then dipped his head closer to the housekeeper's ear.

"But if you could tell me where she is?" he whispered conspiratorially. "Please?"

The housekeeper pursed her lips and looked about nervously. "In the studio," she furtively replied. "On the south gallery."

Elliot nodded, then gave a little wink. "Thank you, ma'am," he answered loudly. "Do tell her I called." Abruptly, he turned and made toward his horse. As soon as he heard the heavy front door thump shut, however, he spun on his heel and strode through the side gardens, making his way around to the back of the house. Soon he reached the upper terrace, which ran from the studio across the back of the house. His booted heels rang resolutely across the stone terrace as he approached the row of French windows.

"Evangeline!" he roared up at the gallery windows. "Let me in! We must talk."

There was no response. Angrily, he waved a slip of paper high above his head and stared up at the gallery. "Evie, I know perfectly well you are listening. Now, come out and take back this bloody bank draft."

Silence. From the corner of one eye, Elliot saw Theo poke his head out of the rhododendron. The lad tiptoed up the terrace stairs to stand behind Elliot and was soon followed by Nicolette, then Frederica. Elliot shrugged and shot them a weak, embarrassed smile, then returned his attention to the upper windows. Despite the fading light of early evening, he caught a glimpse of movement near the center window.

Elliot decided to try a different tactic. "Evie, darling! I am sorry. I swear it! Do not force me to make a spectacle of myself here in front of the children. Let me in, please?"

"What do you care about the children, Rannoch?" she finally called, opening the rusty casement just an inch.

"You attacked an innocent boy and very nearly broke his nose!"

Nicolette and Theo burst into giggles behind him as Elliot snorted derisively. "Oh, aye! An innocent boy, Evie? I'll tell you true, Weyden's no boy, and he blacked both my eyes proving it."

From the corner of his right eye, he saw the allegedly innocent boy step out onto the terrace, distracting his attention just as the upper casement flew wide open. Too late, Gus shouted out the alarm. A small clay pot crashed to the sidewalk mere inches from Elliot's feet. He cursed under his breath as bright orange pigment splashed across his top boots and up the thigh of his buff pantaloons. The children fell into peals of hilarity until Elliot shook his fist at the window and roared, "Evangeline! I want my bloody portrait! You struck a bargain in good faith, do you hear? Stop this foolishness, take this money, and give me my painting!"

In the dead silence, Elliot heard nothing but the wind rustling through the late-summer leaves. Elliot swiveled his head to survey the amused quartet now standing just behind him. He turned back to face the window. "Oh, this is grand, Evie! Is this what you shall do when Lady Trent returns?" he bellowed. "Throw paint pots at her? 'Twill be a rather poor defense, Evangeline! She'll not leave empty-handed this time! I think you know what I mean!"

In response, another pot—bright blue this time— soared through the air just as the rapid clippety-clip of a lady's boot heels sounded up the steps. Elliot turned to see Winnie Weyden, her hand looped beneath her brother-in-law's elbow, hurrying onto the terrace. "Good God, Elliot!" she said breathlessly, the other dainty hand clasped to her heaving bosom. "Peter and I could hear you from the river. Whatever is this unholy commotion?"

Elliot jabbed his finger repeatedly up at the windows. " 'Tis that stubborn woman upstairs!" he raged. "And she'll not be giving me my money back! We struck a deal, fair and square, and the least I am leaving with is my painting."

"I think, my dear," answered Peter Weyden, sagaciously eyeing the splash of orange that marred Elliot's otherwise flawless garb, "that his lordship has come to plead his case with Evangeline."

Elliot brusquely nodded his agreement, then exhaled a sharp breath of exasperation. "Damn it, Winnie! Talk some sense into the bloody woman, can you? Look! She's resorted to throwing things," he hissed, pointing to the broken paint pots.

Eyes wide, Winnie pressed her fingertips to the perfect *O* of her mouth just as a giggle escaped. "Indeed? I hardly know what to say, Elliot," she squeaked. "Will she not speak with you?"

He steeled his voice and redirected it loudly toward the windows. "No, ma'am, she will *not* speak with me! And for my part, I've decided I should infinitely prefer to speak with someone sane. Aye, someone"—he raised his voice another notch—"who is not possessed of an artist's irrational temperament!"

"Indeed?" Winnie repeated, her eyes widening, just as another pot sailed wide, crashing onto the flagstone near the rear door. A sickly shade of green this time.

"Yes," he finished, returning his gaze to Peter Weyden. "You, sir, for example."

Mrs. Weyden nodded her head vigorously, looking relieved to have the issue settled. "A wise choice, my lord. I shall take you both into the library."

Evangeline stood in the dim light of the library, biting back tears and staring out the window into the night which now enveloped Chatham's gardens. Suspended above, in a cloudless sky, a brilliant sliver of moon twinkled as Evangeline wished fervently that she were on it. Oh, that she could be anywhere other than this house, trapped with the marquis of Rannoch! Her forced meeting with Peter—that bloody turncoat!—had been almost too much to bear. Her avuncular guardian had suddenly begun to treat her as if she were a petulant child, while Winnie had offered no support at all, insisting that the marquis be permitted to have his say. Worse still, as if Evangeline's opinion counted for naught in her own home, Winnie had insisted Rannoch stay the night at Chatham Lodge.

Repeatedly goaded by Peter's sharp, reproving glances, Evangeline had finally stalked out of their heated discussion, only to spy Elliot in the drawing room, splayed upon her sofa, chattering with the children as if he had never been ejected from her home in shame. As if *he* had been innocent and *she* had been unreasonable. Now the devil was here, ensconced in her own library, and Peter had told her in no uncertain terms what was expected of her.

She drew a deep, resigned breath. "My guardian has reminded me, my lord, that I must do you the courtesy of hearing you out," she began.

Peter had confirmed something else, too, though she was loath to confess it to Elliot. Her commission really was to have been a Mr. James Hart, a London gentleman of Peter's acquaintance who had been unexpectedly jilted by his fiancée just before his portrait sitting. Peter was convinced that Elliot could not possibly have known of Mr. Hart's situation, so if Elliot had indeed pulled off an elaborate ruse, he had been very nearly clairvoyant in doing so.

Her back turned to Elliot, Evangeline struggled to still

the trembling that edged her voice. She was not yet prepared to surrender her martyrdom. "He is right, of course. So pray tell me, if you will, what it is that you have come for?"

She gasped as Elliot's warm hand came to rest lightly on her arm. In her attempt to maintain her aplomb, she had failed to hear him rise from his chair to cross the room. "Ah, Evie! How you wound me with your cool composure," he whispered. "This odd, restrained civility; it has not always been thus between us—"

"It is thus now," she interrupted, her soft voice laced with wariness. Roughly, she dropped her hands from the windowsill and stepped back to distance herself from his touch. "I ask you again, Lord Rannoch, what do you want?"

Elliot watched through narrow, assessing eyes as Evangeline crossed to the opposite side of the narrow chamber and took a seat behind her desk. With deliberate languor, he crossed his arms over his chest and leaned back against the bookshelves, studying her. "First, Evie, I should like to have the portrait I commissioned," he answered quietly. "I paid gold for it, and I agreed to no alteration of our terms."

Abruptly, Evangeline bounced from her chair and tugged upon the bell pull. The elderly butler entered. "Please ask Gus to fetch Lord Rannoch's portrait from my studio," she commanded. Bolton nodded, then pulled the door carefully shut behind him.

"And secondly," continued Elliot, "I ask that you listen to my explanations of the regrettable misunderstanding that has transpired between us." He watched as anger, and perhaps pain, flared in Evie's eyes. Before she could retort, he interrupted. "Evangeline, however angry you may be, I think you owe me that much, given all that we have shared. Indeed, we owe it to each other, do we not?"

Again, Evangeline rose haughtily from her chair and began to pace the room. "I cannot think that I owe you anything, my lord. Nor you me. But by all means, speak your piece and have done with it."

Elliot drew a ragged breath and struggled to summon the magical words that might convince Evangeline of his penitence. She whirled again, moving nervously about the room, revealing a flash of the petticoat beneath the hem of her emerald-green gown. Tonight, she was as beautiful as ever. No, more so, with her flaming eyes and high color. Lord, but she was angry. Moreover, it was a cold, controlled anger, just the sort of defense Elliot found difficult to attack. In his impatience, he burned to dispense with all the foolish explanations, to pull Evie into his arms and kiss her into submission.

Elliot had no experience in justifying his behavior. Indeed, in the last ten years, he had never bothered to explain himself to anyone. But was that not, in large part, how he had trapped himself in this wretched excuse of a life? Pride and temper had most assuredly contributed to his downfall. And now, Evangeline deserved an explanation, pathetically weak though his might be. He drew a deep, unsteady breath.

A sharp rap sounded on the door, and Gus carried in the portrait while Theo followed with a sturdy easel. Without comment, they reassembled the pair, then promptly quit the room, leaving Elliot to stare at the amazing work before him. He had seen glimpses of it before, in varying stages of completion, yet the piece that stood before him now was wholly dissimilar to the one he had seen.

The pale marble stairs on which the late Elliot Roberts had stood, with one knee elegantly bent to the step above, had been transformed to a rocky Highland outcropping darkly etched against a gathering gray storm.

His blindingly white linen was similar, but his black wool coat was greatly altered, his shoulders widened. Gone, too, were the buff riding breeches and glossy black top-boots, now obliterated in favor of thick woolen stockings and an opulent kilt of black on emerald, the Armstrong tartan. It tossed about his thighs as if caught in some hellish gale. His hair, too, tossed dark and wild on the wind. A thin silver sword hung from his hip, and a fur sporran completed the clan regalia. His eyes glittered, black and wicked. Aloft and pointed heavenward, he held a long, heavy claymore.

"Mother of God, Evie!" In light of the painting, the rest of Elliot's ill-prepared speech of contrition vanished like smoke. "When . . . why . . . ?" he stuttered, his queries fading as he gaped at the portrait. The man in the painting stared coldly back, his expression immutable and unforgiving. The broad hand at his waist was sinewy and taut, as were the lean, solid muscles of his legs. In the flickering lamplight of the library, the canvas sprang hauntingly to life, exuding enmity and tension, as if the observer should be wary lest the subject pounce from his craggy perch in attack. The stubborn, bladelike nose, the wild dark hair, the overly strong jaw . . . it was unmistakably Elliot.

And yet it was not. At least, Elliot did not want it to be. This man, with his resolute pose and evil eyes, looked nothing like the man in Evangeline's first version. And yet, beyond the altered clothing and the arsenal of weaponry, her changes were amazingly subtle. A hint of shading here, a harsher line there, and in due course, good-natured Elliot Roberts became the cold, overbearing marquis of Rannoch. Was it just that simple? Was it just that appalling?

Good Lord, was this how Evangeline saw him?

"Evie," he began softly, "I cannot think what to say.

Your artistry is, as always, overwhelming, but I cannot fathom how . . ."

"I have not slept well of late," she interposed in an odd, tight voice. "I was driven to repaint it. Winnie said—oh, hell, Rannoch! Just take the dratted thing and go!" Abruptly, Evangeline whirled toward the side table and reached for the decanter of madeira Elliot knew Winnie always kept at hand. With a grip that was less than steady, Evangeline poured one glass almost to the brim, then paused, extending it toward him with an impatient look of inquiry. When he shook his head in refusal, she drank purposefully from the glass, set it down, then immediately took it up again.

Elliot, still holding her gaze, jerked his head toward the portrait. "Is that the man you think me, Evangeline? Such cold, harsh images—is that how I seem? Is that how I feel to you when you are in my arms?" Uncertainly, he came away from the wall as if to approach her.

"Please don't, Elliot," she whispered, her empty palm extended as if to forestall him. "If the portrait is what you have come for, just take it. Just take it and go."

He moved toward her, ignoring her entreaty. "Evie, please," he said softly, "tell me that I am not that man. Tell me that I am—or that I have some chance of again becoming—just Elliot. To you."

"No." Her response was a weak whisper in the pale lamplight. Like a terrified animal, she held his gaze as he slowly closed the distance between them.

"Evie," he replied, reaching out to touch the strands of hair that lay soft against her temple. "Can we not put this misunderstanding behind us?"

"Why?" she bit out, pulling away from his hand. "Why did you do it, Elliot? Explain yourself, if you can. I should like to hear the truth for once."

"I have, believe it or not, told you nothing that was

patently untrue," he answered hollowly, turning away from her. He drifted toward the hearth and sank down into the wing chair. Mentally grasping at the seemingly futile words, Elliot held his hands open before him and studied them intently. At last, he speared them through his hair in frustration and lifted his gaze to her. Evangeline stood by the side table, refilling her glass. "Evie," he said softly, gesturing toward the opposite chair, "can you not sit by me? Just for a moment?"

Warily, she nodded and came to join him. Elliot drew a deep breath. "Evie, I never meant to mislead you. I only—well, I suppose that is not entirely true. I admit to being less than honest, but I had lost my way in the rain the day I came here. It is hard to explain, and I am not at all sure I can."

"Try," she responded skeptically, her mouth drawn into a tight line.

Elliot forced a weak smile. "Yes, well . . . I was riding to Wrotham Ford on a rather unpleasant errand, and I felt, quite simply, miserable. When I saw this place, well, I stopped for directions. Despite my protestations—and admittedly, they were weak ones—I was immediately mistaken for someone else. Why I did not correct the oversight is something I cannot easily put into words."

"Try again," she repeated, her voice still cool.

Elliot shrugged in resignation and looked away. "I just wanted to stay here," he answered quietly. "I was so wet, and just so bloody weary. . . . No, that's not it at all. I was unhappy. The weariness was inside me, Evie. Can you understand?" He flicked his gaze to catch hers. "No, you cannot, can you? You have not let your life flounder, only to be wasted out of bitterness. You have had the strength to go on, while I—well, I have not been so wise. When I found this place, these people—such warmth and welcome—for the first time in my adult life, I found myself questioning my life's direction."

"You will excuse me, my lord, for saying that seems a trifle maudlin, not to mention implausible, given your history." Evangeline's tone was only slightly less chilly. She stared at him in icy cynicism. "Moreover, I cannot think what sort of errand a gentleman such as yourself might have in a backwater like Wrotham Ford."

Elliot sucked in his breath sharply. This was a question he had never expected to face. "I was searching for someone, Evie," he answered quietly. "An acquaintance. My—a woman. A woman I needed to speak with about . . . a personal matter."

Evangeline's chin came up a notch. "Is *mistress*, perhaps, the proper term?"

Elliot ran one hand wearily down his face. "I'll not discuss this with you, Evie. It would be inappropriate to do so."

"Ah, yes! Conveniently so!"

"Very well, damn it! *A mistress*. She had family there. She and I had a long-standing arrangement. An arrangement I chose to terminate. In such cases, it is customary for a gentleman to . . . that is to say, I wished to speak with her. I—I was angry. I wished to make certain she understood that it was over."

"I am not sure I believe you," she responded coldly. "Indeed, I collect that your most recent paramour met with an untimely death."

Elliot went rigid with shock. It seemed that in a very short time, Evangeline had more than compensated for her lack of knowledge about him. "As it happens, you are remarkably well informed," he answered grimly. "She is, regrettably, dead. Moreover, someone most assuredly murdered her, but it was not I. In any event, most of my time has been spent here. With you." A sick feeling unfolded in the pit of his stomach. "Who dared make such vile suggestions to you, Evangeline?"

"My step-grandmother says the talk is all over town, my lord," she answered flatly. "As well as a few other stories. And one thing is certain—you were not with me when you received that gunshot wound in the shoulder."

Oh, God, thought Elliot, *could it get any worse? Damn Lady Trent straight to hell, the meddling witch!* Elliot pulled himself stiffly erect in his chair, watching as Evangeline downed the better part of her second madeira. "I was challenged, Evangeline, and I was left with no honorable alternative. That is all I have to say." He averted his gaze toward the floor, feeling the nerve in his jaw begin to pulse angrily.

"Was it over a woman?" she snapped back.

Elliot's head came up in a flash. "In a manner of speaking, yes," he answered tightly, "and it is over. Do not raise the issue again. I forbid it."

Evangeline was out of her chair at once, amber dregs sloshing from her wine glass. "You forbid it? You *forbid* it? You must be mad, Rannoch, to think that you can command me like one of your servants—like one of your whores!"

"Damn it, Evangeline," he hissed, rising to his feet. "Do not taunt me! I warn you. I am trying to swallow my pride and make my peace here. God knows I should, but I'll not have my past examined in every minute detail."

"Hah!" She stalked toward the table to take up the decanter again. "From what I have heard, my lord, your past can scarcely withstand the light of day."

"That may be, Evangeline. But it is, however, precisely that—the past. And upon my honor, when we are wed—"

"Wed?" Evangeline laughed throatily. "You really must be mad, sir. And as to your honor, some would say you have none. Indeed, I know but one reason why you might wish to wed me! You think to exact some sort of revenge upon my father's family by thwarting their plans for Michael. Confess it."

Roughly, Elliot grabbed her by the shoulders and pulled her nearer. "That is naught but another of Lady Trent's lies, Evie! She would do much to keep us apart, whereas I would do nothing to hurt Michael. After all that has passed between us, if you do not know that much about me, then perhaps I am indeed wasting my time here."

Evangeline's face suffused with color. Abruptly, she looked away, hands trembling. "I—yes, I do know it. You have been exceedingly kind to the children. Forgive me."

"Evie," he whispered, tilting her elegant chin up with his finger, "whatever my past sins, and there are many, I meant you no harm in coming here. Not the first time, and not now. I care for you, and for Nicolette and Michael. I think it best we marry, and I have told Mr. Weyden so. Come, we have his blessing! Will you not agree?"

She looked away, her face still rigid with pride. "I—no, I cannot!"

"Look at me," he commanded, turning her face back toward him. "It is for Michael that you worry, is it not?"

"Oh, Elliot!" Her voice began to break under the strain. "You know that my step-grandmother will stop at nothing to get her hands on the Trent heir, so that she may continue to wield her power. Already she controls my uncle like a lapdog."

"Yes," murmured Elliot, setting the other hand lightly upon her shoulder, "and Nicolette will soon make a pretty pawn on the marriage market. Lady Trent will leap at the opportunity to advance the Stone dynasty by means of an advantageous marriage."

Evangeline's eyes opened wide. "Good Lord, that had not occurred to me!"

Elliot looked at her intently. "Rest assured that she will be no threat to them once we are wed, Evie. Perhaps we may both take some small comfort in the knowledge that my ruthless reputation shall at last prove invaluable," he added bitterly.

"Why, Elliot?" Evangeline pulled incrementally away, but Elliot tightened his grip on her shoulders. "Why do you pursue me so?"

"I love you," he said simply, searching her face for any sign of affection.

Evangeline's blue eyes flared wide as she tilted her head back to stare up at him. "I cannot believe you are a man much given to that emotion, my lord. If it is not revenge against my uncle, what do you truly seek from this alliance?"

"You will not believe, then, that I am capable of love? Very well. Perhaps I want only to possess you," he answered with a quizzical smile, "much as one might covet an exquisite work of art. I've been collecting a few, you know. Or perhaps I seek a mother for Zoë. God knows she deserves it. Or mayhap I have grown jaded with my existence and want nothing more than a life of rustic tranquility. And perhaps there is some small measure of truth in all of these things."

"I am afraid, my lord, that you must do better than that."

Elliot let his smile fade, his words soft yet certain. "Very well, Evie, I shall be painfully blunt on a more practical point. What if you already carry my babe? I'll not have another child of mine born a bastard, and you cannot avoid that fact by escaping to Ghent."

Her sapphire eyes darted nervously over his face, then dropped to his shirtfront. "I do not believe you would stop me," she said in a small voice.

"Come now, Evangeline," he answered grimly, letting his hands slide down her arms and giving her a gentle shake. "I think you do. Furthermore, you still desire me, I believe. As I desire you."

Abruptly, she tried to pull away from him, but Elliot merely tightened his grip on her upper arms. "Listen to me, Evie! I want you, and I am willing to protect you. 'Tis as simple as that. Marriages have been made for far worse reasons. Carefully consider that with your grandfather in his grave, Lady Trent is already moving to solidify her position. She shall never be satisfied with a dowager's life. Michael is her means to power."

"Oh, God, no," murmured Evangeline, an expression of weary resignation shadowing her lovely features. One hand fluttering anxiously at her temple, she brushed past him to resume her stance before the window, yet she did not pull away from him when he came to stand close behind her.

"What better alternative remains, Evangeline?" he asked softly, placing one hand lightly upon her shoulder. He felt a stirring of optimism when she did not push it away. "I shall try to be a good husband, I swear it. What other course of action will leave your family's peace undisturbed? They are happy here; indeed, I was happy here. Is it fair to insist that your family sacrifice a life which they have come to love and return to a homeland they can scarcely remember?"

In apparent capitulation, Evangeline dropped her hand from her forehead to the windowsill. "You do not fight fairly, Elliot." Her voice was a choked whisper.

"No," he answered gravely, "I do not. I cannot afford to. I need you too desperately."

Evangeline felt the heat of his breath sear her skin long before he opened his mouth against the curve of her neck. She simply understood the inevitable and gave herself up to it. Lifting her gaze to their pale reflection in the window glass, she watched as Elliot reached around to place his other hand on her upper arm, effectively checking any movement. With agonizing deliberation, Elliot moved to brush his mouth against the turn of her jaw, his tongue hot and teasing, his teeth nipping gently into her flesh.

Evie's mind felt defeated and confused, but her traitorous body was neither of those things. Involuntarily, her head tilted to the left to allow him access, even as a sigh of acquiescence escaped her throat. She felt so reckless, so wicked. Ah—yes, so good. He was controlling her, bewitching her once again, and she felt no inclination to resist him.

"Surrender, Evie," he whispered, nuzzling her neck. "Surrender, love, and we both shall win this battle."

She was so weak. Endless days of sheer fatigue and consuming grief were now exacerbated by too much wine, melting Evangeline's defenses into a puddle of warmth in her belly. Elliot battered at the armor of her logic even as he ravaged that of her heart. She wanted him. Such blind need was foolish, she knew. Yet at this moment, she did not care. As his free arm came up to bind about her waist and pull her back resolutely against him, she knew that despite all that he had done, it was her own lust that would now truly betray her. At the insistent touch of his tongue and teeth, pulling and suckling at the tender lobe of her ear, Evangeline gave up all pretext of refusal and moved against him, feeling his hard length press into her back.

Enthralled by his slow, calculated seduction, she watched in the glass as his hand slid across to tug gently at the bodice of her dinner gown. Was ever a man so wickedly tempting? With agonizing slowness, Elliot pulled the fabric inexorably downward until her breasts were bare, her nipples teased into hard, ripe buds by the sliding silk. Shaping first one breast then the other in his broad palm, Elliot still did not lift his mouth from her throat. His hands were unhurried and erotically abrasive against her skin as he took each swollen bud in turn, caressing them hard between his fingers, biting at her throat, and sending shafts of pain and pleasure coursing toward her stomach and lower still.

He went on and on, relentlessly, until Evangeline's breath became rapid and shallow. Then Elliot stopped and lowered his hands to capture hers. Roughly, he pulled them up and folded them against her chest. "I want to see your hands on your breasts," he whispered, his voice dark with hunger. His eyes held hers in the glass even as she felt his fingers pulling urgently at the back buttons of her dress. "Touch yourself," he commanded. "Yes, tease me."

Instinctively, she obeyed.

When Evangeline's garments felt loose at her waist, Elliot, still watching her reflection, slid his hands up her back and into her hair and slowly pulled the pins from it. The loosened tresses tumbled to her waist. "Stay here," he whispered hoarsely in the dark, moving swiftly across the room to put out the lamp, drowning her in desire and darkness. A scrape of ancient metal sounded as Elliot turned the key in the lock. And then he was pulling off his coat, loosening his cravat, and pressing her urgently back onto the heavy mahogany desk. In heated confusion, she felt Elliot shove up the froth of her skirts and tear at her drawers.

Dimly, Evangeline knew she should protest, but reality now seemed beyond her control. She had to have him inside her and was beyond caring about the consequences. Whatever he was, whoever he was, he had burned away all reason. His enticing promise of pleasure heated the darkness as Elliot yanked free his shirt and tore at the close of his trousers. In the pale moonlight, she felt herself sliding inescapably down into his carnal netherworld, even as his manhood rose, hard and powerful, from the crumpled fabric of his clothing. Abruptly, Elliot shoved two fingers into her. Gasping at the sudden intrusion, Evangeline was stunned to find that she was already wet with need.

"Ah, yes," she heard him rasp, "you are ready for me, sweet Evangeline." Smoothly, he urged her back and came almost on top of her, the warm, probing weight of his heavy shaft demanding entrance. He shoved himself into her, stopped, then abruptly pulled back, leaving her whimpering with frustration.

"No," he whispered. "I am mad for you, Evie, but I want you writhing with hunger for me." So saying, Elliot lowered his mouth to the joining of her thighs and returned his teasing fingers to her feminine depths. Clever hands, enticing tongue; they were hot inside her, in stark contrast to the cool wood beneath her hips. He was everywhere, urging her deeper into the blackness, driving her mad, just as he had vowed. She cried out into the night as the orgasm swept over her in a crashing wave of ultimate capitulation, drowning her, washing her in warmth and light as she burst free of the darkness.

Elliot heard her cry of submission, the half scream of surrender that tore through his deteriorating self-control. Again, he came up to shove himself inside her, feeling the heat of her slickened flesh as he anchored against her thighs. Within, she still throbbed with release, pulling hungrily at his swollen shaft. Oblivious to the papers and ledgers that tumbled from the desk, he buried himself deep in her warmth and began to move inside her.

Elliot felt like a man driven to desperation. The need to bend Evangeline to his will, to again lay claim to her, had quickly shifted to the need to lose himself in her. "Ah, take me, take me, Evangeline," he whispered desperately. "Take me, please." Unsure even of what he was asking for, Elliot murmured the words like a mantra against the dampness of her brow. Her strong, capable hands came up to tangle in his hair, to turn his mouth to hers so that she might draw his tongue inside. As he thrust himself over and over inside her, she matched his rhythm, intently seducing his mouth stroke for stroke, sweetly undermining his control, until he poured his very soul into her in a pounding rush of molten pleasure.

Elliot collapsed against her crumpled clothing, drawing deep, ragged breaths laced with the fragrance of spent passion. Inside, he still throbbed. His heart pounded, his chest choked with warmth. Slowly, however, his breathing calmed, and rational thought intruded. He lifted his face from her shoulder and looked about the room in bewilderment.

Good Lord, he had bent Evangeline across her desk and taken her in the middle of the library. He was little better than a rutting animal. Beneath him, Evangeline moved restlessly, and Elliot stood, pulling her up with him into his arms. Then, settling into the chair by the fireplace, he held her in his arms until her head slumped against his chest and her breathing shifted to the slow, deep rhythm of sleep. Neither had spoken, yet Elliot could sense that he had won the battle for Evangeline, but only in the short term.

Satiation began to battle with his apprehension, however, until Elliot straightened their clothing, gathered Evie into his arms, and carried her through Chatham's darkened corridors to the safety of her bed just as the clock struck midnight. Evangeline had surrendered to him, or, rather, had surrendered to his practiced seduction. It was more than he had dared to hope. For a time, it would suffice.

Bending low across Evangeline's bed, Elliot pressed a kiss to her brow. Tonight she had been blinded by lust, a useful but limited tool. He took comfort in the knowledge that even in anger, Evie was vulnerable to his seduction, yet it was far from enough. Indeed, he may have persuaded Evangeline to wed him, but he had not persuaded her to love Elliot Armstrong.

There was, perhaps, some hope. She had loved a part of him once, albeit briefly. And the gentle, good-natured Elliot Roberts was, he now understood, the better part of the man he had once been. A little more naïve and a little less jaded, perhaps, but an integral part of him, nonetheless. The trouble was, would Evie ever believe it?

Weakened by a choking rush of emotion, Elliot watched Evangeline snuggle deeper into the pillow and part her lips in a whispery sigh. She was so beautiful. Wise yet innocent, a rare and enchanting combination. He shoved his hands into his disordered hair and wondered what had become of his innocence, his wisdom, his very Scottishness. He thought again of his portrait, of the metaphorical changes Evangeline had made.

And as for metaphors, what had become of his black and green plaid? Had Kem truly burned it, as he had threatened so many years ago? Elliot could not suppress a smile and then grew somber once more with the realization that he had not seen his Scottish homelands for two years or better. He had not paid his respects to his mother. He had not knelt in prayer at his father's grave. Simple things, proper things, things he now knew he should have done. Yes, his mother had been cold, his father pious, and while they had not taught him to love, their woefully repressed emotions were no excuse for his failures. Indeed, it was not as if he had never known love, for he had grown up surrounded by two maiden aunts, a devoted nurse, and the land he had cherished.

What vagary of fate had impelled him to the edge of moral and emotional ruination? Had it been Cicely? Elliot was forced to admit that it had not. His yearning for her had been genuine, but it had been the incipient desire of a green boy, not the abiding love of a real man. Yes, Cicely's deception had cut him deeply, but was it the source of his destruction? No. His own failings, false pride and a false heart, had been the real cause. And as fanciful as it seemed, on a rain-soaked Essex night, the softly glowing windows of Chatham had become the windows to his soul. Through a cold mist, he had peered into their warmth and seen what he had once been, what he had so rashly given up, what might yet be salvaged.

Yes, soon he would wed Evangeline and take her to Strath to assume her rightful position as marchioness of Rannoch. The dowager countess of Trent be damned; Elliot took immeasurable satisfaction in the knowledge that Evangeline would outrank every member of her toad-eating Tory family. In Richmond, he would give Evie time and distance, until her anger diminished.

As for himself, Elliot had offered Evie and the children the protection of his name, and he now bore an obligation to make it a name worth having. He therefore resolved to dispel some of the uglier accusations hanging over his head—those that were undeserved, at any rate. Then he could begin his courtship in earnest, wooing his wife slowly and somehow convincing her of his willingness to change.

No, not to change. He would convince her—somehow—that a part of him was, in truth, the man she had fallen in love with.

&14&

The quality of mercy is not strain'd, it droppeth as the gentle rain . . .
—WILLIAM SHAKESPEARE

On the occasion of Lord Rannoch's wedding day, the skies poured forth in torrents. A bad omen from heaven, some said. Not a bit of it, countered his friends. 'Twas the devil shedding tears for the loss of his emissary on earth, since the marquis, or so they held, was a changed man. Rannoch, however, was left alone to stare blindly through rain-washed windows in a state of suppressed agitation, counting the hours until the appointed moment, his knuckles white with a worry he dared not name. His was a dangerous gamble, and for once Rannoch was all too aware that he cared very deeply about what was at stake.

His vigil was scarcely a solitary one. Every determined dowager and inveterate gossipmonger in London waited, too, with one ear pressed to the ground in a fervid effort to confirm the most titillating scandal to reach London in a month or more. The rumors spun wild and fast, shouted in gaming houses, then whispered in drawing rooms, each more outlandish than the one before.

The marquis of Rannoch had compromised a country innocent . . . The marquis of Rannoch was finally marrying his mistress . . . No, not the one he'd murdered, some silly foreign chit who'd foolishly flung herself beneath his boots and was now about to be well and truly trampled . . . No, indeed, that was not it at all! The marquis was taking revenge on the earl of Trent by seducing his niece and seizing his heir . . .

The talk went on and on, with far too much of it, in the bride's conflicted opinion, all too true. For her part, Evangeline tried to spare no thought for the machinations of the *beau monde,* focusing instead upon the weather, which she, too, feared was something of a portent. Numbly, she rose, bathed, and dressed, going through the necessary motions, until at last, mere moments before the ceremony was to begin, she found herself staring through the rain at the church, terrorized by doubt. And what should she expect, given the way she had allowed herself to be seduced into accepting Rannoch's marriage offer?

As she stepped into the crumbling old church in Wrotham-upon-Lea, a visceral stab of fear pinned her feet to the threshold. On the second rush of uncertainty, she wondered if it was too late to cry off. Standing close behind, as if frustrated by Evangeline's cowardice, Winnie gave an impatient shove against the small of her back, and Evangeline stepped tentatively through the door and into the unknown.

The marquis stood before the altar, looking resolute and resplendent in clothing far more elegant than anything Elliot Roberts had ever worn. Rannoch's every garment, from the perfectly tailored trousers to the rich superfine coat, bespoke his true standing as a wealthy, privileged peer who would be denied nothing. How easily the contents of a portmanteau had transformed the handsome but otherwise unremarkable Mr. Roberts into the indomitable marquis of Rannoch! How hard, how determined his eyes now looked . . . and what a pity she had not noticed them sooner.

As if he could hear her thoughts, Rannoch lifted his gaze to meet Evangeline's, heating her with his intensity. Evangeline tried to steady herself and look past him, deep into the shadows of the chancel, determined that the marquis would never know how profoundly he affected her. But he did affect her, damn him. It was beyond her understanding, this perplexing mix of need and desire she felt but would never confess. Despite his deception, Evangeline found herself obsessed by a man reputedly so depraved that, under ordinary circumstances, she would have walked a wide circle merely to avoid brushing him with her skirt hems. But the circumstances in which she now found herself were far from ordinary. She was walking toward the altar. Toward *him.*

Panic surged through her again, and Evangeline tried to force herself to relax. She drew a deep, deep breath. She told herself not to be foolish. She reminded herself that she was marrying for her brother's sake and that whatever Rannoch's purpose in wedding her, Michael would be a vast deal safer with the marquis than with her father's family. Of that much she was unaccountably certain. Perhaps Rannoch did indeed wish to annoy Lady Trent, but he meant Evangeline's brother no harm.

After what seemed an eternity, Evangeline reached the altar. Rannoch stood more stiffly now, his expression guarded, his narrow eyes assessing her. Gus stood at his side, but otherwise the marquis was completely alone. No friend or relative had darkened the church door. Why was that? Evangeline dimly felt her breathing grow shallow. Was Rannoch truly so wicked he had no friends? No family who cared? And what was she about to leap into?

Think, breathe, don't panic, she ordered herself, but her mind would not obey. What did she know of him, really? That he had a child . . . Zoe. An uncle . . . wasn't it Hugh? And a mother, the dowager. But where were these people? She was surrendering her very life to . . . to whom? A veritable stranger.

In a great black cloud, doubt and fear swirled up to seize her. Evangeline scarcely realized her knees were beginning to buckle until Elliot slid a strong, steadying hand beneath her elbow, pulling her up and drawing her to his side. To the casual observer, the gesture might have seemed possessive, almost sweet.

"Breathe!" He softly mouthed the word, his eyes narrow, his expression inscrutable.

Suddenly, Evangeline felt the air rush back into her lungs. A faint sound of relief escaped Elliot's lips. As if on cue, the vicar flipped open his prayer book and began.

Passages were read, responses were exchanged by rote, and Evangeline remembered little else about the ceremony until sometime near the end, when a protracted silence fell over the church. Elliot stared expectantly down at her, his mouth tight. Had she done something wrong? Behind her, Winnie gave an impatient hiss. Elliot's jaw was rigid, one small muscle jumping almost imperceptibly. Finally, he simply reached around to take her left hand in his right, lifted it, and slid a wide band of sapphires onto her finger.

Blinking uncertainly, Evangeline stared down at the ring, only vaguely aware of having spoken her vows. She stared up at Elliot, and the magnitude of what they had just done hit her. Quietly, his gaze drifted over her face, as if searching for something. Fleetingly, the mask of ruthless arrogance slipped, and for one infinitesimal moment, Evangeline saw uncertainty in his eyes.

The knowledge brought her a small measure of comfort, and she watched in fascination as he looked up from her hand, closed his eyes, and swallowed hard. A few more words, the vicar snapped shut his book, and Elliot's eyes flew open to stare into the depths of her own, then quickly shifted away. Evangeline choked back her own fear and studied him—*her husband*—more closely, increasingly certain of what she had glimpsed.

It was that tender, perplexing mixture of confusion

and desire which she had so often seen in young men, like Gus or even Theo. An awkward, almost adolescent rush of doubt, which could cut an inexperienced lad to the quick, leaving him feeling insecure and inadequate. Most assuredly, it was not the sort of emotion one would ever associate with the marquis.

Doubt returned. She must have been mistaken. And indeed, Elliot's sense of determination seemed very much intact. Evangeline could feel it, thrumming through the stillness about them while he gripped her elbow stubbornly, as if daring her to step away.

The vicar waved his hand one last time, and Elliot bent to kiss her quickly, sealing their vows forever with lips that were cool and firm. *"Courage,"* he whispered grimly as his mouth left hers, and Evangeline managed an unsteady smile. And then it was done. She was Elliot's in the eyes of God, and now she must make the best of it.

Together, they dashed out into the downpour, Elliot's arm wrapped securely around her, his ring snug about her finger. Someone—perhaps one of the conspicuously absent relatives—had had the forethought to send Elliot's enormous traveling coach up from Richmond. The sight of the elegant equipage, with its subtle but unmistakable Armstrong crest, had caused quite a stir in the tiny Essex village. He urged her quickly into it now, clambered up after her, and settled onto the opposite seat. Then, in a tender, companionable gesture, he draped his hand lightly across Evangeline's knee and leaned forward to watch Winnie bounce up into Peter Weyden's barouche.

Through the fabric of her clothing, Evangeline felt Elliot's touch warming her skin. Outside, the cold rain pelted down in a steady tattoo upon their carriage roof as, across the narrow churchyard, Evangeline saw Etienne staring disconsolately at the back of Winnie's cloak.

Then, slowly, he, too, turned away to climb up into a third carriage with the others.

It really was over. Elliot's coachman gave a shout, and they lurched forward into the rain. Evangeline gazed across the narrow compartment to study her husband's profile, which seemed oddly softened by the light of the overcast morning. Tentatively, she brushed her hand across his, just as she heard Etienne's door thump closed.

Elliot dropped the curtain and lifted his gaze to stare at her, his expression almost vulnerable, as if her simple touch had been a needed sign. Then, without another word, he pulled Evangeline across the width of the coach and into his lap, just as he had in the library but a few short days earlier. Elliot cradled her, her head upon his shoulder, his left hand threading lightly through her hair, as they made their way back to Chatham Lodge.

They were halfway home before he hesitantly spoke. "I truly feared you might refuse me, Evie," he whispered into her hair. Elliot's lips brushed lightly against the pulse of her temple, and one hand came up to lift an errant strand of hair to his lips. "It seemed you might bolt back down the aisle and out of my life—or refuse my ring." She angled her head to look up at him.

Finally, he spoke again, staring not at her but into the depths of the carriage, the strand of hair still wrapped loosely about his long fingers. "I could not have borne it, Evie," he quietly added. "I could not."

Evangeline did not know how to respond. Impulsively, she touched her lips to the hard line of his jaw, drawing in the warm scent of his skin, feeling a hint of stubble against her lower lip. Sharply, Elliot exhaled, then made a little choking sound in the back of his throat as he turned his lips to take hers. Evangeline came up to meet him, one hand sliding up his lapel and around his neck.

He kissed her once, lightly, almost gratefully. And

again, much deeper, more demanding. Willingly, Evangeline opened her mouth, drawing him into a kiss rich with need. Elliot answered, surging inside, crushing her mouth hungrily beneath his. His fingers skimmed the turn of her jaw, slid through her hair, then cradled her face, and Evangeline purred with pleasure. His mouth was sweet and hot, his breath warm and fast. She pressed one palm against his shirtfront, thrilling at the rapid beat of his heart beneath her hand.

Whatever he was, whatever he had been, she could not deny her desire for him. She simply prayed that it would be enough, then gave herself up to Elliot's ravening mouth and let his caresses soothe her uncertainties as his words could never have done. Impulsively, Evangeline let her fingers slide seductively down to skim beneath the bearer of Elliot's trousers. Abruptly, he sucked in his breath, the raw, ragged sound of a desperate man, and Evangeline decided that, for the moment, she would allow herself the luxury of believing that perhaps—just perhaps—she was the luckiest woman on earth.

It was nearly dusk before the progression of traveling coaches and baggage carts straggled through London and rumbled over the river, and it was past dark by the time they reached Richmond. In a whirlwind of frenetic activity, much of it directed by Evangeline, the children were unloaded, the baggage carts emptied, and the wide-eyed servants brought forth to make their bows. A bevy of housemaids escorted children up to bed, footmen toting trunks in their wake.

To Evangeline, it seemed the day might never end, despite Elliot's admonitions to go up to bed, and it began to feel as if she might soon see dawn's light while still in her wedding dress. Already weary from the wedding, Evangeline breathed a sigh of relief when at last she found herself alone, able to collapse onto the drawing-room sofa with a much-needed glass of wine.

After ordering Evangeline to rest, Elliot had gone off in search of his uncle Hugh, who apparently did indeed exist but who had made it a lifelong policy to avoid churches in general and weddings in particular. The children were undoubtedly asleep, and at last a sense of calm had settled over the house. Languidly, Evangeline let her eyes drift over the well-appointed room. A bank of four deep, well-dressed windows overlooked a landscaped lawn which rolled toward the Thames. The walls were hung in a soft yellow wallpaper, and the Turkey carpet might have ransomed a minor sultan. Strath was vast, but managing such a place little worried Evangeline, who had supervised large, cumbersome households since her mother's death.

The thought, however, of being alone with her new husband had given her pause. Two days before the ceremony, she had announced that the children would accompany them to Richmond. Only Winnie would remain behind at Chatham with Gus, who was studying for his return to school at Michaelmas term. To her surprise, Elliot had cheerfully agreed and immediately solicited everyone's help in acclimating Zoë to family life.

Evangeline tried to relax. After putting down her wine and toeing off her slippers, she tucked her feet beneath her skirts and let her head drop down onto the softly padded arm of the sofa. From this new angle, however, something very strange caught her eye, and all thought of relaxation vanished.

On the dimly lit wall to the left of the sofa hung a huge painting. The work was richly mounted in a gilt frame which was elaborately carved and at least twelve inches deep. The cost of the frame very nearly exceeded the price of the painting, for Evangeline could fairly guess at the value of such a fine mounting . . . and she knew to the very ha'penny just what the marquis of Rannoch had paid for the canvas.

How could she not? The painting was hers.

Evangeline closed her gaping mouth and stared in astonishment. Of all her works, she knew that *The Fall of Leopold at Sempach* was her very finest, the long-awaited culmination of years of painstaking study. Evangeline had been a little saddened while watching Peter's workmen crate it for the trip to London, and a part of her had hoped that he would be unable to sell it for the impossibly high price she had set. Her prayers had been in vain, for the work had been snatched up, still in its original crate, by a nameless man who paid Peter in gold and carted it away, sight unseen. At the time, it had been most puzzling.

Before Evangeline could assimilate the extraordinary happenstance of finding the battle of Sempach raging across her husband's drawing-room wall, a soft knock sounded, and a round-faced chambermaid poked her head through the door. Despite her confusion and fatigue, Evangeline managed to dredge up a name to go with the face. "Yes, Trudy?"

The girl bobbed a quick, deep curtsey and looked around. Obviously, she had expected Elliot. "Beg pardon, my lady, but his lordship said as how I might bring Miss Zoë down to him? She's a bit too excited for sleep just yet."

From behind Trudy's starched skirts, a tiny face in a white nightcap peeped out.

Evangeline came swiftly to her feet and flew across the distance to the door. "And who wouldn't be! After such commotion, I daresay I shan't sleep, either."

Trudy wavered uncertainly in the door as Evangeline knelt to look at Elliot's daughter. Zoë Armstrong was plump and china-doll pretty, with a perfect bow mouth, wide brown eyes, and a mop of wild chestnut curls no nightcap could ever suppress. They sprang out in all directions, giving one the impression of having disturbed a woodland sprite from her slumbers.

Evangeline extended her hand. "Good evening, Zoë," she softly said. "I am . . . Evangeline."

For the space of two heartbeats, Zoë stared at the outstretched hand, then crossed her arms stubbornly over her tummy. Her bottom lip protruded into a querulous expression, which made her look so much like her father that Evangeline was compelled to choke back a giggle.

The girl narrowed her gaze skeptically and stared at Evangeline. "My papa," she finally proclaimed, "says that I am to have some cousins to play with. And a mother, too."

"And so you shall," agreed Evangeline. "As to the mother, why . . . I suppose your papa meant me. Shall you mind it very much?"

"Have you brought the cousins?" asked Zoë intractably, as if negotiating with a horse trader. She studied Evangeline with unveiled suspicion, and this time Evangeline saw her husband's flashing eyes.

"Oh, indeed I have," answered Evangeline gravely. "A whole carriage load. More than you can count, I daresay."

"Hoo!" said Zoë dismissively. "I doubt that! I am seven years old. And I can count to five hundred. *And* do sums."

Evangeline strove to look mightily impressed. "Can you, indeed?" she asked.

Zoë nodded and finally took the outstretched hand. Evangeline rose from her crouch on the floor and steered the child toward the sofa. "I confess, Zoë, I am all astonishment at such skill. I was given to understand that you had no teacher, and so I have brought one with me. But perhaps you have no need of him?"

"Well, I don't know," Zoë admitted, as she clambered

up onto the sofa. She wiggled back and forth until she was comfortable and sat, bouncing one foot up and down with restless energy. Evangeline took the seat beside her. "I suppose I might need one," the child continued, "for I've not had a governess in ever so long . . . not since Papa set Miss Smith on fire." The minx beamed mischievously.

Evangeline inadvertently hiccuped with laughter. "Oh-ho! Set her on fire, did he?"

Trudy rushed into the conversation. "Oh! Not set *on* fire, my lady!" she interjected. "*Fired.* His lordship discharged Miss Smith, that's all."

Zoë looked askance at her maid and huddled closer to Evangeline. "Oh, Tru! I know he didn't really do such a thing," she peevishly responded, in the small, brittle tone of a child who was badly in want of sleep. Her foot was barely bouncing now as she stretched, then scrubbed a fist over one eye. "But I am glad that she's gone, just the same."

Evangeline watched the girl's eyes grow heavy. "Don't worry, Zoë," she said softly, smoothing down her nightcap with one hand. "You shall like Mr. Stokely. I promise."

Zoë barely nodded. Her foot had ceased to move. "Your hair really is the color of our yellow wallpaper," the child muttered, her head falling somnolently against Evangeline's shoulder. "And you're pretty, too, just as Papa said. Am I to call you Mama?"

"As you wish, Zoë," whispered Evangeline as the child's eyes dropped shut. "Sleep on it. You need not decide just now."

For a time, Evangeline sat perfectly still, quietly looking down on the child as she drowsed, searching Zoë's expression for more bits and pieces of Elliot. She found them, too—in the turn of Zoë's cheek, the tilt of her brow, and the long sooty lashes that fringed the girl's eyes. Gently, Evangeline crooked one arm around to tuck back a loose curl that tickled at Zoë's nose.

"You make a lovely pair, Lady Rannoch," drawled a soft voice from the shadows of the corridor, and her husband strolled into the room with his deliberate, long-legged gait. "I begin to think that perhaps my daughter needs you almost as much as—" And then, apparently noting Trudy's presence, he shrugged his broad shoulders, smiled faintly, and let the words slip away.

Elliot had shed his coat and turned up his shirtsleeves to reveal the hard tendons of his forearms. In one hand, he held a half-filled tumbler, deeply etched with his coat of arms, and in the other, he carried a tattered book of bedtime stories and a rag doll with one eye missing. Evangeline was pleased to see that he looked relaxed, almost happy, in fact.

For a long moment, Elliot simply stood there, silently watching his wife and his daughter, transfixed by the overwhelming sense of comfort the scene evoked. His *wife*. His *child*. In his home. Yes, this was what had been missing.

Such thoughts were silly and sentimental, he knew, yet he did not give a damn. At last, this nerve-wracking day was over. Evangeline was his now, his warmth and serenity, his haven of peace in a cold, mad world. And as for Zoë, even in sleep, she was a bundle of vibrant energy. Together, Elliot found them perfect, flawless in their symmetry, a sonnet made of flesh and blood. For the third time since meeting Evangeline Stone, Elliot found himself fervently wishing that he were an artist, capable of committing such beauty to canvas.

"She is asleep," said Evangeline. Trudy stepped closer.

"So she is," answered Elliot softly. Quietly, he leaned forward to set down his glass and the toys, then scooped up his daughter with one arm. "I shall tuck her in. Trudy, you should take yourself off to bed as well."

Trudy nodded and exited into the corridor. Elliot watched her go, then slowly turned to face Evangeline. "My dear, I shall return in a few minutes." He looked her up and down. "A few *short* minutes," he belatedly clarified, "if you will wait for me."

Evangeline struck a haughty pose, folding her hands demurely into her lap. "That would depend, I suppose."

"On?" Elliot crooked a dark brow at her.

She lifted her chin disdainfully. "On whether or not you really said I had hair the color of your *wallpaper*."

Elliot shot her a boyish, sideways grin. "If memory serves, it was very costly wallpaper. Does that in any way mitigate the insult? Or must I grovel?"

"Grovel, I daresay."

Elliot nodded gravely. "Yes, your ladyship." And then he was gone.

Left alone, still inwardly laughing, Evangeline began to muse over the man she had just married. Had she really made such a bad bargain? At times like this, when Elliot seemed more like Mr. Roberts than the marquis of Rannoch, it surely seemed she had not. Michael was safe, and, in truth, she was not, at this moment, unhappy. Clearly, there were many aspects of Elliot's personality she had yet to discover.

As for his part, tonight Elliot seemed almost lighthearted. She listened as his heavy tread echoed up the winding staircase, and she wondered, too, just what Elliot had been about to say before seeing Trudy standing beside the sofa. *Did* Elliot need her? He had repeatedly said as much, so why could she not let herself believe him? Did he *love* her? Certainly, he was capable of love, far more so than she would ever have thought possible of him. For it was clearly love that shone in his eyes when he looked at his child. And one more thing was equally clear: both Elliot and his daughter were desperately in need of a normal, loving family.

What a fortuitous coincidence. He had just married one, had he not?

The next several days, however, left Evangeline with little time to woolgather. Because it had been uncertain how long the family would remain fixed at Strath, Evangeline had ordered that lessons must go forward as usual, which meant blending Elliot's daughter not only into the family but into the schoolroom as well. A makeshift studio was established for Evangeline's work and the small schoolroom carefully dusted and stocked. And throughout the rush and routine, Evangeline could not but notice that Zoë watched her almost constantly with a vague, rather wistful expression. Clearly, the child yearned for maternal companionship and family structure.

Almost as disconcerting, in Evangeline's opinion, was the child's woefully neglected education. Her childish bravado notwithstanding, Zoë's education was hardly what it ought to be. Not only had her instruction been sporadic, but her many governesses had apparently been more concerned with embroidery than geography. After the first day, Evangeline instructed Harlan Stokely to work with Zoë, for the express purpose of evaluating the child's educational needs.

Consequently, she and Mr. Stokely now reclined in the afternoon shade of Strath's expansive rear garden, casually chatting. A brace of liveried footmen lingered dutifully in the background, and all of them watched as the children desultorily whacked a tattered shuttlecock back and forth against the glistening backdrop of the river. Despite the beauty of the scene, the summer heat in and around London had become oppressive.

It was a sad truth that ennui had pretty promptly set in at Strath. During the first week, there had been high talk of visits to Astley's to see the trick horses, to Hatchard's for new books, and to Gunter's for flavored ices. To his credit, Elliot had indulged the children in their every whim without complaint. Inwardly, Evangeline chuckled at the stir the wicked marquis and his newest entourage were undoubtedly creating among the *ton*. Nonetheless, even as Elliot persevered in his paternal duty, the attractions of town faded for the children, and the day before, they had begun to mutter discontentedly about a return to the country. Zoë, once reassured that she should accompany them, quickly fell in with the grumbling.

Evangeline sighed.

Seated beside her, Mr. Stokely gravely cleared his throat and poked his spectacles back up his perspiring nose. "To return to our discussion, Miss—er, *my lady*—it is my considered opinion that Miss Armstrong is highly intelligent. Though the child has had little direction, and no classical education to speak of"—he paused to sniff disdainfully—"she is possessed of a sound logic and an imaginative mind. She will catch up and be a welcome addition to the schoolroom."

"Hmm," mused Evangeline, watching as Theo Weyden struck the shuttlecock a wild blow, sending it flying in the general direction of Mr. Stokely. It fell a few yards short, however, and disappeared into a tangle of flowering shrubbery.

The younger children leapt into the bushes, vying for possession. Suddenly, a cry of pain rent the stifling air. With instincts attuned to any childhood crisis, Evangeline was out of her chair before the screaming stopped. As she reached the rattling greenery and bent low to peer into the branches, Zoë bolted forth, one tiny arm extended, tears streaming down her face. Frederica and Michael followed on her heels.

"Mama! Mama!" she screeched, launching herself at Evangeline. "It bit me! It bit me!" A wrenching sob tore from her chest and set her lower lip to trembling.

"A bee!" explained Michael breathlessly, drawing up just as Evangeline folded the crying child into her arms.

"A bee!" confirmed Frederica, her glossy curls bobbing. "It stung her pointy finger."

"See?" wailed Zoë, tugging her hand from the folds of Evangeline's embrace to produce the wounded digit.

Her index finger really was swelling prodigiously. Gently, Evangeline grasped the hand, pulling it to her lips "Oh, yes, sweetie, you are hurt," soothed Evangeline, whirling up and about with the child in her arms. So she was *Mama* now. It had taken less than a fortnight to win such high praise. Secretly, Evangeline was pleased.

She stroked her cheek against Zoë's hair. "We must have a poultice straightaway. Let's find Mrs. Woody, hmm?" Evangeline continued to murmur to the distraught child, brushing the hand across her lips again. Her attention fixed on Zoë's tear-stained cheeks, Evangeline strode up the garden path, never noticing her husband until she had very nearly bumped into his massive frame.

Elliot stood just an arm's length away, looking down at her with an expression of barely leashed rage. Thinking perhaps that she had somehow overstepped her new role, Evangeline held his daughter out to him uncertainly. "Zoë's been stung," she managed to stutter. "A—a bee. In the shrubbery."

"Aye, I heard," he responded, his face relaxing slightly. Effortlessly, he pulled the child into his arms, smoothing back the wayward curls from her face with his big hand. "I'll take her to Mrs. Woody. Freddie can come with me," he added, nodding at the worried girl beside Evangeline.

"Is something amiss, Elliot?" Evangeline asked.

He nodded brusquely, the dark look returning. He flicked an anxious glance at the children. "I cannot speak plainly, Evangeline, but there is a Mr. Jones to see you in the library. My man of affairs, Gerald Wilson, is there and will stay with you. Please just answer Mr. Jones's questions, however . . . offensive they may be."

"He wishes to see me?" she repeated, feeling quite confused.

"Yes," he answered hollowly, then held her eyes firmly for a moment. "Evie—I'm sorry," he whispered.

Evangeline stared after him in bewilderment, but Elliot and Frederica were already trailing up the path toward the kitchens.

Inside the library, the silence was thick with dread. Gerald Wilson turned anxiously from his position by the window and stared at Albert Jones. The Bow Street runner had snapped rather respectfully to his feet when, not five minutes earlier, the marquis of Rannoch had angrily pounded his fist upon the desk and then stalked out of the room. Now, Jones still stood stiffly beside his chair.

Wilson crossed the distance between them and looked pointedly at the man. "Mr. Jones," he said, trying with little success to mimic the haughty glare his employer so often used to such an intimidating effect, "I am reminded of something we discussed once or twice before. It concerns the missing bracelet. Have you made the inquiries we spoke of?"

The runner looked up from the toes of his boots, his eyes focusing suddenly on Wilson. "Indeed," he answered with measured reluctance. "Based on the information you relayed to me, I revisited Miss Fontaine's mother in Wrotham Ford. Mrs. Tanner was adamant. She insisted that his lordship left the note—which she described as 'threatening'—and nothing more."

Wilson snorted derisively. "And do you believe that?"

Jones shrugged equivocally. "I recognize Mrs. Tanner and her ilk for what they are, Mr. Wilson. And I am not fool enough to believe that if she pinched a ruby bracelet, she'll be wracked with sudden guilt."

Wilson's cynical rejoinder was cut off when MacLeod pushed open the library door to admit the new marchioness. Briefly, Wilson let his gaze catch hers. Lady Rannoch always moved with an efficient, fluid elegance, giving one the distinct impression that she was both capable and confident. Today, however, she gave the further impression of being very, very annoyed.

Wilson chuckled softly to himself. Rannoch and, at present, Mr. Jones had their hands full—that was Wilson's bet. Ten days earlier, the marquis had turned the entire household upside down when he had arrived with a new bride, four children, and a tutor in tow. It was, on the whole, the most shocking spectacle Wilson had ever witnessed, and there had been some exceedingly shocking spectacles at Strath over the years. The servants' chatter had been unremitting ever since the three carriages had been unloaded at the doorstep.

If gossip had the right of it, Rannoch's bride was something of an enigma. No schoolroom miss was she; the beautiful lady with the subtly foreign accent was obviously a few years beyond the customary age for marriage. Furthermore, Wilson had it on good authority that she was a famous artist—E. van Artevalde—of all things imaginable! At last he had an explanation for his lordship's newfound preoccupation with the Flemish masters, for in the past, Rannoch had been more disposed toward the blacker arts than the higher arts.

Yet Strath House had been recently adorned with

three of van Artevalde's finest works, and though they had come dear indeed, Rannoch hadn't so much as twitched upon being presented with the staggering bills. And even stranger, perhaps, than his lordship's new wife was her brother. The sweet-tempered lad was reportedly the heir to Lord Trent, that hapless cuckold who had managed to lodge a ball of lead in the master's hindquarters, a regrettable misadventure which inevitably bode ill for the staff whenever the weather turned damp.

But it was a funny thing, that. For months now, Rannoch had been of a remarkably agreeable disposition. What was it that dry-witted valet kept muttering? *Cherchez la femme?* Indeed! As Lady Rannoch swept across the room toward them, Wilson decided he need look no further for the reason behind his master's sudden change in temperament. Instead, he seriously considered kissing her ladyship's skirt hems.

In the past ten days, the household had been tossed into an uproar, with children scurrying everywhere, room arrangements shifted, servants reassigned, scullery maids engaged, and menus altered. Henri, Rannoch's treasured French chef, quit in a huff after only two days, insisting that he simply could not continue "cooking coddled eggs for a gang of rapscallions," a description that, in Wilson's book, was more aptly applied to Rannoch's old friends than his new family. Kemble seemed constantly on the verge of ungovernable mirth, while Mrs. Woody was exceedingly pleased, telling anyone who would listen that the new marchioness knew "just what was what" about running a proper household.

Wilson's ruminations about his new mistress ended as her ladyship approached them. With a sharp little cough, Wilson stepped forward and made the introductions, then watched in admiration as Lady Rannoch's brows shot up one elegant notch.

"I collect that your husband has explained the purpose of my visit, my lady?" Mr. Jones began.

Lady Rannoch's expression did not alter. "I am afraid that he has not, sir. I was seeing to my stepdaughter's bee sting when my husband arrived. He took charge of the situation and merely bade me attend you."

The runner looked a little nonplussed at that, Wilson noted. It was, however, a brief reaction. Politely, the man handed a piece of foolscap to her ladyship. "Then I apologize for the intrusion, Lady Rannoch. Your husband agreed that I might speak with you about these dates."

She took the paper, her sharp blue eyes flicking down the page. "And so you may, sir. Though I have no notion what they might represent."

Jones made an odd choking noise in the back of his throat. "I merely wish to confirm that your husband was with—er, in your company at your home in Essex on these dates, my lady."

"Really?" Her voice was arch. "Why do you not simply ask him?"

Jones dipped his head deferentially. "We did discuss it, my lady. His response was—ah, something to the effect that if I had any further inquiries, I might ask the lady in question," answered the runner, his lips twitching in obvious bemusement. Wilson coughed again at the man's diluted version of the marquis's rather graphic terminology. "I believe his lordship did not take kindly to being questioned," Jones added.

"No," murmured Lady Rannoch with a faint smile. "I daresay few would." She bowed her head and skimmed the dates more slowly. Unexpectedly, she set aside the paper, rose from her seat, and went to the desk to take up a leather notebook, which she flipped open. Then, shutting it with an efficient snap, she returned to her chair. "My calendar indicates that Lord Rannoch was visiting at our family's estate on each of the dates you have listed, Mr. Jones," she answered coolly, handing back the paper. "Have you anything further?"

Once again, the runner seemed at a loss for words. Plainly, he had expected Lord Rannoch to tell his wife precisely what to say, and he had expected her to say it unequivocally. Instead, the lady was calmly pulling out notebooks and behaving as though Bow Street had inquired about the date she had last inventoried the third-floor bed linens.

"No, Lady Rannoch," he responded at last. "I do not. I apologize for the intrusion."

Her ladyship rose graciously from her chair. "Not at all," she murmured softly, then lifted her piercing blue eyes to Mr. Jones's face. "A murder is a serious thing, is it not? And I have little doubt that that is what brings you to Strath." The runner merely nodded. "We none of us here want an assassin running loose amongst us, Mr. Jones," she added gently. "Rest assured that Lord Rannoch and I wish you every success in your duty."

Albert Jones nodded once more, then rose from his chair.

Evangeline watched in silent relief as both Jones and Wilson gathered up their respective files, murmured polite good-byes, and quit the room. As soon as the door was whisked shut behind them, she drew a deep, steadying breath, counted to ten, then bolted for her bedchamber. No one noticed as she slipped inside and collapsed into a chair, fighting to still the trembling of her hands. Though she knew she hid it well, Evangeline felt thoroughly overwhelmed by the sudden changes in her life. It was all too much. A house full of people. Strangers to meet. *His lordship. My lady.* The incessant bowing and fawning.

When she had stepped into Strath House, her world had seemingly spun right off its normally sturdy axis. First, she had seen Zoë, who had fallen asleep on her shoulder, immediately captivating Evangeline's heart. And then there had been her paintings! Three of them, adorning the grandest rooms of Strath, and those rooms were very grand indeed. How and where had he obtained them? And what did it mean?

When she had asked him, he had been vague, almost uncomfortable in answering her. Such purchases might have been a small thing to a man of Elliot's wealth, little more than a whim, perhaps. But Evangeline did not think so. Indeed, she did not know what to think; she only knew that the fact that he had wanted them tugged at her heart in a way she did not comprehend.

Oh, Elliot! That was the most imposing change of all. The wicked marquis of Rannoch was now her husband. And lest she forget just whom she had married, some contretemps of fate had sent a Bow Street runner to remind her. And amid all these disconcerting changes, Evangeline had discovered that insomnia and inappetence—those faddish plagues of flighty, overbred females everywhere—had become her boon companions.

Two weeks ago, marriage had seemed the only solution. Indeed, it still seemed so. Evangeline drew some small comfort from her inability to think of any better alternative. And to her surprise, she was not, precisely, unhappy. At times, it seemed that Elliot was determined to win her heart again, and she was relieved to realize that her handsome roué of a husband had not yet grown weary of her. But he would. Oh, yes. She very much feared he would. A man like Elliot rarely reformed.

But she loved him. God help her, she did love him still. And in her rare moments of clarity, Evangeline admitted that she had always longed for a husband and children of her own. Inwardly, she gave a bitter laugh. If her recent morning sickness was any indication, she was well on her way to her second objective, close on the heels of the first. Perhaps Elliot had been right all along in saying that an expedient marriage was for the best.

Oh, Elliot. Evangeline squeezed shut her eyes and let her nails dig into the padded arms of her chair. Lord, how he could make her want him. It was shameful. The man had earned the appellation of *rake* quite honestly. It was, Evangeline sometimes feared, her husband's only honest accomplishment. Clearly, Mr. Jones suspected as much.

Every night Elliot came to her bed, and every night she welcomed him. Rarely did he leave before dawn. What else was she to do? She could not help but respond to his skilled seduction. Moreover, she had granted him the privilege of her bed when she had stood, visibly trembling, inside the tiny chapel of Wrotham-upon-Lea and whispered her vows. She had taken those vows very seriously, for it was only right, she told herself.

Yes, it was right. But was it wise? To give one's heart to such a man? For that was most assuredly what she had done. She, an abundantly prudent woman, had fallen hopelessly in love with a handsome, calculating rogue. Yet she could not honestly use the excuse that he had tricked her. She now admitted that she loved this man for himself, a reckless mistake which she knew would inevitably break her heart. Even his wickedness held a strange, spellbinding appeal. One night in Chatham's library had shown her that much.

When she paused to consider the enormity of what she had done, Evangeline was seized by a choking terror. She had surrendered her heart, her body, indeed her very life, to a man who had many enemies, most of them deserved if rumor had the right of it. Her husband was caught up in a scandalous murder investigation. His mistress had been horribly strangled. In this one thing, however, Evangeline held steadfast. Despite his reputation on the field of honor, Elliot would not kill in cold blood, of this she was inexplicably certain.

He might be wicked and vengeful, but it was not in his nature to be deliberately cruel. Elliot's propensity for carousing, gambling, and dueling, however, was another thing altogether, and Evangeline was filled with a chilly certainty that he would one morning find himself standing ankle-deep in dew-soaked grass, faced off against another armed and irate husband, but one with far more proficiency than her Uncle Stephen had possessed. It would kill her to lose him. She would kill him if he were unfaithful. Men like Elliot were never faithful. God, what an endless coil!

Indeed, throughout their impassioned lovemaking, Elliot had never once mentioned the word *fidelity*, and had he done so, Evangeline would have choked on a swell of doubt. She reminded herself that only a few short weeks ago, Elliot had dueled with a man named Cranham over a woman and then refused to discuss it with her. Perhaps she should strive to view his obvious disdain of hypocrisy as one of his finer qualities.

Though Evangeline nurtured hope in her breast, for without it she could never have surrendered to him, when seen in the light of day, it was a fragile hope indeed. She recognized it as that same naïve, impetuous emotion inevitably seized upon by every silly female who had ever dared to both love and wed an inveterate roué. How bittersweetly unbearable his touch would be when her frail, foolish optimism was crushed. It was true that Elliot had said he loved her. But no doubt he had used those very words to many others, including the young lady who had very nearly borne his child. The woman who, now ten years dead, should have been long since forgotten. Evangeline, however, had not forgotten. So often now, she found herself haunted by the remembrance.

At the soft sound of footsteps on carpet, she lifted her gaze from her white-knuckled hands to find that the object of her obsession now stood in the center of her bedchamber.

"I knocked," he said softly, "but perhaps you did not hear?" In truth, Elliot looked sick with worry.

"I—no, I did not," she answered, still trying to fathom his look of distress. Her eyes searched his face. "Is aught amiss? Is Zoë recovered?"

"On the mend, I think. She and Frederica have gone to the schoolroom with Stokely." Her husband sank down into the narrow settee across from her chair, looking, as he always did, far too big for the delicate furnishings of her bedchamber. This afternoon, however, he looked rigid and unsettled. He leaned stiffly forward in his seat rather than reclining languidly, with his muscular arm stretched out along the back of the settee, as was his habit.

"Jones has gone?" he asked in an uncharacteristically hollow voice as he roughly shoved back his hair with one hand.

Evangeline forced her hands to unclench and ran them up and down the fabric of her skirt. "Yes," she finally replied.

He slid forward in his seat to pull one of her hands into his and began to rub it gently. "So cold, Evie," he murmured, almost absently. "So damnably cold, you feel nigh bloodless. I have distressed you yet again, have I not?" He continued his gentle ministrations, taking first one hand, then the other, without looking into her face.

"I'm perfectly well," she eventually answered. Unwittingly, she began to respond to his warm, comforting touch.

"I am so sorry about Jones," Elliot whispered, bowing over her hand, refusing to meet her gaze. "About his coming here today. He should have sent word . . . I could have met him elsewhere."

She shook her head. "Elliot, it was not an inconvenience."

"No, indeed. It was not! It was an impertinence!" He squeezed her hand so hard it hurt. "I should never have permitted him to speak with you. I cannot think what was in my mind. 'Twas my temper, I suppose, as usual. But he made me so damnably angry—"

"That's understandable, Elliot. But I answered his questions. It was no hardship."

Elliot did lift his eyes to hers then, a rueful expression flashing across his solemn face. "Sometimes I fear that this marriage will be nothing but a hardship for you, Evie. I suppose I had some foolish dream of protecting you from the harsher realities of life. Perhaps I have merely drawn you into something worse."

"Elliot, please do not—"

"No, Evie, let me speak." He let go of her hand and threw himself back against the chair, a look of unutterable weariness etched upon his visage. "These damnable lies, and I assure you they are such, shall be set to rights. I will find the truth, one way or another."

"You are quite serious," answered Evangeline, surprised by his odd intensity.

"Aye, about many things," he replied softly, then pulled her onto the settee beside him. He wrapped his arms about her and crushed her to his chest, burying his face in the top of her hair. "Will you make love to me, Evie?" he whispered hoarsely.

"Now? It's—"

"—the middle of the afternoon. I know," he answered, lifting her from her seat and carrying her toward the bed.

With his free hand, he pushed away the bed hangings. Then he laid her gently on the coverlet and followed her down into the softness.

Evangeline wriggled away slightly. "But someone might—"

"No," Elliot rasped, suddenly intent on loosening her hair. He paused just long enough to stare down into her fathomless blue eyes and felt his heart melt. "They won't. I left word that we're not to be disturbed. I wanted to speak with you, yet now I find that words fail me. Let me love you instead?"

"Yes," she whispered, already arching eagerly against him.

She was so beautiful, his beloved bride. Elliot lowered his head, opening his mouth wide over hers, coaxing her lips to part. Evangeline opened to him willingly, quieting his apprehension, suffusing him with relief. And relief smoothly shifted to need, which bloomed in his chest and drifted lower.

Lord, he had never had a more sweetly complacent woman in his bed. Once inside her mouth, he explored her languidly with his tongue, as if they had all the time in the world. And he thought of her, this woman, his wife. He considered what her life had been like, difficult, filled with obligation. And he realized again how desperately he wanted to strip away those burdens and give her back her girlhood in some small measure. To bring joy to her heart. To make smooth her path through life. Love her, and be loved by her.

She had hoped to marry someday. For love, she had said.

And then duty had called in the form of family obligation, more than once, and time had begun to pass her by. Well, she was surely wed now. To him. And though it was not perhaps the love match she had wished for, Elliot fought to believe he might still have a chance at making her dreams come true. Today, he had been losing the battle. Until this moment. Lovemaking had become much more than physical release; it was his lifeline between hope for the future and despair of the present. Only blinding passion could quiet the uncertainty. Each time Elliot sheathed himself inside his wife, hope became a tangible, living thing which vibrated about them like the heralding hum of a lightning strike.

He slid his palm up her neck to cup lightly the elegant turn of her jaw. Evangeline was tugging at the fastening of her dress and turning to press her breasts to his chest. Hard beneath her chemise, the dark areolas of her breasts tempted him, the stuff of his dreams. Pleasure and fulfillment. He shifted his weight onto one elbow, then spread his mouth wide to capture one swollen nipple, suckling hard through the thin fabric until it clung damply to her skin. Beside her, Evangeline's left hand fisted in the coverlet as her head tilted back into the pillow.

Elliot paused just long enough to pull away her clothing, then took the other nipple in his teeth, biting hard until she whimpered, then suckling and soothing her with his tongue. He heard her moan. Her sounds of lust and pleasure were familiar to him now, yet still sweetly exquisite, as they would be into eternity.

Elliot refused to hurry; he felt driven to make her desperate with need. Evangeline's hungry hands, quite warm now, came up to pull at his shirt, tugging it free. Deftly, she loosened the close of his trousers and eased her hands down inside, palms stroking his belly as they went. His groin was tight with desire as she slipped one hand down to cradle him. He moaned, pulled away, and rolled off the bed to stand in a low shaft of afternoon sun.

Elliot undressed slowly, loosening the tie of his drawers and letting them slide away to reveal his shaft, thick and throbbing with desire for her. For Evangeline. His wife. Elliot had no need to touch her, to test her readiness for him. Evangeline was consistently, reassuringly eager. Yes, that, too, gave him hope.

With his head bowed, Elliot stood beside the bed and slid one hand back and forth along the smooth surface of his erection, willfully tempting her. He watched her eyes open greedily, saw her tongue flick out to touch one corner of her swollen mouth. He reveled in the vision of how solid and sleek his shaft would feel when he sheathed it deep inside her, then withdrew, only to plunge deeper still. He looked down at himself. The means by which he would join himself to Evangeline. One body, one flesh. He turned his head to look at her as she lay naked upon the bed, her glistening yellow hair spilling across the pillow, her heavy breasts still taut with unslaked desire, the enticing curls that teased at her already open thighs.

"Oh, God, Evangeline. I am truly lost," Elliot heard himself rasp, for yet again, he had become the victim of his seduction. "I have wanted you all day. Since the moment I left your bed at dawn until this very minute, and every one in between. I think I love you to utter distraction."

Her lips curving into an enigmatic, feminine smile, Evangeline touched herself in blatant invitation and extended her other hand toward him. Squeezing shut his eyes, Elliot eased his palm down his hardened rod again, thrilling in the sensation as his blood thickened, then almost stopped, when he imagined his manhood driving into her, spilling his seed, and filling her with his child.

Evangeline's riveted gaze still held fast to every movement of his hand. Her blue eyes, already wide and unfathomable, became softly luminous with an unmis-

takable hunger. Then, just as Elliot bent his knee to join
her on the bed, intent on burying himself inside her, she
gave a small, choking cry and came onto her knees before
him, taking his swollen shaft into her hands.

"Beautiful," he heard her whisper as she bent low to
flick her tongue lightly across his heated flesh, sending
fire coursing deep into his belly. Then she looked up at
him in innocent wonder, her full mouth parted invitingly, and Elliot could do nothing but groan and nod his as-
sent. He stood beside the bed, one knee resting on the
mattress, as the low, exquisite torture began in earnest.

Evangeline drew him deep inside, loving him with her
mouth and tongue and fingers until the pulse pounded
wildly in his temple. Suddenly, with a roughness he could
not control, Elliot shoved her backward on the bed,
hauled himself on top, and pinned her slender wrists
above her head. "Evangeline, promise that you are mine,"
he whispered as he urged her thighs apart with his knee,
then pushed into her mercilessly. "Say that you love me."

She stared back at him, her eyes open yet impenetrable.

"Yes! Say it," he commanded as he embedded himself
deeper into her warmth. "Say it, Evie. For God's sake,
please tell me," he rasped as he deepened his thrust.

As if in answer, her legs came up to twine about his
waist as she began to tremble beneath him. Her arms
pulled against his grip as Elliot drew back, then sheathed
himself deeper still another long, powerful stroke.

Evangeline's breath came out in a little gasp as she
shifted her hips and urged herself hard against his flesh.
Elliot thrust inside the slick, hot welcome and began to
pound rhythmically against her womb. She sighed and
arched against him, stroke for stroke, rising up to meet
his thrusts, her head tipping backward into the pillow,
her mouth open with pleasure.

Time seemed suspended until Elliot at last became aware of her low, ragged moan of incipient release. Easing his hands beneath her bottom, he lifted her higher, then suddenly, possessed by the demons he could not control, Elliot paused in mid-stroke and squeezed shut his eyes. "Just say it, Evangeline," he rasped. "I have to hear the words again."

Beneath him, Evangeline whimpered, a hungry, urgent sound, but Elliot's perverse resolve did not falter. He held himself stubbornly in check; his own need was a hot, heavy ache in his groin.

"Yes," she gasped at last when he did not move. Her words sounded as if they had been ripped from her heart. "Yes, I love you, Elliot. God help me. I love you." She began to pant desperately. "Please—oh, please—I love you. You know I do," she repeated, and a wicked satisfaction edged with rapture knifed through him.

With a hand that shook, Evangeline threaded her fingers through the hair that had tumbled across his forehead. Then, as he continued to drive himself relentlessly inside her, she pulled his panting mouth to her breast. Her trembling deepened, dragging him with her to the brink of fulfillment.

Suddenly, he felt her orgasm begin as Evangeline cried out his name again, her voice rich and throaty. He watched as awe flashed across her face, and then she was clutching at him wildly, her legs lashing tighter about him, her sweet insides pulling and pulsing and drawing him over the edge. Splintering him and pitching the shards into blissful infinity, the pleasure carrying him into eternity.

At last, he collapsed against her breasts, bearing his weight marginally forward on quaking elbows and dropping his brow to touch hers. Gasping for breath, Elliot rolled to one side and waited as his beating heart calmed.

He lay limply upon his wife's bed, staring up into the canopy, and considered what he had just done. For the second time in a fortnight, he'd done something that had stunned him into utter silence. First, he had taken a wife. Now, he had begged, cajoled, and tormented her into saying something she had not wanted to say, and might not have meant. It had been wrong. But at the moment, Elliot was beyond caring.

Inside, the room was soothingly quiet. Outside, through the open casement, Elliot could hear the busy warble of a dove on the sill and the cheerful clamor of children playing in the afternoon sun. He found the sounds foreign and unexpectedly intense yet infinitely soothing. Fleetingly, he wondered if he had ever listened before. Or had there, until Evangeline had come into his wretched life, been nothing to hear?

Lord, it felt good to lie down with her. The tangle of sheets about his legs felt crisp and cool. The sun still shone across the bed, a bit lower now. In the shaft of heat and light, Evie's hair was warm. She smelled sweet, safe. He pulled her close against his side, and they burrowed into the covers to drowse.

⸭15⸭

Did ever a woman interrupt a man with such a silly question?
—LAURENCE STERNE

When Elliot awoke, the sun was well past the window, casting the room in soft shadow. A cooling breeze drifted in through the window, fragrant with the scents of a summer evening. The doves, the river, and the children, all had fallen silent. On the bed next to him, Evangeline had levered herself onto one elbow and was staring down into his face. With a stroke of her long fingers, she brushed the tangled locks of his hair backward, then lowered her lips to his forehead.

"Let's get up, Elliot," she said, her mouth soft against his skin. "We should dress and go downstairs."

Smoothly, he shifted to one side to face her, capturing her hand in his. "Oh, Evie, I love you! Did I remember to tell you?"

"Oh, yes. You did." In the soft light of evening, her eyes were soft and faintly moist. "I love you, too," she repeated, with an unmistakably bittersweet smile. Her gaze drifted up and across the bed hangings. "I said it. I suppose there is no point in pretending I have not fallen in love with you. What difference would it make?"

Elliot caught the note of regret that edged her voice. "All the difference," he answered, roughly pulling her against him. "All the difference in the world to me. Those three words from your lips changed my life. Do not keep them from me, Evie. Ever."

She rested her head against his chest and fell quiet for a long moment. Slowly, Elliot let his hand slide around to caress her, pulling her hips hard into his. He wanted her again, wanted to chase away her regret with his desire. He would make love to her so intently and deeply, and so very thoroughly, that there could never be any lack of understanding between them.

"Elliot?" He felt her breath stir the hair on his chest.

"Yes, Evie?" The edge in her voice stilled his wandering hands.

"I would like your answer to a particular question."

"Sweetest," he interjected gently, brushing the back of his hand against the softness of her cheek, "there is nothing you cannot ask."

There was a long silence in the room. Not the sort of silence Elliot always longed for, that intimate, peaceful quietude that lingers between lovers once sated, but a silence heavy with uncertainty. Evangeline drew a deep breath. "Elliot, do you mean to be faithful to me?"

Elliot bolted upright in the bed, dragging his wife up with him. Sharply, he turned her toward him. "What sort of question is that, Evangeline, to spring on a man whose heart has been very nearly ripped from his breast? Aye, I mean to be faithful! Why else should I have begged you to marry me?"

Evangeline watched his expressive face, the hawkish brows drawn tautly together, the deep furrows of his frown, and her mind spun into yet another whirl. Why else, indeed? There had been some reason, some suspicion, had there not? But it had slipped from her mind now, borne away, apparently, on the wings of passion.

The fleeting intimacy that had lingered between them was gone. She had shattered it. "I—I don't know, Elliot," she stammered, absently shoving her heavy hair back over one shoulder. "It's a reasonable question. More wives ought, perhaps, to ask it."

"Well, my wife needn't ask it," he huffed, seeming genuinely affronted. "What did you think, Evie? That I would keep my bachelor ways and take a wife as well?"

Evie felt her face suffuse with color. "I never thought . . ." she mumbled weakly, but her expression undoubtedly answered his question.

With a grunt of manly resignation, Elliot collapsed back into the pile of bed pillows and drew his arm over his eyes. He lay across the tangle of sheets for a time, then heaved a weary sigh. "Bloody hell, Evie! We've been married nigh a fortnight, and we make love every evening. Sometimes twice! I sleep like a dead man. I stagger when I walk. And I hardly stir from home." His Scots accent broadened as his words flew. "Lord, woman! We've got a gaggle of children who keep me worn to a frazzle—and I am not complaining, mind—But God's bones, I'm no' a young man! I'm all of five-and-thirty! Now you've taken to seducing me in the middle of the afternoon, right under the servants' noses. Now, do tell me, lass, just when, and by what miracle of nature, am I to service this—this mistress—or whatever it is you imagine I've the energy or interest left for?"

He did not realize he was shouting until a sharp rapping sounded on the connecting door. Her face flushed with embarrassment, Evie dived beneath the covers.

"Those *servants' noses,* my lord?" sang Kemble through the thick slab of oak. "Even as we speak, one of them is pressed resolutely against this door. Now, pray get up! It is time I dressed you for dinner."

Godfrey Moore, Baron Cranham, reclined indolently in his chair by a deep, arching window, impatiently dangling his quizzing glass by its black satin ribbon. As always, Brooks's was lively, but tonight he had not come to play. No, he had come at Lord Linden's behest and found himself a little plumper in the pocket for the inconvenience.

Cranham swung the glass high, then neatly caught it in the palm of his hand. What a pity he could not catch Rannoch so easily. Curling his lip into a sneer, he stared at Linden. The fool. Let the viscount whisper and gossip and drag him from pillar to post if he wished, but the bloodthirsty strangler was not apt to show himself by leaping upon them from the shadows of London's clubs, hells, or whorehouses, no matter how diligently Linden trolled his bait through town. No, Cranham's would-be murderer lay snug in his bed in Richmond with his new bride, whether anyone wished to believe it or not.

He yawned discreetly, then strolled into the card room to watch the charismatic viscount drift companionably from table to table. One could almost see the aura of charm that surrounded him as he slid from table to table, wine glass in hand. Cranham leaned subtly into him as he strolled past.

"Linden, are we nearly done with this preposterous sham?" he hissed. "I feel as if a bloody ax hangs over my head."

"My dear fellow!" whispered the viscount in a tone rich with sarcasm. "The center must hold. I pray your nerve shall not fail you whilst success is within our grasp!"

"Damn your impudence," answered Cranham in a growling undertone. "I have little use for you and your cursed duplicity."

"Better my way than yours, I should think," commented Linden dryly. He stared over his wine glass and let his eyes drift over the crowd. "Perhaps I *should* let old Elliot shoot you, Cranham, purely as a matter of principle. I begin to find you tiresome."

"Hmph," snorted Cranham derisively. "I do not fear that bullying Scot. Not in the light of day, at any rate."

At this, Linden arched his brows elegantly. "Do you not? Then you are more the fool than I thought. I can only hope you've held firm to our little Banbury tale these last three nights."

"I have," admitted Cranham tightly. "For all the good it shall do us, since I cannot imagine anyone witless enough to believe that Rannoch and I have suddenly become bosom beaus."

"Convince them, damn it," commanded Linden softly, his threat implicit.

"What of Lord Rannoch?" growled Cranham. "Will he do his part?"

"Rannoch will do whatever it takes. He has a new bride to impress."

"When, damn it?"

"Tomorrow night, *mon ami*," answered the viscount, staring coldly through the window into the darkened street. "Tomorrow night, I think we shall all go to Vauxhall."

Evangeline spent the following morning with Mr. Stokely and the children, who were industriously engaged in mapping Hannibal's route across the Alps. Her thoughts, however, were far less orderly. Elliot's words yesterday had thrown her into a quandary. He insisted that he loved her and swore his fidelity. He said she had very nearly broken his heart.

She was afraid to believe any of those things, yet despite all her pointed barbs about his honesty, Elliot did not strike her as a man normally given to lying. He seemed far too arrogant to resort to prevarication—and rather adamantly, at that—when haughty condescension or circumspect evasion might just as easily suffice. Instead, he had appeared both hurt and angered by her question.

In the afternoon, just as she began to consider the remote possibility that her husband's indignation had been genuine, she met Elliot in the corridor outside their bedchambers. He looked decidedly uncomfortable. "Evie, might I have a word with you?"

"Certainly," she answered, coming to a halt just outside his door.

He rubbed one finger down the side of his nose uncertainly. "Linden is downstairs. He has asked me to bear him company for this evening's festivities at Vauxhall. We have taken a supper box for the evening. I wanted to let you know that I was leaving."

"Vauxhall?" She almost winced at the sharpness in her voice. "But it is hours yet until dark—"

"Well, yes, I know. Linden has some plans for the afternoon as well. Forgive me for failing to make that clear. We shall be quite late, I am afraid. Do not bother to wait up for me."

"Very well," she said coolly, and turned to go.

Unexpectedly, he seized her arm and turned her back toward him. "Evangeline? Are you upset? Please do not be angry with me."

"I am perfectly all right," she lied as he pulled her abruptly into his arms and held her tightly for a long moment. She felt her taut shoulders relax as he leaned down to rest his forehead against hers.

Finally, he spoke. "Evie, I shan't make a habit of staying out most of the night, I promise."

"I am sure, my lord, that your social life is none of my concern. I should hope I have a clear understanding of how society works in town."

"Evie, darling, I am sorry," he soothed, pulling back to look into her eyes again. Absently, he traced his finger around the angle of her jaw and chin. "I did give Aidan my word. He seems to think it very important."

"Lord Linden thinks Vauxhall important? Why? Or dare I ask?"

Elliot shrugged his shoulders. "Just one of Linden's wild ideas," he answered vaguely. "Let's just say it is a sort of celebration to mark the end of my bachelor days. You'd not begrudge your husband a spot of relatively innocent fun with old friends, would you?"

"No, I suppose not," she grumbled.

"Good," he answered, his gray eyes suddenly twinkling. "For just the briefest moment, I thought you might be jealous."

"Don't be foolish."

"Ah, Evie, but I am! Foolish for you, that is," he responded, dropping his head to kiss her soundly. Gradually, he let his hand slide down to nestle in the small of her back and pull her firmly against him. Just as Evangeline surrendered to his seduction and felt Elliot deepen the kiss into something more intense, a sudden, horrified gasp sounded behind them.

"*Pas devant les domestiques,* my lord, *s'il vous plaît!*" hissed Kemble in feigned mortification. The valet stood in Elliot's doorway, an evening coat dangling casually from the tip of his index finger. "Now! Off with that dreadful rag you're wearing! I must insist upon the black coat, given your plans for the evening."

"Ah, duty calls," said Elliot softly, still looking into her eyes. Eventually, he let his arms fall away from her waist. "Sleep well, wife. I shall see you at breakfast tomorrow morning. You have my promise."

Though it was Elliot's first extended venture from home since their wedding day, Evangeline was not surprised at his sudden departure in such company. She had met Lord Linden, and Major Matthew Winthrop as well. Bowing, winking, and grinning, the pair had called at Strath the preceding week, ostensibly to pay their respects to the newly married couple, but Evangeline had scarce been fooled by their good looks and courtly graces. She could always spot a pair of rogues—even personable, handsome ones—when she saw them. Indeed, until Elliot had slipped through her defenses, Evangeline's instinct had been unfailing in that regard.

Therefore, as she watched Kemble lead Elliot away to be dressed, she resolved to think no further of his sudden plans. Her husband had a part of his life that did not include her, and she had married him to protect her brother. Evangeline tried to take comfort in those beliefs.

Unfortunately, it was a task more easily said than done, and she passed the next hour in a foul humor.

It had become her custom to take tea in the library with Sir Hugh at half past four each afternoon, and, to her surprise, she had discovered she rather liked the old rogue. It seemed she had developed quite a taste for rogues in general, she decided with an inward sigh. Evangeline descended the steps rather early, in hope of searching the library for suitable bedside reading. With Elliot away for the evening and her emotions in a turmoil, a diversion would be much needed. Halfway down the twisting staircase, however, she was surprised to see MacLeod arguing rather sternly with a strange young woman who stood bracketed in the open doorway below.

"I tell ye plainly, madam," the butler was insisting, "seekers o' household wark are tae go 'round back and speak wi' Mrs. Woody."

The woman shook her head. "Sir, I thank you, but I've no need of employment. 'Tis his lordship I would speak with if he's at home?" The soft-spoken woman wore a plain black dress and walking cloak, with her red hair caught back into a starched white cap. She appeared young for a housekeeper; nonetheless, her attire and demeanor hinted at just such an occupation. The careful tucks in her simple bombazine disclosed something else, too. The woman was just beginning to grow round with child. Evangeline stood in the shadows of the landing, watching the scene unfold. A feeling of apprehension began to draw tight about her chest.

"Verra sorry, madam. His lordship is no at home," the butler answered firmly. "Ye may speak wi' Mrs. Woody if ye please. Howiver, her bein' the housekeeper at Strath, she doubtless ha' no need of anither."

"I *must* see his lordship," the young woman insisted, her soft voice growing anxious. "I've no want of work,

sir. In truth, I'm on my half day, and 'tis a personal errand which brings me."

Forcing a calmness she did not feel, Evangeline descended the remaining stairs. "Pardon me, MacLeod," she
interrupted, giving the elderly retainer her most brisk
smile. "Might I be of some assistance?"

Amazingly, the redhaired woman turned whiter still,
yet she managed to execute a graceful curtsey. MacLeod
drew himself up to his full height. "I wouldna trouble ye,
Lady Rannoch," he answered with a stiff formality, all but
ignoring the young housekeeper in the doorway, but the
butler's fearful suspicions were writ plainly upon his face.

At the mention of her name, Evangeline heard the
woman's soft gasp. She watched the visitor carefully, her
growing curiosity exceeded only by her unease. The woman
was far from pretty, and past the first blush of youth. But
her voice was sweet, and her rather ordinary face was offset
by a pair of remarkable eyes. Almost silver-gray in color,
they were round, and far too large for her pale face.

"I am Lady Rannoch," Evangeline said at last, still
looking pointedly at the woman. "Is this matter something you would care to discuss with me?"

The visitor bobbed again, her eyes now fixed firmly
upon the rug at her feet. "I, ah, beg pardon, m'lady. I
should not a' come here."

Evangeline's discomfort grew. Clearly, this woman had
not expected to find a wife in residence. She nodded
sharply at MacLeod. "I have a few minutes before tea
with Sir Hugh, MacLeod. Will you please show—?" She
stared at the woman pointedly. "Forgive me, I did not
hear your name?"

"Pritchett, my lady," supplied the woman in a whispery
voice. "An' Mary's my Christian name."

"Pritchett?" echoed Evangeline. "Very well. Please
show Mary Pritchett into the library, MacLeod."

With a distinctly disapproving expression, the butler glanced at the visitor and then returned his gaze to Evangeline. Clearly, he did not consider a mere servant fit company under any circumstance. Evangeline, however, was determined to ascertain what manner of errand brought a pregnant flame-haired housekeeper to her husband's doorstep.

The caller, however, looked no more disposed toward this arrangement than did MacLeod. Bobbing another curtsey, she pulled a small velvet case from the folds of her cloak. "Beg pardon, m'lady. I just wanted to set things aright, but . . . but I should not have come," she repeated softly, handing the bag to Evangeline. "Just return this to him, please, m'lady, an' say that I'm ashamed of what happened and that there'll be no more trouble."

Then the woman spun hard on the heels of her sturdy shoes and slipped out the door into the brilliant afternoon, leaving Evangeline and MacLeod to stare after her. Knees weak with dread, Evangeline watched as the woman climbed into a waiting hackney coach, which promptly lurched forward with a creak and a rumble.

"I believe," she finally managed to say, "that I shall take a dish of tea at once, MacLeod." Without further comment, Evangeline strode into the library, went directly to her husband's desk, and, with fumbling fingers, tried to open the velvet box. It flew apart in her hands, its contents spilling onto the desktop in a clattering cascade of red-gold fire. Mounted in a heavy, ornate bracelet, a dozen rubies splayed across Elliot's blotter, winking up at her impudently in a shaft of late-day sun.

"Well!" she remarked softly, collapsing into the desk chair.

There seemed nothing more to say. The cold, sick feeling continued to roil in the pit of her stomach. Evangeline was wise enough to know that she was ignorant of a great many worldly things, but there was no mistaking what had just happened. Nevertheless, this woman had been quite a contradiction to her idea of the sort of woman Elliot might seduce. Indeed, this sweet, doe-eyed innocent was far worse than anything she might have imagined.

Evangeline suppressed the urge to burst into hysterical laughter. Would it have been any better, she bitterly considered, had her husband's conquest been a different sort of woman? A full-blown courtesan, for example, with the clothes and hair and attitude to match his generous gift? Would her heart have ached a little less had the woman been another actress or dancer, rather than a naïve servant who had almost certainly been seduced? Who was now, by her own admission, ashamed? And who had been proud enough, or perhaps imprudent enough, to reject a gratuity that would have fed and clothed her unborn child for months to come?

Beneath a pale moon, all but obscured by fast-moving clouds, the specious gaiety of Vauxhall was hurtling toward its crescendo. The dancers dwindled, even as the raucous laughter ascended to a fevered pitch. Already, some of the Garden's more circumspect patrons had departed, taking with them a bevy of impressionable daughters and virtuous wives. Only the more carefully chaperoned, or in some cases the most thoroughly hardened, of ladies remained as the orchestra began to wind down in anticipation of the evening's finale.

The men, however, were plentiful enough. With the unmistakable signs of both desperation and inebriation etched upon their faces, many still prowled the dimly lit walkways in search of companionship for the evening. Letting his eyes drift across the crowd, Elliot sprawled a little lower in his seat, stifling a yawn as he did so. A trio of boisterous, garishly dressed demireps frolicked past Linden's box, whispering, elbowing, and cutting hopeful glances in the direction of its occupants.

Winthrop jerked to his feet, looking like a raven among the peacocks of Vauxhall. "I say, Linden," mumbled the major, one eye on the women, "this has become rather dull work. Believe I shall leave you to it, since the evening's near done."

Languidly, Lord Linden crossed one elegant knee over the other and lifted his haughty chin. "Lud, Matt! Have you not learned your lesson? Go after either of those three, and I vow you'll not get a drop of sympathy from me when you find yourself pissing fire."

Unexpectedly roused from his ennui, Elliot gave a harsh bark of laughter. "Aye, Winthrop! You'd be screaming bloody murder over the chamber pot in a fortnight, I don't doubt."

Still looking at Winthrop, Linden dropped his voice. "In any event, old boy, it's your turn to follow Cranham." He motioned impatiently at the baron seated nearby. "Up, up! The both of you. Go prowl around the South Walk. You're to lead by twenty paces, Cranham."

Major Winthrop stifled a groan, and Linden jerked his head toward the row of elms that edged the Grove. "What? Must I do it myself?"

"No," grumbled the major. "I shall go, but I'll tell you plainly, Aidan, I'm bloody tired of watching Cranham's back. And I have no notion what we're to look for."

"Then for once we find ourselves in agreement," snapped Cranham, shoving back his chair. "I, too, grow weary of Linden's games."

Linden let his bored gaze drift over his three companions, then took up his wine glass, swishing the ruby dregs about desultorily. "As I have said time and again, gentlemen, we do not know precisely whom we seek. If we did, we'd hardly have wasted an entire evening hanging about in this very boring, very public place, now would we?"

"Oh, be damned, Aidan! I said I'd go," groused Major Winthrop, shrugging into his greatcoat, "but I surely do feel stupid in this coat." With that remark, he finally ambled off, falling into step behind Cranham.

Elliot passed the next quarter hour in a sleepy haze as he idly considered how quickly one became accustomed to country hours. Indeed, the mere thought of the country improved his sour mood. God, how he hated town, especially Vauxhall. How thankful he would be when the household could remove to the peace and warmth of Chatham Lodge.

Fast on the heels of that sentiment, however, came a far more frustrating thought: the image of his warm wife, snug in her bed at Strath. After nearly two weeks of marriage, he was loath to leave her, even briefly. Yet she would never believe that he had had no real desire to visit this loud place filled with drunken dandies and garish whores. Elliot had seen the ugly assumption that had flared in her eyes as he left her.

Ah, yes. There had been no mistaking that blue-white fire in Evie's eyes. Inwardly, Elliot grinned. He fully expected to suffer that look often, and perhaps to occasionally deserve it, throughout the coming years. The thought did not overly concern him, for he would be a good husband, even if his bride did not yet believe it.

Elliot was yanked from his contemplation of his wife's smoldering eyes by the reappearance of Cranham and Winthrop. He surveyed the baron suspiciously as the pair stepped into the box and took their respective seats. Something about the bizarre situation made Elliot unnaturally edgy. He had all of Linden's assurances that this effort to lure forth the killer was the right thing to do; nonetheless, his every instinct warred against their actions.

No one really believed that he and Cranham had reconciled their differences, did they? Elliot knew Cranham for the duplicitous bastard he was. Suddenly, he felt weighted down by hopelessness. Everyone, perhaps even his own wife, thought him an out-and-out cad. Worse, it had become increasingly obvious that many believed him guilty of Antoinette's murder, and that had dredged up all the old gossip about Cicely. Yet his innocence could no more be proven now than ten years ago. What did Linden hope to achieve? Elliot was no longer sure, and as the dancers whirled their last in the lantern light, he began to feel like a flagging hunter, propelled toward a fence which he knew he should not, could not, jump. This dreadful evening could not possibly end soon enough.

"Look there," interrupted Major Winthrop, pointing toward the orchestra which was now dispersing into the crowd. "Is not that—" But his words were split by the sound of the first of the evening's fireworks. Screaming glitter shot through the night sky, blazing a trail of red and gold, then tumbling inescapably earthward in a shower of multihued sparks.

Smoothly, Lord Linden rose from his seat. "Let's call it a night, gentlemen," drawled the viscount. "It would appear that my hopes were misplaced. One more meander through the Grand Cross, then we will reassemble at the Rotunda, shall we?" The group, Elliot included, grumbled reluctant agreement and set off in a laggardly trail. Cranham preceded them by drifting in aimless patterns through the crowd, just as he had done to no useful effect all evening. No one out of the ordinary had approached them. No one seemed threatening.

Elliot delayed just long enough to shrug into his greatcoat, then set off after Cranham, Winthrop but a few feet behind. Yet they were exceedingly discreet; only the sharpest of eyes would ever have suspected that they were all watching and following one another. As they pressed their way through the gasping throng, now held transfixed by the shattering bursts of fireworks, Elliot let his eyes drift across the faces of the crowd. Despite Lord Linden's advice, he could see no one, nothing, that looked odd or out of place.

From time to time, he returned his gaze to Cranham's back as they moved down the graveled path that stretched out before them. No one approached the baron; indeed, few gave more than a passing nod in his direction. Soon, Elliot saw Cranham turn to his left and make his way onto the Grand Cross, which ran the back length of the gardens. The trees and shrubbery felt deceptively thicker there, and as the excitement of the Grove faded into the background, so, too, did the lamplight and the crowd.

In the dimness far behind, Elliot could barely hear the echoing footfalls of Winthrop. Somewhere in the distance, bringing up the rear, would be Linden. They should not have bothered with this last little foray. The crowd, which had shown only mild interest in their little gathering anyway, was now shifting toward the garden exit. Few among the *ton* or the demimonde knew Cranham by sight; therefore, the stir Linden had hoped to create had undoubtedly come to naught. Suddenly, Cranham moved deeper into the dimness, and Elliot lost him.

"Damn the man for wearing such dark clothing," he muttered under his breath, then glanced down at his own black coat with a touch of chagrin. Kemble had been right; it rendered him almost invisible. Ahead on the path, Elliot thought he saw a flash of white linen as the next burst of explosives let loose in the sky.

White linen? That implied a man's chest, not his back,

which made no sense. In the dark, the crunching of gravel and the rustling of leaves seemed suddenly louder, and instantly Elliot felt a strong trepidation, an unexpectedly heightened awareness. The flicker of unease that had plagued him all night leapt into full flame when, ahead of him, Elliot heard a cry. Of anger? Or pain? The night sky was filled with another cacophony of light and sound, revealing that the path before him now lay empty. Cranham had vanished from the walkway.

Simultaneously looking back across his shoulder as he burst into a run, Elliot shouted out a warning to Winthrop, though he saw nothing at all in the gloom behind him. Speeding forward, he had run but twenty yards when the backlash of a flying tree limb caught him full in the face. His right eye welling with tears, Elliot blinked hard against the sting. He darted through the trees on the opposite side of the lane. He struggled to listen, despite another barrage of firecrackers.

As his vision began to clear, another pyrotechnic burst lit the sky. The tangle of shrubbery flashed into stark relief. In that split second of light, Elliot saw Cranham. He was locked in combat with a larger man. Above the baron's head, Elliot caught the fast glint of steel as it bore down toward the smaller man's shoulder. Then, just as quickly, all was shrouded again. This time, Elliot heard Cranham cry out in pain. A string of curses followed, and then the unmistakable grunt and thud of someone falling. Someone heavier than Cranham, by the sound of it.

In the dark, the pistols that both he and Major Winthrop concealed inside their coats were of little use. Instinctively, Elliot bolted into the thicket. He hurled himself in the general direction of the large man, who was already staggering to his feet. Ruthlessly, Elliot thudded into the wall of his chest, taking him back down. The attacker exhaled with a sharp wheeze, then began to thrash ineffectually. Too late, Elliot realized that the man had one hand in his coat pocket.

"*Rannoch . . . pistol!*" rasped Cranham weakly from somewhere in the darkness. Elliot felt the sickening chill of a gun pressed to his temple. Quickly, Elliot weighed his options. The assailant felt corpulent, unconditioned. Certainly, he was big, and gasping for breath. And his grip on the gun was tremulous. Smoothly, Elliot wrenched upward on the pistol, simultaneously rolling off into the thick grass. In the dark, the man cursed and came up onto his knees, somehow holding on to his weapon. Another dazzling burst of colored light, and this time Elliot was stunned to see more than just the identity of his assailant. He saw that the pistol was now wavering in Cranham's direction.

"Oh, God! Don't shoot!" the baron begged. He cowered beneath the shrubbery, still clutching his upper arm with the opposite hand. Elliot could hear Winthrop moving rapidly up the path.

"Put down the gun, my lord," said Elliot softly. "Winthrop and Linden are behind us."

"No!" the attacker hissed. The insanity in his tone chilled the darkness. "You should have stayed out of this, Rannoch. Damn you to hell! I mean only to kill him. But now I must kill you, too!"

Suddenly, the scuttling clouds slid away from the quarter moon. Elliot saw the gun barrel leveled squarely at Cranham's face. Just as Major Winthrop burst into the thicket with his pistol at the ready, Elliot dove for the madman's legs. They went down in a snarl of coats and limbs. The roar of a pistol thundered in Elliot's ears. Not once but twice. How could that be? Hot, blinding pain cut through his body, and Elliot's last lucid recollection was of Winthrop, dragging him from beneath the lifeless form of Cicely's uncle, Lord Howell.

*   *   *

Despite Elliot's command that she not wait up, Evangeline found herself rigidly upright in bed, anticipating her husband's return from his evening's diversions. Inwardly, she admitted that perhaps *command* was too strong a word, but Evangeline was disinclined to think well of her husband on this particular night. Ever the optimist, she had tried. Yet every tender sentiment, every measure of love, and every implausible excuse she could fathom for the pregnant servant upon their doorstep had long since paled by the time the clock struck three. Angrily, she tossed aside her book, jabbed a fist into her pillow, then blew out the candle with a determined huff.

Damn it, she *would* go to sleep. Moreover, she would resolve that in the future, where her husband slept would be no concern of hers. After all, Evangeline reminded herself, Elliot had remained dutifully by her side for almost a fortnight, far longer than she had expected. A warm bead of moisture trickled down her nose, dribbled sideways across her cheek, and landed on the taut linen pillowcase with a *plop!* Damn it, she *would not* cry. But despite all her stubborn vows, the tears rolled, and sleep eluded her. After all, she recalled with a sniff, Elliot had seemed so content. She had clung to that hope.

And could she have been mistaken about the woman and her bracelet? The questions and doubts began tumbling around in her head again. Evangeline drew a ragged sigh. She well understood that the ladies and gentlemen of the *ton,* loosely bound by marriages of convenience, usually led separate lives. Had she somehow deluded herself into believing that a marriage to London's worst blackguard would miraculously be better than the norm? Yes, somehow, she had foolishly managed to do precisely that.

She had begun to slip back into that state of contented happiness that she and Elliot had once shared so effortlessly. Somewhere between her wedding vows and that afternoon's encounter in the corridor, three words had crept insidiously into her heart. *I love you.* Elliot said it frequently, though she had said it only once. He rasped out the words often in the throes of lovemaking; he whispered them into her hair in the early-morning light when he thought her still asleep. And she had begun to believe it. How could she not? She wanted to so desperately.

Perhaps Elliot did love her; perhaps this was just the way of men. Her father had not acted thus, but then Evangeline was forced to admit that the love her parents had shared had been rare, the sort of devotion that transcended life and death. She punched the pillow again. It was now rather damp. Oh, she did not know! She felt so naïve, so blindly stupid. Perhaps the redhaired woman meant nothing to Elliot. Perhaps she was just a woman from his past, and the babe was another man's child. Or perhaps she was just a stranger off the street, someone's idea of a cruel prank—or worse.

Nonetheless, the ruby bracelet she had delivered was no prank. Evangeline was reasonably confident that just one of its stones could have put food in the mysterious Mary Pritchett's cupboard for ages. If Elliot had indeed tried to buy her off with it, why, then, had she not simply sold it? Indeed, was that not the way such things worked? Evangeline wished that Winnie were near so she might ask for advice, then realized with a start that she would be too humiliated to do so. Rolling onto her back to stare up into the darkness, Evangeline struggled to think the best of her husband, and cursed the fates which seemed determined to thwart her. Eventually, she must have dozed into a fitful slumber, because she awakened abruptly as the clock struck four, her belly clenched tight with terror.

It was not the clock that had awakened her, of that she

was unaccountably certain. Her first thought was for the babe she was almost sure she carried, but nothing seemed amiss. As she tossed back the bedcovers and came upright, she realized that she had been awakened by sounds, soft bumps and murmurings that echoed from Elliot's adjoining bedchamber. And there was more. She heard rushing feet, thumping doors, and the incessant rumble of strange voices. Not Elliot's. Many voices, all at once. Abruptly, she sprang from the bed and drew on her wrapper. Before she realized what she was about, she had pulled open the door and was walking in.

Five sets of eyes flicked simultaneously upward from the bed to catch her horrified gaze. Evangeline, however, was quickly drawn to Lord Linden's stricken expression; it told her more than words ever could. Her hand flew to her mouth, and her eyes darted frantically about the room, even as her mind struggled to assimilate what she saw into some sort of logic. Beside the viscount, a short, broad-chested man whom she did not know was bent low across her husband's comatose body; his fingertips trailed expertly down Elliot's neck and arms, pausing briefly here and there.

At the foot of the bed, MacLeod was ripping away what was left of Elliot's trousers and stockings. Kemble was savagely dragging a table to the bedside. Linden was placing Elliot's washbasin upon it. To her right, the door hinges groaned as a footman carried in a copper pot filled with steaming water. Already, Elliot's chest was bare, and Evangeline could not miss the thick crimson compress that Matthew Winthrop held resolutely against Elliot's thigh. Behind him, someone reached through the crowd to thrust another wad of cotton cloth into Winthrop's outstretched hand.

Suddenly, the facts began to swim together in a grim picture. Evangeline thought perhaps that she had screamed, yet no sound came out. Instead, an ominous, hollow voice echoed from deep inside the room, which was now beginning to dim at the edges.

"If that, gentlemen, is her ladyship," said the grim, far-away voice, "I suggest someone see her safely abed. She looks perilously close to swooning."

From somewhere in the distance came a harsh buzzing sound which swelled into a drone, filling Evangeline's ears like the rush of gossip sweeping through a crowded ballroom. But the drone became a roar, growing until it filled her head. A hand came up to touch her forehead. Her hand? Cold fingertips found the dampness of her brow, and then, suddenly, Lord Linden was behind her. One strong arm lashed tight about her waist, and Evangeline found herself dragged down onto a nearby sofa. She was dimly aware of the citrus smell of Linden's soap as his cool hand urged her head forward onto her knees; then, slowly, the roaring darkness subsided.

"Lady Rannoch?" she heard Kemble ask softly. The valet dropped to his knees before her and smoothed the hair back from her forehead with a hand that was cool and comforting. "My lady? Can you hear me? Are you recovering?"

"I—I do not know," Evangeline answered woodenly, her voice muffled into the heavy fabric of her wrapper. "Oh, God! What has happened to him? Just tell me what has happened!"

"Pray keep your head down a moment, my lady," replied Kemble in a soothing voice. "You very nearly swooned."

Beside her, Lord Linden bent forward to speak softly into her ear. "We shall fetch a cool cloth for your forehead, ma'am. I daresay the sight of so much blood is inappropriate for a lady of delicate sensibilities."

"My sensibilities are not delicate," she rasped, addressing her knees. Slowly, she tried to sit up. "Moreover, I have never swooned in my life."

"No, my lady. I am sure you have not," soothed Kemble, easing one firm hand around her upper arm. "But these are unusual circumstances. Come, can you stand?"

Dumbly, she nodded and came weakly to her feet, watching Linden's blond hair return slowly into focus. Kemble rose with her, still holding her arm. Despite Lord Linden's opposing pressure on her elbow, Evangeline turned to stare at her husband. MacLeod had somehow managed to remove most of his clothing. Beside Major Winthrop, the stranger—a surgeon, she now realized— was still bent low over the bed, his fingertips pressed to Elliot's throat, an unsettled look fixed upon his face.

Against her will, the valet and the viscount almost carried her back into her bedchamber. As Linden urged her into bed, Kemble strode across the room and yanked the bell to summon her maid. Pressing her back into the pillows, Lord Linden gave her a crooked grin. "Not sure old Elliot would approve of my taking his wife to bed," he mumbled weakly, "but one does what one must."

"What has happened?" she demanded hollowly as a cool cloth was settled across her forehead. "Linden, you must tell me! How serious is it?"

"Shush," soothed the viscount. "Promise me that you will lie still, and I will tell you all that I may." Evangeline stilled her agitated motions, allowing Kemble to draw up her bedcovers, and Linden continued. "Elliot was shot, my lady."

"Shot?" Her voice came out a disembodied whisper. "I do not understand. Where? Why?"

"At Vauxhall. And I regret that I must be the one to tell you, for it was almost certainly my doing—"

"How, my lord? I do not understand."

"Hush, Evangeline," he said softly. "Elliot will tell you

all, I am sure, when he awakens. But I must tell you that he has lost a bit of blood and will lose a bit more this night if the surgeon is to remove the ball."

"Oh, God," she whispered, and despite her best effort, the tears began to fall in earnest.

Lord Linden sat himself gingerly upon the far corner of her bed. "Ma'am, you mustn't overset yourself. I can assure you that your husband is perfectly indefatigable, and he has been through just this sort of thing before."

Coloring slightly, the viscount had the good grace to look away. "That is to say, he has been shot once or twice and always pulls through. Old Potter is the best of surgeons and has done the honors on Elliot before, so you need have no concern on that score."

"Who shot him?" Evangeline cried. "Why?"

Linden shook his head and leaned forward to lay one hand gently across hers. "It was an accident, Evangeline, and even I do not fully understand what happened. It is all caught up in Elliot's past, and I cannot know what he has told you, so I would rather he explained it, and in his own time. But I can tell you that he was in no way at fault and that he acted very bravely. Now, promise me that you will rest, so that I may go and lend a hand to Potter?"

"Yes, all right," she whispered hoarsely, her mind already clawing toward its own conclusion. But with those same conclusions came a strange sense of calm. Already, her husband lay wounded, perhaps fatally. Evangeline had conjured up many ugly imaginings about what her marriage might be like, yet, regardless of how real her fears became, she had entered into the union of her own accord. She was now his wife.

The phrases *for better or for worse, in sickness and in health* began to echo in her mind. Yet Evangeline ruthlessly refused to consider the last of her vows, for it was unthinkable that Elliot might die. Almost unconsciously, her hands grasped the bed linens and pushed them away. She could not let him die. She had fallen imprudently in love with him, and she had surrendered to her physical desire for him. If fate now required her to pay for her weakness by means of a marriage that fell far short of her girlhood dreams, she must simply remind herself that it was a marriage nonetheless, and she was long past girlhood. For now, duty called, and she would see to it.

Indeed, she harshly reprimanded herself, a wife's place was by her husband's side. She should be ashamed of swooning, babe or no. Moreover, she, of all women, had no business languishing upon her bed like some delicate, overbred debutante. As soon as Lord Linden finished instructing her maid and quit the room, Evangeline slid out of the bed. She had responsibilities.

"Find Kemble," she ordered her maid. "Tell him he is to fetch me as soon as the surgeon has left my husband's bedside." Lips pursed tight in a pale white face, the girl nodded once, then darted off to do as she was bid.

§16§

For secrets are edg'd tools, and must be kept from children and fools.

—JOHN DRYDEN

All of Richmond seemed ominously quiet when Gerald Wilson alit from his lordship's carriage at ten o'clock that morning. The footman, who had come in all haste to fetch Wilson to his master's apparent deathbed, now put down the stairs and stood deferentially to one side. Rannoch's man of affairs stepped out onto the cobblestone drive of Strath House and into a thick, spattering rain.

The summer air held a dreariness that was unusual, even for London. Across the wide stone façade of Strath, not a lamp had been lit to cut through the oppressive gloom of the morning. Wilson trudged up the steps to find that within the grand entrance hall, neither children nor servants stirred, save MacLeod, who pulled open the door with an air of poorly concealed grief. It was true, then. The butler's red-rimmed eyes all but confirmed the worst.

With a deep sigh, MacLeod took Wilson's greatcoat, then handed him back his tooled leather folio. Already, a thick sheaf of papers protruded from one end, for this was not Wilson's first stop of the morning. Indeed, Rannoch's equipage had first conveyed him into the center of the City of London, to the offices of Messrs. Barclay, MacEwen, and Matheson, his lordship's trio of hardened solicitors. Out of sympathy, Wilson mumbled a few banal sentiments to the elderly retainer, then set off down the hall and up the short flight of stairs that led to his lordship's inner sanctum.

Everything about Strath was quietly, soberly familiar, the smell of wax and spice, the opulent blues and golds of the Oriental runners, and the rich brown oak of the library door. Nonetheless, things were not the same, and might well never be so again. Indeed, Wilson found himself realizing that this could be his last such trip. Oddly enough, he rather hoped not, for he had somehow grown very fond of the fellow he'd once thought of as Old Scratch jumped up from the bowels of hell. Swallowing hard, Wilson laid his hand upon the brass knob and entered.

The heavy draperies were already open, to no good effect. The room remained as somber and gray as the mood within. "I've brought the necessary papers from the solicitors' office, Sir Hugh," said Wilson softly, setting down his folio upon the desk.

"Eh?" responded Hugh, stirring vaguely. His bleary gaze drifted up from a low table, scattered with the remnants of an early-morning coffee service. "Papers? What sort?"

Wilson took a quick look about the room and, seeing only friends, spoke openly. "The will, Sir Hugh. And the dower addendum for the young ladies, Miss Stone and Miss d'Avillez. His lordship bade me have it drawn up last week."

Major Matthew Winthrop, his back to the room, stood before the window and stared out into the street below. Slowly, he let his hand slide from the window frame and turned to face the others. "Did he sign them?" he asked hollowly.

"No, Major," answered Wilson, shaking his head. "I am afraid he has not yet had an op—"

"Damn it all, I'll dower them myself," interrupted Lord Linden, setting down his coffee with a violence that shattered the saucer, sending it flying from the table in pieces. No one seemed to notice. "If Elliot dies . . . hell, I'll see to it! 'Tis the least I can do after having led him—led all of you—into this foolish farce."

"Pretty things, the pair of 'em," mumbled Sir Hugh. Absently, he bent forward in his chair, picked up the largest of the porcelain shards from the carpet, and ran his thumb across one splintered edge. "Reckon it won't take a dowry to find 'em a husband."

"Good God, stop it, both of you!" Major Winthrop came away from the window in three quick strides. "He isn't going to die, damn it! Moreover, we are none of us at fault! None of us. Elliot wouldn't tolerate such drivel."

Lord Linden shrugged lamely, then shoved his long manicured fingers through hair that was no longer perfect. Indeed, Wilson noted, the viscount's normally flawless attire was in total disarray, looking very much as if he had slept in it. No doubt he had. A woolen blanket lay crumpled in a heap at his feet. "I thought up this reckless scheme of spreading rumors that Elliot and Cranham had set aside the past," answered Linden softly. "I was certain that the person who tried to kill Cranham murdered Antoinette, and I was so damned arrogant, I thought I could flush out the killer. Good God, I treated it like a lark! I ought to be hanged."

Bracing his hands upon his thick, muscular thighs, Winthrop sank slowly down into the chair opposite Sir Hugh. "But that's just it, Linden! Do you not see? We had to do something. Elliot was forced yet again to live under an insufferable cloud of suspicion."

The baronet made a little choking noise and Major Winthrop scowled darkly. "Do not deny it, Sir Hugh. You know it is true. The conjecture over Cicely's death ruined his life ten years ago. And matters were growing uglier with every passing day."

"But why Howell?" rasped Sir Hugh. "And after so many years? Good Lord! Known 'im all my life! At Harrow with him and all that. Thought him too damn lazy to hold a grudge, and over an *orphaned niece?* But he wanted Cranham dead. And maybe Elliot blamed."

Slowly, Winthrop shook his head. "No, Hugh. I think you're mistaken about the grudge. It had to be something else. Lord Howell's niece was little better than a slut, and he must have known of Cicely's reputation. Many a gentleman among the *ton* had propositioned her, but not for marriage. I had begun to believe that she had accepted one of them, someone who took advantage of Elliot's innocence all those years ago and did not now want the ugly truth to come out."

"As did I," agreed Lord Linden bitterly. "And I had some hope of forcing the gentleman into the open."

"Yes," mused Winthrop. "Do you not find it remarkable that Howell, of all people, remained silent when Elliot severed his engagement to Miss Forsythe? Indeed, he has always tactfully avoided all of us. Perhaps he found it prudent to let Cranham take the brunt of Elliot's rage and suspicion. When Cranham returned from Baipur, the trouble began. You know, Howell refused to see Cranham on at least a dozen occasions."

"Oh, Cranham's a troublemaker of the first order, and no mistake," agreed Linden, sagging wearily backward into the depths of his chair. "And while he admits he bore a grudge against Elliot, he swears he did nothing more, save trying to seduce Antoinette, whom he seemed to think was blackmailing Elliot."

"You believe him?" asked Sir Hugh flatly.

"Oddly enough, I do," murmured Lord Linden thoughtfully, "but only because he could not possibly have stabbed himself."

"Indeed," answered Winthrop, rubbing his wide palm back and forth across his shadowed chin. "It was just as Linden surmised. Cranham and Elliot together—that was the perceived danger. Together, they must have constituted some sort of threat. Something Howell was willing to kill for . . ."

Suddenly, the door swung inward to admit a man Wilson recognized as Potter, the surgeon, having seen him at Strath on at least two previous occasions. Major Winthrop and Lord Linden came swiftly to their feet. "How is his lordship?" asked the major anxiously.

Potter set down his bulging leather bag on a side table and pressed his thumb and forefinger against his puffy eyelids. He shook his head, making his heavy jowls flop like a weary hound. "Weak, gentlemen. Very weak. More blood loss than I have seen in many a day."

"Will he live?" asked Sir Hugh, wringing his hands with uncharacteristic concern.

"Too soon to say, Sir Hugh," answered the surgeon bluntly. "But he is strong, not to mention stubborn. Moreover, the wound, though deep and nasty, is in his thigh. A shot to the chest or belly, now, that would have meant a sure and painful death. As it is, I would have to say he is in God's hands."

"What can we expect?" asked Linden anxiously.

"If he lives through the complications, we may find him crawling out of bed in a sennight," answered the surgeon with an equivocal shrug, "or he may be dead by nightfall."

"Has the bleeding stopped?"

"Aye, and you can thank her ladyship and that eccentric valet for it, too. Both been up all night. Man knows as much about medicine as some physicians I've seen. And her ladyship is a tough piece of work—barking orders, changing dressings. She's already sponging tea into 'im. Got the staff moving like a well-ordered battalion. Wouldn't have thought it when I saw her very nearly faint last night, but if sheer determination can keep a fellow alive, his lordship will make it."

The gray light of late morning seeped into Elliot's bedchamber, casting grim shadows across the already harsh angles of his face. A day's growth of beard merely emphasized the pallor of his normally dark skin. Mercifully, the tourniquets and surgical instruments had been long since carried away, and the seemingly incessant train of servants bearing water, sheets, and bandages had finally vanished.

And Elliot was still alive. The blood loss had been prodigious, and at times his heartbeat weak, but he was still very much alive. Wearily, Evangeline wiped the back of her hand across her forehead and sank into her chair by Elliot's bedside.

" 'Tis almost noon, Lady Rannoch," whispered Kemble as he assiduously rearranged the contents of Elliot's dressing table for the tenth time. "There is little you can do for the nonce. Go to your room, and try to rest."

Evangeline bounced anxiously from her seat and crossed to the other side of Elliot's massive bed. Absently, she flicked up the covers and straightened them with a snap. "You are all kindness, Kemble, but I know I shan't sleep. I must remain here—at least until he wakes." Across the wide expanse of bedding, she saw Kemble purse his lips stubbornly. "He will awaken, Kem," she responded in a firm but quiet voice.

The valet turned to face her, his expression one of concern. "Indeed, all will be well, my lady. Rannoch has lived through worse. But you! You need your rest, for we may have hard days ahead. You, perhaps, more so than anyone?"

Ignoring the thinly veiled question in Kemble's last remark, Evangeline prayed, as she had prayed all night, that the valet's faith in Elliot's strength was well placed. Her husband was a strong, healthy man, was he not? But how much blood loss could a person endure? She had no clue. A clean shot, Potter had said. What a horrid phrase! There had been nothing clean about it.

Since five o'clock that morning, she had not left her husband's bedside, save for a quarter hour spent explaining matters to the children—or perhaps *lying* to the children was a more apt description of what she had chosen to do. How could one explain, particularly to little Zoë, the horrible truth? Evangeline had hardly known what to say, and so she had stumbled through half-truths and platitudes. Afterward, Zoë and the younger children had sniffled quietly, while Theo had stood apart, biting valiantly at his lower lip, old enough to sense what had gone unsaid.

Evangeline gazed again at her husband's face, so deathly pale against the linen, and her unspoken need for him knifed through her heart. No, it was more than need; it was the fear of needing, for what would she do if she lost him now? Despite all that they had been through, and all that she had sometimes believed of him, her love had held fast, almost against her will. Gently, she brushed his hand with hers. Elliot's long, graceful fingers lay limply atop the woolen coverlet. The light dusting of dark hair across the back of his hand was just beginning to be visible in the feeble daylight. Elliot had such big hands, such capable hands. How it hurt to see them so lifeless yet so strikingly beautiful.

As if in response to Evangeline's thoughts, the fingers of his left hand began to move restlessly against the bedcovers. Her gaze flicked back to his face. Beneath his lowered lids, she could see his eyes move back and forth. Then, gradually but unmistakably, the movement of his hands and eyes stilled, and his breathing eased. What had been a shallow, uneven pattern shifted to deeper, more restful inhalation. It was, she fervently believed, a positive sign.

Oblivious to Kemble's puttering in the background, Evangeline absently picked up Elliot's left hand and pulled it to her lips. Her worry abated for just a moment as she realized that his skin felt surprisingly normal against her mouth. Indeed, his fingers were warm, rather than the cool, seemingly bloodless hands of early morning. Better still, he was not feverish, and she could only hope that he would remain so. Gently, Evangeline reached across the pillow to place her free hand against his brow. Warm, yes. But not hot. Evangeline gave a little sigh of relief and dropped her hand away just as Elliot's eyes began to flutter.

They had not opened far when he winced, the muscles in his jaw bunching in obvious discomfort. "Ummm," he groaned, almost inaudibly. Evangeline wanted to cry out with joy at the sound.

"Elliot?" she asked quietly. "Are you awake?"

She felt his fingers curl weakly about her thumb. "Evie?" he murmured, his voice a nearly inaudible whisper. "Took—took it in the leg, did I?"

Kemble moved to the other side of the bed and braced his arms against the mattress as he leaned across to study Elliot's face. Elliot's eyes were still closed, his face fixed in an expression of stoic resolve.

"Yes, in the thigh," she answered softly. "But it's a clean wound, though Potter says you've lost a good bit of blood."

His lips tried, with limited success, to turn up into a weak grin, while his feeble grip on her thumb tightened another notch. "I'm nothing but trouble, Evie," he whispered, clinging to her hand, "but I love you."

As Kemble turned away to give them privacy, Evangeline let her gaze drift over Elliot's face, the fear and anger suddenly melting in the crystalline light of her love for this man. The sting of disappointment eased, and Evangeline grappled with the words she knew Elliot needed to hear. When she did not respond immediately, he finally forced open his heavy eyelids.

"I love you, too, Elliot," she managed weakly, but Evangeline knew she had hesitated a moment too long. Yet how could she express, in mere words, the complexities of her feelings for him? His gray eyes, deeply set, dark, and wearied by pain, dropped shut, his disappointment all too obvious.

Evangeline reached out to smooth the tangle of thick,

dark hair from his brow and set her cool palm against his forehead. "Does the leg hurt?" she asked gently, fumbling for something to say.

"Aye," whispered Elliot, his voice kind but unmistakably indifferent. Suddenly, his face contorted in obvious discomfort as his back arched off the bed.

"Potter left a bottle of laudanum," she responded, shooting a quick look at Kemble, then jerking her head toward Elliot's night table. "Kem will give you a bit. Can you take it?"

"I'll try," he answered, his clenched jaw relaxing once again.

"And some warm, sweet tea?"

"Aye," he tried to respond, but his respiration was already settling back into the deep, rhythmic breathing of a body exhausted by trauma. Suddenly, a light knock sounded on the door, and Kemble slid quietly across the room to admit one of the footmen.

"I do b-beg your pardon, your ladyship," stuttered the servant as he presented an outstretched salver. "MacLeod took himself off to—to retire to his rooms. I did not know what might best be done . . . but there's a caller below who begs to see you for a moment."

The word *no* was almost out of Evangeline's mouth when the footman interjected, "I am afraid, ma'am, that she's terrible overset, and desperate to see you. On account of his lordship, she says."

Evangeline quickly changed her dress, twisted her hair into a severe arrangement, and strode toward the blue drawing room in a state of agitated resentment. Her nerves were worn raw; furthermore, she had not slept. She had no recollection of the lady who awaited her beyond the drawing-room doors. She had barely glanced at the card, and the unfamiliar name had flown from her addled mind as soon as she set it down again. Resolutely, she pushed open the door and entered to find her guest anxiously pacing the floor. The scene made Evangeline feel, by comparison, utterly composed.

The tall, broad-shouldered woman careened to an abrupt, teetering halt in the center of the carpet. Clearly, she was nearly wild with anxiety. The woman could never have been described as handsome; indeed, her long, heavily boned face would have been decidedly unattractive, even under the best of circumstances. Today, however, her nose was raw, her eyes swollen, and she gave every appearance of having spent the night on the edge of hysteria.

At the moment, however, she seemed almost resigned to a horrible fate as she bowed formally and announced herself as Lady Howell. She then paused expectantly, as if she had anticipated a less than welcoming response from Evangeline.

Evangeline, emotionally drained and sleep-deprived, recognized neither Lady Howell nor her name. Before she had time to consider the matter carefully, however, Lady Howell closed the distance between them and caught Evangeline's hand in a desperate grip. "Pray forgive me, Lady Rannoch," she whispered, her voice suddenly catching in her throat. "My call is ill timed, and I know the pain you are suffering, but I beg you for five minutes. I would speak my piece and have done with it— please?"

Evangeline pulled her hand gently from the woman's clasp. How could this woman know about Elliot? And yet his injury was almost certainly the circumstance to which she referred. Given such knowledge, what matter could be so urgent as to compel her to call in the midst of a tragedy? "I am very sorry, ma'am," she answered with as much patience as she could muster, "but I really cannot spare—"

"*Oh, please?*" interjected the dour woman. There was a wrenching agony in her voice, and Evangeline was shocked to see tears pool in her eyes again.

Nervously, Evangeline smoothed her hands down the silk fabric of her skirt front. "Yes. Yes, of course. I did not mean to be unfeeling, but as you must undoubtedly understand, I wish to be at my husband's bedside."

"Oh, yes," murmured the woman weakly, "Yes, I am but too well aware."

"Please," offered Evangeline, with a flick of her hand, "do take a seat. And pray excuse me for remarking that you seem not at all well yourself."

The woman, trembling now, sank with apparent gratitude into a nearby chair. She withdrew a small scrap of linen and blotted quickly at her eyes. When she looked up at Evangeline, her hands still shook, but she looked somewhat more composed.

"Lady Rannoch," she began in a hollow voice, "I beg your forgiveness, for I must tell you that I am responsible for your husband's accident."

Evangeline was rocked by confusion and fatigue. While she had certainly supposed that a woman was involved, the lady before her was most assuredly not what she had expected. Uneasily, she began to mutter, "Why, I am sure, ma'am, that you cannot be!"

"Oh, my dear girl, you cannot know how I wish that were true! You must let me speak. My only regret is that I did not do it weeks ago—no, *ten years ago!*"

"Ten years?" replied Evangeline softly. "I am not sure I understand, ma'am. Indeed, I think we need not speak of this at all. Not until you are more . . . yourself."

Evangeline's guest wrung her handkerchief wildly. Suddenly, she looked almost mad. "*No!*" she wailed pitifully. "Others have paid the price for my silence, when I should have spoken out. I can hide my shame no longer. Now your husband lies near death, and the blood of that—that actress—Antoinette Fontaine—is on my hands."

"I cannot think what you mean," Evangeline began to interject, but one look at Lady Howell's tortured visage forestalled any further comment.

The woman's plain face twisted in agony, and she reached out to grasp Evangeline's arm, her long, thin fingers digging into the flesh despite her gloves. Evangeline winced, but the woman seemed beyond noticing. "I must tell you a dreadful story, Lady Rannoch," she whispered furtively, her eyes growing increasingly frantic as she tried to pull Evangeline forward in her chair. "It all began ten years ago, when I took on a new housemaid. A plain girl—a country girl. I insisted upon it, you know, for I had good reason."

"Yes," muttered Evangeline, now thoroughly confused. *Was* Lady Howell demented? Evangeline was growing increasingly disturbed by her wild eyes and tormented voice.

"I was fond of her," continued Lady Howell in her veiled tone. "And she quickly became an excellent servant. Yet, not six months later, I returned from a visit to my father's estate, only to discover that my husband had turned the girl off without notice. Oh, he was very cool about it! He insisted that Mary had stolen a gold watch chain from his room. Immediately, I knew it for a lie."

Evangeline stared at the woman's expression, transfixed. Perhaps she was indeed raving mad. Yet she did not look exactly deranged; she looked . . . guilty. And clearly, she believed that she was imparting critical information. "Yes, do go on, Lady Howell," she said softly.

"Well, you see, I fear that I knew rather too much

about my husband's proclivities. I was convinced he had seduced the girl, then found it necessary to rid himself of her. It would not have been the first time . . ."

"I—I do not know what to say, Lady Howell . . ." And, indeed, she did not.

Evangeline's visitor continued as if no one had spoken, her eyes darting anxiously about the room. "She was so young, so rustic. I asked myself, what if she was with child? Or starving? Oh, I knew my husband, you see, and I put nothing—*absolutely nothing*—past him."

A feeling of great unease began to settle about Evangeline. "I cannot think what bearing this has on my household, ma'am, but pray continue if you feel you must."

"I must," she insisted, returning her wide-eyed gaze to Evangeline as if she had forgotten to whom she spoke. "I called at the agency from which I had hired her. Of course, without a reference, they had refused to place her again. But they did give me her direction, and on pretext of visiting Papa, I went there instead. To Wrotham Ford. I still don't know why I did it."

To Wrotham Ford? Evangeline hid her surprise. "And did you find her?"

"Oh, God, yes! Mopping floors in her father's filthy taproom. Beaten black and blue." In the woman's lap, one gloved hand began to open and close spasmodically. "At the very sight of me, she was seized by fear. But I had to speak with her! Then there was a terrible row with her parents, but finally, when I encouraged her, she began to babble. My husband had indeed lied to me, while her words were, I somehow knew, horribly close to the truth."

"The truth?"

Lady Howell suddenly froze and looked across Evangeline's shoulder into the distance. Her gaze was detached and unfocused. "She denied being with child. She swore my husband had never touched her."

"Was—was she a thief?" Absently, Evangeline pressed her fingertips against her temple and rubbed hard.

"No," answered Lady Howell in a disembodied voice. "What she was, was *a witness!* She had seen something she ought not to have seen. I am haunted by that poor child's huge gray eyes, for I begged her—I *begged* her to tell me the truth! Only then did she confess that she had seen my husband engaged in—in wickedness. In his bedchamber with . . . with his niece, Cicely Forsythe." Lady Howell had begun to sob quietly through her words.

Evangeline gasped. *Cicely? Elliot's dead fiancée?* The thick air seemed to press in around her, hot and urgent, yet before she could make sense of it all, Lady Howell drew a ragged, hitching breath. "Oh, yes! In truth, I was not terribly surprised. I think I knew it all along. And poor little Mary was so reluctant to hurt me, despite her own wretched situation! Turned off by my husband, beaten by her parents . . . so I gave her a reference to a dear friend in Mayfair. They were in want of a scullery maid. I took her back to London and begged her never to tell what she had seen. And she didn't, but I fear that her family had overheard much of our conversation."

Somewhere deep within Evangeline's subconscious, this nearly deranged woman was beginning to make frightening sense, yet she could not quite bring the facts together. "Oh, Lady Howell, I cannot think what to say."

Lady Howell lifted up her head. Her eyes were still distant. "I make no claim upon your sympathy, Lady Rannoch. Believe me when I tell you that I neither need it nor deserve it. In truth, I had long suspected why my husband brought Cicely into our home. Ha! She was hardly a green girl. But at Howell's insistence, I humiliated myself by taking Cicely into society, until her constant flirtations became too much to bear. By the time I learned the truth from Mary, it was too late. Cicely was with child, and may God help me, I suppose I knew it was Howell's."

"Oh, no," whispered Evangeline. The room began to tilt, and Evangeline felt her nausea returning.

"Oh, yes," she whispered hollowly. "And then marriage became a necessity. Given Cicely's flagrant flirting, however, finding a husband was no simple matter. No decent mama would let her son wed her. Yes, Cicely and Howell were desperate, and soon they began to quarrel over who it would be. She laughed at Howell and told him she'd have nothing less than a wealthy husband. Indeed, she said she deserved it, if you can believe that." The woman began to sob quietly. "She thought herself so very, very shrewd."

"I—I am so sorry, Lady Howell," murmured Evangeline, but she was almost certain that her guest had ceased to hear anything save her own echoing voice.

Lady Howell drew another ragged breath. "At last, it appeared that Godfrey Moore—Lord Cranham's bastard—might offer for her, though he had neither title nor fortune to recommend him. Cicely had flirted quite coyly with him throughout the season, yet she turned up her nose when he finally came to the point. I flew into a rage! I told Howell to make her accept him. To get her out of my house! God help me, I even asked Papa to pressure Howell, and so he did. He threatened to cut Howell off. And that made him desperate."

"And then what happened?" Evangeline's hands, too, had begun to shake.

"Within the week, Lord Elliot Armstrong arrived from Scotland. He was wealthy and handsome, but in truth little more than a country innocent. He knew nothing of town, for his father had not been disposed toward London. But his parents decided it was time he wed, and his mother insisted on an English bride, and so he was sent down for the season."

"Oh!" answered Evangeline in a strange, tight voice.

"Yes. Lady Rannoch had planned to attend her son, but her husband fell ill, and it was agreed that her ladyship's brother would keep an eye on the boy. How laughably ironic! Sir Hugh was too busy light-skirting to worry about his nephew. By the time he realized what was afoot, Elliot had sent the betrothal announcement to the *Times*."

Evangeline gasped. "What did you do, Lady Howell?"

"Nothing," she answered in a grim whisper. "I did nothing then. And I did nothing when Rannoch returned from Scotland to find my niece's belly beginning to swell with child." Lady Howell exhaled suddenly, her eyes focused somewhere far away. "I must own, I admired that boy's nerve. He may have loved her to distraction, but he was hardly the besotted fool Cicely thought him. He saw the way of things at once and stormed out of the house. But he made one faulty assumption and challenged Godfrey Moore. Again, another irony . . ."

"In what way?" asked Evangeline, her hand fluttering weakly to her temple.

Lady Howell gave a sharp, bitter laugh. "Cicely could have had Godfrey, but she held out for Rannoch's money, and that stung Godfrey's pride. By the time she realized Rannoch wouldn't have her, Godfrey had been shipped off to India to avoid Rannoch's challenge—or the scandal, rather—for his father wouldn't have much cared if Godfrey'd been shot dead."

"And then what happened?"

"I don't *know!*" Her haunted voice broke then, and she began to sob in earnest. "Cicely never deserved such a fine young man. His storming out that night was the last straw. I ordered Howell to get the girl out of my house. A few weeks later, I learned of her death." Lady Howell's voice began to rise, taking on a hysterical edge. "After that, I wanted to know nothing further! I never asked!"

"Calm yourself, Lady Howell," insisted Evangeline, struggling to maintain her own composure. "You are not at fault."

"But I am! Had I done as I ought, and spoken out—"

"Oh? To say what?" challenged Evangeline softly. "That your husband was an incestuous pig? Had you any proof?"

"No, but by saying nothing, I let an innocent man suffer. And now we see what has come of heaping silence upon sin!" Her already homely face had crumpled into a hideously swollen mass, and tears were streaming down her reddened cheeks. Violent, choking sobs began to wrack her broad shoulders, jerking her repeatedly as she bent almost double.

Wordlessly, Evangeline left her seat and slid onto the sofa next to Lady Howell. She wrapped her arm around the wretched woman and tried to make some sense of all that she had heard.

There was some truth in what the woman said. An innocent young man had been allowed to pay the price for another's grievous sin. It horrified her, and she wondered to what extent, if any, this poor woman was to blame. What, given such terrible circumstances, would most wives have done? Evangeline did not know the answer to that question. But as she watched Lady Howell, tormented by guilt, she realized that whatever crime this woman might have committed, she was now paying a horrific price. No doubt, she had done so for many years and would continue to do so for as many more.

Slowly, Lady Howell collected herself and began to

wipe her face. "Oh, Lady Rannoch! I pray you will forgive me. Please forgive me for everything that I have done. Everything that I have allowed to happen——"

Evangeline took her hand into her own and pressed it encouragingly. "You are indeed forgiven, Lady Howell, for whatever part is mine to forgive. But indeed, ma'am, I do not understand why you are telling me this today, after all these years."

Lady Howell's face drew into a taut, bitter expression. "Because it will all come out now. I cannot help it. Moreover, I no longer care. I shall go abroad as soon as the funeral is over. My husband's death releases me from any obligation I may have had to protect him."

"Your husband's death?" Evangeline stared at the woman in horror.

Lady Howell lifted her gaze to hold Evangeline's. Her bleary eyes were wide with alarm. "Yes, my lady, his death. Have you not understood me? My husband attacked Lord Cranham. At Vauxhall last night. Rannoch tried to intervene, then Matthew Winthrop was forced to shoot . . ."

As Lady Howell's words faded away, Evangeline felt caught in a tangle of emotion. She struggled to understand the implications of Lady Howell's convoluted tale. "Why would Lord Howell——?" she managed to whisper.

"Oh, his vile deception began to crumble when Cranham returned from India. He began stalking Cranham; he was obsessed with where he went, to whom he spoke. Yet publicly, Howell avoided him." Her voice turned to an almost steely whisper. "You see, Cranham made no secret of the fact that he wanted to make trouble for Rannoch. Howell was afraid to answer Cranham's questions, for the man was like a loose cannon. I tried to warn Cranham away, to no avail. I suspect my husband knew that a meeting between Cranham and Rannoch was inevitable, given their animosity. And then, they might realize the truth: that Cicely had another suitor. Neither of them. A lover to whom she had easy and unsuspicious access . . ."

"I am not sure I understand."

"Oh, my lady! The scandalmongers would have ruined Howell had his incest become public. And, of course, there was his dishonorable conduct in allowing an innocent young man to be blamed for Cicely's death. He would never have been received in good drawing rooms again."

"I see," whispered Evangeline.

"But as long as her suitors remained on separate continents, it was easy for them to go on blaming each other. Then that actress—Antoinette Fontaine—managed to learn the truth somehow. I think she was blackmailing Howell. I found her name and direction in Howell's ledger. He had begun to spend large sums of money, larger even than his outrageous gaming debts. He killed her . . . yes, I really think he killed her."

Fontaine. Tanner. An inn near Wrotham Ford . . . what was the connection? Suddenly, Evangeline felt her throat begin to constrict.

The strain of the last several hours was telling. She felt driven to escape. To return to Elliot's side. She needed to touch him, to talk to him, to persuade him to fight to get well. For them, and for their child. Moreover, as much as she knew she should be grateful to this guilt-ridden woman, she was still seized by an irrational, nearly overwhelming urge to flee from her presence.

It was simply too much, too much ugliness to comprehend in one such tragic day. Abruptly, she rose and muttered what were almost certainly incoherent words of sympathy and thanks. Then, fighting the inclination to break into a run, Evangeline picked up her skirts, rushed from the room, and up the two flights of stairs to Elliot.

Evangeline spent a restless night by Elliot's bed, carefully considering what Lady Howell had said yet saying nothing that might distress her husband. By the following morning, Elliot was well enough to slump weakly against a stack of pillows, drink a bit of beef tea, and spend a quarter hour sequestered with Gerald Wilson.

By that afternoon, however, matters took an altogether different turn. The dreaded fever seized hold with a vengeance. His huge body was wracked, first by chills, then by scorching heat. Potter returned to shake his head and make soft, sympathetic noises but otherwise did little. Kemble mixed up a bitter tea of bark and herbs which Evangeline dutifully sponged into his mouth during his more settled moments. They shared the task of changing the bandages and applying the appropriate compounds, for the wound must, the surgeon emphasized, be kept free of putrefaction at all cost. Evangeline remained by her husband's bed, sleeping on a cot MacLeod had sent up.

Throughout the first full day, the worst throes of fever would seize Elliot, seemingly out of nowhere, and together Evangeline and Kemble would be forced physically to restrain him. Twice, they were required to ring for footmen. Elliot would thrash about violently, and each time Evangeline feared that the sutures in his thigh would rupture. Within twenty-four hours, Elliot's fever began to spike faster but less frequently, and for the most part he slept restlessly, his breathing rapid and shallow. During the febrile spells, however, he would first rage wildly, then cry out for Evangeline.

Occasionally, he would carry on entire conversations, almost coherently. When his temperature dropped and the chills took hold, Elliot would plead with her to come to bed. Evangeline did so, gingerly at first, fearing that she would somehow worsen the wound, yet the heat of her body seemed to ease his otherwise uncontrollable shivering. The cycle went on and on into the second day, until both she and Kemble were on the verge of collapse and Elliot severely weakened.

It was following just such an episode when Evangeline awoke, somewhere near daybreak, to find herself tightly ensnared in Elliot's arms. After three days of sleeping only intermittently, Evangeline realized she must have dozed off. She came fully awake with a start. Elliot had managed to roll toward her and now lay on one side. Sliding one hand up against his massive shoulder, she tried to press him back down against the mattress, but his eyes flew instantly open.

He blinked once, twice, then focused his smoky gaze upon her with a breathtaking intensity. "Evie . . . ?" he whispered. The desperation in his voice was almost tangible. His eyes searched her face with a strange urgency. "I thought—that is to say, I dreamed—that you were gone."

"Gone?" she answered uncertainly.

"That you had left," he muttered vaguely, lifting an unsteady hand to touch her face. "Aye, gone away . . . before I could explain . . ."

"Shush, Elliot," she softly replied, touching his fingertips lightly to her lips, then placing his hand back atop the coverlet. "You must lie still. You have been feverish for quite a while, but I am here."

As if perplexed, Elliot lifted his hand again and scrubbed the back of it across his four-day growth of beard. He eyed her speculatively across the pillow. "Aye, quite a while indeed," he murmured. Then his mouth turned up into a weak, roguish grin, but his words were laced with doubt. "Had you worried, I hope?"

Evangeline rolled up onto one elbow to look down into his haggard face. Elliot had always been dark, his beard heavy, but he now gave every appearance of being a dockyard thug. A faint purple bruise colored the outer edge of his left brow, while harsh black stubble covered his face. His cheekbones, more pronounced than usual, were slashed with deep hollows beneath. And now that he was fully awake, Elliot's eyes seemed darker, sunken, and ringed with shadow. Her expression apparently betrayed her thoughts.

"Umm—that bad?" One eyebrow went up as he struggled to maintain the grin.

Still propped up beside him, Evie shook her head. "A little gaunt, perhaps. And yes, you had me worried."

Elliot reached out with surprising strength, circled his arm about her waist, and pulled himself a half inch closer before the pain obviously overcame him. He looked at her with a grimace. "Very worried?" he asked softly.

"Terrified, truth be told," she answered grimly.

"How long?" he asked tentatively. "How long since Vauxhall?"

Evie pulled her gaze from his and pushed the bedcovers incrementally away. "This is the fourth day," she answered.

"And you have remained here every moment, have you not?" He reached out to touch her chin lightly and turn her face back toward his. "Look at me, Evie. I know it. 'Tis as if I was aware of you throughout . . . throughout whatever it is I have been through these many days and nights. Aye, I sensed your presence. And then I dreamed—well, I cannot say quite *what* I dreamed. Just don't leave me, Evie, promise that you will not?" He swallowed hard, and as she watched the faint movement of his throat, Evangeline was flooded with an overwhelming sense of relief and gratitude.

"I will never leave you," she answered with unwavering certainty.

Mutely, Elliot nodded, fell back against the pillow, and dragged his arm across his forehead. For a long moment, he was still, and she thought he was sleeping. "Do you know, Evie?" he asked at last, the question punctuated by a little grunt of discomfort. "Did they tell you about Howell? I remember now . . . the bounder meant to shoot Cranham. And I think he shot me, too, though I'm damned if I know why."

Gingerly, Evangeline moved across the bed and tucked in close to his side. "She came here," Evangeline answered softly. "Lady Howell. Her husband is dead, Elliot. Did you remember that Major Winthrop had to kill him?"

Elliot's soft voice was slow and uncertain. "I—don't know what I remember. If he is dead, then I am not much saddened by it . . . but why would Lady Howell come here, Evie?" he asked, his voice suddenly protective. "Did she distress you in any way?"

Elliot lifted his arm and turned to look at her as she shook her head. "No, not distress. Upsetting, yes. She was that. But she was driven by grief and guilt. She came only to confess. To say that it was Howell who—who—"

Evangeline fumbled weakly with the end of her sentence, for she and Elliot had never openly discussed the death of his fiancée. "It was Howell, Elliot. It was Howell who got Cicely Forsythe, his niece, with child," she finally managed to say. "You have a right to know the truth, though you should not hear it from me. In fact, you are too weak to have this discussion at all."

Suddenly wincing, Elliot sucked air through his teeth and squeezed shut his eyes. A moment passed before he spoke again. "Aye," he said bitterly, "that may be, but I've got a bloody hole in my leg for my trouble, Evie, so I'd like to know why. Go on."

"Well, that's about it," she concluded softly. "I take it that theirs was a long-standing affair. You—and Cranham, too, for that matter—were merely used."

Elliot remained quiet for a protracted moment until, at last, Evangeline sat up in bed and looked down at him. His eyes were closed, his face fixed in an expression of unmitigated grief. Had he loved her so very much then? Did knowing the name, not to mention the utter perfidy, of one's betrayer make it worse? Of course it did, she acknowledged.

Elliot had a troubled past; she had known it, and been wounded by it, when she wed him. What she had not known, and had not bothered to consider, was just how badly his past had wounded him. Far more, Evangeline was beginning to realize, than she had ever imagined. She had been wrong about a great many things, and perhaps she had unwittingly wronged him in the process.

Though the artist inside Evangeline well understood that life was never black and white, the woman who had fallen in love with Elliot Armstrong had been unwilling to tolerate shades of gray in her life. Perhaps, she suddenly realized, that was just a bit too much to ask. Elliot was not, and never would be, perfect. He was just a man. A strong, good man who was honest at heart yet fraught with inner demons and insecurities which he was at last struggling to overcome.

Smoothly, she leaned forward to touch her lips to his forehead. "You were ill used, Elliot," she whispered against his forehead, "and I know you must hurt. I wish it had been otherwise."

For a moment, he said nothing. "Aye, I hurt sometimes, Evangeline," he finally admitted, his voice soft. "What's worse, I've hurt you as well. And right now, I fear that nothing I may do will rid us of the past and make us free."

"Perhaps we need not hide from it, Elliot, but merely get beyond it?"

His eyes flickered open, and in their smoky depths Evangeline suddenly saw it all, the sorrow, the doubt, the love, and the seemingly eternal weariness that lingered there. "Do you think we can manage it?" he asked hesitantly.

With infinite care, Evangeline slid down into the bed and moved her head to share his pillow. "I love you, Elliot," she answered, curling one arm across his chest and setting her lips close to the turn of his jaw. "I have always loved you. Together, perhaps we can overcome anything. We can try."

"*Do* you love me, Evie?" he asked solemnly, his eyes focused on the ceiling above. "I must confess, I cannot go on teasing such words from your lips, no matter how desperately I need to hear them. And on the one occasion when you said them from your heart, you said them to another man. Not to me."

"No, I think you are wrong about that," she softly countered.

Elliot exhaled a long agonizing sigh. "Tell me true, sweet, for I think I very nearly made you a widow before you'd hardly become a wife. I will confess, that fact has rather unnerved me, and I want nothing more standing between us."

"What are you saying?"

"Life can be short," he answered gently, "and when I met you, I discovered a newfound desire to know where mine was headed. This throbbing pain in my leg makes for quite a reminder. So what I am asking is, can you set aside my past, which has admittedly been less than virtuous? And can you forgive me for pushing you into this marriage too quickly?"

"Yes," she answered simply. "And yes. But as to whether

or not we wed too quickly—" Evangeline paused to run her free hand down her belly. "That remains to be seen."

Elliot turned to look at her, his expression suddenly one of gentle astonishment. "Evie, I—why, I cannot think what to say. Do you mean it? All of it?"

Evangeline shot him an enigmatic, feminine smile and tilted up one eyebrow. "Certainly, I mean the *yes* and *yes* part. We shall shortly know about the last part." She watched, enthralled, as utter amazement, then joy, chased across the gaunt angles of Elliot's face.

With a little effort, he shifted his weight toward her, then trailed one big hand slowly down to rest across the flat plane of her belly. Smiling in obvious contentment, Elliot let his heavy eyelids fall shut. "Aye, if not now, soon," he whispered. "Soon, love. I promise."

They remained thus for a time, wrapped in each other. Elliot seemed to drowse, his breathing even, his hand still lingering restfully upon her stomach. Eventually, however, his fingers came up to slide through the hair at her temple. "Evie?" he whispered.

"Umm?"

"Let's go back to Chatham. As soon as I may stir from this bed, let us leave."

"Yes, of course," she answered uncertainly. "But why?"

"If you are indeed with child, you'll have need of Winnie and plenty of clean, country air. And for my part, I feel a need to be there just now. 'Tis a healing place, Evie. You know that, do you not? I will recover, we will recover." He turned to smile softly at her. "And with any luck at all, I shall be able to watch your lovely, lithe figure grow round and fat."

"Oh?" she said archly. "Fat, is it?"

"Aye," he said arrogantly. "And I'll likely make you paint, as well. I shall stand over you like a good Scottish husband and make you work. I'll be wanting another portrait, of course. One that doesn't look so bloody grim. And you'll need your exercise, of course, so I'll have you walk with me, Evie, through the woods, by the river . . . mayhap we'll even go swimming, eh?" He shot her a wicked, suggestive wink, then shut his eyes.

"Oh, Lud!" she breathed. "Did you know about that?" But Elliot, feigning sleep, would not answer.

❧ Epilogue ❧

On these small cares of daughter, wife or friend,
the almost sacred joys of home depend.
—Hannah More

*A*utumn at Chatham Lodge was the most beautiful of seasons under any circumstance. This year, it was glorious indeed. The smell of late-summer flowers drifted through the air, carrying with it the exuberant voices of the children who played in the gardens below. Indolently, Evangeline reclined in her chair upon the terrace and watched as Zoë whacked a croquet ball soundly against Theo's booted ankle, setting off a theatrical howl which the remaining players summarily ignored.

The match had been in progress off and on for the better part of the afternoon, interrupted only for arguments, accidents, and a bounteous al fresco luncheon which Mrs. Crane had laid out in the rose garden. Evangeline patted her growing stomach and wondered if the tray of cold ham had been taken in yet.

"Oh, my," drawled a languid voice behind her. "Quite a rackety lot, are they not? Too early for it, my lady! Far too early in the afternoon for such vigorous merriment."

"Aidan!" Evangeline leapt from her chair to kiss Lord Linden enthusiastically upon one cheek. Behind him, she saw Elliot closing the distance more slowly. In his left hand, he held a gold-knobbed walking stick, but he bore very little weight upon it now.

"Discretion, my darling!" whispered the elegantly attired viscount as he pulled away from her embrace. "I don't think the old boy yet knows about my having taken you to bed."

"Go bed someone else's wife, you lecherous dog," muttered Elliot, sinking into his chair with a grunt. He tossed the cane into the grass in feigned distaste. "I grow weary of you and Winthrop gawking at my wife. Besides, she's big with child, for heaven's sake. Have you no restraint?"

"I am hardly *big* with anything as yet," Evangeline retorted, grinning at her husband. "Linden, it would serve him right if I grow as large as a house, would it not? And speaking of Major Winthrop, why has he not come with you? Was that not the plan?"

"Matt sends his regrets, my dear, for he was called home to his family seat," answered Linden, but Evangeline did not miss the telling glance that passed between the viscount and her husband.

"To Cornwall?" Elliot's brows lifted in mild surprise. "Family trouble?"

"Hmm," droned Linden absently as he watched the croquet match with newfound interest. "Something like that, I suppose. But I did not come to discuss Matt's troubles. I came, rather, to discuss yours, old man."

"Then it shall be a short visit, Linden, for I haven't any," replied Elliot cheerfully. "Cannot an injured man retire to his country home to recuperate? After all, I have only another week before Mother arrives from Scotland to cut up my peace."

"That's *make peace*, darling," corrected Evangeline gently. "Recollect, if you will, that the two of you have agreed to set aside your distinctly different personalities on behalf of your heir."

Linden smiled, pulled out his ever-present snuff box, and flicked it open with an expert finger. "Familial concerns aside, you shall both rest more peacefully in your marriage bed when you hear what I have learned. Congratulate me, for I have discovered the identity of Evangeline's mysterious Mrs. Pritchett!"

"*No?*" interrupted Evangeline, who then blushed effusively. Confessing her assumptions to Elliot had been difficult enough, but the appearance of the ruby bracelet had required something by way of explanation. Knowing that Elliot had shared with Linden the tale of the redhaired housekeeper's visit, however, was worse still.

Linden continued, oblivious to her discomfort. "Do you not wish to know who she is?" he crowed, then did not bother to wait for a response. "She's Mary Tanner, Antoinette's sister! Can you credit such a thing? As different as night from day!"

"How do you know?" asked Elliot, his face fixed in an expression of utter amazement. "And how did you find her?"

Linden hesitated, then gave a lazy shrug. "Well, actually, Winthrop came up with the idea. We just asked Kemble. MacLeod gave the old boy her name and description, and Kem was easily able to tell us the name of her employer. We put a few facts together, then had an easy job of running down the mother."

"How charming!" interjected Elliot dryly.

"Indeed," answered Linden, his lip curling into a slight sneer. "She now operates a decrepit alehouse in Cheapside, by the by. We dropped in, made a few pointed remarks about the dreadful ramifications of jewelry theft, not to mention the stupidity of lying to Bow Street."

"And?"

"And *voila!* The old buzzard sang like a spring robin, swore she'd never meant to steal the bracelet; she'd merely forgotten its existence. Then, *saints be praised*—those were, I recollect, her very words—the eldest daughter discovered it, inadvertently buried in Mama's portmanteau. Realizing the grievous error, Mrs. Pritchett delivered it up to his lordship himself."

"A likely story," snorted Elliot.

"Oh, but it improves! Matt and I called upon the daughter as well, who just happens to be the devoted housekeeper of Lord and Lady Collup in Albemarle Street. Mrs. Pritchett, nee Tanner, was recently wed to the loyal butler, one Elam Pritchett, and the whole lot of them live snug as bugs in a Mayfair town house."

"Is there a point to this story?" asked Elliot dryly. "Other than to display your astounding knowledge of London geography and your speaking acquaintance with the greater portion of its domestic service?"

"Well, yes!" answered Linden with a flash of white teeth. "Lady Collup, don't you know, is first cousin and bosom-bow to Lady Howell. Over the years, they've traded horses, recipes, and even—on occasion—servants."

Evangeline gasped audibly. "Lady Howell told me! Mary was the girl Lord Howell dismissed . . ." She let her words trail off awkwardly, but Linden picked up her thought.

"Just so, Evangeline! Both Antoinette and her mother were present all those years ago when Lady Howell came to speak with Mary. At some point, probably after listening to Cranham rage on and on about the past, Antoinette must have finally put the pieces, or at least the names, together. And when it turned out that Cranham couldn't really afford Antoinette, and Elliot would no longer have her, she evidently decided to cash in an old marker. It was, we now know, a fatal decision on her part."

"And what of the woman, this Mary Pritchett?" asked Elliot.

Linden cut an appraising glance toward Evangeline, then hesitantly spoke. "Mrs. Pritchett was, I daresay, rather ashamed of her family. She admitted that her sister came to Albemarle Street several weeks before she died, asking pointed questions about Lord Howell. Afterward, I believe that Mary meant to do the right thing in coming to Strath, but she apparently had no notion that Elliot had wed. She became very much afraid she had made matters worse for him."

"Will you tell me something else, Linden?" Elliot asked as he stretched out his leg and absently massaged his injured thigh. Evangeline fought back the urge to reach across and assist.

"But of course," agreed Linden smugly. "I am a veritable fountain of knowledge."

"How did you persuade Cranham to cooperate anyway?"

Uncharacteristically, Linden tossed back his head and laughed aloud. "Like most of his sort, Cranham's instinct for self-preservation was highly developed. When I pointed out to him that you had had more than ample opportunity to kill him on the field, and had neither need nor inclination to go skulking about in alleys, he realized that it was remotely possible that someone else wished him dead."

"Really?" asked Elliot, sounding skeptical.

Linden tossed off an elegant shrug. "Well, that . . . and I bribed him with a bloody fortune. By the by, old man, if it will make you feel any better, you can reimburse me! I should very much like to have that set of dueling pistols, since you'll have no need of them now . . . and perhaps two months' use of your hunting box for the next few years?"

Elliot snorted incredulously, but Evangeline ignored him. "And how did you know it was Lord Howell?" she asked breathlessly. "No one suspected him!"

"Oh, he didn't," answered Elliot wryly. "Linden merely

stirred up enough gossip to flush the bird from the bush. He had no notion who might fly forth."

Evangeline swallowed hard. "Oh, I see," she murmured weakly.

"Indeed, as do I," mused Lord Linden, his attention now focused elsewhere. Purposefully, he withdrew his quizzing glass and peered through it onto the terrace below. "Tell me, Elliot, whoever is that *jolie femme* with such an outstanding mallet technique? I vow, I have never seen the like of her, ah, her swing."

"Ah, yes," responded Elliot, glancing knowingly across the low hedge to the makeshift croquet field. "That woman with the impressive *swing* would be the merry widow, Mrs. Weyden."

"Indeed?" commented Lord Linden with a small choking sound. "I take it she has put off her widow's weeds?"

"Yes," replied Evangeline sardonically, "about a dozen years ago." Together, the three of them stared down at Winnie, who was industriously engaged in chasing Fritz from a wicket, which he had obviously targeted for some nefarious doggie deed. Today, her face glowed a charming shade of pink, her gold-brown ringlets were piled high atop her head, and she wore a cerulean silk walking dress cut, as usual, just a shade too low. Lord Linden exhaled a long sigh and began to polish his glass rather vigorously.

"She is my dear friend and companion, Linden," scolded Evangeline. "And a bit older than you, I suspect."

"Not to worry," answered Linden amiably. "I find older women charming. I should no doubt make her acquaintance before Sir Hugh insults her obvious good taste with some vulgar overture."

Elliot tilted his head to one side and studied Linden. "A charming lady, old fellow, if I do say so myself. More than up to any challenge you might present, and, I might further add, newly parted from a former admirer." He turned his gaze to Evangeline.

Evangeline could not suppress a sharp laugh. "Honestly, Elliot! Does none of us have a secret you've not become privy to?"

"You, madam, are permitted none," he intoned solemnly. "And as for his, I wouldn't care to know them."

But Lord Linden did not hear this last remark, for he had risen from his seat and was drifting aimlessly down the stone staircase to the next terrace, where he would no doubt offer up his services as chief mallet bearer or dog chaser or whatever position he might otherwise ingratiate himself into.

Smoothly, Evangeline rose from her chair. "Come, Elliot, give me your arm," she invited. "For, unless I miss my guess, our athletes will be engaged for a while, and I have a wifely urge to rub that thigh of yours."

Elliot flashed his wicked grin, took up his cane, and arm in arm they strolled up the steps and along the path that trailed along the terraces, Elliot's rich laughter echoing in their wake and brightening the gardens of Chatham Lodge.

POCKET STAR BOOKS
PROUDLY PRESENTS

Two Little Lies

LIZ CARLYLE

Coming soon from Pocket Star Books

**Turn the page for a preview of
Two Little Lies . . .**

Signorina Alessandri was ill. Again. With one hand restraining the flowing folds of her fine silk nightclothes, she lurched over the closestool in her Covent Garden flat and prayed, in fluent and fervid Italian, for death to take her.

"Oh, please, miss, *do* speak English!" begged her maid, who had caught her heavy black hair and drawn it back, too. "I can't make out a word. But I do think we'd best fetch a doctor."

"Nonsense," said the signorina, clenching the back of the closestool in a white-knuckled fist. "It was the fish Lord Chesley served last night."

The maid pursed her lips. "Aye, and what was it yesterday, miss?" she asked. "Not fish, I'll wager."

With the other hand set at the small of her back, Viviana closed her eyes and somehow straightened up. *"Silenzio,* Lucy," she said softly. "We talk of it no further. The worst is over now."

"Oh, I doubt that," said the maid.

Viviana ignored her and went instead to the washbasin. "Where is the morning's post, *per favore?"* she asked, awkwardly slopping the bowl full of water.

With a sigh, Lucy went into the parlor and returned with a salver which held one letter covered in her father's infamous scrawl and a folded note which bore no address. "Mr. Hewitt's footman brought it," she said offhandedly.

With hands that shook, Viviana finished her ablutions, then patted a towel across her damp face as her maid looked on in consternation. The girl had been both loyal and kind these many months. "Thank you, Lucy," she said. "Why do you not go have a cup of tea? I shall read my letter now."

Lucy hesitated. "But do you not wish your bathwater brought, miss?" she pressed. "'Tis already past noon. Mr. Hewitt will be here soon, won't he?"

Quin. Lucy was right, of course. Viviana laid aside the towel and took the note. Quin usually came to her in the early afternoon. Yes, just as he meant to do today. And oh, how she longed for it—yet dreaded it in the same breath.

She tossed the note into the fire. She had not missed the furious looks he'd hurled her way in the theater's reception room after last night's performance. Viviana had sung gloriously, hitting every high note in her last aria with a chilling, crystal-clear resonance, before collapsing into her lover's arms in a magnificent swoon. The theater had been full, the applause thunderous.

But all Quin had seemed to notice was what had come afterward. The compliments and congratulations of her admirers. The champagne toasts. The subtle, sexual invitations tossed her way by the lift of a brow or a tilt of the head—and refused just as subtly in turn. It had not been refusal enough for Quin. One could hardly have ignored his cocky stance and sulky sneer as he paced the worn green carpet, a glass of brandy clutched in his hand. His uncle, Lord Chesley, had even had the effrontery to tease him about it.

Quin had not taken that well. Nor had he been especially pleased to see Viviana leaving on Chesley's arm, as she so often did. And today, God help them, he would undoubtedly wish to quarrel over it. Viviana was not at all sure she was capable of mounting a spirited defense. But it almost didn't matter anymore.

"Miss?" said the maid. "Your bathwater?"

Nausea roiled in her stomach again, and Viviana moved gingerly to a chair. "In ten minutes, Lucy," she answered. "I shall read *Papà's* letter whilst my stomach settles. If I am late, I shall receive Mr. Hewitt here."

Lucy pursed her lips again. "Aye, then," she finally answered. "But I'd be telling him straightaway, miss, about that bad fish if I was you."

Finally, Viviana laughed.

The fleeting humor did not sustain her as she opened her father's letter. Even the scent of his letter-paper tugged at her heartstrings. She knew the very drawer of his desk from which it had been taken; the same desk in which he kept his tobacco. Then there was the penmanship itself. The broad, slashing strokes always recalled to her his indefatigable strength, the tight loops and curls, his wisdom and precision, and the lyrical words, his artistry. He was one of Europe's most renowned composers, and not without reason.

She drew in the scent once more, then spread the letter across her lap. She read it through once, disbelievingly, then again, very carefully. Chesley, it seemed, had kept his old friend well informed. Already *Papà* knew that tonight was to be her last performance in *Die Entführung,* and that all of London's West End lay appreciatively at her feet. As *Konstanze*, at long last, she had triumphed.

And now *Papà* was writing to tell her she might return home. Viviana closed her eyes and thought of it. Dear God, what a strange confluence of fate and timing this was! It seemed an eternity since she had fled Venice with nothing but her panic, her violin, and her music folio to bear her company. And now, to return! Oh, it was what she had lived for and longed for almost every moment since, save for those spent in Quin's arms. He had been, in truth, her salvation.

But now she could go home. It was a bit of a devil's bargain, what was being offered her. Certainly it was not what she wanted. Nonetheless, as *Papà* pointed out, there were advantages to such an arrangement. Great advantages. It would also make his life a vast deal easier, though her father would sooner die than tell her so.

And so the decision was to be hers. *Nothing would be forced upon her.* Ha! Those were not her father's words, she'd wager.

Apparently, Conte Bergonzi had changed his tactics. Moreover, Viviana could tell by his careful phrasing that *Papà* fully expected her to refuse Bergonzi's offer, and would forgive her if she did so. Viviana set her hand on her belly. She was not at all sure she would have the luxury of refusing.

The water was wonderfully hot when it came, and remarkably restorative. Feeling perhaps a little more at peace, Viviana was still luxuriating in it when Quin came stalking into the room. He looked at once angry, and yet almost boyishly uncertain.

He stared down at her naked body and gave her a tight, feral smile. "Washing away the evidence, Vivie?"

It was a cynical remark, even for him.

For a moment, she let her black eyes burn into him. "*Silenzio,* Quinten," she returned. "I had quite enough of your jealous sulking last night. Be civil, or go away."

He knelt by the tub and rested one arm along its edge. His eyes were bleak today, the lines about his mouth almost shockingly deep for one so young. He smelled of brandy and smoke and the scents of a long, hard-spent night. "Is that what you want, Viviana?" he whispered. "Are you trying to drive me away?"

She dropped her soap into the water. "How, Quin?" she demanded, throwing up her hands in frustration. "*Dio mio,* how am I doing this driving? I am not, and that is the truth of it, *si?*"

He cast his eyes away, as if he did not believe her. "They say Lord Lauton has promised you a house in Mayfair, and more money than I could ever dream of," he answered. "Not until I come into my title, at any rate. Is it true, Vivie?"

She shook her head. "Quin, what would it matter if it were?" she returned. "I am no longer for sale—perhaps not even to you. Why must you be so jealous?"

"How can I help but be, Viviana?" he rasped, brushing one finger beneath her left nipple. It peaked and hardened, begging for his touch. "Men's eyes feast upon you everywhere you go. But at least you still desire me."

Viviana glowered at him, but she did not push his hand

away. "My body desires you, *si,*" she admitted. "But sometimes, *amore mio,* my mind does not."

He plucked the nipple teasingly between his thumb and forefinger. "And what of your heart, Viviana?" he whispered, looking up at her from beneath a sweep of inky lashes. "I have your body ensconced, ever so circumspectly, in this flat which I have paid for. Have I your heart as well?"

"I have no heart!" she snapped. "That is what you told me when we quarreled last week, if you will recall. And you need not remind me, Quin, of who has put this roof over my head. I have become mindful of it with every breath I draw."

As if to torment her, he let his lashes fall shut, then leaned forward to crook his head so that he might suckle her. Viviana sat perfectly still, allowing him to draw her nipple into his mouth, and then between his teeth. At that, she gasped and cursed the old, familiar pull of lust which went twisting traitorously through her body. It curled deep in her belly and left her breathless.

He lifted his head with a satisfied smile. "Where did you go last night, my love?" he asked.

She looked at him defiantly. "To Chesley's townhouse," she said. "We dined with Lord and Lady Rothers, and some acquaintances they had brought from Paris."

"Ah, patrons of the arts, all of them, I've no doubt," said Quin almost mockingly. "My uncle's little coterie!"

"Why must you so often think ill of him? He is kind to me, no more."

"My uncle is a fine man," Quin returned. "It is his friends I do not trust. By the way, my sweet, what is this here, just below your jaw? A bruise? Or something else?"

Her glower darkened as he brushed the side of her neck with the back of one finger. "It is absolutely nothing," she snapped, having no need to look. He was trying to elicit some sort of guilty reaction. "It is nothing, as it has always been nothing, Quin," she went on. "Chesley is my father's friend. My mentor here in London. He thinks of me as his *ward,* for God's sake! How many times must we suffer this foolish argument?"

He broke his gaze and looked away. "I cannot help it, Viviana." He choked out the words. "You—you drive me insane. Chesley runs with a fast crowd. I cannot bear how those other men look at you."

"And how, pray, am I to stop it?" she asked him. "What would you have me do, Quin? Give up my career? Enter a convent? I am a singer, for God's sake, and for that, one needs an audience." She seized her towel from the floor with a snap and pushed him away.

"I—I could pay you," he said. "A little now, and a great deal more—eventually. Then you would not have to sing at all."

She looked at him incredulously. "Sometimes, Quin, I do not think you understand me," she whispered. "I *must* sing. It has nothing to do with money."

He watched her almost warily as she stood to towel the water from her body. Viviana made no effort to hide her nakedness from his heated gaze as it drifted over her. She was, after all, his. He had bought and paid for her. She had let him do it, too—though she had fought it at first like a tigress.

"Lie down on the bed, Viviana," he said when she was dry. "Open your legs for me."

For a moment, she considered refusing. But God help her, she still wanted him. Even though it had come to this. She had wounds and scars to last a lifetime, as, no doubt, did he. Petty jealousies and bitterness had eaten into their hearts. He was too young. Too inexperienced. And she—well, she was simply too lonely. They were just using one another now. Surely he understood that?

Certainly, she did. Yet she craved the pleasure and the peace his virile young body could give her. She craved *him*. And she remembered a time, not so long ago, when it had been enough to sustain her; a time when they had worshipped each other and experienced together all the sweet delights of a first love.

"Lie down on the bed," he said again, more firmly. "You are my mistress, Viviana. I have the right."

And that, too, was perfectly true. Viviana tossed aside the towel, drew back the sheets, and did as he asked.

As the early afternoon light spilt over his shoulder, Quin stripped off his clothes with the practiced ease of a man who was used to having his needs and whims accommodated. He was already hard and fully erect. As usual.

When his snug, buff trousers had been shucked and tossed aside, he crawled across the bed in an almost predatory fashion and mounted her without preamble. Viviana gasped at the invasion, her whole body arching upward.

"You are mine, Viviana," he whispered, thrusting the full length of his erection inside her. "Do not ever forget that."

She was not his, but she did not argue. Instead, she set her feet flat against the bed, and tilted up her hips to better take the deepening strokes.

In response, he clasped her hands in his, palm to palm, and pushed them high over her head and onto the bed pillows, holding them there as he rode her. They had become like cats in heat, she and Quin, hissing and squabbling even as they burned for each other. She could already feel the quickening in his body—and in hers, too, despite the hurt he had done her. What manner of woman was she, to crave and cling to this?

It was as if Quin read her very thoughts. "You are mine, Viviana," he growled, bending over her and staring into her eyes, still pressing her hands high above her head. "You are mine, damn it, and no one else's. *Say* it."

Viviana turned her head away. It was not worth the fight. "I am yours," she whispered.

"Look at me, Viviana," he insisted, quickening his thrusts. "Look at me when I do this to you. Sometimes, I swear, I think you mean to break my heart. Say it again. You are mine, and no one else's!"

She returned her gaze to his, defiant. "I am *mine*, Quin," she said, her voice low and tremulous. "I am *my own person*. But I have chosen to be with you. There is a difference."

But Quin seemed not to hear her words. He had closed his

own eyes now, and the flesh was taut across the hard bones of his face as he rode her more furiously. She felt her pelvis arch to his against her will, urgent and greedy. Oh, God, he had such a gift for this! She wanted to lose herself in this pure, physical act. Wanted to feel nothing but the joining of their bodies.

He sensed it, and the urgency drove him. In this one way, at least, he understood her. *"Si, caro mia,"* she crooned. *"Li desidiro. Li voglio."*

Sweat had beaded on his temples now. His face was etched with strain, stark and beautiful. "God, Vivie!" he groaned. "Oh, God, I worship you!"

She jerked her hands from beneath his and clutched at him, gasping for breath. He thrust again and again, harder still, then one last sweet, perfect stroke. Viviana cried out, her whole body trembling. The pleasure washed over her, engulfed her, drowning out common sense.

He fell across her body, his chest heaving, the weight of him bearing her down into the softness of the bed. She stroked one hand down his taut, well-muscled back and felt tears spring to her eyes. "Oh, *amore mio,"* she murmured. "Oh, *ti amo,* Quin. *Ti amo."*

And in that moment, she did love him. She loved him with all her heart, though she had never once allowed herself to say the words—not in any language he could comprehend. Soothed and spent, she simply listened to the sound of his breathing for a time. It was the simplest of pleasures, she had discovered, to lie in the arms of a beautiful man—no, *this* man—sated and happy, and simply listen.

But the peace, of course, did not last. Soon they were quarreling again about the events of last night. Quin had apparently taken note of every man who had so much as kissed her hand or fetched her a glass of champagne. It was foolish, almost sophomoric behavior which had worsened with her ascending fame, and Viviana gave no quarter. She had reached her wit's end, and she told him so.

Quin reacted badly. "God, how I hate the way we must live!" he finally shouted. "I have the right to protect you. I have the right, Viviana, to show the world that you are mine."

"Quin, *amore mio*, we have been through this a thousand times," she whispered. "Such news would kill my father. He did not sacrifice everything to send me to England so that I might become a rich man's mistress."

Indeed, her father had sent her for precisely the opposite reason. But there was no point in saying as much to Quin. It would only serve to make him angrier.

"Signor Alessandri does not worry about this fast theater crowd his daughter runs with?" he retorted. "He does not care whose eyes are undressing you? And Lord Rothers! Good God, Vivie! His patronage comes at a price. He has bedded half the actresses in the West End."

"Well, he hasn't bedded *me*," she returned. "Nor will he. Nor does he wish to. My God, Quin he was with his *wife*. What do you think happened? A *ménage-a-trios* on Chesley's dining room table?"

His mouth thinned, and he moved as if to turn his back on her. "Yes, go ahead. Make a jest of it, Viviana. Make a jest of *me*."

She laid a hand against his chest. "Oh, *cara mio,* you are so young!"

He turned back to her at once. "Damn it, Vivie, I hate when you say that!" he swore. "Stop acting as if I'm some ignorant pup. I'm almost one-and-twenty now."

"Yes, and we agreed, Quin, at the start of this—"

"I know, dash it!" he interjected, laying his hand over hers and squeezing it almost violently. "I know. I shall keep my word, Viviana. But I bloody well don't like it."

A heavy silence fell across Viviana's bedchamber for a time, broken only by the distant clamor of Covent Garden beyond their windows. Eventually, however, she rolled onto her stomach and propped up on her elbows to study him, as she had done so often at the start of their tumultuous relationship.

Dear heaven, but he was beautiful, this half-man, half-boy she had come to love with such a breathless intensity. And she realized, quite suddenly, that despite it all, she could not bear to lose him. Even after all the harsh words—plenty of them, on both sides—she could not imagine a life without Quin. But was there any hope? She prayed there was, and not just for herself now.

"Quin, *caro mia*," she said impulsively. "Tell me something. Where is life going to take you?"

He lifted his head from the pillow and looked up at her strangely. "What do you mean, Vivie?"

Viviana shrugged lamely. "I am not perfectly sure," she said. "Have you ever considered . . . oh, going away, perhaps? Abroad, I mean?"

"Abroad?" he said bemusedly. "Good God! To where?"

"To the Continent?" Viviana lifted her brows. "To Venice or Rome, perhaps?"

He laughed. "Why on earth would anyone leave England?"

Viviana felt a prick of anger. "Perhaps because it is a stifling, moralizing place?"

"Vivie, it is my home," he said, stroking a hand down her hair. "Let's have no more talk of anyone going anywhere, all right?"

"But what of your future, Quin?" she persisted. "What do you mean to do with your life?"

"Live it, I daresay," he returned. "What else is one to do?"

"But have you ever thought that we might—" She stopped and swallowed hard. "Have you ever thought, Quin, of . . . of marriage?"

His eyes widened. "Good God," he said. "To you?"

She tore her gaze away. "To . . . to someone that you worship," she managed to answer. "To—yes, to me."

His expression gentled. "Oh, Vivie," he whispered. "Oh, if only life were so simple."

She pressed on, fully conscious of the hurt her pride would endure. "Perhaps it *is* that simple, Quin," she answered. "You say you cannot live without me. That you wish to claim me as yours. I ask you, how badly do you wish for this?"

He cut her a sidelong glance. "Is that what all this hesitance is about?" he asked. "Are you holding out for marriage? Oh, Viviana, you knew I couldn't marry you when we started this. *Didn't* you?"

Viviana shook her head. "I am not holding out, Quin," she answered. "It is not like that."

But Quin was still looking at her incredulously. "For God's sake, Viviana, I'm heir to an earldom," he continued. "Have you no idea what an obligation that is? When I must finally wed—which will be at least a decade hence, I pray—Mama will marry me off to some pale, flaxen-haired English miss with a slew of titles hanging off her Papa's name and fifty-thousand pounds in the three-percents, and I shall have little say in the matter."

Viviana's eyes narrowed. "Oh! So I am too old and too foreign and too bourgeois for the grand Hewitt dynasty? Is that it?"

"Now, Vivie," he chided, sitting up fully. "I never said that."

"I think you hardly need to!" Viviana curled one fist into the bed sheet, grappling with the nausea again. Why in God's name had she raised such a topic? He was right. She had known all along this would not last. But she had asked, and there was no backing away from it now.

"In a few weeks, Quin, you will be one-and-twenty," she said, her insides trembling with rage. "We are adults, both of us. Whom you chose to marry is up to you. Do not dare pretend otherwise. You insult my intelligence."

"Aww, Vivie!" He screwed up his face like the impatient young man he was. "We have our whole lives before us! I am not marrying anyone anytime soon. Why spoil what we have now?"

She gave him a mordant smile. *"Si,* it is a tedious business, this future, is it not?"

Quin did not catch the sarcasm. "That's my girl," he said, kissing her again. "Look, Vivie, I brought you something. Something which will cheer you up." He climbed from the bed and rummaged through his coat pockets, returning with a small box. "Open it," he commanded.

Viviana lifted the lid and gasped. The box held a ring; a wide, ornately carved band set with one large, square-cut ruby. It was a truly magnificent piece of jewelry. Viviana started to hand it back. Why did he insist on showering her with gifts? What she wanted was something his money could not buy—and this ring had undoubtedly cost Quin far more dearly than even he could afford.

Quin pushed the box back at her. "Put it on, Vivie," he insisted. "Put it on, but just promise me one thing."

Reluctantly, Viviana slid the ring onto her right hand. "I . . . yes, I shall try."

"Promise me you will keep this one," he said. "Promise me you will never sell it, and that you will wear it once in a while, and think of me."

Viviana was still staring at the ring, and blinking back tears of grief and rage and love and about a hundred other conflicting emotions. "I never stop thinking of you, Quin," she whispered.

"As I never stop thinking of you, Vivie." But there was mild skepticism in his eyes. "Now, what time are you due at the theater?"

"Six," she said hollowly.

"Yes, and I must go soon," he went on. "We are wasting precious time when we could be enjoying each other. I could be telling you, Viviana, that you are the most beautiful creature on this earth. That your eyes make my breath seize, and that your breasts nearly make my heart stop. Lie down, my dear, and let me make love to you again."

So it was *lovemaking* now. Not his earlier, more vulgar phrase.

She should have refused him. She should have told him to leave her bed that very moment. But the memory of a sweeter, happier time had drawn painfully near, and the future stretched out bleakly before her. So Viviana turned onto her back and let him join his strong, vigorous body to hers one last time.

Quin rose from her bed some hours later, his mood improved, but his gaze still wary. She watched him dress, drinking in his lithe, slender beauty, and wondering, not for the first time, what he would look like in the full splendor of manhood. Already, his shoulders were wide, and his face shadowed with a stubble that matched his heavy, dark hair.

He dragged his shirt on over his head, and she marveled again at the perfection which was his face. That patrician forehead, the thin blade of a nose, lean, high-boned cheeks, and the most stunning feature of all, eyes the color of the Aegean at dusk. Oh, it was no wonder he had caught her eye. But how had she been such a fool as to let him steal her heart?

She tried to watch dispassionately as he drew on his stockings and hitched up his trousers. It was not anger which she felt toward him, no. It was more of a resigned acceptance. Nor did she blame him. It was her own passionate, romantic nature which had gotten her into this. Ah, but one could not sing without passion. And one could not truly live without romance. Viviana accepted the fact that, on this earth, one took the bad with the good, and lived a full life in return.

He pulled on his coat, then leaned across the bed, setting both hands on the mattress. He held her gaze for a time, his eyes so intense, she felt, fleetingly, as though he could look into her soul. "Tell me something, my dear," he said quietly. "Do you love me?"

It surprised her a little, for it was a question he had never asked. And she knew what was in her heart, just as surely as she knew what her answer must be. She had at least a little pride left. "No, Quin," she answered. "I do not love you. And you do not love me."

He looked at her with the eyes of an old man. "No. I suppose I do not."

She shrugged. "It is best, *si?*"

He straightened abruptly. "Well, Viviana," he said. "At least you are honest."

But she was not honest. She had just told him a blatant lie. And as she watched him stride toward the door, she wondered, fleetingly, if perhaps he had just done the same.

No. No, it was not possible.

The door slammed behind him. Viviana exhaled the breath which she had been holding, then closed her eyes, willing herself not to cry. She listened to the heavy tread of his footsteps as he left her. One warm tear rolled awkwardly down her nose, then landed on her pillow with a soft *plop!*

Abruptly, she sat up in bed. No, by God, she would not cry. Not for him. Not for anyone. Not even for herself. One tear was too many—and if another followed, there might well be no end to it.

Lucy came back into the room just as Viviana was drawing on her dressing gown. "Shall I tidy up now, miss?" she asked.

"Sì, grazie." Viviana went to the small writing desk beneath the window. "Tonight is my last performance as *Konstanze,* Lucy," she said, unlocking the little drawer which held her meager savings.

"I know, miss," said the maid as she began to neaten the bed. "It's been a grand run, hasn't it? What will you do next, I wonder? Pr'haps you ought to go down to Brighton for a rest. Perhaps Mr. Hewitt would take you? 'Tis beautiful there, I've heard."

Viviana was already relocking the drawer. "Actually, Lucy, I'm to go home tomorrow," she said, handing a pitifully small roll of banknotes to the maid. "Here. I wish you to have this. Lord Chesley need know nothing of it."

The girl looked at her incredulously and pushed Viviana's hand away. "Why, I can't take your money, miss!" she said. "Besides, it ain't like you've got it to spare—which heaven knows it's not my place to say, but there, I've said it. And Lord Chesley pays me well enough to look after you, which I've been glad to do."

With a wistful smile, Viviana put the money in the maid's hand and forcibly curled her fingers around it. "*Take* it," she insisted. "Where I am to go, neither *Papà* nor I shall need it. And I wish *you* to go back to Lord Chesley's estate and marry that handsome footman of yours. This money is my wedding gift. You must buy a cradle, a very beautiful cradle, for your firstborn, and think of me when you use it, *si?*"

Lucy uncurled her hand and stared at the banknotes. "But how can you just up and leave England, miss?" she asked. "What's to become of you, so far away, and in such a foreign place?"

Inwardly, Viviana's smile deepened. The poor girl was so naively provincial—just like Quin. "It is my home," she said quietly. "It is time I returned to it. Now, you must wish me happy, Lucy. I have just learned that I, too, am about to be married."

The girl's face broke into an impossibly wide smile. "Oh, lawks, miss!" she cried, throwing up both hands. "I just knew it! I just knew Mr. Hewitt would do the right thing, soon you told him! I just knew it would all come aright somehow."

Viviana felt a hot, urgent pressure well behind her eyes, and turned at once back to her desk. "I think, Lucy, that you misunderstand," she said, pretending to neaten her pens and papers. "I am returning home to marry someone who used to . . . well, someone I used to know."

"Oh, no, miss!" She felt Lucy touch her lightly on the arm. "But . . . but what about Mr. Hewitt?"

Viviana regained her composure and turned around again. Opera required one to be not just a good singer, but a competent actress as well. "Oh, I think we have come to an understanding, he and I," she said, forcing a smile.

"Well, I can't see what it could be!" said the girl.

"Hush, Lucy." Viviana set her hands on the maid's shoulders and swiftly kissed both her cheeks. "I am leaving England, my faithful friend. Do not grieve for me. All good things must come to an end, *si?*"

Breathtaking romance from

LIZ CARLYLE

Beauty Like the Night

My False Heart

A Woman Scorned

A Woman of Virtue

Pocket Books
A VIACOM COMPANY

3089-01

Visit
❖ **Pocket Books** ❖
online at

....

www.SimonSays.com

....

Keep up on the latest new
releases from your favorite
authors, as well as author
appearances, news, chats,
special offers and more.